Wyatt in Wichita

Wyatt in Wichita

A Historical Novel

John Shirley

SKYHORSE PUBLISHING

All rights reserved. No part of this book may be reproduced in any manner without the express written consent of the publisher, except in the case of brief excerpts in critical reviews or articles. All inquiries should be addressed to Skyhorse Publishing, 307 West 36th Street, 11th Floor, New York, NY 10018.

Skyhorse Publishing books may be purchased in bulk at special discounts for sales promotion, corporate gifts, fund-raising, or educational purposes. Special editions can also be created to specifications. For details, contact the Special Sales Department, Skyhorse Publishing, 307 West 36th Street, 11th Floor, New York, NY 10018 or info@skyhorsepublishing.com.

Skyhorse® and Skyhorse Publishing® are registered trademarks of Skyhorse Publishing, Inc.®, a Delaware corporation.

Visit our website at www.skyhorsepublishing.com.

10 9 8 7 6 5 4 3 2 1

Library of Congress Cataloging-in-Publication Data is available on file.

Cover design by Rain Saukas

ISBN: 978-1-62914-313-2

Printed in the United States of America

For Micky

Special thanks to Paula Guran

—⎯∽∾∽⎯—

Preface: The Legend of Wyatt Earp

—⎯∽∾∽⎯—

Wyatt in Wichita is a novel about a historic figure: Wyatt Berry Stapp Earp. The work you hold in your hand focuses on the young Wyatt Earp. But it's still a novel and, inevitably, quite a bit of this tale is fiction, including the murder at the heart of the plot. Even so, many of the events in this novel did happen, and I tried to portray him in a way that seems to me close to the historic young Wyatt Earp. He was *capable* of doing all he does in this novel. And a number of the remarks he makes in this novel—and those made by certain others—are in fact quotations, statements made in real life.

The legend of Wyatt Earp has gone through cycles, spinning like a Peacemaker's cylinder. Early on, the first "popularizer" of the Tombstone story, Walter Noble Burns, called him "the lion of Tombstone," and Earp's myth-maker, Stuart Lake, made him the archetypal "Frontier Marshal." After a spate of overly reverential mid-century Hollywood movies, the 1960s brought a series of biased attacks on Earp's reputation. The anti-Earp crowd claimed that Lake and Earp made many of his exploits up, or wildly exaggerated them. These writers had a way of quoting Earp's enemies; they chose their documentation very selectively, and sometimes they made things up themselves—or exaggerated more than Lake did, but in the negative. One of the principal anti-Earp authors is from Texas, where people still grumble about how Wyatt Earp treated some of their grandfathers who were troublesome cowpokes in Dodge City and Wichita. Wyatt had a short way with rowdy drunks and Texas has never forgiven it.

In recent years, the cylinder has spun again. Serious, deep-delving researchers like Bob Palmquist, Allen Barra, John Gilchriese, Casey Tefertiller, and Glenn Boyer have found evidence strongly supporting Earp. Stuart Lake exaggerated and he certainly cleaned Wyatt up, but he had some of it right. For example, Earp *did*, after all, ride shotgun out of Deadwood; he *did* arrest Shanghai Pierce; and Earp's courtroom testimony concerning the gun-fight not-quite-at-the-OK-Corral has been confirmed by forensic research. The most negative tales about Wyatt S. Earp have been cast into doubt or largely refuted.

It's also true that Wyatt Earp was no angel—he was a complex man, and he had his dark side. We see that dark side in this novel: Earp was involved with a prostitution ring, in 1872. But he put this behind him and, despite some very human ethical stumbles, became a good lawman. It turns out that, despite the redundancy, he really was, as the old TV theme song had it, "brave, courageous and bold."

Some historians suspect Wyatt Earp killed more men than is generally acknowledged—Johnny Ringo might've been one of those men—but Wyatt's fights in which Wyatt fires his gun, in this novel are fiction. *Wyatt in Wichita* is about the young Earp, and takes place before Tombstone.

Many of the men Wyatt faced down in this novel were real, and Wyatt's basic conflicts with them were much as I describe them. The tale of Bat Masterson and Corporal King is true too.

While the characters Dandi LeTrouveau, Sanchez, Swinnington, Johann Burke, Toothless Mike and Montaigne are made up, Bessie Earp was a real person, as were Celia Ann "Mattie" Blaylock, Sallie Earp, Charlie Utter, Dave Leahy; so were Mike Meagher, John Slaughter, Ida May, Dunc Blackburn, Mannen Clements, Thompson's enemies in Ellsworth, and Isaac Dodge. And of course Bat Masterson was real; so was his close friendship with Wyatt Earp. The novel's newspaper quotations are also genuine. They are given verbatim.

The young Henry McCarty (also, William Henry McCarty), who later became well known under a different name, was in Wichita at the time Wyatt was there. No one knows if they met. They could have. Wyatt did have a fight with Doc Black like the one I describe in the novel, and for the reasons I give. Wyatt said he first met Wild Bill Hickok in Kansas City. Opinions vary, but I believe Wyatt could have run into James Butler "Wild Bill" Hickok in Deadwood too. And Wyatt's riding shotgun for Wells Fargo, the subsequent encounter with outlaws on the trail to Cheyenne, and how that wound up, did happen much as I described it, though I have woven the real event into my fictional plot.

Early on, I had to skip ahead in time a bit—and over some mighty eventful times. A few events in Wyatt's real history, depicted here, have been chronologically shifted for dramatic purposes. But a great many incidents in the novel really happened, as for instance the Ida May's piano story, the confrontation on the bridge over the Arkansas River, Smith's calumnies, Wyatt's thumping of him, and Abel Pierce's arrest in Wichita.

When I could, I stuck to facts.

Two Real-Life Testimonials About the Historic Wyatt Earp

"Earp is a man who never smiled or laughed. He was the most fearless man I ever saw. He is an honest man. All officers here who were associated with him declare that he was honest, and would have decided according to his belief in the face of an arsenal."

—Dick Codgell, Wichita Police Chief, 1896

"Wyatt Earp was a wonderful officer. He was game to the last ditch and apparently afraid of nothing."

—Jimmy Cairns, former Wichita Deputy, in a 1929 interview

PROLOGUE

Missouri, 1870

In the wet early morning, as the wind from the plains searched between the frame houses of Lamar, Missouri, Urilla Sutherland Earp followed her baby to the great beyond. The wind had risen all night, while Urilla lay there shivering and sweating, and then she took a final shuddering breath and was gone—as if the wind had blown her soul clean out of her weakened body.

Urilla's doctor, name of Chas Hackett, was a round-faced, snub-nosed man in a mud-speckled frock coat, his face set permanently in an expression of sympathetic resignation. He smelled of drink and shoe polish. The doctor set the stillborn child in a wicker basket, to await burial. To Wyatt, the mottled infant curled in the basket looked like a dead baby bird in a nest. Then Doctor Hackett drew the sheet over Urilla's white face, covering her sinking eyes; he patted Wyatt on the shoulder and went his way . . .

"Was it the fever or the child-bearing, took her?" Wyatt asked, his voice sounding toneless in his own ears. He sat in a straight-backed chair beside the bed; he'd built the bed-frame himself.

"Hard to tell, Mr. Earp," said the doctor gently. "Could have been the typhoid or the loss of blood in childbirth, or both."

Wyatt sat a while longer with Urilla, getting his weeping done—the last he would ever do for Urilla.

Then he stood stiffly up, and walked slowly out of the little house they'd shared for so short a time, feeling half along to dead himself after sitting up with Urilla for four days. Coming into the blowing damp he took dull note of Urilla's two brothers muttering to one another outside the front gate—the gate Wyatt had built and white washed himself. It wasn't a bad effort, that gate, but never did hang quite right.

The Sutherland boys were a couple of corn-fed, stocky, dark-eyed young men; the older one, ham-fisted Rafe, had the scraggy beginnings of a black beard; the younger, Caleb, was clean-shaven and pimply, wore a straw skimmer starting to sag in the thin, inter-mittent rain. Some of his acne was bleeding where he'd scraped it with a razor.

"She's dead ain't she?" Rafe said.

But Wyatt didn't answer, seeing his older brother Virgil riding up saddleless on one of his father's plow horses; the hooves of his pale, bulky horse splashing in the muddy road as the rain slackened off, its mane streaming in the wind.

"How's Urilla?" Virgil asked.

"She's gone," Wyatt said, his voice cracking. "And the baby."

"Dead!" Rafe exclaimed. "You are the son of a poxed whore, Wyatt Earp."

"A steaming mule dropping is what he is," said Caleb, clutching his hat to keep it in the wind.

Wyatt only watched the top of the poplars toss; the receding rain scratching the sky. Urilla was gone. The baby . . .

They had talked for a whole evening of that baby's future, just a month ago; if a girl, how she would have great learning and gentility, and—this was Urilla's notion—and perhaps she would write stories, like Miss Louisa May Alcott; Wyatt had allowed that it was perfectly all right with him if the girl wrote tales, so long as she did her chores for her family and her husband. If they had a boy, they decided, after much grave discussion, he would go to Harvard College, which was rumored to be on its way to becoming an institution of merit, back East. After university, the boy would return to Lamar and become mayor.

The baby was now a tiny blue-skinned corpse in a basket.

"I knowed you was a son of a poxed whore," Rafe was saying musingly. "I knowed it when you busted up our still—acting the Constable only to protect that Nicholas Earp's whiskey makings. Your paps can make whiskey but not us. And now you've let our sister die. You overworked her and you let her die."

Virgil got down off the horse, his boots squelching in the mud as he approached the Sutherland brothers. "That is every bit of it a lie," Virgil declared. His voice was calm but decisive. "There's not a particle of truth in it. Our father only made whiskey for himself, and the family—a few friends—and outside town limits. Your still was *inside* town limits and you were selling them spirits and that's against the law. Wyatt did right to fine you. And he never overworked Urilla. Now you two go home and let the man grieve for his wife."

But a keening fury was rising in Wyatt now, as the rising wind shrieked furiously between the fence posts. He wanted to rage at the dirty world, a world crawling with sickness like a stray dog with fleas. He was more furious with the treacherous world that had taken his Urilla than he was with the Sutherland brothers—Urilla, a trusting, doe-eyed slip of a thing who'd never done a wrong. Now she was dead with his child . . . and perhaps some of the fault was his.

And he knew he would be punished, if he got in a fight with the Sutherland boys. It seemed right that he should be punished.

Because he'd gone on that trip to Kansas City, when she'd asked him not to, and he'd fallen into the cards again, and delayed. And while he was gone she'd taken sick. But the Sutherland boys acted like he'd wanted her to get sick. Like he'd known she was poorly. It was not so. And to say he'd overworked her—as scurrilous a lie as ever man spoke.

"I do not care what these jug-headed idiots suppose," Wyatt said, his voice so measured and hollow that Virgil looked at him with surprise. "But I will not have it said I worked my wife to death. It is a wicked falsehood."

And with that he strode down the walk—it was made of flat pieces of tree-trunk he had set into the ground himself—and pushed through the picket gate with his left hand; the other, fisted, caught Rafe smartly with an uppercut. Rafe pitched backwards, to sit blinking and mud-splashed in the mucky road.

"Oh, hellfire," Virgil said, resignedly, and swung at Caleb, as the younger Sutherland started toward Wyatt; Virgil fetched him an audible thump on the side of his head, so that his hat flew off into the mud and Caleb staggered to keep from falling.

Rafe was on his feet again, and the Sutherland boys were quickly swinging back at the Earps. Two sets of brothers flailed across the mud, with Wyatt concentrating on Rafe. Swinging in wordless anger, Wyatt took blows to his face and ribs without feeling them. Mud splashed with their staggering and falls till the brown-black Missouri ooze made it impossible to tell one man from another.

Scrambling to his feet, sliding in the mud, Wyatt was dimly aware that his half-brother Newton was riding up on his tall black horse. Wearing an oiled leather coat against the rain, Newton was bearded, with tufted eyebrows and piercing blue eyes. He was known to everyone as a Civil War hero and a deadly shot. His arrival—and the shotgun cradled in his right arm—made them pause and back off a few steps. He was sure to have a pistol under his coat.

"I have it from the doctor that we have lost Urilla," Newton said, in his gravelly voice. "I presume this skirmish is the consequence."

"He . . . he let my sister die!" Caleb said, pointing at Wyatt.

"And the baby!" Rafe added, spitting out a broken tooth.

Those words penetrated to Wyatt's heart as if they were bullets fired from Caleb's pointed finger.

"You given vent to your feelings," Newton said. "At this time, you will get yourself off to that fleabag your father calls a hotel where you will pray for your sister, and the child, and send the undertaker. We ourselves will pay the undertaker. And I will hear no more of this nonsense. Or your folks will have more grieving to do."

He set the shotgun emphatically on his knee, pointing at the sky, but ready to drop and fire in an instant.

The Sutherland boys considered Newton, and his reputation. Then, pausing only to hock bloody sputum at Wyatt's feet, they turned and struggled up the street toward the center of town.

CHAPTER ONE

Soon after losing Urilla, Wyatt S. Earp sells the house and rides to Fort Gibson, Arkansas. It seems far enough away from Missouri. He is thinking of starting afresh, but the ache in him will not let him find his way. Instead, for a time, he spirals downward.

In Fort Gibson, bitter as the dregs of a vinegar barrel, he takes to drinking. Though Nicholas Porter Earp liked to make his own corn whiskey, Wyatt's father didn't approve of drunkenness, never commencing before the supper bell rang, and he had warned his sons, "A man whose head is spinning with spirits cannot make a wise judgment. He will find himself trusting the wrong men, and he may fight with men who should be his friends."

Wyatt discovers, not for the last time, that his father is right. Half starved and fully drunk in Arkansas, Wyatt falls in with a couple of shady characters, Ed Kennedy and John Shown, who bilk a man of his horses. Wyatt is arrested with Kennedy and Shown—Wyatt once a Constable, arrested!—and his father has to bail him out. The evidence is shaky, and the authorities never get around to pursuing the case. But Wyatt knows . . . Riding way from Fort Gibson, Wyatt knows what he's done.

For lack of another direction, he rides to Henry, Illinois, to see his Uncle Lorenzo. Any destination is better than returning to his father's chilly supervision; his silent disapproval.

Illinois is no better. Still troubled by drink, and twisting inside over Urilla, Wyatt falls out with his uncle—and in with a procurer named Walton who watches as Wyatt gets into a fist-fight with a train's brakeman; the fistfight flares into gun play, Wyatt wounds the brakeman with a cavalry pistol Newton has given him . . .

Walton, a pimp, is impressed with young Earp's nerve and invites him into his business, offering a cut of the proceeds, culled on what were called "gunboats" on the Illinois River . . .

1872

"I don't know why they call them gunboats," Cudgin said, not long before the ruckus. "I was in many boats, and this here's a ketch, and not far from a yawl, neither. 'Round forty foot, with yon fore and aft masts, d'ye'see?"

Wyatt Earp nodded, looking at the Illinois River in the moonlight. Mist curled along the surface, lit up by the moon, which seem to roost in the thinning branches of the trees on the far bank. The gunboat was tied up at a dock, not so far from Peoria, that'd been used by a lumber camp, now abandoned; but there was still a road to the dock, and the customers came, now and then, in their buggies and on horseback. Wyatt was sitting on a deck chair—anyway, it was a chair on the deck, though it was more like something found in a kitchen—and he was looking over the side, into the syrup-slow Illinois River. They'd had a fortnight of rains, with little respite, and the river was up high, embracing now the gray-white trunks of beeches, and lapping around the darker, muscular trunks of hickory trees. Fallen hickory leaves dimpled the water, barely moving in a current that could scarce be seen close to the banks. Wyatt thought it looked more like a pond than a river. But it was plenty deep here, deep enough for drowning.

"Walton says they were gunboats in the Civil War," Wyatt remarked. "There's a piece of iron on the deck up front where a cannon was—"

"Up *forward*, boy! Not *front!*" Cudgin interrupted, with exaggerated disdain, and slapped at a mosquito on his neck. He was a narrow shouldered, big-bellied man in a tattered, floppy hat, a matted beard; a man with blackening teeth and yellowing eyes, Cudgin believed that bathing more than once a year endangered the vital humors. Wyatt relished neither the man's conversation nor his proximity. Theoretically Amos Cudgin was the boat's pilot, though his being a near-sighted drunk seemed to suggest he wasn't right for the job. The boat's rightful pilot, a man named O'Herlihy—who'd performed a kind of marriage ceremony for Wyatt and Sarah—had been tossed in jail, a fortnight earlier, for shooting a deputy in the leg.

Sarah's voice fluted from below decks, dutifully crying: "Yes sir, that's what I call lovin'! Go and get what you're a-for, it's all yours!" There were three closet-like chambers below decks, two of them cabins, the third containing liquor and coils of rope and about six inches of sloshing dirty water, kept from the rest of the boat by a dike of oily rags; Sarah was in the nearest "business cabin" with a sheep-breeder from the outskirts of Hennepin; the new girl, Prudence, was in the farther cabin with a man who seemed too tall and wide to fit back there, but somehow they managed. As Wyatt listened—while trying not to listen—there came a certain thumping against a bulkhead, probably the belt on the back of someone's open trousers, that confirmed a customer getting what he was a-for.

Cudgin grinned at Wyatt; downwind, his grin had a smell. "There they go, to beat the Dutch! Which'n ye think tis thumping so? The little half-nigger—or your Sarah?"

Wyatt shrugged. He had developed the ability to steer his mind around that snag, and he had gotten quite good at it. He never did picture Sarah with the customers anymore. He had trained his mind to go blank when it came to the actual *doing* of Sarah's work. Still, he didn't like to hear them, below . . .

"You some kind of husband to that Sarah, aire ye?" Cudgin went on.

"Some kind," Wyatt said.

When was Walton coming back? He would provide some relief from Cudgin's company. And Wyatt had a burr under his saddle about his pay. He thought it ought to include some regular money as well as the cut, because he seemed never to have enough to put aside. He had said as much to Sarah, and she'd said, as women tartly will, *"Perhaps if you put them cards aside you can put some gold aside . . ."*

Cudgin fished in the big pockets of his long ragged brown coat, first one side and then the other, at length producing a small jug. "Will you take a pull?" he asked.

"I thank you, no," Wyatt said. He was trying not to drink. The memory of his drunken fiasco in Fort Gibson was still painfully fresh.

Cudgin sucked at his jug, snorted, shuddered, and slapped a mosquito. "Do ye think the constable will come out, some night? To arrest us—or mayhap to have a poke at them girls?"

"Could be. But Walton uses gunboat so we can move around, go from one county to another, to dodge all that. Friends who give us warning of the law . . ." Wyatt fell silent, waving away a mosquito humming past his ear. The law was another subject he didn't like.

The boat drifted in the faint wind and the fainter current and thumped against the pier, then swung outward again, like the hand on an uncertain clock. "That's right, that's right, my big black beard!" Sarah said. Her voice seemed so small and piping, coming from down there. Perhaps he might again approach her about going away from here. She seemed to misunderstand his intentions, before. They were not really scratching out much this way, though it all seemed so easy.

Then came a roar from below, and the squeal of a frightened girl. A moment later the big man—a tree-cutter, his long brown mustaches seeming to jet from his nostrils—was squeezing himself out of the hatchway. There was a thumping on the narrow, steeply-pitched stairs, and Wyatt was on his feet, seeing that the lumberjack was pulling the girl up by the wrist like a one-armed man dragging a feed sack.

"Don't—!" she yelped, as he heaved her up to the deck. It was Prudence, a short, stocky, colored girl with the wavy black hair, wearing only a slip now, and that torn.

"What's this shindy?" Cudgin was saying, looking more pleased with the show than outraged, as Mule—that was the moniker of this lumberjack—dragged the girl toward the aft of the boat.

"This whore sought to refuse me, after I paid my gold!" Mule bellowed, dragging the thrashing girl. "I told her she'd go swimming if I didn't get mine and still she refused me! 'You is crushing me,' she whines, 'crushing me! I cain't breathe!' Breathe underwater, nigger cow!"

"You! Stop yourself, right there!" Wyatt shouted. Adding, even louder, as he drew his pistol, "Not a step further!"

"Ahoy, Mule, here comes the shavetail!" Cudgin called in glee, as Wyatt shoved past him and ducked a boom to reach the two figures struggling at the end of the boat.

But Mule was lifting the girl like a chunk of wood. He tossed her overboard. Mule watched her splashing, and laughed.

"Damn you!" Wyatt said, and fired a shot past Mule's head to get his attention.

Mule jumped and touched his ear; the bullet had carved the shape of a quarter moon from it. He turned and rushed at Wyatt, roaring moonshine fumes; Wyatt sidestepped and tripped him, sending a kick into his rump to help him along. He heard the girl thrashing in the water.

"Sarah!" she yelled. "Mister . . . !" The rest was lost to bubbling.

"Get that girl up from the water!" Wyatt shouted at Cudgin. Wyatt was occupied with Mule, who was getting to his knees.

"I cain't swim!" she shouted. "I cain't . . ."

"Get her out, Cudgin!"

"Why, I . . ." Cudgin said, scratching in his beard.

Wyatt pressed the muzzle of his gun to the back of Mule's neck. "You feel that? You won't rush me another time. That ball will go right through your spine! Now if you want to walk again, get up and walk off this boat. Go—and do not turn around!"

Wyatt's heart was pounding. He was not at all sure he could bring himself to shoot this man through the back of the neck. And if Mule chose to spin around and grapple, the burly lumberjack would have the edge.

Mule growled, "I will return and see you sunk, or in jail!"

He stalked off, the boat jittering in the water with his heavy tread; Wyatt followed him to the dock. Still shouting threats, Mule leapt onto the pier and made for his horse.

Wyatt turned back to find a black-bearded face—so heavily bearded the nose and eyes were near overwhelmed—glaring up at him from the hatch.

Sarah leaned to look past the corona of her client's beard. She was wearing only a shift, one freckled shoulder exposed, her curly red-gold hair adrift around her head. "I cannot reach the end of my ride with all this caterwauling!" the sheep-breeder complained. "I need me a refund!"

"He reached it all right," Sarah said, pushing past him. She lifted the skirt, showing her pale skinny legs, her knobby knees—and the snail track of semen running down the inside of her thigh.

"You skedaddle too," Wyatt said, cocking his gun in the sheep-breeder's face. The man's eyes got wide, and he scurried off the boat, making for his buckboard.

"I told you," Wyatt said to Sarah, "you are to use the lamb's slipper." Condoms of lamb's intestine were used here at Wyatt's insistence.

"I did! But it went bust! He's got a pecker like ten dollar lumber!"

"You've been re-using them, Sarah? The Doctor told you not to do that. They'll bust, he said."

"Them things is dear, Wyatt! We can't afford a new one every time!" She looked around. "Where's . . ."

Cudgin had come forward, was gaping after the buckboard clattering up the trail. "You think they'll bring the constables?"

Wyatt stared at him. "Where's the girl, Cudgin?"

"Why, I . . . it'd be worth my life to leap into them waters, the humors—"

Wyatt shook his head in disgust. "You didn't even look, damn you . . ."

"Prudence!" Sarah yelped. She ran to the other end of the boat and knelt. "Prudence girl!"

They found her after about thirty minutes of searching, Wyatt and Cudgin—who had to be persuaded by a clout on the head to come along—and Sarah, had to pick their way through the brush along the flooded bank.

It was Wyatt who spotted her. Prudence was floating face-down under the roots of a fallen tree tipped into the river . . .

After that, Wyatt felt he had just go ahead and bury her, because she had no kin locally that they knew of, and by the time he was done forcing Cudgin to dig the grave, and they wrapped Prudence in a sailcloth and said their goodbyes—Sarah's freckles went glossy with weeping; Cudgin ogled at the grave open-mouthed, as if he expected Prudence to climb spectrally out and drag him under for letting her drown.

The Constable drove up in a buggy, followed by Mule on his horse and two deputies and all the lies Mule had prepared. The constable's arrival was all that saved Cudgin from the beating Wyatt was planning.

They were afraid they'd be charged in the girl's death if they spoke of it, and it ended that they were jailed in Peoria for unlicensed procuring and whoring, and it took all their money to work a release . . .

* * *

"Sarah," Wyatt said, when they were walking down the street in the thin late-September morning sunlight, weary from a sleepless night in the stifling Peoria City Jail, "I believe the both of us need a new profession." A stout woman stared at them as she passed on the wooden sidewalk; she peered from under her flowery hat, from within a flouncy yellow dress with the biggest bustle Wyatt had ever seen. She seemed to be biting her lip to keep from calling them names.

"Your own mama, Sarah," Wyatt went on, lowering his voice, "only got herself sick and a slave to opium. I don't want that for you. Think of what happened to poor Prudence! That is no business for any sensible woman. And the judge here knows us now, and hates the sight of us. We will go to stay with my family, and get a new start. I could find a partner, do some freighting, save my money—"

"You have thought it all out!" Sarah said, her hands trying to make some sense of her hair as she walked. "But you have not thought about my first husband! I was married at fourteen; I already tried me the life of a country woman, the mistress of a farmer—"

"I have not asked you to farm."

"It amounts to the same kind of life. He made me work my fingers till I was sore and asleep standing up. Before we was married, told me he wouldn't make me do that—same as you say now. So don't you bother to lie about it, I know what men do. Your father is a farmer; I know how it'd go. I run off from my husband and I'm glad to be shed of him. I am saving money for a house in St. Louis, where I will never have to touch a man, but only order the girls about."

"You have put money aside, and not told me?"

"My mother keeps it for me."

"And you think it's still there? Your mother will have spent every penny."

"Shut your bazoo, Wyatt Earp, do not blacken my mother, who did the best she knowed!"

And so it went, their friendship deteriorating, their intimacy gone. It made Wyatt sick to his stomach, thinking of that bearded gnome's ejaculate running down Sarah's leg.

Being arrested on the boat had shamed Wyatt, though he kept a defiant face before the judge. Wyatt had seen enough of laudanum-addled whores and greasy procurers and stiff-necked judges sniffily handing out inflated fines. He was determined to change directions.

Sarah was obdurate; she would not go with him. Wyatt was stung by her refusal: she should have trusted him, should have followed him wherever he went.

He pondered her shrugging him away, lumping him with some pig-farmer, and left her within the week.

Wyatt got up before noon on a Sunday, while she was still asleep, and put a few things in a bag, slung it over his saddle, and rode to the south, and the west . . .

CHAPTER TWO

About two years later

"Bat," said Wyatt Earp, as he shifted on the seat of the wagon, "I am fed up with shooting buffalo, fed up twice-over with *skinning* buffalo, and will have no more of it." As he remarked on this to Bat Masterson, who rode his white-faced mare alongside, Wyatt guided the two oxen to the top of the low rise and saw the dusty wooden buildings of Ellsworth, Kansas, clustered on the flat prairie less than a quarter mile away. He stopped the freight wagon, a massive oaken dray piled precariously high with roped-down buffalo hides, to consider the prospect of Ellsworth in summer of 1874.

Blocky and false-fronted, built mostly of uncured green lumber, with the occasional hump of a sod-roofed dug-out on the fringes of town, the buildings seemed huddled together for protection from the big emptiness of the plains. To one side curved the Smoky Hill River, a thin twist of glossy-brown in this time of drought. Ellsworth had begun to replace Abilene as the major cattle market and hundreds of longhorns roiled in cattle pens south of town— which was downwind most of the time. He could just hear the distant lowing of the cattle, and faintly, the moan of an accordion from one of the saloons. Ellsworth seemed quiet enough, in the late afternoon but Wyatt knew it could be uproarious at night.

William Bartholomew "Bat" Masterson reined in beside Wyatt, and looked down on the little town with satisfaction, removing his bowler hat to slap away the trail dust. He was a medium-sized wide-shouldered man with mischievous blue eyes, a drooping black mustache, and, generally, a genial expression. "It could be that after a bath, Wyatt, maybe two baths to get it all off, and we eat something besides buffalo and sage hen, why, you'll say to me, 'Bat, I need another five hundred dollars to go into the freighting business, and the buffalo have got my money . . . '"

"Buffalo are getting scarce anyhow. I'll have enough money in hand, already, come sunset, which looks to be in about one hour," Wyatt said.

"But you know how you like to turn a card, Wyatt. And if you lose your poke . . ."

"I will not lose my poke. As I'll prove to you if we can only go and claim it. Let us get a wiggle on." With the wagon halted, the reek of the hides drifted strongly around him, and he yearned to be shed of them.

He clucked at the two oxen, cracking his whip, and the wagon started rattling down the hill, following the trail through rabbit brush and buffalo grass. Bat rode close beside, his horse clopping. He hummed "Little Brown Jug" as they went.

When they were nearly to the wooden freight docks at the railroad tracks, near a fly-haunted mountain of stored hides, Bat said, "Those hides, so many as that together, smell so bad, the smells fled around from sour and nearly gone to sweet again. The nose cannot register it."

Lost in thought, Wyatt didn't reply. Bat looked at Wyatt and chuckled.

"What's so whimsical?" Wyatt asked, coming out of his study with a frown. He was sensitive to being laughed at.

"Why, I was just thinking I shouldn't expect any more talk from you—for a few minutes ago you spoke several sentences to me, like you were in haste to come to a grand total of a hundred words for the totality of our hunting trip."

Wyatt snorted. Bat was voluble, sometimes wrote long letters to the newspapers under imaginary names—as they say Ben Franklin had done, to get his start in journalism—and aspired to be a journalist. On occasion he spoke of moving to New York City, a prospect Wyatt found repugnant. "You talk enough for two, three, and four of us, Bat. Just like your brothers."

But the next afternoon, though still a bit achy from weeks sleeping in a wagon, a bathed and fed Wyatt Earp was at table in the Generous Lady, chatting amiably enough with a young woman.

The girl was Celia Ann Blaylock, a stolid blond in a red satin gown that exposed her wide, pale shoulders; she was familiarly called "Mattie," and she was not especially fetching. There was cold coffee at Wyatt's elbow, and a deck of cards fluttered absently in his hands as he glanced around the bar. The cattle being penned for the freight trains, and end-of-drive money frittered away, most of the drovers had moved on. Only one other table was occupied: a group of gamblers sat near the dust-coated window. One of the poker players was a city policeman of Wyatt's acquaintance. Dour and sometimes belligerent, "Happy Jack" Murco had pocketed his badge for the moment, as he sat drinking whiskey and playing poker with John Sterling—a local baggy-pants gambler who was sometimes a deputy—and Ben Thompson, a cattleman known for his moodiness and his eagerness with a gun. In Thompson, easy affability alternated with a taste for feuding.

Thompson saw Wyatt look his way, and gave a curt nod, for Wyatt had once backed his play in a hair-trigger stand-off with a group of drunken *vaqueros*. No gunfire had ensued, but Thompson had noticed Wyatt's dislike of seeing one man facing four alone.

"What did you do with your team and wagon?" Mattie asked. Her gown—her only gown—was starting to lose its color from many washings; he noticed she'd repaired the seams, in places, with some hasty stitching, the threads not quite matching. There was a finger-shaped bruise on her left shoulder, inadequately covered with a cosmetic powder. One of her customers had gotten too rough.

Wyatt felt a pang, looking at the bruise—and wondered how Sarah Haspel was doing in Illinois. Was she being ill-treated too? He thought of the girl Prudence, floating face down in the river . . .

"You going to sell them oxen?" Mattie persisted. She was probably wondering if he had already sold them and thus had the cash on him: totting up in her mind all that he'd made with buffalo hides and oxen. She took no money from him, but it was the habit of a bar girl.

"Oxen aren't suitable for long-distance freighting," he said, cutting the cards and idly dealing himself a hand, "though I've seen it done. Mostly they're too slow. I'll sell them in the morning and buy a team of horses." He spoke as if he were a flush businessman, who knew his trade, but in fact he was afraid of getting euchred, for he knew little enough about freighting. He took a sip of coffee and grimaced at the taste. He supposed he might call for some condensed milk, he had seen the Borden's can back of the bar, but it had likely sat there, open, for a day or two. He would stick with the plain arbuckle. He never drank liquor anymore, other than an occasional short glass of beer. After what'd happened in Arkansas, he'd sworn off strong spirits.

It was time to say something or seem offish—he knew people thought him offish—so he said: ". . . I'm sure sick of killing buffalo." He had started to wonder if the general slaughter wasn't a mistake; if perhaps the government might not take a hand. A power of buffalo were being killed—all that meat wasted. It was said the Plains Tribes resented it, and he could understand that.

"You could stick here," Mattie suggested. "Huck Buford wants someone to buy a share of his saloon. You could go in with him."

Wyatt didn't like Huck Buford, and he knew, anyway, why Mattie was making the suggestion. She and Wyatt had kept company, a time or two, on his visits to town. Mattie had taken to granting him her favors gratis, like the Generous Lady namesake of the saloon. She was hoping he'd be around long enough to make her a habit.

Right now Wyatt was wishing Bat had waited for him. He wanted advice. But Bat had set out that morning to see his own brothers, Jim and Ed, over in Dodge City. Perhaps, Wyatt thought, I might send telegrams to Virgil and James, make an effort to get them into the freighting business.

Taking care of business didn't include going upstairs with Mattie Blaylock—for she was not a woman who rushed through a job of that kind, at least not with him—and he was casting about for a polite way to cut her loose. He told himself he had left that life behind; he wanted no more special understandings with Ladies of Easy Virtue. Yet he could not suppose himself morally in the clear, after his time on the gunboat. And he thought of most prostitutes as women of simple practicality: for many an abandoned woman, whoring was the only road out of starvation. His own brother James had married a whore; "white-washing a soiled dove" was not uncommon. Sarah had spurned her chance for another life. She had spurned Wyatt with it . . .

He grimaced. He suspected that Mattie had set her cap for him, as Bessie Earp had for James. Keeping company could become keeping hearth and home.

Home. Shuffling the cards to no purpose, Wyatt remembered all the days Urilla had tossed in the fever of typhus. It was a mercy that Urilla had been delirious during the delivery; that she hadn't known her child had been born dead.

Thinking of the dead child, he remembered Prudence's body floating facedown in the muddy green water, like something washed from the scupper, her hair swirling about her head mingled with leaves and twigs. He should never have trusted Cudgin to see to her . . .

"What is it, Wyatt?" Mattie asked, now. "You looked like you expected a peach and bit into a lemon."

"So it was too," Wyatt murmured, sitting up straight. "Two such sour peaches, in fact. I will see you later, Mattie—it's early yet, and I've business to do." He slid her a double eagle. "For the comfort of a lady's conversation."

Mattie tucked her chin, looking at him closely to see if he were making a game of her, and smiled when she saw no mockery. The gold piece vanished into her bosom, neat as a magic trick.

"You, John Sterling, are a scabrous rascal and a cheat!" said a low voice that had a tinge of British nestled in its Texas accent: for Ben Thompson and his brother Bill had been born and partly reared in England. "And I believe you are in it with him, Murco! You signaled him when you dealt those cards!"

Wyatt turned to see Ben Thompson glaring at John Sterling. Thompson had drooping mustaches, and his receding hair emphasized the roundness of his large head.

"You will withdraw that foul lie, Thompson!" Sterling shouted, standing suddenly enough to knock a whiskey bottle to the floor. The bottle did not break and there was a moment when the three men glared at one another and the only sound was the whiskey gurgling from the overturned bottle.

Sterling was a plump man with a tinhorn's checked suit and too many rings on his fingers, but his hand had gone with practiced ease to a gun in his waistband. Murco, a ferret-faced, snaggle-toothed man who seemed to sleep in his disheveled clothes—despite his being a city official—had a hand in the pocket of his long black coat.

"I am not heeled," said Thompson. "I have no weapon about me. But if you'll lay those guns aside my fists will teach you not to cheat a gentleman."

"The devil you will," said Murco, swaying. "Go get your weapon, if you haven't pawned it, and you can bring that no-account brother of yours too."

Wyatt knew Murco for a coward and a back-shooter, and also knew he would not be challenging a known gunman like Thompson—who had been warned by Sheriff Whitney not to carry a pistol in town limits—if he were not drunk.

Thompson's voice a cougar's purr. "Sir, you have declared for your own end."

And Thompson stamped out through the doors, seeing to it that they banged loudly behind him.

Wyatt found he had his own hand on his pistol; he'd instinctively been prepared to defend the unarmed Thompson.

Now he dropped his hand from his gun, as the drunken gamblers stumbled to the bar and shouted for rye. "We'll get some of my friends on the police force," Murco was saying, in a low voice to Sterling, "but you'll have to pay them for their help. They'll back us up if Thompson comes looking for a fight."

Wyatt told himself it was best to stay out of this affair entirely.

* * *

Frontier shooting affrays are not likely to culminate neatly, and the participants, if they lived, invariably thought back on the event with puzzlement and regret. What had they been fighting about? Drink was almost always implicated.

Billy Thompson had been drinking gin since his noontime breakfast of steak and eggs. Ben had limited himself to a single brandy in his coffee, and on entering Brennan's saloon he was disgusted to see his younger brother Billy—slender, pale, with scraggly mustaches—swaying at the bar and leering at the barmaid.

"Billy," Ben said, striding up, brandishing his Winchester, "I need you sober now. We have business at the Generous Lady." He had gotten his gun belt with its two six-shooters from his hotel room, and the Winchester for good measure.

"Ha!" Billy crowed, "Sober! You've found me full drunken, and rejoicing in it, by God!" He kicked at a brass cuspidor, sending it spinning with a clatter.

"Then you'd best stay here," Ben said flatly.

But it was then that Billy took full notice of his brother's Winchester and pistols. He patted Ben's rifle. "Why you are loaded for bear! What's the trouble? Who has insulted my family? I will line the buggers up and blow holes in them!" Billy grinned—it made one eye squeeze small when he grinned that way— and pulled back his long, beer-stained suit-coat to show he had a small pistol hidden in a holster on the back of his left hip. He turned and swept up a double-barreled shotgun leaning against the bar. "I was going to go out and hunt jackrabbit, but by God we can hunt sons of bitches just the same . . ."

"Billy, wait—"

But Billy was already striding to the front door and out onto the sidewalk—almost missing the door in his drunkard's walk—and Ben saw with dismay that he had cocked the shotgun and was glaring around the street. He stalked off across the dusty street toward the Generous Lady, with Ben hurrying to keep up.

"Billy, now hold on—ease the hammers off that shotgun—" Ben said, joining him on the wooden sidewalk a few steps from the Generous Lady's front door. "You're too drunk to have a cocked gun in hand . . ."

But Billy spun at a creaking on the sidewalk and the hammer fell, discharging one of the shotgun barrels to blast a splintery hole in the sidewalk at the feet of two startled cavalrymen. "Don't shoot us, friend!" cried one of soldiers, stumbling back. "We are not armed!"

"He did not mean it, gentlemen," Ben said, turning to his chuckling, swaying brother. "Billy, now you see you've nearly shot two innocent men . . . Come on with me, we'll sober you up a bit, and then perhaps we'll demand an apology and my one hundred and forty-seven dollars from the crooks who took it at cards . . . It's that Murco and Sterling, I should never have played a single hand with them . . ."

"A couple of vermin, those two!" Billy declared, cocking the shotgun again "Crikey, they'll shoot you in the back, Ben—you've got to keep a watch on the whole 'orizon for 'em!"

"Ben Thompson!" shouted Sheriff Whitney, approaching. He was an older man with graying temples and a beard mixing white and stained yellow; one hand was on the butt of his pistol but the other was raised in a gesture of conciliation. "Who are you shooting at here?"

"Oh, Billy's gun discharged accidentally, Chauncey," Ben said. He liked Chauncey Whitney—the sheriff had always been patient with Billy and amiable with them both. "We've got to have words with some card cheats—"

"You will leave the card cheats to me, Ben!" Whitney reproved him, gently.

"They are yours already, for one's a town policeman and the other sometimes a deputy—and crooked as most of the so-called lawmen in this town!" Ben said angrily. Adding in a lower tone, "Present company, sir, excepted."

"Tell you what, Ben—you and Billy come with me into Brennan's, and we'll have a few drinks and talk it over, and I expect we'll come to an understanding."

"Well Chauncey, if you think you can obtain a fair—"

"Look out, Ben!" shouted Wyatt Earp, stepping out of the tele-graph office two doors down. Drawing his pistol, Earp pointed toward the saloon with his other hand.

Ben turned to see Murco and Sterling lunging toward him from the Generous Lady, both of them even drunker than he'd left them, their pistols in hand; Murco raising his pistol, firing at the Thompson brothers.

Two bullets whined past—one of them close enough to the sheriff to make the old lawman bridle in surprise and anger. "What the devil!"

Ben snapped off a shot with the Winchester, the round neatly drilling through the corner of a wooden post near Sterling's head, so that the gambler ducked back with an unmanly squeak, and Murco—looking surprised that someone was shooting back at him—turned and ran back into the bar. Acrid gunsmoke hung pur-ple in the air. Seeing the gamblers had retreated, Wyatt holstered his sidearm. But Ben was cocking his gun—

Sheriff Whitney rushed to push Ben's gun down. "No, that's full enough shooting!" And then there came a thunderous discharge. Whitney made an inhuman sound between a grunt and a squeal, and staggered back.

Ben turned to see blue-black smoke drifting from the muzzle of Billy's shotgun—as Sheriff Whitney fell, shot where the shoulder meets the neck. Billy had tried to move into a shooting angle to fire at Sterling but in his drunkenness had squeezed the trigger too soon, hitting Whitney instead.

"You've shot me, Billy!" Whitney cried, sinking to his knees, gushing blood.

Ben stared, amazed. How had it come to this? He saw Whitney pitch over groaning, face down in a growing pool of scarlet. The shot had been at close range, the wound was big, the copious blood suggesting a blasted artery—Whitney was likely to bleed to death.

Billy was staring down at Whitney in shock. Ben shook his head grimly. "Billy, you're going to have to leave town, and fast."

"What about those two dogs Murco and Sterling! This is their fault!"

"For God's sake leave town! You've shot our best friend!"

"I don't give a damn!" Billy said, though the quaver in his voice testified differently. Then he got some of his bravado back and shouted, "I'd have shot if it'd been Jesus Christ!"

Ben thrust a small bag of silver dollars into Billy's hand, "Here's money and there's your horse. Get you on it and ride like Hell! I'll find you somewhere near Abilene! Go!"

Billy dropped the shotgun and backed away from the sheriff, then turned and ran to his horse, and in seconds was galloping out of town. Dust from his horse's hooves mixed with gun smoke.

Wyatt and Deputy John DeLong were hurrying up to the sheriff, and Ben Thompson—glancing at the Generous Lady and seeing no sign of Murco and Sterling—hastened to his hotel as quickly as dignity permitted.

Ben just didn't know where else to go—but he knew he had to cover Billy's exit from town.

* * *

"I heard some more gunshots," remarked Wyatt, emerging from the doctor's office. "Quite a few." He was speaking to Town Marshal "Brocky John" Morton who was standing at the corner of the next building, peering from the shadows at the hotel down the street. Morton was a lean, pockmarked man with sallow skin. Wyatt had never been impressed with him. Like the other local constabulary, apart from Whitney, Morton only enforced the law for the highest bidder. Wyatt had heard him deny that the roulette wheels in the gambling halls were rigged. But Mattie had quietly warned Wyatt that they were indeed rigged—and he knew that Morton raked a percentage of the game.

Morton turned to look Wyatt over. "Why yes, Ben Thompson has been firing at the door of the livery stable—and at every hitching post on the street—to keep a deputation from fetching their horses."

"Trying to keep them from going after Billy, I expect," Wyatt murmured, nodding to himself. He understood, well enough. There was little he would not do for his own brothers, or they for him. The Earps were a curious mix of independent and clannish, and he never went long without seeing family, whatever differences he might have with them. "Where's Thompson shooting from?"

"Just inside the hotel door, over there."

"What about Sterling and Murco?" Earp asked. "They still shooting at him?"

Morton shook his head. "Murco's gone to ground somewhere, and Sterling took the train out of town. Say, how's Whitney?"

"The wound is stanched," said Wyatt. "But he has lost a power of blood. He will be dead within the hour, so the doctor says . . ."

Another shot rang out, scoring a hitching post across from the hotel, and making a pinto pony rear and snort. Morton stepped back into the alley. "You see that saloon over there—Brennan's? Abel Pierce and five of his men are in there. Sheriff Whitney was a good friend of Pierce's. He wants to hang both the Thompson brothers . . . And he hates Ben Thompson anyway—he had some kind of bad cattle deal with him. Some of the cattle died and Ben wouldn't pay up."

"That's *Shanghai* Pierce?" Wyatt said, thinking of the big man with the fancy boots who liked to cut such a dramatic figure in the Kansas cow towns. "I thought the drovers moved on."

"Pierce is still here with some of his men—he's waiting on payment from a Chicago buyer."

"Bat says Pierce thinks he's emperor of Texas."

"He's emperor, anyhow, of a good many gunhands—and he'll go after Thompson, soon enough . . ."

"This's got to end, Marshal," Wyatt said. "Thompson's going to hit someone with that Winchester, whether he intends to or not . . . And if it isn't that, it'll come to a gunfight with Pierce."

"Thompson'll run out of bullets, in time," Morton said.

"Not before he hits someone," Wyatt insisted.

Morton turned a glare at Wyatt. "Well then why don't you go over there—disarm him, shoot him down, whatever you like? Here . . ."

He took off his badge and summarily pinned it on Wyatt's shirt. "Go ahead, 'Mouthy' if you're so full of suggestions. I heard you were a constable, one time . . . let's see you constabalize."

Another shot—and a window shattered. A woman screamed in fear.

Morton stuck out his hand. "Or give me the badge back and shut your mouth, boy!"

Wyatt snorted. He had been about to do just that until Morton sneered at him. And if someone didn't do something they'd be lynching Ben Thompson before this was over . . .

Wyatt shrugged and stepped out into the main street. He began to walk toward the hotel, going diagonally down the road, affecting a serenity he didn't feel.

He squinted against the glare of the late afternoon sun. It would have been better to have the sun behind him.

A bullet kicked up dust at his feet, and he heard its report a split-second later. Thompson firing at him from inside the hotel. His gait only hitched a little at that. But his mouth went dry and metal-tasting. He knew, in the marrow of his bones, that it was important to seem unafraid. It didn't matter if a man was quaking inside, so long as he could seem like a park statue on the outside. It was his brother Newton who'd told him that. *If you got to go at 'em, keep your head—and if you've got to fire, aim slow and careful.*

But he hoped he wouldn't have to use his pistol. He and Thompson knew one another. Ben Thompson wouldn't shoot him down. At least, he didn't think so.

Another small geyser of dust spat up near his right boot. That one was closer. "Ben Thompson!" Wyatt shouted, reaching the wooden walk on the other side of the street—and the welcome shade of the overhangs and false fronts. "Ben! It's Wyatt Earp! Don't shoot me, I'm just here to have a word with you!"

He strode onward, and reached the hotel, paused at the corner of the building. The downstairs front window shattered, glass flashing outward to tinkle on the sidewalk—whether from bullet or gun-butt, Wyatt wasn't sure.

"Ben!" Wyatt shouted again. "Just a word or two!"

Then he saw Thompson stepping into the doorway of the hotel, smoking Winchester in his hands, the muzzle pointed toward Wyatt. "How's Chauncey, Earp?"

"Not good," Wyatt admitted. "He won't make it."

Thompson sighed and shook his large round head. "I'm sorry for that. But it wasn't me who shot him."

"That's something the court'll surely take note of, Ben," Wyatt said, coming closer. "You probably won't get in any serious trouble . . ."

Thompson raised the Winchester to his shoulder. Wyatt was looking down its muzzle. It was infinitely black, down that muzzle. "Hold it right there!" Thompson barked.

But Wyatt kept coming, raising his hands up in front of him, walking slowly, locking his eyes on Thompson's. He kept his voice as amiable as the tension allowed. "Got to come and talk to you Ben. Got to. Shanghai Pierce is pouring whiskey into his men, working them up to rush you."

"This affair'll be his excuse to get me," Thompson said, shrugging. "That's all it is, Wyatt."

Wyatt suspected, then, that Thompson could be made to surrender—an angry man who'll talk without cursing you will usually come to terms, if you're patient with him. So his father had told him.

"Don't give Pierce the excuse, Ben. Listen, I understand what you're doing for your brother. But he's long gone by now. They won't take out after him—they're all half drunk and ready for their suppers. He'll get to where he's going. You can surrender now and not worry about him."

"Suppose Pierce wants to lynch me right out of the jail? Or Murco, some of Chauncey's friends?"

"I guarantee you'll not be harmed," Wyatt said. "I'll stand a watch."

Thompson grunted. "I'm sure sorry about ol' Chauncey. Billy didn't mean it—he was full as a tick, Wyatt. Didn't know what he was doing."

"I'm sure of it. Folks in town know that. Now toss out your weapons and I'll see you safe to the calaboose . . ." He set his hand on his gun, signifying his willingness to blaze away if he had to, even though Thompson had the drop on him.

Thompson smiled. "You've got some sand, I'll give you that." He leaned the Winchester against the doorjamb, and unbuckled his gun belt, tossed it aside. "But I want a cup of coffee, once we get into that jail. Sweetened with brandy."

"Sweetened with brandy it is, Ben."

* * *

"I estimate it this way," said Abel "Shanghai" Pierce. "It's clear to me and it's clear to everyone here, that both brothers are responsible for Chauncey's death, Billy and Ben: the two of them are to blame, and both should hang." He stood with his back to the bar, elbows propped on it, a flute of champagne looking lost in his big right hand. A prosperous cattleman from Texas, Pierce was six foot four, a rawboned man with a voice that boomed no matter what he said. It was the parade trumpet of his pugnacious bearing. He had a shock of reddish brown hair, matching red mustaches, a high-crowned dove-colored Stetson; on his feet were finely figured stovepipe boots, with higher heels than most, and jangling spurs of silver and gold. He was called "Shanghai" by some because with his oversized golden spurs and general oversized demeanor; he was said to strut like "a Shanghai rooster." He didn't like champagne much, but he always drank some when he closed a deal, and he'd made eight thousand dollars that afternoon, thanks to Sternbrest, the Chicago stockyard buyer for the U.S. Cavalry.

"You got it right, boss. The Hell with them Thompsons." This from Pierce's ramrod, Grigsby, sitting nearby playing cards. He was lanky and red-faced and missing every third tooth. Grigsby was known for his highly developed sense for cattle and no other kind of sense at all.

Ranged at the bar and the table, the six rumpled, unshaved men with Pierce, still wearing chaps against the thorn brush, were trail hands in various stages of grime and drunkenness—they'd all come from cutting cattle for the freight train just minutes after Whitney had been carried off to the doctor's office. Normally they'd be heading for the barber and a bath, but the Thompson business had detoured them to this waterhole for a pondering session.

"But then borrowin' trouble seems like asking for what nature give us already," said old Dudley mildly. He was a time-worn Texas cowboy known as a purveyor of gnomic pronouncements and homilies. As he spoke, Dudley was trying to throw darts at a target; his wayward darts had chivvied the drinkers at that end of the bar to another corner. "Sorry . . . I'll get 'er yet . . ." He wore a rust-colored sombrero over his stringy gray hair and a Mexican shirt sewn with crude images of guitars and dancing senoritas. The other cowboys told him he was dressed "too young for that leathery rump of yours." He squinted at the dartboard. "Yes, borrowin' trouble saves a penny for Hell . . . that's what my ma used to say . . ." Dudley was often the voice of moderation, and forgetting to agree with Mr. Pierce had cost him his ramrod job. But he stuck with the outfit; there wasn't much else, at his age.

"Ol' Dudley, he's always quotin' his mama," snorted sour-faced Creighton, aiming brown spit at the cuspidor and missing. "Mr. Pierce is right about Thompson, that's my view."

"Sure Mr. Pierce is right!" said the stick-slender young cowboy named George Hoy, drawing two cards. "Damn, I'm out, Grig, I got nothin', nor even hope of fooling you."

"I agree with you too, Mr. Pierce," said a dark figure sitting in the corner, hunched over a cup of coffee. "If his name's Thompson, why, he needs to hang."

"Well now, that's Happy Jack Murco speaking up," said Hoy, looking over. "And Murco owes me twelve dollars."

Murco didn't address the twelve-dollar debt. "It seems to me that, what with the various friends Thompson's got in this town, he's going to wing it out of here with his skin intact, soon enough. They'll slide him out of the jail when the night's dark. Unless someone was to get to him in that jail, first . . ."

"Now how would you propose a man could do that short of shooting his way in?" Pierce asked, cocking his head, putting his champagne glass on the bar. "Morton and that new deputy's guarding him. I'd hate to have to dodge the U.S. Marshals all the way back to Texas."

"Well sir, if someone was inspired to it, I expect he could get those deputies out of that jail, long enough for somebody else to get in there and finish up their business . . . There is a way, I believe. As I said, it's a matter of inspiration."

Pierce leaned back against the bar, idly spun the spurs of one boot on the brass foot-rest, and considered his choices. Murco made it sound effortless, but this was a risky undertaking. The law was already concerned to question Pierce about some rather precipitous hangings, on his holdings back in Texas; it wouldn't be wise to burn his bridges in Kansas too. But on the other side of it, he hated that son of a bitch Thompson.

Who was Thompson to buck him? Abel Pierce had shaped the Texas cattle industry; had worked to make his mark since running off from Rhode Island at the age of nineteen. He'd stowed away on a ship bound to the Gulf of Mexico and was unceremoniously pitched off the ship near the town of Houston. In Texas he'd learned all there was to know about cattle, working for W.B. Grimes. He'd learned other sorts of things in the Civil War. Despite his Yankee origins, he'd signed onto the Confederate Army—for his Uncle Fergus had convinced him the Bible endorsed slavery. He'd butchered cattle for a whole Army and had been impressed with the vast amounts of money spent on beef. Back in Texas after the war, he'd carved out an empire—and he demanded deference from every man he worked with. Was he not a direct descendant of John Alden? Was he not kin to old President Franklin Pierce? Closest thing to American royalty.

Along came Ben Thompson, innocently asking to run his cattle with Pierce, then demanding a second count at the end of the drive. He came within a hair of accusing Pierce of stealing several hundred head. Didn't matter if it was true—Thompson had called him low-down, and a thief, and they'd nearly dueled over it. Thompson then told a cattle buyer over in Dodge City that Pierce could not be trusted, costing Pierce a lucrative deal.

Ben Thompson deserved to die for that effrontery alone. And here he'd been in complicity with the murder of the sheriff—Whitney had always shown Pierce the respect he deserved—and he'd shot up the town to cover the murderer's escape. The more Pierce thought about it, the more he felt his blood rising in him. Ben Thompson had blackened Shanghai Pierce's reputation and Bill Thompson was a murderer. Both of them deserved a summary hanging—had for a long time. Ben Thompson had killed a number of men himself, before coming to Ellsworth. Gunfights? Executions, if you were fighting a man who couldn't shoot straight. And now people knew what Pierce's preference was, in the matter of Thompsons. They had heard him declare it. Making Thompson his enemy, anyhow. That alone was reason enough to see it through. Once the deed was done, the town would back him up. . .

Pierce made his decision. "Let us go over to the Ellsworth Inn, Murco. We'll stop by the hotel safe, and then we'll speak of what inspires a man."

* * *

Wyatt Earp and Ellsworth's Town Marshal were not congenial companions. The two men sat silently in the cramped office of the jailhouse, a structure of wood and stone no bigger than a typical log cabin, Morton on a chair, boots up on the desk, and Wyatt poised awkwardly on a stool. It was evening, the sun not long down, and it was painfully quiet in the office. From outside came the distant sound of a saloon accordion, a fiddle sawing away; the laughter and clip-clop of two farmhands riding past the jail. Sometimes Wyatt could hear the faint sound of moths batting themselves against the kerosene lamp on a cabinet for forms and circulars. Morton was smoking a rolled cigarette, drinking from the brandy bottle that was supposed to go to Thompson, now and then giving a sharp sideways glance at Wyatt.

They simply didn't like one another. Morton seemed to think Earp had been showing off, or insane, taking Thompson in; Wyatt thought of Morton as a bent lawman.

It could be he judged Morton all the harsher because of his memories of what he'd done himself, in Arkansas and Illinois. But he had made up his mind that there were laws, and then again—there were laws. Some laws mattered a lot more than others. And laws against promiscuous shooting, and lynching—those laws mattered.

In the cell behind them, Thompson was reading a three-week old newspaper from Wichita, yawning with boredom.

"When's the judge coming?" Thompson asked, for the fourth time, rustling the paper as he turned a page.

"I sent the message," said Morton, pouring another tot of brandy. "If he ain't indisposed, he'll come. But it'll be in his own good time."

"You're drinking up all my brandy, Marshal . . ." Thompson began. But broke off when Happy Jack Murco creaked open the heavy oaken door from the street. "Murco!" Thompson shouted, coming to white-knuckle the bars. "It's your fault Whitney's died!"

Murco ignored Ben Thompson. "You two better get over to the Generous Lady. There's a half crazed cowboy threatening to kill that yellow-haired female workin' there."

"He's threatening Mattie?" said Wyatt, getting up. He strode quickly out the door, before Murco could answer—but Morton was close on his heels. Morton had to take two strides for Wyatt's one to keep up as they crossed the dark street. The only light spilled onto the walk and the rutted road from the windows of saloons and the hotel.

"See here, Earp, you are deputized by me, and I decide what goes here, dammit!" Morton said, when they'd reached the front door of the saloon.

At just that instant Wyatt spotted Mattie, forty yards down the street, waving cheerfully at a drover and stepping into the little rented cabin she slept in, probably to make herself some supper— or lunch, considering her hours. She was in no danger, it was clear. What was Murco so worked up about?

Wyatt had a thought, and turned to look at the jailhouse. "Marshal, I believe I'll let you handle this after all."

He turned and walked back toward the sheriff's office.

The Town Marshal shrugged, surprised at Earp's unpredictability, and went into the saloon to look for a dangerous cowboy who'd never been there.

Wyatt returned to the jailhouse, slipping through the darkened doorway, just two minutes before Murco returned with Shanghai Pierce and five of his men.

* * *

"Where's Dudley?" Pierce asked, looking at his followers congregated outside the little jail. The others shrugged. Pierce reckoned Dudley had had the sense—and Pierce knew it was good sense, despite himself—to linger at the bar.

Pierce nodded at Murco. Hiding the act from the street with his body, Murco slipped Pierce the key to the jail cell; Pierce passed it to Grigsby. "Grigsby, you and Creighton and Hoy, go ahead on in—keep your pistols about you, though Thompson won't be armed—and drag that hound out here. Give him a thump on the melon if he sets up a ruckus. We'll take him out to those cottonwoods by the river and hang him there."

Grigsby nodded, led the other two into the jail's office. The door closed behind them. A few moments of quiet were broken by a muffled shout, a thud, a grunt, and the sound of a man falling.

"Lord they worked fast, getting him out of that cell," Pierce muttered.

Murco frowned and drew his gun, stepped into the office. He nearly tripped over two men on the floor, one lying atop the other: Grigsby and Hoy. Creighton was draped over the desk. Creighton was groaning; Hoy beginning to stir himself. None was worth a damn at the moment. None seemed to have been shot—just badly thumped.

Thompson laughed at Murco from the jail cell—and then looked to the shadows in the corner by the door.

Murco never did see Wyatt Earp buffalo him with the barrel of his pistol. He was out cold before he knew what hit him.

But Pierce knew what had hit Murco—as soon as he and Jim Banner stepped through the door and found Wyatt pointing two pistols at them, three inches from each man's nose.

Wyatt cocked the pistols. "Boys, it is illegal to take a prisoner from the jail without the consent of the judge or the Marshal. Murco hasn't got the stature. And I won't allow it anyhow."

"Who the hell are you to not allow it?" Pierce demanded.

"My name's Earp. I've been deputized, and I'm going to have to insist that you take these beautiful dreamers out of here, and make yourself scarce. That means leave Ellsworth, and now."

* * *

It was in the bright morning light streaming through the window of the jail house that Wyatt woke in the office chair to find Morton taking a thick handful of currency from Ben Thompson. The gunfighter was handing the cash through the bars of the cell.

Hearing Wyatt get to his feet, the Marshal turned, pockmarked face made uglier yet by a scowl. "Earp . . ." he muttered, tucking the money out of sight in a coat pocket. "I spoke to the judge, who has granted me the power to fine Thompson twenty-five dollars for disturbing the peace. He has now paid his fine." He turned the key on the jail cell, and opened the barred door. "Okay, Ben, head on out. Your brother was seen riding toward Abilene . . . You'd best follow him and hope Marshal Hickok hasn't shot him dead yet."

Ben grinned and clapped his top hat on his head. He came to Wyatt and placed a hand on his shoulder. "Wyatt, I'm just about cleaned out of money, for now, but if you'll come to Abilene . . ."

Wyatt shook his head. "You owe me nothing."

"We'll see about that," Ben said, chuckling. He slapped Wyatt on the back and headed out the door.

Wyatt stretched, grimacing. He'd slept badly in the chair and his bones ached. He turned to see Morton glaring at him. "I understand," Morton said, pausing to sip coffee from a tin mug, "that you buffaloed one of my men last night. He's laid up with an aching head and will be of no use to me. I could arrest you for that."

"Did I do that? That was no twenty-five dollars you just took from Ben Thompson, Morton. It was a good deal more. You want to talk about that?"

Morton's eyes narrowed. "You want your share, do you?"

Wyatt stared. He didn't see what was so bad about taking a little extra in "fines" from an unlicensed gambling house or a freelance whore, as he'd seen Jim Masterson do. He was not above shearing a fool at poker. In the recent past, he had been no angel. But outright bribes to get a man out of jail he could not stomach. That kind of thing gnawed at the roots of civilization.

He just shook his head, put on his hat, and went to the door.

"Wait a minute," Morton said, and added grudgingly, obviously not wanting to say it: "The mayor wants you to stay. He's offering you Whitney's job."

"I kind of like Ben Thompson," Wyatt answered. "But he nearly shot me dead and he brought his drunk brother into the street for a fight and he shouldn't be surprised that Chauncey Whitney died in that fuss. Ben needed a month or two in jail, at least, for that foolishness, though it wasn't him that pulled the trigger. Your judge let him go for twenty-five dollars. I conclude this town's not my size. Now goodbye to you, Morton, I've got business over to Wichita . . ."

Half an hour later, riding out of town on a sorrel standard-bred stud, Wyatt felt some relief when he left the smell of Ellsworth behind: the smells of crowded cattle, and mountains of buffalo hides, and overflowing outhouses.

The air was sweet and pure, out here on the plains.

CHAPTER THREE

Abel "Shanghai" Pierce rode a big, gray-white Arabian stallion out onto the plains east of Ellsworth, under blue sky and cottony clouds; rode out to talk to his Uncle Ferg, who had died about fourteen years earlier.

Pierce had taken Old Dudley with him, as he often did on such expeditions, because Dudley seemed to accept the necessity of talking to the dead, as if it were the most natural thing in the world. And two guns were good to have on the plains. Billy Thompson could be hiding out here somewhere.

Dudley, riding a chestnut white-faced mare, asked no questions when they paused atop a modest swell in the plains. A patch of delicate purple blossoms, little trumpets running tandem up stalks of rich green, swayed in the morning breeze.

"Capital grazin' here," Dudley said, blinking around at the flowers, the rippling buffalo grass. He would have preferred to be nursing his aching head in bed at the hotel,

"Wonder what them purple flowers are," Pierce muttered.

"Why sir, it happens that I know," Dudley said. "They are found in Nebraska too, and my Mama, back in Nebraska, she loved 'em so, God bless her." His eyes filled with tears, thinking of his mother, dead of the ague more than six seasons now. When he was hung over, his heart seemed sorer than usual, and at such times he was prone to weeping. His brother had told him of his mother's death— he and Bud had run across one another in an Abilene saloon. She had died and he hadn't been there to hold her hand. The stalks before him shook in the desultory wind with the motion of a woman's disapproving finger.

"Well what the devil are they called then?" Pierce demanded. "Those purple flowers."

"Eh? Oh yes, sir, they're lady's tresses, is what they call 'em."

"Lady's tresses . . ." Pierce realized, then, what it was that drew his eyes to these lady's tresses. They reminded him of that girl in Louisiana; she had a dress figured with purple flowers at the bosom. Had she really laughed at him, when he'd asked her to be his wife? The woman had been a gold-digger who liked lavish gifts. Laughing at a Laird.

He had not had his land then, nor his cattle, but he had known he was a Laird. His Uncle Fergus had told him so.

"You are a Pierce," Fergus had told him, when his father had died. *"You are the one we have been waiting for—the one ready to take the world back again. We had it all, once. We were Lords of the old world, up North in England—they called us Lairds . . . Then come that Bloody Mary, and we had to run from her. And we lost it all . . ."*

"My ma used to say," Dudley began. "That with flowers, why, gather them while ye—"

Pierce gestured for Dudley to shut his mouth and rein in his mount. Dudley immediately fell silent and backed his horse a half-dozen steps, to give Mr. Pierce some semblance of privacy.

"Uncle Ferg . . . it's Abel . . ." Pierce seemed to address the flowery rise in the soil, as if it were his uncle's grave, though that grave was thousands of miles back in the Old States.

Dudley yawned, and dozed gratefully in the saddle, as his boss talked to a dead uncle.

"Uncle Fergus, what do I do, now, with those blowhard politicians in Texas making noise about me? And here I'm made to look a fool up in Kansas too. This boy Earp has struck my men down, and shamed us all. My respect's gone up the spout. But he's an odd stick, and I've found such men to be dangerous. He's said to be the brother of two lawmen, and I've got enough of the law to bribe already. Now you know me, I can take the gaff and I don't give a continental what anyone thinks, but I'm stumped, with the trouble I'm having down south I've got to linger up here for awhile . . . But maybe I should 'shoot, Luke, or give up the gun.' What do you think? Should I have him kilt?"

Dudley came out of his doze with a start when Pierce spoke of killing a man. He noted that Mr. Pierce had gone silent, his head bowed; he knew that meant Pierce was listening to his uncle. Dudley listened himself, then; he'd always hoped to hear a ghost, like the spiritualistic people did. He heard only the nickering of the horses. But as if the horses were translating for Uncle Fergus, Mr. Pierce said, "I see. I see. Yes sir, when you're big as the plains, you can afford to wait. Too much worry from the law already. Don't be wakin' snakes till you got to. Yes sir. I'll wait. We'll look for our chance, and it'll come, and we'll punish that boy, and it'll be him taking the gaff. Yes sir. Yes sir I hear you. And I'll need that Burke anyway, for some other business . . . I'll send for him, sure . . . I thank you."

Pierce tipped his hat, and rode back toward town. Dudley drifted after him, noting, in the distance, the silhouette of a rider heading in the direction of Wichita—a tall, slender rider on a fine long-legged sorrel.

* * *

Wyatt had been the Faro banker in his brother James's gambling hall for almost two months before he heard the story.

"That's right," said the wheezing bourbon peddler with the mutton-chop whiskers, placing his bet on the Faro table, "I saw Ben Thompson himself playing Faro in Abilene. Not a week later I was up in Ellsworth and I heard this Wyatt Earp shot it out with Thompson—and the way I heard it, he hauled him, covered in blood but still kicking and a-howling, right to the calaboose. Then this Earp shot it out with Abel Pierce over a lynching! Left a pile of corpses on the ground!" He added in a confidential tone, "I understand he's a cousin or something to the very fella that owns this gambling emporium."

"Is that so?" Wyatt said, paying off in chips when the man won the round.

"That's right . . ." The peddler paused to wheeze. "I'll place my bet right there . . . Say what's your name, young fella?"

Wyatt just smiled. His brother James, the owner of the establishment, came over to inspect the game. James was a bit stooped; he drank more than he ate, as attested by the broken veins on his red nose and his gaunt frame. But he wore a fine dark blue three-piece sack suit, the best Wichita could offer, and a matching homburg. "I'll take over, for awhile, Wyatt," James said. "You look wore to a thread."

Wyatt was more jangled than tired. He liked saloons and gambling halls, for their action and easy manners, but the constant pall of cigar smoke—James was puffing his own stogie, adding to it—and the incessant shouts of glee and disappointment and the thumping of the small brass band in the corner got to be a bit much after seven or eight hours. His eyes were watering and he was developing a cough and his ears buzzed.

"I'll take you up on that, James. I'll send Percy in if I see him . . ."

James nodded, tilting his hat back and clamping his cigar on his mouth. "Who wants to get luckier than a cowboy with a spring widow?" James called out. "Place your bets!"

"Say did you call him *Wyatt?*" the peddler asked, with some mortification, before his voice was swallowed up by the noise. Wyatt made for the door.

The street could contend with the gambling house for noise, and though it was September, it hadn't rained for a while and the moody plains wind was whirling up yellow dust devils. Texas drovers, in sombreros and vaquero hats, whooped as they staggered from a saloon toward the bridge over the Arkansas River. They were off to Douglas and Main, Wyatt supposed, to find the bawdy houses down in Delano. James's wife Bessie had one of the less showy establishments there, with several girls who'd taken the last name Earp—taking the name of the Madame of the house was a common practice. To Wyatt, who was trying to put his past behind him, this was a source of unexpressed misery: Several local whores calling themselves Earp. James really ought to put a stop to it, he reflected.

He found himself strolling almost instinctively for the center of the hubbub. A couple of gunshots echoed from across the river—probably just playful shooting, though Wyatt well knew it could wind up in unintended killing.

A bullwhacker drove a couple of oxen by, snapping his whip, nearly running over a drunken Texas cowhand who was laughing as he chased a wheeling, wind-flipped sombrero down the street. Wyatt continued up the wooden bridge over the shallow Arkansas River, thinking he would just see if Bat Masterson was still playing cards in "Rowdy Joe" Lowe's place. Maybe he could persuade Bat to take the air with him. They had things to talk over.

He had reached the Delano district, where sporting women, faces garishly painted and some wearing only their slips, leaned out the upper windows of the Gay and Winsome Dance Hall, calling out to passing prospects. It took him a moment to realize that, "Hey, tall and slim, come on in and show me if you're that bony all 'round!" was directed at him.

He waved in friendly but noncommittal response, and was just about to enter Rowdy Joe's when two men came tumbling out the door, flailing wildly at one another. The smaller one, sprawling in the dirt, was trying to grab a fallen pistol with one hand, kicking at the other drunk the while. Wyatt picked up the gun and tossed it out of reach, thinking to stop at least one killing.

The men rolled about on the ground, thrashing at one another and cursing, right to the toes of Wyatt's boots, forcing him to step over them. He was tempted to step in—something in him fairly ached to do it—but he reminded himself he was no longer a constable or a deputy anywhere. He was just an unconvicted horse thief and a former bawdy house bouncer. He sighed, and walked into the saloon.

Every poker and Keno table was thronged with dusty, mostly drunken men, and wreathed with smoke set off by yellow rings of lantern light. A patchily bearded old man in a blue Union Army cap, which he might or might not have worn in the war, was sawing on a fiddle in the corner; with the laughter and catcalls and groans of the men gambling and the old man's loosey-goosey playing it was impossible to make out the song.

Wyatt had to weave his way through the crowd for a couple of minutes, carefully sidestepping drunks. It would be a shame to get into a fight for a mere jostle.

His way was blocked by a grubby, squat man with a burlap shirt and mismatched shoes—Wyatt knew him to be Luc Montaigne, a half-crazed French Canadian known in Wichita as "Champagne" Montaigne. The Canuck waved an old Champagne bottle filled with water, or beer—never champagne. James claimed Montaigne had been carrying the same bottle, its label peeling away, for more than a year. Montaigne had rheumy blue eyes and a mouth wide with the meaningless, perpetual grin of a hound. "James Earp's son, Wyatt! Have a drinka champagne, *mon ami*!" Montaigne crowed.

"I'm James's brother, not his son. What you got in there today, Luc?" Wyatt asked.

"Champagne, by way of beer, *c'est* superb!"

"Well you're cutting a swell, for sure. That's too fine a drink for me, I'll leave it to the aristocrats." He patted the rummy on the shoulder and slipped past him, peering through the smoke.

He found Bat Masterson at a table in the far corner playing poker with a cattle buyer in shirt sleeves and a gambler in ashy-blue frock coat. Bat was wearing his coffee-colored derby and three-piece chocolate colored suit, though it was warm in here. Like Wild Bill, he sat in a saloon with his back to the wall—Bat's gunfight with Corporal King had convinced him to sit where he could keep an eye on the whole room.

Wyatt walked up to stand where he couldn't see anyone's cards and caught Bat's eye. Bat nodded and threw down his cards with disgust. "One of you gents has stolen a precious item from me!"

The tinhorn gambler across from him looked up in alarm. "What's that? Stolen what, sir?"

"My luck! Either that or it has deserted me out of sheer boredom with this lackadaisical game!" Bat grinned to show he was joking and the other men laughed in relief.

He got up, picked up his remaining chips and took them to the chip counter, cashed them in with the pretty but child-sized Chinese girl who wore a black dress and black-plumed hat.

"Drink?" Bat asked, returning to Wyatt. He walked with a slight limp, a legacy of King's bullet. He tried to disguise the limp with a gold-headed cane he carried in his left hand.

Bat had asked about the drink out of ritual politeness; he wasn't surprised when Wyatt shook his head.

Outside, as they strolled down the boardwalk toward the bridge, Wyatt observed, "I've never seen you play anything but poker . . ."

"I've got more sense than to play Keno—seeing as it's 'adjusted' to improve the odds for the house."

Wyatt nodded. "Could be I'd own a saloon sometime. But I'd have more windows, and keep 'em open."

"Does get devilishly close in there, especially when some of those fellows choose to play cards right off the trail, before they think about bathing. If they ever do."

"They should be dunked in that river right there—" Wyatt broke off, hearing a gunshot, turning to watch a small crowd shoving its way out of "Red" Beard's place, across from Lowe's. Five women in drawers and slippers, two of them bare breasted and one in a tattered approximation of a scarlet ball gown, were lining up in an unruly row in the middle of the street. Trail hands, whistling and laughing and waving money in the air, mobbed the boardwalk to watch the whores. A man carrying a snare drum, and a trombonist from the saloon's small brass band took up positions behind the row of women. The percussionist commenced a drum-roll as a short cowboy with knee-high boots and a tall white hat, raised his gun in the air, shouting something hard to hear in the hullabaloo. ". . . if yew gents have . . . bets . . . is ready to commence the race!"

"You don't mean to tell me . . ." Wyatt said, shaking his head.

"I do," Bat said, laughing as the mustachioed cowboy fired his gun in the air and the women, as drunk as the men, began gracelessly running toward the bridge. Two of them stumbled and fell almost immediately—one laughing as she tumbled, the other bursting into tears. Four made it to the bridge led by a fierce-looking red-head, the girl with the tattered gown, the skirts held daintily up with her hands so she could run, white legs flying as she tapped the bridge post and returned, nimbly dodging another woman's attempt to trip her. The redhead triumphantly leapt into the arms of the mustachioed cowboy and the trombonist made a donkey braying sound with his horn to announce the end of the race.

"She done it again! Hilda's took the record, sure!" the cowboy shouted, firing his gun again. Blue gun smoke drifted above the false fronts, and the crowd began to work its way back into the saloon for celebratory drinks, the trail hands arguing about their bets. The losers in the race straggled after, forgotten.

"Started about a week ago," Bat said, grinning. "Whore races."

Wyatt snorted and walked up onto the bridge. He didn't think it was funny, himself. Someone's daughter, turned into a racing beast. Another thought of Sarah—quickly pushed away. "You done for the night?" Wyatt asked. "Ready to head back to the other side of town?"

"I am. It's early but I'm still shaky from last night. Jim and Ed were in town and we tied one on." Nearly to the bridge, hands raised against gusting dust, they passed a rectangular building, still yellow from the newness of its unpainted wood, the sign on its false front declaring it the Evening's Contentment Hotel. More than two dozen cow ponies were tethered out front on a hitching post made for ten; they stepped on each other's fetlocks, shifting irritably, ears flicking, blinking in the wind.

"I considered staying at that hotel," Bat remarked, "when first I started coming to this side of town—just to save money—but I was told I'd have to share a room with five cowboys. When the season's on, they sleep half a dozen and more to a room, trading lice."

"They ought to put those ponies in a livery somewhere," Wyatt grumbled. "That's no way to treat a horse."

Sensing Wyatt's mood, Bat said nothing more, and they walked in silence across the bridge and along the main street. The clamor of the party end of town diminished to a distant mutter and tinkle.

They passed a closed ice cream parlor, a lady's milliner, a gentleman's pool hall, and were nearly to their hotels, which stood across the street from each other, when Wyatt suddenly said, "Look here, Bat— James has offered to invest some money in the freight business but it's not enough for me to pay for all the horses I need, the newspaper notice and employees too, so I was looking to take a partner for a little investment and to help me drive. Virgil's riding shotgun for the stage, Morgan's off somewhere . . . Might you want to partner up with me?"

"I might too," Bat said, "if it comes to that." The ambivalence of this response was not lost on Wyatt.

He was ambivalent about it himself. Not sure what he ought to go into, now. But he knew there weren't enough freighters in this part of Kansas and he had a fear of missing the best chance. There were men making powerful money in Wichita, and there were men who languished and were always hungry—and there wasn't much in between. You had to watch for an opening and take your best shot. But he also knew himself to be restless, like his father, and wondered if he could stomach the tedium of a hauling business. But what else would he do?

A shout from across the street drew their attention: a big, bellied, balding, lantern-jawed man, in trousers barely kept up by red suspenders, was thrashing a spindly boy on the front porch of Black's Hotel. It was Doc Black himself doing the thrashing. The boy was shoeless, wearing a ragged shirt that might've been white once, and a pair of fraying trousers held up with a belt of twine.

"Why that's 'Doc' Black," Bat said. "It seems he—"

But Wyatt had already started across the street and heard nothing more but a roaring in his ears.

Black had knocked the boy down, and was dragging him to his feet by his collar. "So you're stealing food from my larder!" Black snarled. "I hire you off the streets and you steal from me!"

He shook the boy by the collar and raised his hand to slap him again. Wyatt saw that the boy's face was bloody.

"Drop that hand, Black, and leave the boy be," Wyatt said tonelessly as he stepped onto the porch.

Black dropped the boy instead and whirled, the raised hand becoming a fist which he shook under Wyatt's nose. "Poke your long nose some place else, feller, or I'll break it for you!"

"You've got no call to beat a boy half to death!" Wyatt snapped. He was dimly aware that Bat had come to stand close by with a hand to the gun he kept under his coat, just in case he had to back Wyatt's play.

"I hired him to empty the toss pots and clean the floors and he steals meat from me!"

"He . . ." The urchin was sitting up now, wiping blood from his nose. He was a thin, buck-toothed kid, who might be anywhere from eleven to thirteen, with a prominent chin, a tousle of curly black hair and no sign of weeping about him, despite the beating. He glared defiantly up at the two men. "He said he'd feed me and he didn't—I ain't eaten nothin for two days! I only took what he said he'd give me anyhows!"

"Well," Wyatt demanded, looking sharply at Black, "what about it? The boy says he was owed some food. You starve a boy, you make him desperate!"

"Why I gave him a piece of bread and butter this morning—or I meant to. Now get your skinny rear off the porch of my hotel!" He turned to reach for the boy again.

Bat chuckled, knowing what was coming.

Wyatt caught the big man's wrist in his left hand, spun him back face to face, and swung a right to Black's jaw, rocking him back. "I said *desist!*"

Black got his feet solidly under him, blinking in amazement. Then he roared wordlessly and rushed at Wyatt, who sidestepped and clipped Black on the side of the head as he went by, making him grunt with pain. Wyatt had felt the blow himself: his knuckles were stinging badly. As Black turned to rush him, Wyatt set himself to fight—shaking his head at Bat who looked at him questioningly, wondering if he should step in—and just managed to block a left-hand jab from Black. He wasn't so lucky with Black's roundhouse right, which caught him a glancing blow on the jaw, making him stagger and sending blue flickers through his eyesight. Black bared his teeth—a kind of animal grin—and snatched up a chair, swung it hard at Wyatt's head. Younger and faster, Wyatt ducked and the chair shattered on a post beside him.

The boy rushed in, windmilling his small, dirty fists at Black's side. Black swiped him with one pudgy paw and knocked him back again—Bat caught the boy and dragged him off the porch.

Black turned back to Wyatt in time to encounter Wyatt's right fist, which sank deep into gut just under the sternum, making him bend over gasping, only to meet Wyatt's knee, snapped up to catch the hotelier's chin. Wheezing, Black fell on his keister, groaning.

"You had enough yet?" Wyatt asked. He was implying he could go on all night but he sorely hoped Black was done, as his own jaw ached, his fist throbbed and he knew that if the bigger man got him in a bear hug he'd crack his bones.

Black nodded, making an angry, dismissive gesture, unable to speak as yet. A small crowd of late-night drinkers and strollers had gathered, and now they applauded as Wyatt stepped off the porch.

Wyatt found Bat standing over the boy, wiping blood from his face with a kerchief. The boy grinned crookedly at Wyatt—the right side of his mouth was swollen—and said, "You whupped that son of a bitch good!"

Bat laughed aloud at that but Wyatt frowned at the boy. "Don't use language like that, boy. You sound like a guttersnipe."

"I've heard it said more'n once that's what I am, so I es'peculate I should talk like one."

"Talking like one'll keep you one," Wyatt said. "What's your name? And how old are you? I'm . . . darned if I can tell."

"My name, it's Henry, sir," said the boy. "Henry McCarty. And I'm thirteen. I think."

"Thirteen!" Bat burst out. "Here's proof of what the professors say, that a boy undernourished doesn't fully grow. I'd have thought him eleven at the most."

"Can you still eat through that swollen mouth, Henry?" Wyatt asked. "He pasted you a good one."

"Why sir, I can eat out of the other side of my mouth if that one's no good!"

"Come along, then, we'll detour over to the . . . to my brother's cocktail emporium. He'll fix you up with a sandwich."

"Could he make it two, or three, do you think, mister?"

"My name's Earp, Wyatt Earp. Now just you come along."

CHAPTER FOUR

In fact Henry McCarty ate two sandwiches and a bowl of beans with jalapeños, complaining of the spice but eating them all the same.

Wishing for sleep and wondering what he was going to do with this urchin, Wyatt sat at the oak table with him, in the storeroom, between stacks of liquor crates. James had fetched him a cool bottle of champagne, from the chiller tub in the basement; Wyatt held the bottle, unopened, against his aching jaw.

Maybe Bessie or her maid would look after this Henry. The boy didn't seem like one who'd turn up his nose at an association with a cat-house Madame. There was no local parson to turn to—so far they had only traveling preachers, with their Sunday tents—and at present no Benevolent Society in Wichita. Wyatt would feel a mere hypocrite to throw the lad back to the streets. Henry might be coming up on being a man but he had the stature of a much younger boy and he didn't seem big enough to take on a man's work as yet.

"You say your mother died—where's your father, boy?" Wyatt asked.

"My own father, he died back in New York," the boy said, with never a quaver. "I got a step-daddy, Mr. William Antrim, but when Mama died of the consumption Mr. Antrim took to trying to whip sense into me, that's what he called it, and making me work like his slave, and I run off and come back here from down to New Mexico. This here's the second time I lived in Wichita. I like a lively town. And that's where the freight train was going . . ."

Wyatt smiled. *I like a lively town.*

Bessie came in then, a handsome, full-figured woman with golden-brown hair, lustrous matching eyes and a sardonic way about her. Henry's eyes got wide, taking her in, for she was dressed in the finery of a successful Madame, a flouncy, flowing yellow and gold floor-length gown, with a white bow on its bustle and a plunging bosom trimmed in lace. "Who's this rascal, Wyatt?"

"This is my associate, Mr. Henry McCarty," Wyatt said solemnly. "He backed me up in a fight, not long ago, and I need to do right by him."

Struck by Wyatt's description of him as his 'associate', Henry blinked at Wyatt, and there was just a faint trembling of his lips. Wyatt hoped he would not cry—he disliked gushes of sentiment.

"You both look like you needed a few more 'associates' to back you up," Bessie said. "You're as kicked about as a drunk in a mule stall. Can I get you some lineament, Wyatt?"

"I think we'll live. Say you still got that colored maid, over at your place?"

"Agnes Sanders? Sure, she's living there now, in the sleeping shack, out back. Those no-goods from Texas killed her man, and she's got no place else to go. What a scandal it was. That Bill Smith just stood by and scratched his head. Poor Agnes."

Wyatt knew the story. A Negro hod carrier, Charley Sanders, had come home to find two Texas cowboys manhandling his wife, offering to pay her a nickel a throw. Charley knocked their heads together, then cracked some ribs and broke a nose, and threw them out on their ears. Enraged by being punished by a man black as midnight, the Texans had conferred with their *compadres*. A man named Shorty Ramsey had volunteered to avenge the honor of the white race. Ramsey rode up to the unarmed Sanders, shot him in the back, and rode off war-whooping. Wyatt had heard from his brother James how witnesses had gone to Town Marshal Bill Smith and found he was already with Ramsey—in fact, having a drink with him and three of his cowboy pards. "What can I do, when these boys have the drop on me?" Smith told the witnesses. "Hell he was only a nigra . . ." Shorty Ramsey was allowed to ride back to Texas and hadn't been heard from since.

"My brothers didn't fight in Abe Lincoln's war to come home and hear 'he was only a nigra', when a man's shot in the back," Wyatt said, wincing at the discomfort of talking with a swollen jaw.

"Then you'll be interested to know that the very same Marshal Smith is out there on the floor asking after you," Bessie said. "I was going to ask if you wanted to be found."

"I'll see the marshal," Wyatt said, shrugging. He took two golden eagles from his coat pocket, slid them toward Bessie. "One of these ought to buy some shoes and a set of clothes for a fellow as scrawny as this," Wyatt said.

"I'm not so scrawny!" Henry protested.

"And the other one ought to feed our Henry here for a day or two. And here's a third one—if you'll give this to Agnes for looking after him, Bessie, I'd be obliged. I'll calculate what to do with him . . ."

Bessie looked at Henry with an expression that was as close as she could come to maternal affection: it looked like cynical amusement. "I see Mr. McCarty yawning fit for a Sunday sermon and I think a bed is the first thing. The bath comes in the morning . . ."

Wyatt nodded, stood up—and reached out a hand to Henry. The boy looked at the hand a moment, then realized Wyatt was asking him to shake, the way two men do. Henry McCarty grinned through his puffy lips and shook Wyatt's hand.

* * *

"Marshal Smith? My name's Earp."

Smith turned from the bar, to assess Wyatt, who returned the appraisal. The Town Marshal was a smartly dressed man with a gold-edged and silver badge prominent on his lapel. Mutton chops edged his narrow face; one eye seemed to have a permanent squint. "That'd be Wyatt Earp, brother of James and Virgil?" On Wyatt's nod, Smith continued, his voice nasal and a tad pompous. "I believe there are at least two more Earp boys somewheres, besides those three. I cannot keep track of such abundance in Earps but I pray God the others are more peaceable than the one to hand. You cannot go about drubbing hotel keepers, sir, it does not go in Wichita."

"He was beating a boy to a busted husk, Marshal. I believe he'd have killed him had I not interfered. I might have saved Black from jail."

"That's one way to look at it. Cognac?"

"No thank you."

"You'll forgive me . . . Here's how!" Smith turned and knocked back his drink, cleared his throat, leaned on the bar to look Wyatt up and down with a different kind of appraisal. "Are you also the Earp who arrested Ben Thompson over in Ellsworth? And the same Earp who put a twist in Abel Pierce's tail?"

"I am," Wyatt admitted.

"And here you stand, with no bullet holes in you, tall and only slightly bruised. Doc Black has thrashed some men in his time. You did pretty well with him—and you showed some pluck in Ellsworth. And while I cannot approve of interference in every small detail of shop keeping, such as the beating of a toss-pot boy, it seems to me that you'd make a good deputy. We have a need for several more. It pays pretty well, and you can take a share in the fines—it's all understood. Speaking of fines, I have to fine you ten dollars, and escort you to jail, for beating Doc."

"Doesn't a judge do the fining in Wichita?" asked Wyatt, remembering Morton collecting a "fine" in Ellsworth. Wyatt's own father was a justice of the peace, as well as a farmer.

"The judge approves certain fines after the fact," Smith sniffed. "That too is understood. Now if we take you to the jail, some of Black's friends, who are oiling up their shooters outside even now, will suppose I'm going to lock you up, and the appeasement is made. But give it an hour or so and you can go on home, once things are quiet. And if you're agreeable, and not too eager to flash a gun, why, you can work for me, tomorrow. What do you say?"

Wyatt considered. He didn't like Smith, and he had his freighting company to think of. But the company was so far a pipe dream. And it occurred to him that if he'd been deputized the day that Sanders had been killed, he'd have escorted Shorty Ramsey to the lock-up, with his cowboy friends watching or not. It seemed to him that Smith's presence on the force only meant that another kind of man was needed to balance things out. And he'd noted that Bat had not seemed too enthusiastic about partnering with him on the freighting business. Maybe Bat would like being a deputy better . . .

"Can I bring on one or two fellas I know to be good hands?" Wyatt asked.

"Sure, after I have a look at them."

"Then let's go to the jail. I'm bone weary, and if you leave the cell door open, I'll just sleep the night there, long as your bed has no bugs in it."

"We boil the sheets twice a week. Let me have another drink, then we'll go and tuck you in. But there's one thing I should mention—Shanghai Pierce's outfit will be in town and soon, he's meeting one of his herds. He says he will no longer do business in Ellsworth—you might've been much the reason. You should keep that in mind, if you're going to wear a badge in Wichita. Mr. Pierce is well regarded by the local merchants . . . Indeed, Shanghai Pierce is Aces High here . . ."

* * *

"Wyatt, can you give me a hand?"

It was Wyatt's brother James, early the next evening, tapping his younger brother on the shoulder as Wyatt collected his money from the pay window at the gambling hall. "If you'll only tell me how, James . . ."

"It appears there's a crazed son of a bitch at Bessie's place, and he's been known to wave a knife around so I thought I'd take someone with me. My boys here are all busy, and the deputies will likely demand a fee . . . And as you are to be a deputy anyhow . . ."

Wyatt nodded and gestured for his brother to lead the way. They wended through the gambling house, out into the cool night air, heading for Delano. Dust devils swirled in the street. A buggy rattled by. Spits of rain drove the dust back down, but it kept rising up again.

"Weather's cooling," James remarked.

"You know, I might be able to get my badge now and bring it along . . ." Wyatt felt some reluctance to take a hand in a whorehouse, again; it was too much like what happened on the Illinois River. He had hoped to distance himself from Bessie's establishment.

"Oh, there's no time for that," James said. "Come on, if you're coming . . ." He waved to a gangly young man in shirt sleeves and the beginnings of a beard, delivering whiskey barrels to Delano. "Hello there, Harl Buscomb! How about a ride over the bridge! We've got some urgent business!"

"Sure, come on, James, but hold on tight, I'm late!"

"Suits us! Come on, climb up, Wyatt!"

With Wyatt and James aboard, the wagon rumbled down the street, over the bridge, and carried them all the way to Bessie's establishment. The business was done in shanties out back, set aside for "the ancient industry"—as the Wichita newspaper liked to call it.

James didn't keep "upstairs girls" at his gambling hall—he would pay regular fines, so-called, to city officials if he did so. If he kept them here, on the dark side of town, they were genteelly overlooked.

They approached the small, ramshackle but newly painted white and red house carefully, Wyatt with a hand on his six gun, James with a palmed two-shot derringer.

They could hear incoherent shouting from inside. Seemed the troublemaker was still there.

"You know who it is?" Wyatt asked.

James shook his head. "I got a message from that boy Henry that someone was raising hell . . ."

Without having to arrange it ahead of time, they flattened to either side of the door, close to the wall; James knocked. "Bessie!"

"James, get this horse's ass out of here!" she yelled through the door.

The door banged opened and a man glowered out. He was bristling with hair like a brown bush around a feather-festooned, dented bowler hat, his gray-streaked hair merging into a spade-shaped beard. Wyatt knew him slightly: Plug Johnson, always with a plug of tobacco in his cheek. He wore the hat with its sagging eagle feathers twenty-four hours around. He had Indian beadwork on his shirt and Indian bracelets, and knee-high rawhide boots. His game was craps, mostly played out behind the halls so he didn't have to give the house its share of the winnings. He was widely suspected of using loaded dice.

"Who the hell are you and what the hell you want?" he said, squinting at Wyatt. "You that Earp kid?"

"Come out here and I'll tell you what I want," Wyatt said. "I understand you're raising hell here."

"I won't come out! One of these girls has done picked my pocket, is what, and I want my goddamned money back and I ain't leavin' till I get it! I demand to see the owner of this re-stablishment!"

He thrust his head out the door to make this declaration and James pressed the barrel of his derringer against the side of Plug's head, just behind the ear. "That's the owner's derringer you're feeling there, you shit-heel! Shall I pull the trigger?"

A red flicker in Plug's beard. He was licking his lips as he thought about it, afraid to move. "I'd re-preciate it if you didn't do that, mister. But I ain't lying. Twenty dollars she took—and I was already paid up!"

Wyatt spotted Plug's knife, a big bowie affair, and he plucked it from the man's belt with his right hand as his left grabbed the back of Plug's neck and shoved him out onto the street. Plug staggered, but kept his feet. "Plug, if we tell you to leave somewhere, you leave. You don't hold hostages."

"I ain't leavin' without my twenty dollars—and that knife was given me by the chief of the Kiowa!"

"I wonder whose body he took it off," James remarked, looking at the knife in Wyatt's hand. Not the sort of thing you saw on Indians much. "Maybe more like 'chief' of the buffalo hunters."

Bessie appeared in the doorway. "I don't know if the girl took the money or not. She says not. But she's gotten kind of low."

"Who is it?" James asked.

"She goes by Sallie."

"This high-smelling rat of the plains touch you, Bessie?" James went on. "Hurt anyone?"

"No—but he brandished that goddamn knife, shouting he wouldn't leave till he got his money back . . . So I sent that Henry to tell you . . ."

"Search that freckly whore!" Plug shouted. "She got muh money!"

James shrugged. "If we search her and find twenty dollars, well, the money could've come from anywhere. I'll pay twenty dollars for a little peace and quiet." He fished in his vest, found a twenty dollar gold piece, and flipped it to Plug who caught it in the air. Wyatt threw the knife—it stuck in the ground at Plug's feet. Plug scooped it up, hurried off down the street toward the saloons.

"That's no way to settle things, waving a knife!" Bessie yelled after him. "You don't come back here, you feather-head son of a bitch!"

"I wouldn't come back there no-how!" Plug shouted, turning around. He caught the look in Wyatt's eyes and turned away, scurried down the street through dust-devils, holding onto his hat with one hand.

"Well come on in a minute, in case he decides to hie hisself back here," Bessie said.

James and Wyatt followed Bessie inside. The sitting room was decorated with a cloth-covered chair, a silk settee, framed daguerreotypes on the wall—of full-bodied ladies in ankle-length negligees—and a candelabra on a lace-covered table, all but one of the candles lit. The room had the false look of a mask.

"I don't know if she done it," Bessie said. "I've got a bottle of wine open in the kitchen if you boys want. We sure thank you, Wyatt . . ."

"I'll have a glass of wine," James said. Wyatt had never seen him turn down a drink.

Two girls looked out from the beaded curtains that led to the back corridor—and one of them locked eyes with Wyatt.

Sarah Haspel.

The other girl, young and diminutive and scared, he didn't know.

Wyatt's heart sank. "How are you, Sarah?"

"That how you know her, Sarah?" Bessie said. "She goes by Sallie . . ."

Sarah swallowed. "Wyatt . . ." She glanced nervously at Bessie.

"Go ahead on back if you want to catch up," Bessie said.

Wyatt nodded, started toward the back room as Sarah disappeared from the beaded curtains. Bessie stopped him with a touch on his arm, whispering, "See if you can figure did she steal the money . . ."

Wyatt gave a noncommittal grunt and pushed through the curtains. He found Sarah waiting in a small bedroom, off to the left of the corridor; she was perched Indian-style on a small brass-framed bed—not the bed she did her work on, from the look of the room. This was where she slept. Most of rest of the room was taken up by a bureau, with a kerosene lamp on it, and second bed where another girl would sleep. There was wallpaper figured with lilies; over the bureau was a framed tintype of Queen Victoria. A chamber pot, painted with roses, was tucked away in a corner.

"Nice little room," Wyatt said, coming in. But mostly he was looking at Sarah: She wore a white dressing gown; her feet were bare, her toes painted red. Her hair was curled in sausage ringlets that seemed utterly foreign to her; her skin so pallid now her freckles, hard to see most times, stood out in a dark spray across her nose. Her fingernails, he saw, were chewed up, the thumbnails downright mangled. She seemed heavier, but it wasn't the plumpness of health, but the sag of drinking.

Sarah shrugged, glancing around as if considering the room for the first time. "I guess it's okay."

"How long you been here?"

"Not long. Less'n a week. I had a friend knew Bessie was looking for girls. You run out on me but you was always good to me before then. I figured an Earp would be right enough."

He winced. "I asked you to come with me. You didn't want to."

"Didn't want to farm. That what you doing?" she asked.

"No. Helping my brother in his saloon. Funny thing is, appears I'm starting up lawing again."

She laughed—and the laugh cut off suddenly. She looked at him narrowly. "You going to arrest me?"

"My brother owns the place, Sarah. Of course not. Nor would I arrest you, in any case. Hell I've been arrested *with* you . . ."

"You should call me Sallie. I go by Sallie Earp."

"Sallie *Earp?*"

"Because of Bessie Earp—that's what girls do. They take her name."

"I know. I just . . . never mind." Why was she here? Hoping to get back with him? He'd given her a chance to go with him, start over. She wouldn't do it. Surely he'd done the right thing, in leaving. But she had that look of mute accusation as she looked at him now. Maybe she'd taken up with Bessie in the hopes of being a burr under his saddle. Make him sorry. He sighed. Too late to change anything. He looked her in the eyes, and asked, "Sarah—did you steal that man's money?" He was conscious of his hands, hanging by his sides. He didn't know what to do with them. He put them in his pockets, and then took them out again.

She shook her head, opened her mouth to deny it, but he held her gaze, and she couldn't quite utter the lie. ". . . I . . . 'spect I did take it. Don't you want to sit down, Wyatt?"

He sat on the other bed. "You can get people in a killing-fight, stealing from them in this business, Sarah."

"Call me Sallie, in Wichita."

"I can't seem to. Don't think I will, Sarah. You steal from customers, here, why, you're hurting my brother and my sister-in-law."

She squirmed on the edge of the bed, and then sat very still, staring at her button up boots. "I'm sorry. I'll give you the money.

I just hated that Plug so much." Her nose wrinkled. "When he took off them boots, I thought I'd throw up from the smell. And I needed the money, I haven't put away much, and I'm sickly . . ."

"You need a doctor?"

She nodded mutely. After a moment she added, in a low voice, "I need the mercury treatment, Wyatt. It takes some time. The doctor wants to be paid in advance . . ."

The mercury treatment. So that was it. She had "the blood disease." Syphilis. "You'd better be using those shields here . . ." If she gave one of Bessie's customers the French pox there could be a reckoning.

"Bessie sees that we use the lamb's slippers. For some things . . ."

Wyatt thought about the mercury treatment. From what he'd seen, it could cause your hair to fall out. You could run paralytic with it, and start drooling, lose your sense. It killed people as often as cured them. But the syphilis untreated would bring madness and death.

He stood up and dug out his billfold, counted out three twenties, pressed them into her small, clammy fingers. "Here. You see a doctor."

"You won't tell Bessie?"

He shook his head. "Good luck to you, girl." He started for the door.

"Wyatt? I wished I'd . . ."

He turned and smiled at her, feeling it an untrue smile even as he made it. "Just save your money as you can. And get that treatment. Then maybe we can find you some better line of work." He waved goodbye.

He had run out of advice. He nearly ran from the room too.

Wyatt located his older brother sitting at a table in the lamp-lit kitchen, drinking red wine with Bessie and the new girl. The small kitchen was furnished with a hand-pump and did double duty with a tin bathing. James put his wine glass aside and got up to go with Wyatt, pausing to kiss Bessie on the forehead. Wyatt waved at his sister-in-law and hurried out, his mind burdened so that he scarcely noticed Dandi LeTrouveau, seated across the kitchen table from Bessie . . .

* * *

"Mrs. Earp," Dandi said, when the two men had gone, "I am in my time, and not suitable for men, but if you will let me wait a day or two . . ."

A delicate-looking little woman, Dandi wore a frilly yellow dress, cruelly tight at her tiny waist. She sat stiffly, with her hands folded in her lap. Her hair was a luxuriant spill of lustrous brown around a wide forehead, large earnest dark eyes, and delicately round, naturally-rosy cheeks; her petite lips were rouged to seem a little larger than they were.

Dandi's girlishness would appeal to many customers, Bessie thought. But clearly the girl was no whore. Still, she might be taught . . .

"There are things you could do for a man while waiting for the red flag to go down," Bessie pointed out, pouring herself another glass of wine. "But you may wait, if you choose, this once, till you get settled in."

Dandi leaned forward, lowering her voice, speaking with a touching earnestness. "Mrs. Earp—I have come to town for a purpose. When you offered me work—well I was looking to come to Wichita . . . and I am grateful for your . . . for your patronage."

Bessie smiled at Dandi's affectation of high-toned diction. ". . . but I cannot forget my purpose. All else must surrender to that purpose."

"And what is that purpose, Dandi?"

Dandi hesitated, pursing her lips. At last she allowed, "I am searching for a Texan—Mr. Abel Pierce. His ranch is in Texas but I heard from a man in Kansas City that Mr. Pierce was known to spend a season in the vicinity of Dodge or Wichita. I thought it might be wiser to approach him there, than at his home . . ."

"Pierce comes through town sometimes. He's a moneyed man. You have an ambition to marry yourself a wealthy man?"

"That's not it, no ma'am. He . . ." She broke off, and seemed to fall into a reverie, gazing at the quivering light of the lamp on the table.

"Perhaps you met him before—did you have a child by him?" Bessie asked the question as if it were her right to know, by preeminent domain.

"I . . . no I did not have his child. I prefer to keep my own counsel as to why I wish to speak to him, if you please, ma'am. I can only tell you that I wish to speak to him privately. In some discreet place. But . . . you have not seen the gentleman of late?"

"I have seen him across the street once, but I don't know as he has sported with us. And I do not know if he is in town right now." Bessie and frowned. "When I asked if you was ready to come out here for the job, you said . . . what was it you said . . . That you had 'the necessary experience of men.' Maybe I mistook your meaning, girl. How many *customers* have you had?"

"Customers . . ." She looked downcast. "Why . . . none."

"None!"

"The only work I've done is a tutor for young ladies . . . a governess. And that taxi-dancing in Kansas City, that's as close as I got. I had a beau, in New Orleans, and we were . . . we did not wait till our wedding. But once he had me, he lost interest and I saw him no more . . ."

"No customers! No wonder you have such tender sensibilities. Why, the girls here have at minimum two men a night—two an hour is a better number!"

Dandi swallowed. "I have no other means . . . But—I do not think I can do the job. I heard Mr. Pierce sometimes availed himself of your girls and . . ."

"You hoped to meet him here before you had to do any real work?" Bessie sniffed censoriously. "That is less honest than a whore, girl."

Dandi winced. "Please forgive me—I simply could not take money to . . . But . . . I can be of use!" She brightened, sitting up straight. "I can cook! I can keep house, I can sew—the colored girl has too much work, and her cooking is . . . she only knows a couple of recipes. Why, I know a great many, and all thrifty! I can keep books for you, and watch over the girls when you're not here—and I will take no payment at all! I wish to be here, until he . . . until the gentleman . . ."

"You can do all those things? Is that right? And did you say, no payment at all?"

"I did! I need only a roof and meals!"

Bessie nodded slowly. "Well . . . it appears, girl, you may be of more use to me on your feet than on your back . . ."

CHAPTER FIVE

It was a soft, windless early evening when Wyatt Earp next walked the crowded boardwalk to the Delano District's "Keno Corner". He was noting all the six shooters, sassily carried in waist sashes and holsters by cowboys tramping eagerly from rickety hotels and bursting corrals. And he was thinking about what Marshal Smith had said a few days earlier, upon presenting Wyatt with a badge, *I want you to be reluctant to shoot that gun, Earp. That's policy. We want the law enforced, when it's practical, but we don't want dead cowboys. They get mad when their pals are shot down. Then they get themselves a mob and Hell breaks opens a station in Wichita. Another consideration, to wit: The Town Council simply does not like the bad publicity. We've got competition with Abilene, and Ellsworth, and they're starting up big in Dodge City now too. If they take their herds there because they hear that the Wichita police are blazing away at any fool of a drunk cowboy, why, everybody loses money. Gunplay looks bad in the newspapers. Much of the time, the reporters cooperate with us, but not always. Don't fire that gun, Earp. Unless you have to. And boy, it'd better be "have to". Make peace—but not by firing that peacemaker.*

Wyatt had his Colt Conversion Revolver on his hip—but he had no true freedom to use it.

"Wyatt Earp!" Piped up a reedy voice, from behind.

Wyatt spun on the boardwalk—to see a boy grinning up at him. The boy was wearing new button-up boots, dungarees, a new white cotton shirt, and had his hair clipped and combed. It took a moment for Wyatt to recognize him—the crooked buck teeth finally did it.

"Why Henry McCarty!" Wyatt said. "You're a new man!"

Henry beamed. "Ain't I a gent? And I come to help you with your work!" His eyes dropped to the Deputy Marshal's star Wyatt wore on his waistcoat now. "You could get the Marshal to deputize me!"

"You're young to be a deputy, Henry—you're still between hay and grass. But you can help out at the office, sweeping and bringing in food and such, and I'll pay you a half-dollar a day myself—if the Marshal does not object to you."

"I'm your *associate*, you said!" Henry complained, disappointed. "You need someone to watch your back!"

"I can watch his back, Mr. McCarty, if you'll allow me," Bat Masterson said, sauntering up. Seeing the boy's skeptical look he added, laughing, "I'm more use than I might've seemed the other night. That's Simon Pure too."

"Henry, let's hope he's more use here than he was at skinning buffalo," said Wyatt. "Didn't like to get his hands dirty."

Henry wrinkled his nose. "I wouldn't like to skin no buffalo neither. Emptying chamber pots was bad enough. I ain't *never* doing that again."

"I sympathize," Bat said. He looked up at the sound of a gunshot from Rowdy Joe's.

Wyatt had already started across the street, one hand to the butt of his own gun. "Tell you what," Bat said, giving Henry two bits. "Go get me a cup of coffee from the café there, and you can keep the change."

Bat started after Wyatt, who was already obliquely scanning the interior of the saloon through the window. It wasn't wise to rush in if guns were being fired. A second shot banged into the ceiling—Wyatt spotted the source, a trail hand he recognized from Ellsworth, one of Pierce's men, wreathed in gun smoke. Hoy, or Hoyt, was his name, wasn't it? One of the cowboys Wyatt had struck unconscious in the Ellsworth jailhouse.

Just now Hoy was pointing a silvery pistol with a short barrel at a man who looked to be somewhere between Indian and Spanish. "Next one goes through your goddamn heart, if you don't apologize!" Hoy said, slurring his words.

Wyatt noted that Hoy was turned half away from him. He started to draw his Colt—then remembered what Bill Smith had said.

Wyatt dropped his hand from his gun and pushed nonchalantly into the saloon, as if he were heading for the bar.

"I cannot think of nothin' to say 'sorry' about," the man with the long, raven-black hair was saying, his face creasing dourly. He looked like he might be a half-breed; part Apache judging by the headband and his mix of Mexican and Indian garb.

Wyatt began sidling his way toward them . . .

Hoy pointed the gun at the other man's forehead and cocked it. "Think again, you Mexy son of a bitch." His hand was unsteady with drink but he couldn't miss at that range.

"Why George, he didn't insult us, to my mind," said an older cowboy, with shoulder-length graying hair and bushy brows, seated at the poker table. "Leastways not enough to shoot him over."

"Damn you Dudley, he *said* that Texas is stolen, and Davy Crockett was a sniveling coward!"

"My Grand Uncle, he is Mexican," the man said, calmly, as if there weren't a pistol pointed at his head. "He was at the Alamo battle, I just tell you what he said, they find this Crockett hiding—"

"Now that's a dirty lie!" Hoy fired—but into the ceiling, as Wyatt Earp had stepped up behind him and struck his arm upwards with his right hand, crooking his left arm around Hoy's neck from behind.

Bat Masterson was stepping up to Hoy's left, his gun drawn but held casually, pointing nowhere special, as if he were going to twirl it to amuse himself. But his readiness to use it if needed came across to Hoy's friends.

"Cowboy," Bat said, "this is no way to debate history. What if the university professors was to go at it that way? Bullets would be flying through the lectern!"

There was laughter at that, and the older, long-haired cowboy smiled and deftly plucked his friend's gun from his fingers. "I'll hold that, George, so's you can get it back later. They got the drop on you sure."

Hoy struggled to break loose—and felt no give in Wyatt's grip. "Let me loose, damn you, I'm not heeled now!"

"In a moment. Bat, pat him down, just for luck," Wyatt said.

Bat holstered his gun and patted Hoy down. He nodded to Wyatt who released the furious cowboy.

Hoy turned to see who'd grabbed him. "Who the hell snuck up like a goddamn red savage—Oh shit!" He rolled his eyes. "It's that Yurrip! From Ellsworth!"

"My name is *Earp*," Wyatt said, correcting his pronunciation, "and mostly I'm from Iowa, by way of Missouri."

"You're the son of a bitch who cracked my head in Ellsworth!"

"I'd-a rather not had to," Wyatt said. "Come on, we'll go outside and cool down. Maybe Mr. Lowe doesn't mind that hole in the ceiling much . . ."

Hoy and three of his friends looked at Bat's gun, and at Wyatt's hand settling casually on his own pistol, and after a few moments of grumbling indecision, they reluctantly filed outside. Wyatt and Bat followed, watching them closely.

The older cowboy, Dudley—no one was never sure if it was a first or last name—remarked, "Mr. Lowe don't care about another bullet hole in the ceiling more or less—we was counting them last night. Fifty seven!"

"Them ceilings," one of the cowboys offered, "is double-thick oak, 'cause there's rooms upstairs."

"Some calibers, I hear, can go right through," said Dudley.

"We won't experiment with ceilings and caliber any further," Bat said. "Not tonight nor anytime in Wichita."

Wyatt nodded. "It's all over. You boys are too eager to pull your pistols. Wanton shooting can kill folks unintended. I won't have it."

Hoy, all this time, was glaring at Wyatt. But now the cowboy hooted with laughter. "He *won't have it!* You ain't much older'n me, and you're a Deputy? You ain't the Marshal nor the Mayor neither! Just exactly who the hell *do* you think you are?"

"I told you how to pronounce my name," Wyatt said mildly. "You behave yourself or I'll knock your heads together just to see what sound it makes." He put out his hand to Dudley for Hoy's gun, locking eyes with the old Texan, and after a moment's hesitation Dudley surrendered it. "I'll keep the smoke-wagon at the jail, you can get it in the morning. You boys keep the peace now and we'll all get along."

"What the hell," Bat said, trying to defuse the tension, "I'm buying drinks—who's with me?"

"I never turned down a free drink yet," Dudley said.

Grumbling, the Texans went back inside, Bat riding herd on them from behind. Hoy paused at the door and, lacking a gun, shot a dark look at Wyatt, just before plunging back into the saloon.

You, the look said. *There'll come a time.*

Hoy was sure to tell Pierce about this, Wyatt reflected. And he would make it sound as if Wyatt had played a dirty trick on him; as if he'd been disrespecting Texans. Pierce would have another reason to think of Wyatt Earp as an enemy.

He saw someone standing in the shadows of the alley beside Rowdy Joe Lowe's, then—watching him. Knowing Wyatt had spotted him, the man stepped into the light that spilled from the saloon's window. It was the half-breed from the saloon.

"I am Tomas Sanchez," the man said; his accent was a curious combination of Mexican and Indian. "They call me Tom around here. I owe you some debt, Deputy. I carry no gun. He maybe have kill me."

Wyatt shrugged. "I just don't want these boys debating with bullets, whoever they're shooting."

"Anyway—I'll be about, you need me to be. I owe you."

"Well—I don't want you back in that bar, Tom Sanchez, not tonight," Wyatt said. He didn't say anything about Sanchez's declaration of loyalty. It felt dangerous to him, somehow.

Sanchez nodded, lifted his hand—and melted back into the shadow. Wyatt could see his silhouette at the back of the building, turning toward the corral.

Wyatt started toward Red Beard's place—and almost ran headlong into Bessie Earp, walking with another woman toward Bessie's cat-house on the edge of town. The other woman he vaguely remembered from the night he and James had sent Plug Johnson on his way. She was compact enough to be almost doll-like. Young, not much above eighteen. The age Sarah had been in Illinois . . ."

Her hair was piled up on her head, a bit unruly but shiny-brown, wavy; her pale skin contrasted with the rouge on her cheeks and lips. Wyatt stared at her in a kind of sickly fascination—she reminded him of Urilla even more than Sarah. The girl must be a prostitute, of course, if she'd been in Bessie's place—something Urilla had never been, nor could have been. Urilla would have starved first.

The girl stared at Wyatt. "I believe we have met, sir?" Her Louisiana accent was like a perfume on her words.

"Dandi," Bessie laughed, "that long skinny fella, you'll notice, is almost as handsome as my James, and that's because it's his brother

Wyatt. He was out to our house to help us with that scalawag waving the knife, the other evening. Wyatt, this is Dandi LeTrouveau, late of Kansas City. She got here on the stage just the day you saw her. She comes from Louisiana, some time before Kansas."

Still struck by the resemblance to Urilla, and the connection to Sarah, Wyatt found his voice was caught in his throat, so he merely touched his dark, broad-brimmed hat and nodded reassuringly.

A smile glimmered on the girl's petite lips. Bessie looked between Dandi and Wyatt, her eyebrows lofted. "You watch your back out here, now, deputy," Bessie said. "We must be off."

Wyatt found his voice. "Have a grand evening, Miss . . . LeTrouveau."

Dandi nodded goodbye to Wyatt and followed Bessie, who took to the boardwalk, in her flaring floor-length gown and bustle, like a majestic ship sailing through a channel, making all lesser vessels steer aside. Cowboys stepped off the boardwalk, whistling as she went by, and Wyatt thought he heard her say, "All in good time, boys."

Wyatt sensed someone at his elbow, and found Henry standing there with a mug of coffee in his hand.

"This coffee's for Bat," Henry said. "It's gettin' cold."

"What, I don't get any?" Wyatt asked innocently.

"Well—I reckon you could buy it from Bat."

Wyatt rarely laughed—but he almost did, then. "Bat'll come for it. Let's go in the café—I'll get my own coffee and we'll see about your dinner."

* * *

"You got a firm way about you, in handling men, Wyatt," Bat was saying as—nearly two hours hour after disarming Hoy—they strolled to the farther end of Delano, "but I'm not sure it's the way to go every time. I mean the way you spoke at Pierce's boys in

Lowe's. *I'll knock your heads together just to see what sound it makes?* There's a time to talk hard to 'em, my brothers say, and a time to gentle 'em up. Like training a horse."

"That *was* my 'gentle'," Wyatt said, looking up at the stars. It was good to see the glorious spread of stars over the prairie, more visible here at the edge of town.

Bat laughed softly, deciding Wyatt was not serious. "Okay. But these boys are mostly just drunk . . ."

"That's why you got to speak to them with authority," Wyatt said. "Nothing else much penetrates. They're drunk with freedom too, when they get here. But there are limits to that. They have to know you're not going to bend."

"Take no offense, Wyatt, I beg you, but you're not as experienced as all that. This isn't Lamar. And not everyone's going to react the way Ben Thompson did. He's got a temper but he's no fool. Too many of these fellows here are fools with a gun."

"It is true, this isn't Lamar, and I'm not an old hand at this job. But—it's just the way I *feel* the job. It feels right that way." He was weary of talking—this had been a good deal of conversation for him, and he fell silent as they reached the edge of the town. The prairie was a dark sea with prominences glazed blue-white by starlight: the occasional dwarfish tree, copses of grass, a rise in the ground like a low, frozen wave. He'd seen the sea, as a boy during the family's sojourn in California; an awesome sight. He longed to see the Pacific, again, someday.

At Wyatt's back was the racket of the town, sounds that inflamed curiosity, made a man's heart beat faster, while ahead was the peace of the prairie. He felt torn, for he was drawn to both. He remembered the seemingly endless, creakingly slow trip in the wagon train with his family, out to California—before his restless father, disappointed with the prospects on the California coast, had returned to the Midwest. Still, on that journey west Wyatt had looked out at the trackless plains, the mountains, the young naked body of the West with scarcely a human mark on it. A man could go in any direction he chose, out there, with no fences or toll roads. It was a land largely without borders—something that attracted him, and disturbed him both.

The land didn't need laws. But people did.

He wondered why he had been attracted to "lawing"—for he had run afoul of it often enough. He'd started lawing early, in Lamar. It hadn't been particularly rewarding work, not in any way at all. He had been tasked to chase down runaway pigs and he had dragged an occasional drunk to the jail. Once he'd caught a thief, and put him in their poky but it was scarcely more than a shed and the man had wormed his way out some loose boards in the night, and escaped. A dull and frustrating job, but not dangerous. And very exacting—he'd been slow to turn in some of the money he'd collected in taxes, just one time. He'd borrowed the money briefly to help his father out—without his father's knowledge—and would have made it good in a few days, but the law saw it as theft and he'd lost the job. Now he knew, the law had been right. Still—he wasn't sure he was right to be the law. In places like Ellsworth and Wichita and Dodge City a man stood a good chance of being shot dead by a drunk; his last view of the world could be spittoons and the muddy legs of the saloon crowd. The pay was middling at best. So why not go back to that freight venture?

Wondering, he seemed to see his father's face, again, grim and sorrowing, after that arrest in Arkansas. And he remembered how the judge in Peoria had looked at him—a round-faced judge with bushy side whiskers, who looked not at all like Wyatt's father but who had nevertheless looked at him just the way his father would have.

Maybe he had gone to work for Walton, on that boat, because he knew his father would not approve; because there was a kind of strange romance to the demimonde of brothels that seemed so in contrast to the black and white starkness of his parents' view of the world; and having gone too far into that, finding himself mired and blighted, he had veered hard the other way. He had to prove to his father—to himself—which side he belonged on. Prove that he was, after all, the man his father had wanted him to be. Why not? It was like he was serving his own sentence, that way. It was just and fair that he should have to prove himself now . . .

"Making sure they know you're to be obeyed is good, Wyatt," Bat was saying. He went on in his platitudinous way: "But making enemies isn't. Now it seems to me—"

"O! She's dead, the child, she's dead!" a woman shouted, from a house not far away. The voice sounded like Bessie Earp. And indeed it was the house run by Bessie Earp, Wyatt realized, as he and Bat loped toward it. They were met at the door of the brothel by Bessie herself, a lantern in her hand—she'd been about to go and find help. She seemed surprised to see them rushing up.

"There you are, quick enough, sent by Providence—come on, one of my girls is killed! And she did not die natural."

They followed Bessie's bustle and the blob of lantern light through the dimly lit parlor, to the sparse kitchen and then along an enclosed boardwalk that went to the sporting buildings out back.

In a room not much bigger than two horse-stalls, lit by a single candle-stub, they found the sprawled, barefoot body. The dead girl's long wavy brown hair was loose, spilled over the boards of the floor. Wearing only a cotton shift hiked up past her hips, she lay on the floor beside a mussed bunk. Her eyes were slightly protuberant, her tongue caught bloody between her teeth; her throat swollen purple. There was a sheet twisted beside her.

It was Dandi, the little woman Wyatt had seen on the street with Bessie. Someone had strangled her.

Wyatt knelt beside the body, instinctively tugging her shift down to cover the girl's groin, his other hand taking hold of her wrist. He confirmed what he'd already known: there was no pulse. The skin, though cooling, was not quite down to room temperature—it stood to reason she hadn't been dead long.

He withdrew his hand, rocked back on his heels and stared at the body, a sickening shiver running through him like a ripple along a whipped saw. He had lifted his hat to her on the street a couple of hours ago, and now she was murdered. He could not help but think of Urilla lying dead too. And of Prudence floating in the Illinois River, face down.

His heart seemed to squeeze like a white-knuckled fist in him, and he looked away from her. "Who found her?" he asked hoarsely.

"I did, Wyatt," said a familiar voice—not Bessie's. "I didn't hear anything for so long . . . Bessie went out till just a few minutes ago . . ."

He looked up to see Mattie Blaylock from Ellsworth. She was standing in the doorway, her makeup streaked by tears. She was wearing a dressing gown, hanging a bit too loosely for Wyatt's liking. "Mattie! When did you get to Wichita?" "Just this morning. I was . . ." He suspected she had been going to say, *I was looking for you* and he was grateful she hadn't, with Bat here. "I just started . . . started here this afternoon. This girl, she said she was going to take care of a couple of fellas. She heard them talking and said they was the ones she'd start with. Said it was her first go! I thought two was a lot for a first go . . ."

"When was this?"

"Why, not more than forty minutes ago. She went in here and— I couldn't make out much of it. Some noises, but you couldn't tell what kind of noises they was. If she was making the Go Darlin' sounds or—"

"The *what* sounds?" Bat asked. Wyatt, with his gunboat experience, already knew what she meant.

Bessie, putting her arm around Mattie, smiled sadly. "Oh—'Go Darlin', it's what we call it around here, noises to pretend they're enjoying themselves when the gents are at their business."

"Oh! So you couldn't tell . . ."

Mattie shook her head. "There coulda been others too, was here. I thought I heard others. I was in the front room and I heard her talkin' to somebody."

"Bessie—who was she with? Which man hired her?"

"There were two men—a man used the name Johnny Brown to make the appointment for both and said there'd be another gent along. I don't remember much about the man who set it up—didn't know him. I wasn't here when they showed up. Dandi let them in, I expect . . ."

"An hour ago," Wyatt said thoughtfully. "They're long gone." He glanced at Bessie. "Who else could've been here? How about Sarah? I mean . . . Sallie."

"Sallie!" Bessie called out, over her shoulder toward the main house. When there was no response she stalked back there, arms crossed.

Wyatt pulled a blanket off the foot of the bunk, covered Dandi's face with it. Two minutes later Bessie returned, her arm through Sarah Haspel's, helping her walk. Barefoot in a nightgown, Sarah looked dreary and disheveled and pallid.

"Wha's' it?" Sarah asked, her voice slurred, as she swiped a wisp of hair from her eyes. She squinted, seemed to be trying to see Wyatt; it was as if her eyes wouldn't focus.

"You didn't hear all the commotion?" Mattie asked. "Bessie was hollerin'."

"No, I'm . . . I'm gone to sleep . . ."

"The doctor gave her a powerful dose of mercury salts," Bessie explained. "And something to sleep. She slept right through it."

Wyatt looked at Bessie. "You knew about that—the mercury?"

"The girls can't keep secrets from me long."

Wyatt nodded, thinking Sarah surely looked sickly. "So you heard nothing tonight, Sarah—saw no one?"

Sarah shook her head. She looked at the figure on the floor and looked quickly away. She asked no questions. He figured she didn't want to know.

"You go on, then and . . . rest," Wyatt told her.

Sarah looked at Wyatt a long silent moment. Then she gazed, blinking, at the covered figure on the floor. And turned to drift away, back to bed. Bessie started to help her along but Sarah shook free, waved her away, and went alone.

"You said they make appointments for this house?" Bat asked, from the doorway, frowning at the body. He sighed, and abruptly looked away from it. Wyatt guessed Bat was thinking of Molly Malone.

Bessie leaned against the doorframe, nodding. "That is my preference. But sometimes they just show up—if they look like they got some real money, sometimes I let 'em in."

"But if there're generally appointments," Bat persisted, "then you know who she was with . . . maybe who did this thing."

"The appointment was to be with a small woman—but we didn't have Dandi scheduled. She'd done some taxi-dancing in Kansas but nothing more. She just stepped into this appointment on her own. I didn't know this 'Johnny Brown' at all, when he come to make the appointment. Just the name, a quick look. And he was bringing someone else with him."

"Now surely," Wyatt said, standing, "'Johnny Brown' was not his real name."

She waved a hand dismissively. "I don't suppose it was. We are not much attached to real names, here. His voice, and the way he dressed—it seemed Texan to me. His name—who knows? Sometimes they use real names. But they always use fake names when there's something special to do here . . ."

"Something special?" Bat asked.

"Oh you know. Like some of them, the men dress up like women—that's more something you find out in Louisiana, where Dandi come from, or with men from London—and then some of the boys, they like to be spanked . . ."

Wyatt blinked. "Spanked?" The gunboats had answered more basic needs. "Why would they . . ."

"And some of them like to *do* the spankin'. And they'll do more'n that. They can be pretty rough. Well this one had a request for something special, someone who seemed like a little girl. Dandi—she was more a housekeeper here. No real working here—I mean, not that way. She was to be a cook. But she must've decided to be the one for this man. She was small enough . . ."

Bessie's veneer of calm was cracking. Her lower lip quivered and she put her hands over her face. Mattie put her arm around her and both women began to cry.

Wyatt pulled the blanket back, took a last look at the girl's body. He saw nothing else useful of note. Then he draped the woolen blanket over her face again. He straightened up, and took a long, deep breath.

Bessie was dabbing at her eyes with a white cotton kerchief. "She hadn't been here long . . . to come out here and die like that . . ."

Bat removed his hat and ran a hand over his hair. "Where'd you say she was from, Louisiana?"

Bessie nodded, just once. "She said she was . . . Looking for someone."

Wyatt looked at her. "For who?"

Bessie opened her mouth—and then shut it, pursing her lips. She shrugged. "Oh I . . . don't know really . . ."

Wyatt thought she was keeping something back. He didn't like to press her—she was James' wife, after all. Given a little time, she'd come out with it on her own.

He saw someone peering around the edge of the doorway, behind Bessie, mouth agape.

"Henry," Wyatt said, "come in here . . ."

Wearing trousers, an untucked shirt, untied brogans without socks—he'd shoved them on like slippers—Henry sidled in, looking nervously at Dandi's body.

"Is that . . . who is that?"

"That's Dandi," Mattie said.

Henry's looked at the body solemnly. "We talked, a few minutes, on this and that. She spoke kindly to me."

"You hear anything—anytime in the last hour?" Bat asked. "Like a fight over here, shouting? A name?"

"I heard . . . somebody yelling let's go. Maybe 'Let's go, Joe.' I'm . . ." He shrugged.

"You look out of your cabin, see anything?" Wyatt asked.

Henry caught the tip of his tongue between his front teeth. He looked at the floor, as if thinking—there was something play-acting about it, Wyatt thought. "Well . . ." Henry said. ". . . No."

"Nothing?"

"No."

"You sure?"

"Um . . . yes sir. I mean—no. No there wasn't any . . . I mean yes I'm sure."

Bat snorted. "You sure you're sure—or you're sure you're *not* sure?"

Henry scowled. "I didn't see nothing."

Wyatt knew that kind of declaration. People who lived on the rough had said it to him often enough, as if it were a matter of principle. He'd get nothing more out of the boy, even if there was more to get. "All right, Henry . . ."

Henry slipped out of the room clomping away.

Wyatt looked at Dandi again. His voice was steady when he said, "Let's wake up the undertaker. And then we'll talk to some Texans…"

CHAPTER SIX

"Well now that's a damn shame," Marshal Smith said. "That's a melancholy shame indeed." He pulled the sheet up to cover Dandi's dead, collapsing face: her lips were drawing back, in rigor, shrinking to show her teeth.

The room was warmer than a morgue should be, and there was another body, a shopkeeper who'd been trampled by a horserace he didn't expect to find in the streets. The smell of death cloyed the room. Wyatt felt like forgetting his abstention from strong drink. He needed one. He was standing on the other side of the table from Smith and a young, brisk, plump-faced newspaperman, Dave Leahy, a reporter for the Wichita Beacon. Leahy wore a brown and black suit, stovepipe hat, and held a kerchief to his nose.

"The question is," Dave Leahy said, his voice a little muffled by the kerchief, "what are you going to do about it, Bill?"

"Why ever would you ask such a question?" Smith asked, lighting a cigar. He blew smoke across the space between them as if trying to mask the smell of decay. "As night follows day, I'll get on their trail, whoever's done it. If they *left* a trail."

"We know they were Texan," Wyatt said.

Smith grimaced. "You don't know that. Bessie Earp's *guessing*. She only saw this man Brown once, if that was his name, which isn't likely. I asked her about it: she said he had some kind of buckskin trousers. We see buckskin trousers on many men who come and go. Texas accent, if she's right—so what? We have nigh as many Texans in town as Kansans. And there's the possibility she killed herself—the whore could've hung herself on that sheet, it coming down at the end . . ."

Wyatt shook his head. "I spoke to the Coroner. He found the finger marks on her throat. I don't think she strangled herself."

Leahy grunted at Wyatt's dry sarcasm. "Yes I suppose we can rule that out . . ."

"You want to look at the finger marks, Marshal?" Wyatt asked.

"Ah. No, I believe not. The coroner is a university man . . ."

Wyatt looked at the body; an inert outline under a sheet. "Let's get some air," Wyatt said. Something bothered him more than the presence of a couple of corpses. He felt prodded, in some way, inside . . .

The others readily agreed and they adjourned to the boardwalk outside, to stand mutely in the greasy yellow light from one of Wichita's few oil-burning street lamps. Leahy puffed his cigar, watching a buckboard creak slowly by, driven by a farmhand, looking slumped and dispirited, probably from losing his sparse wages at the gaming tables.

Finally, Wyatt said, "Well, I'll nose around, see if I can get something more definite."

Leahy nodded at Wyatt with approval. But Smith squinted at him through a velvety coil of cigar smoke. "Did I appoint you some kind of town detective, young fella? I don't think so. You're barely a policeman here. I will see to this matter myself."

"Seems to me," Leahy said, "that Deputy Earp here is already involved. He was on the scene, it only makes sense he should poke around a mite more."

"That house is run by Bessie Earp, I note," said Smith, looking at his shoes with his lips compressed, as if unsatisfied with the shine. He leaned against a porch post and rubbed dust off the shoes on the back of his trouser legs, one at a time, as he spoke. "Bessie's the wife of Wyatt's brother. Now those folks can be seen as responsible for this girl, and she died when they should've been watching over her. I'm not so sure young Earp here can be . . . objective."

Wyatt felt anger rising in him, his arms and shoulders tensing. He often felt anger that way. As if his limbs wanted to be used to act on the anger. He held himself in check, but his voice was taut as he said, "What is it you're suggesting, Marshal? That I would cloud the facts for my family? I will ask you to retract the imputation." Wyatt had for a time studied to be a lawyer, and retained a store of such language.

Smith looked at Wyatt with surprise, at hearing so formal and wordy a challenge from a man he'd taken to be a former farm boy turned moderately competent street brawler. "Now see here, Earp . . ." But the look in Wyatt's eyes made him change his mind about his response. "Oh, I didn't mean to suggest anything . . . just that people might, ah, misunderstand the connections . . . Well, anyhow, if you want to look into it a bit more, why, that's no skin off my beezer. But you'll report to me, and I'll decide if there's any arresting to be done, Deputy Earp."

And Smith scowled, hearing the reporter chuckle . . .

* * *

"I guess I did hear a name said, the night Dandi was killed," Mattie said, softly. "Thinking about it last night, it come to me." They were standing together on the porch of Wyatt's hotel. In the quiet morning they could hear cattle lowing with worry from a crowded pen out on the edge of town, two blocks away.

Wyatt had encountered Mattie on his way to breakfast. He was surprised to see her up so early—ten-thirty in the morning. But judging by her red, weary eyes, she'd had a restless night, and she'd probably given up trying to sleep.

"What name did you hear?" he asked.

"Just the name . . . it sounded like *Joe Hand*, or something like that. One of the men calling to the other. 'Come on, Joe Hand, damn you, we've got to be gone from here,' he says. That's all I heard."

Wyatt nodded. It seemed he'd heard rumors of a Joe Hand, somewhere. A nickname for some *pistolero*. "Texas voices?"

"Seemed to me. I sure hear enough of them to know."

Wyatt was thinking about what she'd heard . . . *damn you, we've got to be gone from here.* It seemed to Wyatt that was the cry of one guilty man to another. It spoke of fear and haste, and it seemed to implicate these hypothetical Texans even further. Not that Smith would think much of it.

"Would you be embarrassed to have breakfast with me, Wyatt?" Mattie asked almost inaudibly, looking down the street toward Murchison's cafe.

"Would I be . . . ? No! If you'll meet me in Murchison's, I'll buy. My privilege. I've got one stop to make first . . ."

He'd asked the hotel's groom to saddle his horse, and it was waiting at the hitching post. He waved to Mattie, mounted, and cantered down the street, weaving through the morning freight traffic, buckboards and ice wagons and delivery carts. He had to give the stagecoach a wide berth, its big team of horses commanded much of the road—he looked for his brother Virgil riding up top, and saw instead a shaggy man in an old and dusty cavalry jacket. A different shotgun messenger, on this leg.

Bessie's place was only a quarter mile from his hotel, but he wanted to get there before any remaining sign was gone. He might see something he missed in the darkness.

He rode the horse across the bridge, past two miserable-looking cowhands leaning on the rail and squinting in the cruel morning sunlight as they stared down into the shallow river. "Hell, Lemuel," said one of the cow-hands, "there ain't enough there to drown yourself in."

Wyatt circled around to the dirt alley between the two lines of buildings constituting the South side of Delano, and reined in a dozen paces from the back door of Bessie Earp's place, not wanting his horse's hooves to disturb any tracks that might remain. He dismounted, tied up his horse, and approached the low buildings, shaped like freight cars, where the girls plied their trade. The nearer one was where Dandi had died. Farther back was an out-house, and over to the edge of the property, on the edge of the prairie, was a shanty, ten by twenty, where Bessie's black maid Agnes stayed with Henry McCarty.

Mattie had said the men had gone out back, and down the alley, and Wyatt found the boot tracks in the dry, gritty earth, sure enough. There were three sets, however. One set coming around the corner of the building crossed the other two at a diagonal. Another set of boot tracks, coming from Bessie's place, was followed by a dotted line in the dirt. The marks came and went with the texture of the ground. Rowel marks, he figured—big rowels, by the look of it. They didn't make many that big.

The tracks seemed to jitter in confusion for awhile, then led past the out-house to the alley back of Delano's main street. Wyatt followed the spur marks, and in the alley found only that plenty of horses and wagons had passed this way since, obliterating the tracks once they reached the alley. He returned to look at the tracks behind the cathouse.

He decided to follow the diagonal set. They went to the reeking outhouse, which was presently unoccupied except by flies, and then trailed unevenly down the alley to the back of the livery.

The marks led right up to Sam "Champagne" Montaigne. He was lolling over a couple of bales of hay, clutching his empty bottle and snoring.

* * *

"Your mind is somewheres in China," Mattie said teasingly. She glanced out the window of the café. "You are surely not here. Maybe you're in Louisiana. I guess you're thinking of that poor Dandi."

Wyatt nodded distantly, and put his coffee cup down on the table, beside the remainders of his breakfast. Mattie was acting like she expected his attention as her due. Kind of early for that. Still, he had been feeling his loneliness for a woman and was tempted to keep company with her. She had made it clear, once more, over breakfast, that he was not to pay her. And the relationship would simplify things. He would not have to court anyone. He would have to see to it they never failed to use a "johnnie"—there was no telling if she'd been any more careful than Sarah.

"Any notion who kilt that Dandi?" Mattie asked, suddenly.

Wyatt shook his head. "Montaigne might've seen the one who did it—he was sleeping out back. I took him over to the jail so when he sobers up Smith can ask him."

He glanced at Mattie, wondering, suddenly, what Urilla would've thought of her. But he knew. He had been thinking of Urilla, since seeing Dandi lying there. It was foolish to compare the two—his wife had been a churchgoing young woman of determined respectability, despite her oafish brothers and her shabby father. But Dandi surely had not been a prostitute long—and she'd had Urilla's delicate, brave vulnerability. And looked rather like her too. As if, seeing Dandi's dead face, he were being reminded that he had indeed let Urilla down.

Urilla had been healthy, when he had gone to St. Louis. He was there to serve a warrant for his father, and he'd ended up staying longer than he should have. After doing the errand, Wyatt found himself in a gambling hall, playing cards. He'd intended to play but a few hands. Apart from a hasty break for the piss-pots they kept behind a screen, it was twenty-seven hours before he left that table, having lost what he'd gained and forty-eight dollars more. Then, stunned with exhaustion, he'd rented a room and slept twelve hours through. He'd awakened realizing his wife had expected him back a day earlier.

Wyatt had returned to Lamar quickly as he could—muddy roads made it slow going—only to find her already fallen ill. She'd been sick alone at home for a least a day and part of a night. She'd not wanted to leave the house, she'd said, for fear he would come home and she wouldn't be there waiting.

Suppose he'd been with her, when she'd first gotten sick? He would have brought the doctor far sooner. She wouldn't have been weakened by fretting on the whereabouts of her husband. Maybe her brothers had been right after all. . .

"Wyatt?"

He looked up at Mattie, blinking, feeling like he'd flown back to Kansas from Missouri in the interval of a moment. "Yes . . . Mattie?"

"It ain't China anymore: You were sitting at breakfast with some other lady in your mind, just now," she said—smiling, but chiding him all the same. "That sad look in your face . . ."

He said, "Can I order you some more tea?"

* * *

Wyatt was leaning against the bar, waiting for Bat in Red Beard's saloon, and had almost talked himself into breaking his liquor fast and having a serious drink. The bar that night was crowded with cowboys—and the occasional shopkeeper hoping his wife wouldn't come looking for him. A barefoot saloon girl, who'd won the race, was banging away on the piano in the corner, caterwauling about the man on "The Flying Trapeze". Wyatt was feeling restless, still seeing that other girl's face in his mind's eye; seeing Dandi's lips receding in death. Maybe a glass of whiskey and water. Everyone else in Wichita drank a bit on duty. What was a drink or two?

He signaled the bartender, pointing at a bottle. The bartender, a portly man with an apron and mustaches oiled into black curls, knew him well enough to look at him with surprise. But he shrugged, set the bottle up on the bar, a little to Wyatt's right, and bent to get a glass . . .

The bottle exploded, spraying amber liquid and spinning glass fragments. Wyatt had felt the air crease with a bullet and turned to see a giggling, pig-eyed, mutton-chopped cow-hand, sitting at a poker table, his seat turned to face the bar; a Dragoon pistol smoked in his left hand; in his right was a half empty shot glass of whiskey. He was wearing fringed batwing chaps and a wilting, sweat-stained trail hat—and he was cocking his pistol for another shot. The man sitting across the table from him was a gaping, pock-marked drummer who'd been selling patent medicines on Main Street earlier that day—the peddler stood up and backed away from the table.

"Now," said the cowboy, speaking carefully so as not to slur his words, "I am a-gonna hit that glass righ' next to where th' bottle was. Bartender, move yourself outter th' way, and you, the tall som-bitch with th' yeller mustache, you move too, and I'll show you how we shoot in Texas."

Wyatt sighed. Texas.

Noting the man was left-handed, Wyatt raised his hands and took a long step sideways, to the cowboy's right, as if he were merely getting out of the way of the gun.

"You don't mind," Wyatt said, "if I move away from the bar before you let fly, just in case there's any ricochet after you shoot that glass?"

"Why sure, boy, go ahead on," the cowboy said, closing an eye and aiming the gun, as Wyatt glided around to one side of him. The cowboy tilted his hat almost to the back of his head and steadied his pistol, his tongue stuck out on one side of his mouth. The room got real quiet . . . The bartender ducked under the bar . . .

Wyatt had less than two seconds to consider his options. He couldn't let this man shoot up the saloon. It wouldn't do to shoot the drunken fool, of course. If he hit him with his fist and didn't put him down thoroughly with one punch, the cowboy would still have that gun and might use it on him. And if he grabbed for the gun, the cowboy might fire in a panic. Might hit anyone.

It occurred to Wyatt there was one way to take the cowboy out of the action reliably, and fast, without shooting him. As the Texan was squeezing the trigger, Wyatt drew his own gun and raised it high with as much speed as he could put into the movement, and brought it down with a *crack* on the cowboy's forehead. The cowboy's eyes crossed and he went over backwards, chair and all, out cold.

Wyatt scooped the gun from the cowboy's nerveless fingers, uncocked it, carefully lowering the hammer. He stuck the gun in his own belt, then took the drover by his greasy collar and began to drag him to the front door.

He was suddenly aware that the room had burst into a noisy response—and it was not a consistent one. Two men in silk high-hats—men he knew to be associated with importing dry-goods—were applauding, grinning from their table in the corner, and the bartender was applauding too. Three cowboys from Pierce's bunch were swearing, and one of them spat at Wyatt's boots as he dragged his charge toward the door. Other men at the tables were laughing, slapping the tables in their delight at the young deputy's slickness.

"Lookee there, he busted open his scalp! Boom! He's bleedin' like a stuck pig!" The dance hall girl had her own particular response, her breasts heaving, her lips parted.

Wyatt dragged the cowboy outside. He found Bat strolling up with his hands in his pockets.

"What's this, another charitable contribution for the calaboose, Wyatt?"

"It is. Promiscuous gunfire in the saloon and destruction of property. I'd appreciate it if you'd watch my back. He's one of Pierce's boys and there are others in Red's place. Not too happy with me . . ."

Bat put his hand on his holstered gun and followed along, walking backwards a ways to keep his eye on the saloon's front door. The cowboys glared after them from the doorway, but no one followed.

Wyatt was thinking about that drink—and the bottle. The bottle had exploded just before he'd reached for it. His mother would've called that the intervention of the Meek and Loving Jesus. Maybe— anyhow, that drover had done him a favor.

Then again, if his drunken aim had been off, that cowboy could have put a .45 slug into Wyatt's back.

Wyatt continued on his way, dragging the unconscious cowboy down the street by the collar, the cowboy's boots making two long skid marks in the dirt, all the way to the jail.

* * *

Mattie managed to just sort of run into Wyatt, stepping out of a doorway just as he was going into his hotel some time after two in the morning. "Wyatt—I need a new place to stay. I got in a tiff with the landlady. I wonder . . ."

"Come along," said Wyatt, who was feeling restless. Some feminine company suited his mood. She silently followed him to his room.

But as she fell asleep beside him, some time later, he lay awake in the moonlight streaming through the window, wondering if he'd made a mistake. Still, there was something comforting about having her snoring softly beside him; about knowing she'd been there of an evening. His feelings for her were muted. There was some sensual desire, and something protective. But he was sure he'd never feel about anyone as he had Urilla. His ability to feel that much for a woman had died like that small shriveled blue thing curled up dead in a wicker basket.

* * *

They had breakfast about ten-thirty the following morn. It was blustery; the wind rattled and hummed at the eaves. Mattie complained at being awakened so early, but Wyatt had things to be about.

She didn't eat much breakfast. She was drinking tea, and looking out the dusty window. "I do think they might take some soap to these windows," she said. Glancing at him sidelong—and then away. "Housekeeping's important in a business. I wouldn't mind keeping a café myself, some time." She glanced at him again. And again away.

He decided there was something she wanted to talk about, only she didn't know how to bring it up. "Whatever it is, Mattie, go on ahead."

She blushed, but she didn't deny it. "I feel like . . ." Her voice was hushed; he had to lean close to hear her over the noise of the café. ". . . you maybe don't have all the regard for me you could, and I know why." She dropped her gaze. "I can't say as I blame you much . . . for not giving me your heart . . ."

"Now that isn't true, that I . . ." He glanced around at the other people self-consciously. He disliked mushy, emotional talk, especially in public.

"It *is* true. It's the way I've been living. You know—" She licked her lips, glanced around. "I wouldn't have gone into working for . . . into this work, if not for the fever taking my family. My father was in debt when he died, and selling the land brought nothing. I went to the church, back home, to ask for help—and Reverend Costingale said for me to pray. I did, I prayed, but . . ." She looked down at her plate, and whispered, "God didn't buy me breakfast. Only gentlemen have done that for me."

He nodded in sympathy. "Out here, there's not much work for a lady."

She looked at him directly. "But a lady is meant to be a wife, Wyatt. To care for a man. That is her proper occupation."

"Not everyone thinks so," he said, stalling. "There is suffrage and such. But to me, the traditional way always seemed natural."

"I want nothing more, Wyatt. And if a . . . a gentleman was interested enough, I would not insist on . . . on the . . ." Again she lowered her voice so he could barely hear her above the noise of the other diners in the small eatery. "I would not insist on . . . on matrimony. But . . ." Her voice trailed off as she looked for the words or the courage to say them.

"You might consider . . ." He had been about to suggest she might be a "mail order bride" for some settler out in Oregon, but then he realized that would only hurt her feelings. And there was no mystery about what she was coming to. She wanted to live with him, with a view to someday becoming his wife.

She was looking at him steadily, her eyes big and round. "Yes? I might consider . . . ? What, Wyatt?"

"Ah . . . we might consider that we . . ."

"Yes?"

He didn't really want to do it. But she was biting her lip, as if she might burst into tears, in front of all these people. He thought of Urilla, and Sarah. And poor little Dandi—who would be alive now if someone had taken her as wife.

Perhaps his thought passed somehow, unspoken, from his mind to hers—or perhaps it was coincidence when Mattie said, scarcely audible: "I'm scared I might end up like Dandi, Wyatt."

"It seems she wasn't making a living that way . . ."

"But it was in one of those places she died. Working for them, however she did it. And there's Prudence. And Molly Brennan—I knew Molly. She was shot by that Corporal King . . ."

Wyatt cleared his throat. He had known Molly in passing: a soft-hearted, willowy girl who was only occasionally a prostitute. The cavalryman had become obsessed with her, and found her sitting with Bat Masterson in a saloon in Sweetwater, Texas, acting as Bat's good luck charm as he played cards. King had come roaring in, pistols blazing, wounding Bat in the leg—Bat had pulled his pistol and returned fire. What Mattie didn't know, and what Bat had told no one but Wyatt, was that Molly had been killed when she'd tried to intervene between the two men—killed by a wild slug from Bat's pistol. Bat shot King dead only to find Molly bleeding to death on the saloon floor. Fortunately, the town blamed King. But Bat knew the truth.

Wyatt thought about Urilla; Bat about Molly Brennan.

Wyatt smiled, wearily amused at the way Mattie had played the Dandi card and then the Prudence and Molly Brennan cards. Three ladies. And her set of queens beat his hand, for he now found himself incapable of leaving her in the life that had those three ladies—that might well kill Sarah Haspel. And perhaps the ghost of Urilla was urging him on too.

"I think we might try it," he said, taking Matti's plump little hand. "We'll see how it goes."

* * *

The wind soon died down but a kind of translucent chill seemed to thicken the air, as Wyatt and Bat set out to see the Marshal, hoping to catch him at his office—Smith had a way of taking three- and four-hour lunch breaks, in various saloons, eating sandwiches, playing cards, and drinking. Afterwards another hour or so was spent napping.

Near the Town Marshal's office, they came upon Dave Leahy outside the haberdashery. Leahy was looking critically at his own reflection in the shop's window, adjusting a new raspberry-colored derby. He had a newspaper under his arm, which slipped to the boardwalk as he tilted the hat—Bat bent and picked the newspaper up.

"Have you written about the killing, Dave?" Bat asked, glancing at the front page.

"I have not yet written it up," Leahy replied, sighing. He removed his new hat, meditatively flicking a speck of dust from it. "I would have composed it immediately but the Marshal came over and asked me to hold my fire."

Bat nodded. "You cut a fine swell in that new derby." Bat looked at the hat with an expert eye. "I may go into the men's clothing line myself someday. Hats, possibly."

"Why'd Smith do that, Dave?" Wyatt asked. "Tell you not to write about it, I mean. Your editors ought to be fuming. Even in this part of Kansas, a murder is news."

Leahy shook his head sadly. "It's your noise about the Texans, I expect. Smith—him and the mayor, they don't like to make the outfits mad. Smith says he wants to make sure of his facts before anyone speaks their suspicions. And—well—there's that 'she was only a whore' way of thinking."

Wyatt snorted. "The newspaper always do what the Marshal says?" Wyatt asked.

Leahy didn't like the sound of that and he gave Wyatt a sharp look. But after a moment he had to shrug a concession. "More or less. The owner of the *Wichita Beacon* is on the town council. It's that kind of connection. I did write something about you, though, Wyatt. I trust you saw it?"

Wyatt shook his head. Leahy took the newspaper from Bat and opened it to a small piece on page three.

On last Wednesday, policeman Earp found a stranger lying near the bridge in a drunken stupor. He took him to the "cooler" and on searching him found in the neighborhood of $500 on his person. He was taken next morning, before His Honor, the police judge, paid his fine for his fun like a little man and went his way rejoicing. He may congratulate himself that his lines, while he was drunk, were cast in such a pleasant place as Wichita as there are but few other places where that $500 bank roll would have been heard from. The integrity of our police force has never been seriously questioned.

"Now where'd you get that story?" Wyatt asked, frowning, as if annoyed. Of course, he was secretly pleased with it.

Bat whistled and rocked on his shoes to burlesque playing the innocent.

"There's your culprit!" Leahy said, grinning, hooking a thumb at Bat. "But say—it's true isn't it?"

Wyatt nodded curtly. "I don't think it should be a remarkable thing . . ." Though in truth he knew that it was at least worthy of remark. Bat would have done the same, he figured, but some deputies would have pocketed that money and claimed the drunk had been pick-pocketed in a saloon.

Leahy looked at his pocket watch. "Not quite noon—we might find Smith in. What say we go over to the Marshal's office and see if I can write that story about the girl. You haven't got any more on her?"

Wyatt decided to play his cards close to his vest. He had no evidence that could back up a definite accusation. Many people wore spurs. And a set of tracks, in this case, proved nothing. He could imagine the defense attorney's caustic comment: *Are you saying, Mr. Earp, that it is remarkable to find boot tracks outside a cat-house?* And he could imagine the jury laughing.

"Nothing definite yet," he said at last, as they started off for the jailhouse. "We found a drunk out back of the place, but he wanders by there all the time."

"Have you considered that someone may've come to town looking for her?" Leahy pointed out. "She could have been on the run from a jealous lover."

"True," said Bat, carefully stepping over horse droppings as they crossed the sun washed street. "That jealous lover may've found her too, and done her in."

"Could be," Wyatt admitted. "We don't know that much about her. Bessie says the girl came out of Louisiana and her family name was LeTrouveau. Wasn't in the profession—she was here on some personal errand, doing some cooking for Bessie to pay her way. Closest she got to whoring was a little taxi-dancing in Chicago . . ."

"Dandi LeTrouveau? What a name!" Leahy exclaimed, with a newspaperman's delight in color. "I must persuade them to let me write it up!"

When they reached the jailhouse, Bill Smith was just getting up from his desk and reaching for his coat. He had the mischievous air of a man about to look for a drink and a game. He grunted in irritation when Wyatt, Bat and Leahy came in

"Afternoon, Bill," Leahy said cheerily. "Hoping you might give me my story at last."

Smith looked longingly at his coat. "Well now, as to that . . ."

Leaning against the closed door to the cells behind Smith was Carmody, a broad, muscular man in blue woolen shirt and denims that he never seemed to change; he was more jailer than deputy, though he sported a deputy's badge. His thinning hair was greased back, and his concession to vanity was his long, upturned mustache, the ends waxed and blackened to extend a full two inches past his round cheeks. He was chewing a sandwich of beef and bread, and glaring at the three men as they crowded the small office.

"You're supposed to be out in them streets looking for hellions, Earp," Carmody said, his voice almost lost in his sandwich. "You too Masterson." Carmody imagined his seniority gave him rank.

Wyatt ignored him. It was that or slap the sandwich from his hand—which is what he really wanted to do—and that wouldn't have been wise. He turned his attention to the Marshal. "Bill, I've been thinking about this LeTrouveau girl. Could be that whoever killed her is someone that does it . . . from what Bessie said . . . well, for pleasure. That being the case, they'll do it to someone else. I was thinking that if we talk to that bunch who came in with the cows on Friday—"

Smith was putting on his coat, adjusting his top hat. "The matter is already resolved, so far as you're concerned, Deputy Earp."

Wyatt looked at Bat, who shook his head in puzzlement. It was a long, tense moment before Wyatt asked, "How's that, Bill?"

Smith looked at the door to the street. "We got a man locked up for the killing, looks to be our man."

"*J'suis malade!*" came the muffled shout from the cells, behind Carmody. "*C'est tout la merde! Tout la monde—c'est merde!*"

"Montaigne," Wyatt said.

"That's who it is," Smith said. "Sam Montaigne. You found him behind the cathouse not so long after the killing—was you told me he was there. Did you suppose we'd let him fly free?"

"I thought he might be a witness," Wyatt said. "Never figured him under suspicion."

"Certainly he's under suspicion. Seems a certainty to me that he's our man."

"Montaigne sounds like he's delirious," Leahy remarked.

"Yuh," Carmody put in. "Doctor said it was 'delirious trembles' he's got."

"*Delirium tremens,*" Bat corrected him, getting only a blank look in response.

"Just finding him outside that cathouse is no proof of anything," Wyatt put in. "Half the men in Delano pass by there. You have something more, I expect?"

Smith sighed. "Well sir, if you insist. Some months ago, over by the lady's dry goods emporium, Montaigne came upon Mrs. Hauptmann—kind of an armful, she is, a German matron. Her husband Helmut owns a lot of land here. Well ol' 'Champagne' makes a grab for her bosoms! Now they're not inconsiderable bosoms, and it's hard to miss them, on a narrow sidewalk, but ol' Champagne he up and sticks his face in those bosoms and gives each one a mighty squeeze and shouts 'Magna-feek!' or some gibberish like that and, well, we had to haul him down here and kick him around a trifle, cool him off for a day or so."

Wyatt shrugged. "It's a far piece from that kind of coarseness to strangling a girl to death."

"T'isn't just that. Another night, Montaigne was following one of the dance girls from Heinemann's. She was not a whore, mind you, just a girl that does a dance for a dime. Montaigne was following after her, making noises like a rooster. Well sir, she was pretty nervous by the time she came upon Carmody here and Champagne had to get another licking. We should have drummed him out of town. Some places, they'd have hung him for what he did to Mrs. Hauptmann and don't think Mr. Hauptmann didn't want us to do it."

"Those are the reasons you figure Montaigne killed that girl?" Wyatt asked. "Because he gave a woman a naughty squeeze and mooned after another? Why, any number of cowboys do the same, after a drink or three, if we don't keep them the other side of the bridge."

"It is more than that," Smith said. "He *confessed* to me. Anyways he said he knew he'd 'done evil' that night the girl died—those were his words. 'Jay-mal'! he says, in that French Canadian yammer.

Hammond, who sells books, he says he thinks it means 'I am bad.' Or 'I've done bad.'"

"But he didn't actually say he'd *killed* anyone—"

"Earp!" Smith said, flushing, glancing at Carmody meaningfully. Carmody came to stand close beside him. "You going to continue to take on with me like a cross-examining lawyer? You were hoping to take credit for an arrest yourself, I've no doubt. Maybe thinking of running for Town Marshal?"

Wyatt shook his head. "No. I'm thinking that you can't be sure that Montaigne did it."

"He did it, sure enough," Carmody said. "He's weeping about bein' evil and such. He did it."

"And that's that, young Earp," Smith said flatly. "You want to keep that badge? Because I'll tell you, I've had some questions. Your Bessie Earp was arguing with Carmody here about the licensing fees. We permit some sporting if the proprietors pay a fee. The fee was raised and she's kicking. Says she pays it when she hasn't. She supposes herself too lofty to pay for her sporting license! That makes her and her girls illegal. Now we're giving her time to change her mind but if she doesn't come around, your brother James may have to bail his wife out of this same jail. I've had just about enough of your freshness, boy. Now I'm going to eat my lunch. You want to keep working here, you'll put all this hogwash out of your mind and get back to watching those streets."

With that, Smith stalked out the door.

* * *

Wyatt found Bessie in the back room of James's place. "Bessie. How are you?"

She was seated at the table, with a rack of bottles at her back, a lantern overhead, squinting at figures in a ledger, a pair of spectacles on her nose. She took the spectacles off and looked at him with raised eyebrows. "You never in your life would come to just ask how I was, Wyatt Earp."

"A man can't inquire after his sister-in-law?"

"Not this brother-in-law, here. But sit down, pull up a barrel. Will you take a drink?"

Wyatt sat on whiskey barrel. "No, I'll sit on it but I won't drink it, not tonight."

She smiled. And waited, sharpening the nib of her pen with a small knife.

"Bessie, you've been feuding with the city over, ah, licensing, and they're nippin' at my heels about it. James has the money, if you don't."

"It'll be a double payment, then. Smith conveniently forgot one. But I'll pay it, seeing as it's coming round to you. Next time I'll demand a receipt." She watched Wyatt, as she spoke. When he made no move to leave, she added, "There's something else."

"The girl, Dandi—do you have an address for her family? Did she say anything about a jealous boyfriend— names of any kind, from her life before Wichita?"

Bessie toyed with her nib. "I . . . No, I know nothing of her family. But there was something else. I didn't like to tell you, it's just a kind of instinct you get in my business, to keep your peace. But she mentioned she was looking for Abel Pierce. She had business with him."

"Abel Pierce. Did she say if she'd found him?"

"She did not. I heard no more about it."

"Has anyone mentioned seeing him at the house that night?"

"Not to me."

"What was her business with him?

"She didn't say. Not outright. But I asked if he'd gotten her with child and she said I was not far wrong. That's all there was."

"Abel Pierce . . ."

"Wyatt—if you're planning to accuse him in this, you'd better have yourself some evidence. He's—"

"I know, I know. He's Ace-high around here. I've heard it."

"Where'd you say you found the girl, this Dandi?"

"I was recruiting up in Missouri, a place in Kansas City . . . Faranzano's Dance Hall, it was called. This Faranzano had brought her from Louisiana . . ."

"Faranzano. A pimp?"

"Along them lines, though from what I saw he puts on airs. Way I heard it, he would have the girls dancing with the gents for a dime, for awhile, then, come the right time, he'd push them into whoring. Far as I know, she'd only done the dancing. I didn't actually talk to the man. I spoke to a couple of the girls after hours, when they were on their way home. Dandi caught my eye. She was interested in coming to Wichita. Looking for Pierce I guess . . ." She took a cheroot and a match from somewhere in her bosom, lit the lucifer with a thumbnail, puffed the tobacco alight, and leaned closer to him. "Now, you don't say this came from me. But Pierce was here once, playing cards. One of the whiskey girls told me Pierce said you might be sorry you'd crossed him up in Ellsworth. The time would come, he said."

"When was this?"

"A while back."

"Why didn't you tell me?"

"Because, with men, talk becomes fighting. And killing. Men are stupid that way. And if you get in a hurrah with that son of a bitch, my husband will feel he has to back you up. That's the Earp boys and there's no help for it. And I'm like to end up a widow . . . And with all this . . . you looking into what happened to that poor girl . . . It just seems to me like if you push Abel Pierce, Wyatt . . . he'll come after you. I'll keep James home from a fight if I have to feed him a micky. And you'll be going after Abel Pierce all alone. Put it out of your mind, Wyatt. Forget all about it."

CHAPTER SEVEN

Though Marshal Smith and Bessie Earp despised each other, they'd given Wyatt the same advice. Wyatt did try to take that advice; tried to put the murder out of his mind, but it wouldn't go. Walking along the wooden sidewalk with Bat, that night, Wyatt looked up at the golden moon in the Bible-black sky, and seemed to see first Urilla, and then Dandi LeTrouveau—and then Prudence crowding between them, the three women gazing sadly down at him from the moon as if it were a port-hole in the darkness.

"Starting to get cold at night," Bat said.

Bat was walking with a certain carefulness, because he'd had a few drinks on duty—all in the name, he said, of keeping peace, but he sobered noticeably when Wyatt said, "Bat, I'm going to go in and talk to Montaigne, whether or not that sour bastard Smith wants me to do it. You coming with me?"

Bat sighed. "Tell you what. I'll keep an eye on Carmody, while you're in there. Those cells are small for three, and I don't want to be crowded up to that high-smelling rummy."

Wyatt nodded. They made a quick stop at James Earp's gambling hall, and then crossed the street to the jailhouse. Carmody, sitting at the desk, a pipe clamped upside-down in his teeth, looked up from a catalog. Wyatt could see the pages were open to drawings of ladies in their bathing wear. He resisted saying something about that—but Bat rarely resisted saying anything.

"Why Carmody," Bat said, "are you thinking of going bathing in the Arkansas in one of those frilly bathing suits?"

Carmody slammed the catalog shut. "What do you damn fools want?"

"*J'veux mourir!*" Montaigne shouted from the cell, distant but shrill. "I am in Hell and you are the devils! *J'mourir!*"

"That murderin' loon's been howling like that all night," Carmody said. "I'll be glad, come the hanging and he's gone to his maker."

Bat pulled a deck of cards from his inside coat pocket. "Carmody, Wyatt and I was arguing about if you had any card sense. Wyatt said no, probably not. I said Carmody's seen the elephant and more, and he's got card sense. I propose to test it, with or without the use of cash money."

Carmody scowled at Bat's deck. Then he opened the desk drawer and pulled out a well worn deck with drawings of dancing girls on the backs. "This here is a deck I know to be steady and reliable."

"Do you accuse me of something, Carmody?" Bat asked, pulling a chair up to the other side of the desk, as Carmody shuffled the deck. "I ought to call you out. But I'll let it go, if you'll deal five cards for draw. How about you, Wyatt, will you take a hand?"

Montaigne, right on cue for Wyatt's purpose, let out a long, wordless howl.

"I'll play a hand or two," Wyatt said. "First I think I'll look in on that Canuck and see if I can get him to shut his yap." He made it sound like he was going to clout Montaigne quiet.

"You do that," Carmody mumbled, squinting at his cards in the light of the whale-oil lamp.

Taking the cell keys from the hook, Wyatt went through the door behind Carmody, and followed his nose to the drunk. But he found Montaigne dismally sober, shuddering in DTs on his bunk. A candle burned low in a wall niche across from the cell, its sputtering twitching the shadows of the bars.

Wyatt unlocked the cell door, opened it and stepped cautiously through, keeping a hand on the butt of his gun.

"You know," Wyatt said, "I got into a drinking binge, once. Several months it was—drinking so much that when they chucked me in jail, out East a ways, I was shaking too, come the morning."

Montaigne peered at Wyatt through swollen eyes. They'd beat him about the face, Wyatt saw, when they'd brought him in, and he was far from healed. "You was under the bottle like me?" Montaigne said, sounding skeptical. *"C'est vrai?"*

"Not so bad as you—you've been at it longer. But I was on my way. I stopped drinking, and never had the shakes again."

"Merde—That mean you don't bring me a drink."

"I didn't say that . . ." Wyatt said, winking, and taking out of his coat the pint of Old Overholt he'd gotten from James.

Montaigne stared at the bottle, licking his lips. He had just enough dignity to keep from snatching the bottle. "That Smith, he is going to let me go?"

"Maybe I can get them to let you go—if you talk to me, tell me what happened that night . . ."

Wyatt handed the bottle over and Montaigne drank half the pint off almost instantly. He gasped, sagging with relief. "Oh, *c'est bonne* . . . What happened that night. What happened. I was walking out to the desert, to drink champagne with the stars. Then I got very tired, and I turned to find sleep. Sometimes I sleep behind the livery. I go there, I go to sleep—then you come and say: Sam, come and talk to the Marshal. And the men beat me and put me here."

"I never expected they'd keep you here. I thought maybe you could tell them if you saw or heard something. You were sleeping near the building where that girl was killed."

Montaigne drank off the last of the whiskey. "Some more whiskey, please?"

"That's all I've got. You hear anything that night?"

Montaigne considered—but addressed something else entirely. "Do you know how I got here, to Wichita? The truth? I don't know, myself! I only know: *Le Cree*! I was taking their furs, they said—these *sauvages*, said I took their furs. Only because I trap a few animals. And they kill my wife and my daughter and my brother too, all together, and I find them dead and I start drinking. And I do not remember how I got to Kansas . . ."

"I understand, Sam. Now tell me about the night you were arrested. You hear anything when you were bedding down?"

Sam looked at the bottle, upended it on his tongue, waiting out the few last drops. He shook the bottle and sighed, and then looked at the candlelight through the bottle glass. At last he said, "That night . . ." Maybe. I hear a man shout, 'Come on!' Cursing the other man. I hear spurs walking by. I keep my eyes closed because the voices sound angry and sometimes they'll beat me, if they're angry and they notice me. Because I am someone for them to beat. 'Here is Sam, someone to beat.' they say." He bent over till his head was nearly touching his knees. He rocked gently, clutching the bottle. "Here is Sam, *le imbecile . . .*"

"That's all? You hear a girl scream? Hear a name said?"

"No. Just a man saying 'Yes sir'. He is speaking to his boss . . . Then I go to sleep and then you come and the Marshal and Carmody beat me and say I have kill a girl."

"You go into that cat-house at all that night?"

"They do not permit me there! Those women would beat me too. One time I look in the back door, only look, and Miss Bessie throw a shoe, and hit my nose!"

Wyatt smiled. He could imagine that. "Well look, did you say to the Marshal that you'd done 'evil'?"

"I did not say anything like this, I said only 'Marshal please do not hit me, please stop, I feel bad, I hurt, *j'ai mal*, Monsieur Smith', and they—"

"Earp!" Carmody shouted, stomping down the hallway to the cell. "What the hell you doing back there?"

Montaigne drew back into a corner, like a snail drawing into a shell, and Carmody saw the pint bottle in his hand.

"You're giving him whiskey? Marshal Smith don't want him drinking, he wants him to suffer till he talks!"

Wyatt decided he wasn't going to get any further with Carmody here. All he'd accomplished was to verify to his own satisfaction what he'd already been pretty certain of: that Sam Montaigne was innocent. But he had nothing he could take to a judge.

"Just thought I'd quiet him down," Wyatt said, pushing his way out of the cell. He closed and locked the cell door and made to pass Carmody in the passage. He could see Bat beyond, shrugging. But Carmody blocked his way.

"I heard what you were telling the Marshal, last time you were here," Carmody growled. "You're playing boy detective again and Bill don't like it."

Wyatt kept his temper in check. It took an effort: he didn't like being called *boy* anything. He possessed an inner certainty that he was more a man than Carmody, so he let it go. "I asked a few questions, out of curiosity, while I was here," Wyatt said. "Now move aside and no harm's done."

Carmody stood still for a long moment, then turned sideways, making Wyatt sidle past in the narrow space between the cells and the wall—and suddenly stuck out a boot to trip him. Wyatt nearly fell, but caught himself on the wall. This time, his temper got the best of him. He spun on his heel, cocking his fists in the same instant, and caught Carmody hard on the right side of the jaw, following with a left jab. Carmody was knocked back against the door of an empty cell, sliding down against it till he was crouched.

Unwisely but understandably, Montaigne laughed.

Carmody turned and glared at the drunk. Wyatt reached out a hand to Carmody. Best to help the deputy save face. "Sorry, Deputy—thought for a moment there you tried to trip me. Maybe I misunderstood. Let me help you up."

Carmody ignored Wyatt's hand and grabbed the cell's bars, pulled himself to stand, grunting. He stared hard at Wyatt, lowering his head a little, like a bull threatening a charge. But one hand wandered to his already swelling jaw and he thought better of it. "Get out of here, Earp. Just get the hell out."

Wyatt shrugged and slipped carefully past Carmody, then followed Bat out to the street.

"That wasn't such a good idea, Wyatt," Bat said, as they stood in the road. "Carmody is Smith's bulldog. You hit him, it's almost like hitting Smith."

"I didn't want to. But he tried to trip me."

"You find out anything?"

"Not much. But I don't think Montaigne did it." He took a deep breath of the fresh air—and froze, seeing Shanghai Pierce riding past on a sorrel.

Pierce turned him a slow, hostile look—and nodded firmly to himself, as if making a resolution.

He turned away but Wyatt shouted, "Pierce!"

Bat groaned. "Wyatt . . ."

"You can stay here," Wyatt said, crossing the street to Pierce.

The cattle baron was reining in to lean on the saddle horn, smirking down at Wyatt. "What do you want—help carrying that badge? Lot of weight, that job, for a skinny young fella like you."

"Like to know where you and your men were, the other night, when that girl was murdered."

Pierce's face went cold. He waited a slow heartbeat and then he said, "You talk like I'd know what night and what girl—and what murder you mean."

"I thought you might have heard about it. Her name was Dandi, little slip of a thing working for Bessie Earp—but . . . not a working girl." He looked at the big rowels on Pierce's boots. "I met her myself. Thought maybe you knew her."

"Might've met her, some time. I meet a lot of girls. I don't ask their names. So I don't much know one from another."

"Wasn't in the paper," Wyatt persisted. "But it was the talk of the saloon."

"I heard about a whore killin' herself, if that's what you mean."

Wyatt shook his head. "Wasn't suicide. A man's accused of her murder, Mr. Pierce. He's locked up in the jail behind me."

He shrugged. "Then it could be murder. Why tell me about it?"

"She came here to town looking for you. So she said—sometime before she died."

Pierce's face seemed to drain of expression. His horse shifted footing. At last he said, "Many women look for a rich man. My name is around. I did not know any suicidal bar girls. Now I've got a question for you. Do you intend to continue to rough up my men, and make yourself out to be the Ulysses S. Grant of Wichita?"

"I intend to keep the peace, Abel."

"You can call me Mr. Pierce. And you stay away from my men. They are not in your jurisdiction—and I don't care where you're standing. Now go to the devil."

Pierce spurred his horse, tugging on the reins so the horse reared over Wyatt, the animal whinnying, forcing him to step briskly back.

Pierce laughed, and rode off down the road toward Delano. Wyatt could only watch him go.

* * *

Wyatt and Leahy were playing cards in James's place. It was nearly eleven-thirty p.m., late for Leahy but not for Wyatt. They were in a heads-up game now, just the two of them at the scarred wooden table. Wyatt had gone off-duty a trifle early tonight, as Jimmy Cairns had offered to take his place in the late hours—but then again Wyatt never felt really off-duty, unless he was in his hotel room, in bed, and that could end at the distant sound of a gunshot. Even now, playing poker, something that normally absorbed him, he couldn't keep his mind off Dandi's murder. He hadn't really known her—but he felt he had to do something about it anyway.

Wyatt's cards were lukewarm tonight. He felt like he was pouring money down a sump. He had tried to give up gambling, once or twice, because of what had happened, when Urilla took sick. He told himself he could be a dealer without being a player. But gambling had entered deeply into him, and taken up residence and though he'd learned to keep it contained, he could never evict it.

"I'll take two," he said, tossing down his discards.

Ought to get back to Mattie, he supposed. She sulked if he stayed out late playing cards. *Urilla* . . .

Dave Leahy dealt two cards. He held his own rather awkwardly—he was not a habitué of the gambling halls—and squinted at them through the tobacco haze.

"You haven't written your story on the murder yet?" Wyatt asked.

"Boss doesn't want me to, not yet," Leahy mumbled unhappily. "Maybe not at all. And I'll tell you something—that *J'ai mal* business that Smith was gassing about? It doesn't really mean 'do evil'. I looked it up. It means *I hurt*. You know—I'm in pain. 'Course, you can do a literal translation and *almost* make it come out the way the Marshal wants. But my guess is, Montaigne's talking about his drunkard's sickness. He has been deprived of his daily dose. And for all I know . . . could be he *did* kill her. He was harassing the ladies, from time to time . . ."

Wyatt shook his head. "Mattie heard two men, sounding Texan, last to be with Dandi. One of them probably did it. Montaigne has a distinct voice, an accent. And it isn't Texan. And I talked to him. I know when a man's lying. I fold—you've got beginner's luck, Dave."

"I'm no beginner!" Leahy crowed, happily reaching for the chips. "No—I'll let it all stand as my ante. You want to deal?"

"You go ahead." Wyatt's mind was mostly elsewhere. He was watching a man enter the saloon. Dudley, from Pierce's outfit, his clothes as begrimed as they were fancily sewn; his sombrero hanging down his back with his long gray hair.

Dudley went to the bar, dug deep in his pocket, began counting his change. All copper change. He looked sober, and looked like he didn't want to be and couldn't afford much more than a beer.

Wyatt signaled his brother, who was walking by with his hands in his pocket, and when James bent near Wyatt whispered in his ear.

James straightened, looking at Wyatt with raised eyebrows. "You want me to put *what* in it?"

"You heard me right."

James shrugged and went behind the bar. He spoke to Dudley, who squinted through the murk at Wyatt, then nodded brusquely and came to the poker table.

"I heard a rumor about some whiskey and cards offerin', but in fact I have no stake for the game, boys," Dudley said.

"Dave," Wyatt said, giving Leahy a look that carried a silent message. "You won't mind a third?"

Leahy looked at Wyatt, then at Dudley, sensing intrigue. "Won't mind at all." Leahy assumed a nonchalant air that was all too transparent, Wyatt thought, but Dudley, hanging his sombrero from the back of his chair and sitting down, all in one motion, didn't seem to notice. Wyatt moved his chair closer to Leahy.

Leahy almost jumped out of his seat, feeling Wyatt's hand prodding his leg under the table. He looked down, saw five silver dollars stacked on the edge of his chair, beside his hip. Leahy picked them up and clicked them together, stacked them in front of Dudley. "I am willing to stake you this far, my friend—" Leahy said heartily, "—because I sense luck in you. But you must repay me twenty per cent."

"Done and sworn before Jesus, Mary, and Joseph!" Dudley declared; and his grin, with ground-down yellow teeth, etched even more deeply the lines on his weather-seamed face. His shoulder-length white hair swished about his head as he reached for the bottle of whiskey James put on the table. "I lost everything last night—" He looked at Leahy and added hastily, "Not that I'm not feeling lucky today!" He raised his shaggy eyebrows, seeing that James had put two tumblers down instead of shot glasses—and seeing James set down a second bottle in front of Wyatt. "You boys are serious drinkers, by God!"

"That's right," Wyatt said, pouring a tall drink from his bottle. "Here's how." As Leahy and Dudley watched in astonishment, he drained it with three quick gulps. He set the tumbler down with a clack. "Now sir, let's see if Texans can drink like Missourians."

Dudley rocked back in his chair a little at that. "As good as . . . ! Ha!" He poured a tumbler, and drank it off, shuddering afterwards, his face flushing. "How's that!"

"It'll do for now!" Wyatt said. "What do you say to some Draw Poker. Ante up." They anted up, and he dealt the cards.

Dudley, peering dizzily at his cards now as the liquor hit his innards, said, "I'll take . . . two. No, three."

Wyatt and Leahy drew cards. In a moment Leahy threw his cards down with disgust. "I've got but a pitiful hand."

Wyatt nodded approval at him. "And I . . . I'll bet you three dollars, there, Dudley."

"Three! Well, what the hell." He placed his bet. "I call you! I've got three deuces, right there! Three of a kind, one for each dollar I'm winnin' from you!"

Wyatt had a full house but he shook his head sadly and threw the cards onto the table, face down. "Beats me. Time to have another drink."

He drank off more of what was in his bottle, Dudley had another tumbler of whiskey, smiling and pleased. Wyatt watched him, thinking that winning at cards made a man affable and talkative, almost as much as drinking, and Dudley was doing both.

The game continued another forty minutes, Dudley mostly winning, Wyatt never betting big, and drinking from his own bottle as much as Dudley did from his. Leahy, mostly folding each hand, watched Wyatt with evident curiosity. Thirty-two minutes into the game a couple of cowboys stood up from a game at the next table, each cursing the other, shouting about card cheats. The shorter, rangier one swung a long arm, his fist just grazing the edge of the bigger man's chin; the bigger man, balding and chewing a hand-rolled cigarette, stepped around the table and pulled a knife from nowhere visible.

"Hold it, boys!" Wyatt called out sharply, making his voice deep for the occasion. Fists and knife raised, the two cowboys froze and snapped fierce looks at him, as Wyatt pulled his coat back so they could see his badge. Pretending not to notice that Dudley was monkeying with the deadwood, Wyatt eyed the cowboys icily. "You don't want to make me go to work when I'm tryin' to be off-duty over here." He dropped his hand to his gun butt. He made his voice carry real regret as he added, "I'll either crack you over the head or shoot you. Can't quite make up my mind which."

The two men stared at him for a moment, then the balding one blew a long breath out so that his mustaches fluttered. He put the knife away, making it vanish as mysteriously as it had come. "Well Avril," he said to the rangier cowboy, "maybe I mistook you. Let's us have us a drink."

The other man nodded, licking his lips, and they hurried to the bar.

The game resumed. Dudley called for show-down and glee-fully displayed three aces; Wyatt paid off accordingly, and dealt another hand. When Dudley raked in another pot, Wyatt judged the moment had come—just when it looked as if Dudley's face might split from grinning.

"I'll just cut these cards," Wyatt said, "and shuffle them a few times too—might change the luck at this damn table. Say Dudley . . ." He expertly shuffled the cards together with a neat zipping sound. ". . . you still with old Abel Pierce?"

"Me? *Wellllll*, not exactly. Not as you'd say *employed* by 'im. The drive's over, you see, and here I am, not sure where I'm gonna jump. Mr. Pierce tends to put me on drag, and I'm sure tired of eating dust. Up the Western Trail we come—Chisolm's not right no more. But what a ruckus, near a hair raiser, when we got into Indian territory. Cheyenne was hungry, not enough buffalo coming down from up North, and they were trimming out our stock—well sir, we caught 'em about midnight but then they called their pals and nigh caught me and ol' George Hoy out on the wide-open. We had to light for the camp like nobody's business! Cheyenne bullet gouged up George's new saddle too."

"George Hoy, he still in town?" Wyatt asked, as casually as he could.

"He ain't. He lit out. Mr. Pierce's still here, though. He cain't go back to Texas no time soon."

"That right?" Wyatt asked, endlessly cutting and shuffling the cards. "Why's that? And say—have another drink, you're letting good whiskey go to waste . . ."

"My Mama didn't raise me to waste whiskey. She liked a dram herself. Thankee. Now what was we talking about? Oh—Mr. Abel Pierce. *Wellllll*, I shouldn't be windy on that one but I guess it ain't too much a secret. Mr. Pierce lynched a couple of rustlers—and the new law down there, they was going to prosecute him! Can you believe it, Abel Pierce, going to jail! The man owns two hundred fifty thousand acres down there. Owns a lot of people too. Starting up his own town, over in Colorado. Can't imagine him going to jail. Why, one time a preacher asked him to donate some lumber for a doxology works. Mr. Pierce pays for the whole church to be built, every stick of it. Now that gent ain't knowed for his generosity, he'll squeeze a penny till it yowps—so I wondered if maybe he was a member of the church. 'You belong to that doxology works, Mr. Pierce?' I asked him. 'No Dudley,' he says, 'That church belongs to *me.*'" Dudley cackled with laughter. "You see? That's Abel Pierce! He isn't going to sit down for any trial. He owns the world! His Uncle Fergus told him so."

"His Uncle Fergus? How's he figure in?"

"Figures in from the next world. He's dead. But Mr. Pierce talks to him. Hears his voice, carries on conversations. Gets hisself inspired. Fur as I can tell, Uncle Fergus usually gives good advice—whatever any older hombre would say. Wished I had my Pa to advise me that way."

"How's Pierce going to get out of that trial in Texas?"

"Why, he's got friends in the government, down there, they'll get him out of that one. Takes a little time though. Meanwhile, he cools his heels up here . . ."

Wyatt nodded thoughtfully. "But why Wichita? He's done with his business here. Why wouldn't a wealthy man like Pierce go to St. Louis, or Chicago? They've got the comfortable hotels there. Have another drink, Dudley . . ."

Wyatt filled a tumbler for Dudley, then poured himself a glassful from his own bottle and drank it off. Leahy looked at the bottle, probably realizing it wasn't really whiskey. But Dudley, seeing Wyatt draining his glass, had to drain his too.

"So why Wichita?" Wyatt prodded.

"Oh," Dudley said, after a moment, swaying in his chair, "Mr. Pierce, he likes to be where the fun is."

"That right? Too many rules up in St. Louis? He likes to be where the sportin' is right down the street, easy to find, eh?" Wyatt winked and Dudley winked hugely back.

"Thas right," Dudley said, slurring his words now. "Things is cheaper here too. Say, you sure take a long time shuffling. You don't take no chances. Yesh, he . . . you know, he likes what he likes."

"Now me," Wyatt said, lowering his voice, "I like those Chinese girls. If I was to go to a cat-house, I mean. That what Pierce likes? Course, they're kind of small, those Celestials . . ."

"Oh he likes 'em small. Likesh the young girlsh, fourteen, fifteen, petite things. Funny, that, him being such a big man."

"But I expect with such a big man a girl like that'd get hurt some . . ."

"With Mr. Pierce? No, I've been in the same room with him, a-sportin! We had three beds and three women, him, me and old Yo-Hann, one time. Mr. Pierce—not that I watched, but you could tell, all in all—why, he was gentle ash a little ol' lamb with them girlsh."

Wyatt nodded, unconvinced—and sipped the water, colored with a little coffee, that he'd been drinking from the tumbler. The whiskey bottle James had put it in was camouflage.

Then he thought: *Yo-Hann?* "Did you say Yo-Hann?" Wyatt asked, dealing cards. "That an Indian name?"

"No, no, that's a name from out of Germany or Swiss-land or some such. He's half Dutch-y, don't you know. Yo-Hann Burke. Works for Mr. Pierce. Gun-hand mostly. His Daddy was an edu-cated man, named him after some foreign songwriter. Name like Burke but not Burke."

"Bach?" Leahy put in. "He named him after Johann Sebastian Bach?"

"That was it!" Dudley said, raising a finger exultantly. He swigged straight from his whiskey bottle—and then, hugging the bottle, he sagged forward onto the table, head on the cards Wyatt had dealt for him as if they were a pillow. He lay there chuckling and snoring by turns.

"You get any of what you were looking for, Wyatt?" Leahy asked softly, as Wyatt stood up.

"Could be," Wyatt said. *Johann Burke*, he thought.

Johann. Which you could hear another way too . . .

Joe Hand.

* * *

When Wyatt got back to the hotel room a little after midnight, he found that Mattie had cleaned it up, washed and pressed his clothes—or anyways she'd had the Chinese laundry do it—and his other suit was tied up in a neat pressed bundle on a chair. She had picked some daisies from the prairie and placed them in a vase, and set extra candles around the room. Wearing a lavender camisole, she'd arranged herself attractively on the bed: she was the centerpiece of a picture of her creation. She'd let her hair down, and it flowed over her shoulders, shining like brightly-polished brass in the candlelight.

"Well now," Wyatt said, because nothing else came to him. He unbuckled his gun belt, took off his hat and boots. "Why, look at you . . ."

"You had your dinner?" she asked softly.

"I have. You?"

"I ate something. Would you like a glass of wine? I got some of this German wine, the German settlers send for it all the way to Dutch-land over there . . ."

Wyatt hesitated. A little wine, he decided, would do him no harm. "Sure. German wine eh? Germans practically run this part of Kansas," he muttered, thinking of the Hauptmanns.

He pulled off his pants, sat beside her on the brass bed in his long johns. The brass bed squeaked as he shifted to get comfortable, sipping the yellow wine. "They sure know how to make wine. I like the taste of this stuff." In fact he thought it a bit too sweet but he wanted to make Mattie happy.

Wyatt liked being with her in this quiet room, in the candle-light, Mattie with her hair down; away from the noise of the saloons, the drunks; away from the dusty streets with their sudden, illegal horse races; away from the simmering cowboy hostility. Bat was better at seeming like the cowboys' gruff big brother suggesting they all cool down. Wyatt, by contrast, supposed he came off heartless, himself. The cowboys' sullen dislike wore a man down, after awhile. Especially when they assumed he didn't like Texans, or cow-hands. He had friends from Texas— had worked at hunting game to feed railroad workers with some Texans, and he had liked them. But once you got tarred with that brush . . .

He sipped wine, and thought that Mattie, no great beauty, was prettier by candlelight. He supposed he ought to tell her she looked nice in this golden light, but he was afraid he'd get it wrong somehow and end up seeming to insult her. That's what'd happened when he'd tried to compliment Urilla. Women didn't seem to care if he complimented them, anyway. Long as he stuck by them.

"Wyatt . . . there's something I want to ask you . . ."

Uh-oh, he thought. It's going to be talk of marriage and babies already.

But it wasn't that. "Wyatt, when I was with men before, you know, working, why, some were decent, some not—but I was always pretty much the same." She sipped her wine, looking at the candle-light, and went on, "I kind of just waited for it to be over, and made those 'Go Darlin' noises, and counted the money. Of course, there was times I almost felt like something more was there, but it was still like *business* . . . Do you know what I mean?"

He didn't, not exactly. "Um—go ahead on."

"It's just . . . I'd like there to be something more. I mean—I don't know how . . . how to be like a woman should be for her man when he's not . . . when he's not a stranger . . . It's not like I did it all that long, but—it's all I ever knew of being with a man . . . ."

There were tears in her eyes and he thought he ought to say something. "Is there some sort of thing that, um, you want me to . . . to do?"

"If you could . . . you know how you kiss me sometimes, and you just touch my face? If you could start out like that—I like that so much. If you could touch me all over like you touch my face sometimes . . . I just think . . . well . . . after that . . . we'd . . . we'd just *know*."

Wyatt nodded. He thought he knew what she meant, after all. He drank a little more wine and got into bed.

It went the way she thought it would, and it surprised him too.

There's more to some women than a man would think, he decided, later on.

He was leaning back, then, propped on pillows, Mattie sleeping in his arms. He wondered if he could blow out the candles from here without disturbing her.

That's when the rapping came on the door. It was the way someone raps when they're not sure they want to wake you, but they think you might be up.

Mattie moaned, and rolled onto her side, snoring softly, as Wyatt got up, pulling on his pants.

Bat Masterson was standing in the hallway holding a kerosene lamp borrowed from the hotel clerk. "Wyatt? I'm sorry if I woke you. But there's a fella broke into the jail and he's stabbed Sam Montaigne. Stabbed him dead."

CHAPTER EIGHT

"Who the hell breaks *into* a jail, if it isn't a lynch mob?" Wyatt asked, as he and Bat rode down to the jailhouse. They'd mounted up to save time.

"Carmody says it's Plug Johnson, that Swede with the feathers in his bowler and the Indian bracelets."

"I've seen him around," Wyatt said, remembering the man he'd rousted from Bessie's discreet little whorehouse. "Had a big knife on him, near to a Bowie knife."

"That's him," Bat said. "Mostly uses the knife to cut a plug from his chaw, always has one going unless he's asleep and maybe then too. Carmody claims Plug was shouting around town that he loved that LeTrouveau woman and he was going to slice up the man who killed her. Well, Carmody was out back answering the call of nature, and by the time he gets back in, Plug must've gone in and found the keys, got in and stabbed Sam—killed him in his sleep, cut his throat. Carmody saw him running down the street—away off East."

"Now why would he be going around shouting about what he was going to do to Montaigne?"

"Could've been drunk, or hopped up. Some get peculiar when they take that opium from the Celestials."

They reined in at the jailhouse, and stepped down. Bat peered at Wyatt's chest in the moonlight. "You missed a button on your shirt there, Wyatt. You're buttoned up crooked."

Wyatt set about correct buttoning. "Only a clothes monkey like you could see that out here without enough light to confuse a firefly."

He'd just finished when Marshal Smith and Carmody came out of the jailhouse office, shaking their heads dolefully. "Well that's the end of that, anyhow," Smith said, as he took out a cigar. He bit off the end and spat it in the street as he took notice of Wyatt and Bat. He pointed the cigar at Wyatt. "Earp, I want to talk to you, and now. You can't thump on my deputies and expect—"

Just then Bat put a hand on Wyatt's arm, nodded down the street. They could just see the shadowy silhouette of Plug Johnson climbing up onto a horse—the feathers in his hat were unmistakable, though he was a ways off. He set off at a gallop—headed for the Delano bridge and the open plains beyond, Wyatt figured.

"Earp—!"

But Wyatt had swung his horse around, was already spurring after Johnson, with Bat close on his tail.

"Earp you get your skinny rear back here!" Smith shouted. "You ain't authorized! Come back here!"

But Wyatt made as if he hadn't heard the Marshal. Some part of his mind had already worked out the reason he was being called back, and he leaned forward, urging his mount after Johnson.

He and Bat thundered over the bridge, shouting a warning to a group of cackling drunks in the road to get out of the way—the drunks were staring after the galloping Plug Johnson.

The drunks scattered, almost falling under the hooves of Wyatt's horse, and soon he and Bat were riding their snorting mounts on the thin, almost invisible trail twisting out into the Great Plains, following a sketchy shadow in the buffalo grass.

Wyatt lost sight of Johnson for awhile when he rode down into a deep buffalo wallow, and then veered into a creek bed. They slowed to a fast trot to pick up his sign, and it wasn't hard to find. Clear in the moonlight, Wyatt could see the mud raised by Johnson's horse in the creek-water. The billowing mud followed the creek's course toward the Indian Nations.

"He's not going to give up easily," Bat muttered, maybe wishing he hadn't set out on this ride. "And we didn't bring so much as a handful of jerky with us. No, nor have I got a canteen. I suppose we can drink this creek water . . . but I am not enthusiastic about the prospect." He buttoned up his coat. "It's getting cold on this prairie, by God."

Wyatt didn't reply, and they splashed along the creek bed, breaking up the reflection of the moon in the water, for several twisting miles more. It got colder yet; the outbreath from Wyatt's horse was silver in the moonlight, rising in twin plumes from her nostrils. His legs began to ache from holding himself in the saddle, as the horse rollicked along, and he realized he hadn't ridden much for months, and his muscles were out of shape.

"He's changed direction," Wyatt said, at length, pointing at the tracks leading up the clay bank. He rested his horse a moment; the mare ducked her head to drink from the creek. "Trying to throw us off—or else he's got somewhere in mind to go . . . Well, let's see where that is." He started up the bank to the open prairie.

Bat sighed, but trailed his mount after Wyatt, up onto the grassy flatland. They dared not ride at more than a fast trot through the buffalo grass. There was no clear road, not even a trail, and neither wanted their horse to stumble into a prairie dog hole, maybe break a leg.

Another hour passed in the saddle, with Wyatt pausing now and then to squint at Johnson's tracks. "Looks like he's slowed down quite a bit. Doesn't seem to think anyone's following him."

"Could be someone's following us," Bat said. "You hear it?"

Both of them heard the other riders before they saw them, at last: six, maybe eight riders visible as dark shapes against the starry horizon.

"You think that's a posse—after Johnson?" Bat asked, clearly hoping it was, as he blew on his cold knuckles. He'd never much cared for long rides—for one thing, they were tough on the seat of your new pants. And he nearly always had new pants. "They could take up the chase."

"Could be," Wyatt said, spurring his horse to greater speed.

Another four miles, a little more, and they came to a low rise in the otherwise flat prairie. Atop the rise was a sagging, probably deserted sod house.

But it wasn't quite deserted—a movement around the side caught Wyatt's eye: A horse, tied up and restless.

"That looks like Johnson's pony," Bat murmured, as they urged their mounts up the low hill.

They got within twenty steps of the sod-house—a low, crooked construction of blocks of sod cut from the naked prairie—and saw the posse dismounting on the farther side just thirty yards away. Marshal Smith was there, and Shanghai Pierce, and George Hoy, and some men Wyatt had seen but didn't know by name, all of them Pierce's crew.

And Pierce was cocking a shotgun as he stalked toward the sod shanty.

"Pierce, hold on!" Wyatt shouted, dismounting and drawing his gun.

Pierce never looked over, but marched straight into the night darkened doorway. There was the flare of a match as someone, probably Johnson, struck it to see who was there.

"Pierce! What the dirty devil are you about!" Johnson shouted. "Put that away, that ain't the—"

He was cut off by the roar of the shotgun. A muzzle flash lit the interior of the sod hut and in that flickering moment Wyatt saw Johnson flung from his feet, into pitch-black shadow.

Heart thudding, Wyatt hurried to the hut, hunched to step through the low doorway in time to see Pierce standing over Johnson's twitching, booted feet on the dirt floor. Gun smoke billowed in the rectangle of moonlight.

"That's done for the murdering son of a bitch," Pierce bellowed.

"He pull a knife on you, did he?" Wyatt asked, wishing for a lantern so he could see if the knife had been drawn.

"He did," Pierce said flatly. "Now back out of my way before this shotgun goes off again. I've got 'er filed to a hair trigger."

Wyatt hesitated, then felt Bat tugging on his elbow. "Come on, Wyatt. He's dead. Dead is dead."

Wyatt turned on his heel, pushed past Bat and went to find Smith. He found him holding the reins of Pierce's horse.

"Earp!" Marshal Smith crowed. "You rode off lickety split but you got here late!" The Pierce outfit laughed at that.

Wyatt holstered his gun. "Johnson doubled back to this place— how'd you know he'd come here, Marshal? You came from a different direction . . ."

Smith spat the dead stub of his cigar into the grass. "We had word he sometimes stayed out here at this dirt-house. Not that it's any business of yours. Now I've got a question for you. What are you doing wearing one of my deputy's badges?"

"Was you who gave it to me," Wyatt said, his heart sinking.

"And it's me taking it away. You're fired, by God. First you sucker punch my jailer, then you pretend you can't hear me when I tell you to come back! Not that I'd have brought you along, in any case. You were fired from the moment you hit Carmody—struck him foully, with no provocation at all."

Wyatt decided that it was pointless to plead that there had been provocation—Carmody threatening him, trying to trip him. It sounded kind of petty, when he thought back on it. And it wouldn't matter a whit what he said. Marshal Smith was determined to fire him.

"Johnson should've had his chance before a judge," Wyatt said.

"And I suppose I should've let him split me open so he could whine for a jury?" Pierce said, mounting up. "Come on boys . . . Let's leave these intrepid ex-lawmen to finish up. Hoy—you lead Johnson's horse back to town, we'll decide what to do with it there."

Pierce cantered back toward Wichita. Glaring silently at Wyatt, Hoy went to fetch the pony and followed.

Smith seemed about to follow, turning his horse—but he turned back, for a moment. "As for Masterson here," Smith began, "Bat, you can stay on as a deputy, if you're minded to—"

"I'm minded to tell you to go to Hell," Bat said, "and urge you to get there quick as you like. I'll leave my badge at the jail-house when I get back."

"See that you do that little thing, the both of you," Smith said, turning his horse to follow Pierce and his men back to Wichita. He galloped to catch up with them. "Hold up, boys!"

But one of Pierce's men had hung back. Wyatt hadn't seen him clearly before.

The man sat straight-backed on his tall gray and black Appaloosa, bathed in moonlight; his pale hair and carefully trimmed mustache and beard turned to silver. He wore buckskin pants, fringed with leather strips, and a yellow duster over a white pearl-buttoned shirt. An ivory-handled revolver slanted low across his waist: a reach-across draw. He presented a mix of finery and raw frontier outfitting. His deep-set eyes were in shadow, though the rest of his face seemed to glow in the pale light.

But Wyatt could feel the man watching him from those twin pools of shadow. Watching from deep inside . . . And Wyatt Earp shivered.

Looking at the stranger's thick blond hair, it struck Wyatt who this man was. "I expect you'd be Johann Burke," Wyatt said.

Burke's only reply was a short nod. His hands were resting on the pommel of his saddle, holding the reins. One index finger tapped the silver-ringed pommel restlessly, as if he were considering whether to go for his gun. Already, he knew Wyatt for an enemy: someone who had been pushing Abel Pierce and pursuing what he should've let go.

And this man fit the description of the man who had hired Dandi LeTrouveau.

Wyatt dropped his hand to the butt of his own Peacemaker. He thought, *If I shoot this man off his horse, without waiting for him to draw, who, besides Bat, is going to be the wiser? And Bat will say that Burke pulled first.*

He was tempted. This man appeared to be of a breed that Wyatt had only encountered once before—a professional gunfighter. And the chances were, this one was faster and more accurate than a deputy who specialized in knocking men on the head with the barrel of his gun. Still, with his hand already on his pistol, Wyatt might well shoot him off that horse . . .

But after a few moments' reverie, Wyatt had to recognize that it just wasn't in him to simply shoot a man down in cold blood. So he waited.

Several more elastic moments passed; the horses shifted, whinnied softly to one another. There was no other sound.

Burke leaned back in his saddle a little, making it creak, as if shifting to reach for his six gun.

Then Bat cleared his throat—very deliberately, Wyatt thought. Burke turned his head fractionally to take in Bat, who had a Winchester cradled in his arms, and then he looked back at Wyatt—seemed to decide he didn't like the odds. Without a word he wheeled his horse and rode away, hurrying to catch up with Pierce and the others.

"Burke talks even less than you do," Bat remarked.

"He fits a certain description. You notice that? The one Bessie gave us."

"By God, you're right . . . It isn't enough, though, by itself . . . I know at least another two men could go by that description."

Wyatt turned back to the soddy, and went in, striking a match on the wooden frame of the doorway; the actual door had long since blown away. Johnson had been nearly cut in half by the shotgun blast, just above the waist. And his knife was firmly in its sheath.

Wyatt rejoined Bat, glad to be away from the smell of blood and death in the sod house. "Knife's in the sheath."

"You surprised? They wanted to be sure he was dead, seems to me."

Wyatt nodded. "And they knew he'd be here. So they had an appointment with him. Probably to pay him off. He was hired to kill Montaigne, so Montaigne'd have no chance to clear himself. Ending the questions about Dandi. That's my guess, anyhow."

Bat took off his bowler and smoothed his hair back thoughtfully. "Johnson was going to leave the territory, with enough gold to make the risk worth it, you figure?"

"Likely. And when we set off after him, they had to change their plans. Shut him up for good before he could talk to us. That's how it might've been. Hard to know for sure." He hooked a thumb toward the hut. "I suppose it's up to us to bury that dice-loading crook."

Bat cocked his head and studied the sod hut. "I figure," he said after a moment, "if we tie a rope to the center-post of that shanty, and get my horse to pull it down, he'll be buried pretty neatly, and in a trice."

Wyatt nodded. He just wanted to get back to the hotel, to Mattie, and sleep. He had a deep weariness on him. He was thinking of Dandi LeTrouveau and Montaigne and Johnson—and of men like Pierce and Burke.

But a while later, when the moon was sinking past the horizon and they were halfway back to Wichita, Wyatt remarked, "There is one place more I might go, to look into this matter. Kansas City."

CHAPTER NINE

"Seems to me this town grew by half since last I was here," Bat said, looking around. Buildings of many stories rose on either side, and the timber skeletons of new ones stood starkly in every vacant lot. Wyatt and Bat were riding in the comfortably padded passenger seat of a hansom from the Kansas City train station to a quarter near the cattle yards, where it was said the dance halls were located. Wyatt watched the lamplighters go from gas-lamp to lamp, lighting up the dusk . . .

"Thirty, forty thousand live here, thereabouts," Wyatt said. Thinking how it'd grown since he'd been here losing money at poker and forgetting Urilla. He regretted ever having to come back. The memories were sour. But it had grown so fast it seemed almost a different town.

He shivered as rising the wind lifted the horse's mane, and carrying a smell that hinted of snow. Wyatt put up the collar of his coat.

"That bridge over the Missouri River's an impressive thing," Bat said. "I remember, before they built that, what a dickens it was getting across. The damned ferrymen would charge a finger and the end of your nose."

"Made their money from settlers, headin' west—whole town's a kind of toll station."

"Cattle's the thing now, gents!" The hansom driver called over his shoulder. He was an Irishman with curled mustachios and plug hat. "The cattleman's association, they have a building grand as a castle. You can smell the cattle near everywhere in town. Smells like money, in Kansas City."

"What say we find a hotel, before we go on this fishing expedition of yours, Wyatt," Bat said. "I have no desire to take that train twice in a day."

"We'll get a place for the night. But I want to go back to Wichita first thing tomorrow." After a moment, he decided it was time to tell Bat of his plans. "I may be leaving Wichita when the cold lets up, at least for a time. There's money to be made in the Black Hills . . ."

"Wyatt—not you too! Let me get you a cold compress!"

Wyatt smiled. "I have not got the gold fever—though I may prospect while I'm there."

"Going to mine for gold in the miners' pockets?"

"Yes. But my plan is not poker, either. That hotel will do, driver . . ."

Bat insisted on putting on a clean shirt and brushing his hat before he'd set out with Wyatt from the Western Sunset hotel to find the dance-halls, and it was quite dark when they were at last on their way. In a dark blue suit, a gray bowler hat, his mustaches freshly waxed, Bat made a fine figure; a gold-headed cane in his left hand paced their way along the wooden sidewalk. Wyatt, in black but for his white shirt—frock coat, vest and broad brimmed hat— was a dour contrast to his companion. Both men had their guns concealed under their coats.

Horses clacked by on the cobbled street, pulling buggies and ice wagons and drays filled with beer barrels—nearby was a brewery, biggest in the west, adding its smell of rancid hops to the stench of cattle from the yards some blocks away.

"There it is—Faranzano's," Wyatt said, pointing across the intersection.

They stopped on the corner and regarded the establishment, a rather grand concoction of wood and brass with much gold-painted scrollwork around the sign:

FARANZANO'S HALL OF DANCE
~ Where Gentlemen meet Ladies ~

"I might mention," Bat said, his voice low and serious, "that I have heard stories of the Italians, in certain businesses—especially in places like New York and Chicago and Kansas City. They have a kind of loose club called *mafie*—it means 'army'. Been around since the Middle Ages. Not so much an army as a secret society. They have a code called *omerta*. Something about dealing with things amongst themselves . . ."

"What of it?"

"I'm just saying that we may find there is no *one* Italian fella to deal with—sometimes it happens that one becomes many. It seems prudent we step as lightly as we can. For all this is a dance hall, I am not speaking of the steps of the quadrille."

Wyatt nodded, and they crossed the street.

* * *

"You dance a nice waltz, Mr. Earp," said the big-boned girl with the luxurious brown hair.

She was a hefty creature so it was fitting that she came out with such a big lie, Wyatt supposed, working hard to keep from stepping on her prodigious feet with his black boots. She was only a couple inches shorter than he was, a broad-shouldered, wide-hipped, long-faced woman with hands that outmatched his own. Her hair was her pride and she kept flouncing it with tosses of her head as they turned in the waltz. She wore a green velvet ball-gown, which strained at the seams; the crinoline bustle, glimpsed when he'd first paid his money, seemed small on her. He had actually tried to ask a more dainty girl to dance, but this one, seeing him coming, had leapt from her seat, flashing her fan like a bird showing its feathers for mating, and intercepted him with such verve he was swept helplessly to the dance floor.

They were laboring through a three-step played by a quartet of dispirited musicians in the corner. The music was by Strauss—or so the lady, Millicent, had informed him—and apart from that he had so far learned from her only that Mr. Faranzano left the general operation of the dance hall to the scowling white-haired Miss Gillespie, at the door, and Mr. Santilli: a big, round-faced man, falling asleep on a chair in a corner. Wyatt figured him for a bouncer.

"Well Wyatt, have you no respect for Johann the Younger?" asked Bat, grinning, as he whirled by with the very girl Wyatt had been hoping to dance with. "You are dancing in something closer to square dance time."

Johann? The name startled Wyatt, for a moment, till he realized that Bat meant Johann Strauss. There was an unnerving abundance of Johanns.

"Suppose a gent wanted to spend extra time with a lady from this hurdy-gurdy," Wyatt whispered. "Who'd he talk to? That Gillespie woman?"

Millicent colored and gulped. "Why . . . yes, I expect so. I don't . . . You see, I'm Catholic."

"How's that figure in, miss?"

"Mr. Faranzano doesn't permit Catholic girls to, ah, see the gentlemen outside of the Dance Hall. He being a good Catholic himself. The others, being damned anyway, are fair game, he says."

Wyatt found himself looking in fascination at her prominent, crooked teeth as she spoke. "Oh . . . I see . . ."

She danced a little closer, whispering urgently, "But, Mr. Earp, that doesn't mean you couldn't see a lady here, outside the dance-hall, was you to make a discreet . . . rendezvous?" She batted her eyelashes. Her breath had a smell to it that made Wyatt think of a pond when the water's drying up.

"Suppose I wanted to . . . to ask for the hand from a girl here. Maybe Mr. Faranzano might deal with me on that one. Was he to be remunerated."

"Oh!" Her face was fairly scarlet now. "He might indeed. He's up those stairs. There's an office. At this hour he'll be going over his accounts or on the telephone."

"On the what?"

"You have not heard of the telephone! They say there are close to three thousand of the instruments now! He talks to certain members of his . . . an organization he belongs to."

Wyatt cast his mind back. *Telephone.* He had read about them but hadn't yet seen one. "Oh yes. Like the telegraph but with a voice. I don't believe we have them in Wichita yet. Faranzano is up that stairs, eh? Now, a friend of mine met a girl from here, once. Her name was Dandi. Miss LeTrouveau. She was from Louisiana, originally. He spoke warmly of her."

"Oh!" Millicent sniffed contemptuously. "She was not . . . Mr. Faranzano brought her here for the other part of the business. She worked here, yes. He took her out of an orphanage, as with so many other unfortunates."

"An orphanage? But was she not a grown woman?"

"She was in her teen years, when she came here. I understand her mother had died a year before, and she took up residency in the orphanage—as a kind of tutor, for the children, and to give her a place to live. She stayed and stayed and then Mr. Faranzano came to the orphanage looking for suitable girls. And he bought several of them, including that snobbish little Dandi person."

"He *bought* them from an orphanage?"

"It's often done, in that end of the business, I believe. She left us . . . she run off. She never would do more than dance. She kept finding excuses and I thought we was well rid of her. But Mr. Faranzano was furious. He doesn't allow . . ." Her voice trailed off as she realized she was saying too much. And the song was coming to an end. "Would you . . ." She lowered her voice to a whisper behind her fan. "Would you like to . . . That is, before, we were discussing . . ."

"I will take up the matter, I believe, with Mr. Faranzano . . ." Wyatt said, bowing to her. He caught Bat's eye and nodded toward the stairs leading to Faranzano's office.

Bat kissed his young lady's hand and gave her his courtliest regrets, then followed Wyatt to the stairs. They heard Miss Gillespie hiss at the bouncer when they went for the stairs, but they were already up them and opening the door for the office before Santilli was quite awake.

Seated at a small desk, Faranzano was a compact, wiry man with his black hair slicked back. He was sitting with his back to them, as they came in, talking into a black, conical instrument wired to a box. Wyatt supposed it to be a telephone. When Faranzano turned to glower at them Wyatt saw a fox face with the blue-black shadow of a beard. Faranzano wore a high-collared white shirt, garters on his upper arms; he had loosened his silken black bowtie. A big diamond ring shone on the pinky finger of his left hand, and diamond studs set off his shirt cuffs. Wyatt spotted the butt of a pistol in the inside pocket of the frock coat hung up on a brass coat-tree. Faranzano could not easily reach the gun from where he sat. Success can make a man careless, Wyatt observed to himself.

Bat closed the door sharply as Wyatt went to the single window overlooking the street and pulled the curtains. On one wall were

three circular tintypes of people who might be Faranzano's relatives, and on the opposite wall was a framed painting of a haloed
saint kneeling in a ray of divine light.

There came a hammering on the door. "Mr. Faranzano?" That
would be Santilli.

Wyatt opened his coat, put his hand on his gun and shook his
head at Faranzano.

"It's all right, for the moment, Santilli!" Faranzano said, his
Italian accent distinct. "But we will talk, after this."

Wyatt and Bat came closer to the desk, both with coats opened
to show the pistols stuck in their waistbands. The telephone's ear-
piece still in his hand, Faranzano looked at the pistols, and then
at their faces. There was no fear on his own face; just a flaring of
anger in his eyes, like a fire that was on the match but not yet on
the kindling.

A tiny voice, like something from a miniature human being, came
unintelligibly from the telephone. Bat pointed at the telephone, put
the same finger to his lips, then dropped the same hand to rest on
the butt of his gun. Faranzano hung the phone's mouthpiece on a
Y-shaped bracket extending from the wooden telephone box.

"You wish to stand there and admire me," Faranzano said, "or
is there something to say?"

"I'm curious to see a man who buys girls from an orphanage,"
Wyatt said. He didn't think he was going to get anywhere with this
man by persuasion or honeyed words.

Faranzano shrugged. "What you want?"

"*Did* he do that, now?" Bat asked, as if bemused. "I heard
that Al Swearingen up in Deadwood does that. But Swearingen's
a scurrilous, foul, son of a bitch. Whereas Mr. Faranzano—why,
I'd like to think you're a man of honor, sir, according to your
own lights. We will respect your honor—if you will honor us with
some information."

Faranzano glanced at Bat's gun. "What information?"

"You had a girl here, Dandi LeTrouveau," Wyatt said. "You got her from an orphanage. I wanted to know where she came from . . . Where the orphanage was, anything you know about her family."

"Who told you that I buy girls? Where you get this story?"

"A man we met on the street," Wyatt said. His poker face supported the lie seamlessly and Faranzano seemed to believe it.

"What man?"

"Never did know his name. Listen to me now . . . What do you do about girls, like Dandi LeTrouveau, who leave here without your permission? You send someone to make an example of them?"

"If I can find them—sometimes. But I could not find that girl. She leaves town too quick. Now: that is all I am going to tell you. But you are going to tell me who you are."

And he reached under his desk, pulling a hidden lever. A bell rang in the hall.

Wyatt shook his head. "You shouldn't have—"

Then the door burst in. Santilli, red-faced and puffing, shoved in past Bat, a small pistol almost hidden in the bouncer's big hand.

Wyatt had drawn his own pistol, when the door banged open— and he pointed it at Faranzano.

"Wait, Santilli," Faranzano said, nodding at Wyatt's pistol. "I just call you to even the odds."

Bat chuckled. "You haven't succeeded."

Faranzano looked gravely at Wyatt and Bat. "You two men, you don't know who I am, or who is on my side, or you would not come in here like this, talking of honor but acting like roughs—like men with no honor. You will put your guns on the desk and then I am going to call someone and we will decide what to do with you. Maybe you live that way."

Wyatt acted as if he hadn't heard. "This girl, Dandi—did she date a man named Pierce?"

Faranzano shrugged.

"Was she pregnant?"

Faranzano turned slowly in his chair. "Santilli, when I tell you, start to shoot . . . This taller one first."

Santilli was still breathing hard. "Sure thing, Mr. Faranzano."

Eyes darting around, Santilli wiped at his sweat-beaded forehead with his free hand.

Keeping one hand on his gun, Bat plucked a kerchief from somewhere, and offered it to Santilli, smiling politely. "Hard to shoot with perspiration in your eyes."

"Oh, thank you . . ." Unthinking, Santilli took the kerchief and dabbed at his head—then did a double-take, glaring at Bat.

"Idiot," Faranzano muttered. As he said it, he opened a desk drawer, put his hand on a derringer.

"Take your hand from that gun," Wyatt said.

Faranzano shook his head. "You kill me and live, a hundred men will hunt you. They catch you, you wish never had you lived. But probably me or Santilli get you first . . ."

"Just answer the questions and it won't come to that. What orphanage?"

Slowly and steadily, locking eyes with Wyatt, Faranzano shook his head. Between clenched teeth, he said, "Put down your gun. Maybe you live."

The room was quiet, for a moment, but for their breathing. Santilli waited for the order to commence shooting.

Wyatt decided he wasn't going to give up his gun. He didn't think he'd come out of it alive if he surrendered to Faranzano. He had gotten himself into a fix and he was going to have to shoot his way out. He thought he would shoot Santilli first, then Faranzano. He tensed himself . . .

That's when Bat began to hum "Camptown Ladies". The other three men looked at Bat, who was tapping his fingers on the butt of the gun. Then he made a sudden move with that hand—Faranzano opened his mouth to shout—

And Bat drew a roll of bills from the flap of the gun holster, and pointed them at Faranzano in place of a gun.

"Two hundred dollars," Bat said, bowing slightly, "for a small piece of information—very small. That much for one little answer—to show we respect you."

Pale, hand trembling on the derringer, Faranzano looked at the money. He pursed his lips. Then he nodded curtly. "Santilli, put your gun away." And Faranzano closed the desk drawer.

* * *

"What makes you think the U.S. Marshal in New Orleans is going to take much notice of you?" Bat asked, as the train started to pull out of the station for points south, the next morning.

Wyatt leaned back in his seat, stretching. "People take notice of a telegram if you give it the official tone. I dropped my father's name in, 'son of justice of the peace Nicholas Earp', said I was a 'law enforcement officer' in Wichita . . ."

Bat chuckled. "You were rehired when I wasn't looking?"

"Stretching the truth a little. I am hoping the U.S. Marshall will trouble to drop by the orphanage, get the facts from them. Tell me where her family is. I can talk to her family, maybe they'll tell me how she knew Pierce—if she was pregnant by him. Then I'll know if I've got any reason to push Pierce again. I don't want to do it, if I don't have to. I keep hearing about how well-regarded and potent the son of a bitch is . . ."

"He's starting a town called 'Pierce' somewhere in Colorado. You'd think Wichita was called Pierce, the way they act." After a few thoughtful moments, Bat added, "Could be Faranzano lied about the orphanage. He didn't like us much."

Wyatt shook his head. "I don't think so. That was the plac

"You trust that man? What that Millicent told you ma... it sound Faranzano had Dandi killed for running off."

"It crossed my mind. But how would Pierce get involved in that? He seems tied in someway. And if Faranzano had her killed, I don't think two hundred dollars would've gotten us out of there."

Bat nodded. "True enough." They were silent as the train began to chug, picking up speed. After a moment, Wyatt said, "I owe you—you got me out of a tight fix, back there."

Bat shrugged. "We were in it together."

"And I owe you two hundred dollars."

Bat shook his head. "You can stake me at cards when I run out of chips, sometime. You know, it might take a while to get word back from the Louisiana . . . You won't be the first priority the Marshal there has, if he bothers at all."

"I expect it's a long shot. Come spring, anyhow, I'm putting Wichita behind me—for a time."

"So you said. The Black Hills. You do realize they've got no law up in Deadwood. A vigilante hanging now and then, is all."

"A man stays sober and alert, he doesn't need the law, most of the time. And they do have something else in Deadwood . . ."

Bat smiled. He knew what Wyatt meant. Gold.

CHAPTER TEN

Winter in Wichita.

This one was colder than most. They didn't go outdoors unless they had to. Wyatt's routine was a trudge from the hotel to the café, then to James's place. With everyone crammed inside, the windows closed against the cold, the saloons smelled, as Bat said, like a cowboy's boot after a long day. Whenever Wyatt slogged back to the hotel, his eyes were burning from the smoke of leaky pot-bellied stoves. Wood and coal were brought in by sleighs towed by unhappy oxen, their legs bloody from crusty snow. After one protracted blizzard pulled a white curtain on the rest of the world, some of the same oxen became stringy steaks. With Wichita cut off by storms, vegetables and juices were hard to come by, canned goods were running low; the town's two physicians were noting cases of scurvy.

Mattie was bored and irritable. She occupied herself with handwork, tatting of various kinds, embroidery; she sewed up rents in Wyatt's shirts and her own dresses. She read old magazine serials. She sometimes supplemented their income with housework around the hotel, the hotel's mistress complaining of rheumatism. But with the grayness of the days, the confinement, nothing seemed to suit Mattie long. Once he found her nodding over a bottle of laudanum—she claimed to have a toothache. He took it away when she'd drunk half it and she never mentioned her toothache again. She was contrite, after that, for a time. But soon she commenced complaining that Wyatt never laughed, that it was a grand occasion if he smiled. Keeping company with her went from being moderately easy, to being a chore. To Wyatt, it seemed as if her conversation was largely prattle. She liked to play rummy, which Wyatt merely tolerated.

She could read, but not as smoothly as Wyatt, and she asked him to read to her. It helped pass the time after he came back from his work—lovemaking took only so much time, and when you had cabin fever it lost some of its appeal. But the books had to be bright and cheerful. She would hear none of Shakespeare's tragedies—which Wyatt found astonishingly loquacious—and she made him give back a book by Mr. Poe, loaned to them by Bat, long before they'd finished it. "It gives me nightmares just to have it in the room!"

The railroad tracks were blocked by drifts of snow, more often than not, and mail was sporadic. The few newspapers that reached Wichita from the great cities back east spoke of economic depression. Theater troupes did not visit in a hard winter and the nights were glum with a quiet broken only by the occasional gunshot. Most of the gunshots came to nothing, but every couple of weeks a body was dragged from a saloon; and one from the livery, where two men, gambling, had argued over how the dice had fallen on the muddy ground in a horse stall.

A Chinese laundry on the edge of town burned down; Wyatt and Bat and a few others tried to save it, working side by side with the Chinamen, dumping buckets of snow on the timbers. But despite the frozen water all about it, and on its roof, it burned to a sodden black lump. The snow, however, kept the fire from spreading.

Most of the cowboys had gone. Abel Pierce and his men had left Wichita in the Autumn. Wyatt had heard it wasn't safe for Pierce, yet, back in Texas, as the cattleman's legal troubles weren't resolved. There were rumors he'd gone to Chicago, taking Johann Burke with him. Even so, when Wyatt played cards, he sat with his back to the wall. When he was planned to go outside he took a look through the window first.

Daily he expected a letter, or a telegram, from New Orleans.

Daily, none came.

He worked for James and he played cards. His brother Virgil came through, between storms, with news of Newton and their father. Winter was hard in Missouri too, and Nicholas talked of moving to California once more. "The Midwest winters will put California in a man's mind," Virgil said.

Wyatt made plans of his own. He tried not to argue with Mattie. A dozen times he came close to sending her away. But he could not turn her out, not in that winter.

March came blustering in, but toward the end of the month an interval of warmth removed much of the snow, and the roads were open. Supplies poured into town, more travelers, a spurt of commerce. Wyatt thought about all that gold in Deadwood . . .

* * *

The road to Deadwood, Dakota Territory, barely deserved the term, Wyatt thought, driving his team up the ravaged track that misty dusk. The harsh Black Hills winter had rubbed a great deal of the trail away. He was regretting driving a freight wagon up into these hills. It was a long ride to a smithy; if he broke an axle he'd have a hell of a time fixing it alone.

The team was game enough, though, stumbling now and then but never shying. He'd bought the sturdy draft horses with money saved from one very fortuitous hand of poker. His own riding horse, tied to the back of the nearly empty wagon, ambled along behind as he urged the team up an ever-steeper trail—a narrow track streaked with mud flow and studded with fallen chunks of granite.

When they came to a particularly steep grade, Wyatt stopped the horses and looked up the rugged hillside. Maybe he shouldn't try it till the morning. But he was hoping to get up to the hilltop and camp on the other side, at the base of the next, higher hill, where it was more out of the weather. The Black Hills forgot all about it being spring, at night.

Looking at the bleak countryside, he wondered if he should have brought Mattie along, after all. She'd have been some company, and comfort on a cold night. But she wouldn't have handled the wilderness very well. And she didn't like the idea of him spending weeks, maybe months up here cutting wood, hauling it to the mining camp. He didn't care to hear her "told you so" if it went wrong. Still, he had good information that the miners would pay a premium for a wagonload of timber for sluices, and smaller cuts for fuel; they'd scoured and clear-cut the hills close around Deadwood. An industrious man, willing to range farther, could make fifty, seventy-five dollars a day cutting wood for placer mining alone.

He'd given Mattie money, and promised to send for her when the stage line to Deadwood started up again. Mattie pouted, making it clear she felt abandoned—but Wyatt had to get away from Wichita for a while. He had no pressing reason to stay; he had received no reply from the U.S. Marshal in New Orleans. He didn't know how else to pursue the case without causing a feud with Marshal Smith.

He wished Bat had come along. Wyatt would've been grateful out here for Bat's talkativeness. His own thoughts seeming to echo from the deep black valleys as he drove the team up higher and higher hills.

It was ghostly quiet. Nothing but the sound of his horses, shifting; his riding mount snorting wistfully over the sewn-up bags of oats in the back of the wagon.

He raised the reins to drive the horses onward, then hesitated, hearing other sounds echoing from the dark hills behind him: a clicking of hooves on rock, maybe, and a wind-thinned whinny.

He turned in his seat and squinted up at the hilltops. Was that a rider, on the top of the ridge to the southeast? It was darkening back there—hard to tell for sure. But he'd thought more than once, over the last two days, that someone was pacing him; watching him.

The rider could easily be a scout for a Sioux war party. The Treaty of Fort Laramie, drawn up in 1868, had protected the Dakota Sioux's sacred Black Hills for a few years. But then Custer's engineer had found gold up here and the government allowed a flood of miners into the territory. Now the Sioux were retaliating.

The Indians could see that the booming mining camp wasn't going away any time soon. Some of the outlying camps had been raided, settlers and miners killed, and it was said that Custer—who had started the whole thing—was taking up a punishment expedition.

Yes, it could be Indians following Wyatt, looking for the best place to cut him down. Could be someone else too, he reckoned. He'd made more than one enemy in the last year.

He decided that getting over the hill would give him a better shot at the rider than camping out here. Get to higher ground, find some cover. But he'd be a damned good target going up this hill, on his way to the camp—with his back to the rider the whole way.

That ridge top was a good ways off, out of easy rifle range. Wyatt could get up the hill in half an hour, if he pushed it, before the rider got close enough for a reliable shot.

He chuckled at himself. He was probably letting his imagination ride herd on him. Still . . .

He shifted on the seat—which he'd cushioned with folded-over blankets—clucked at the draft horses and flicked the reins, starting up the steep trail.

The going was slower than he'd hoped, with the night falling around him; the sky soon went from dark blue to charcoal, to sable. More than once he had to get down and lead the horses on foot past the touchy spots.

Maybe an hour and a half after starting up the slope, he drove the team into a kind of natural cul-de-sac of boulders at the base of a higher hill, just off the trail. He wondered if he were just trapping himself in here. He couldn't fight off a whole war party alone, and he was giving himself no easy line of retreat. But he needed a place out of the wind.

Wyatt's fingers were stiffening with cold as he unyoked the horses, led them to a pool of water between two craggy outcroppings. It was nearly pitch dark by the time he'd fed them, rubbed them down, and staked them out.

He walked carefully back to the wagon, picking his way over the scree. He felt around for the lantern in the back of his wagon. There it was, cold metal and glass under his fingers. He dug wooden matches out of his vest pocket and lit the wick, keeping it mostly shuttered. He swung it around, letting the feeble ray of light fall into a sheltered place between two wedge-shaped rocks, where he might build a small fire. But it'd be safer to do without a fire, stretch out in the bed of the wagon, try to keep warm under a blanket.

As he tried to make up his mind, Wyatt heard the distinct click of a shod horse on stones. He froze, listening. There it was again. Whoever they were, they were coming slowly, cautiously up the trail. The metal-shod hooves probably meant it was not an Indian.

He set the lantern back down and opened its shutters wide, so it beamed out fairly bright. He pulled his Winchester from its scabbard alongside the seat, and moved off into the shadows to wait. The light burned steadily in the wagon, a lure for whoever was trying to get the drop on him.

The wind rose, whistling through the Black Hills, coming sharply out of the rough-edged stony canyons of the Badlands as if it had honed itself there. He was shivering, though he wore a greatcoat, and every so often he had to flex his fingers to get the feeling back into them. His feet were going numb when he finally heard the sound of someone approaching through the maze of boulders.

It sounded like the stranger was coming on foot, leading his horse: there was a clattering of small stones under boots, a man cursing under his breath, and then the uncertain click of a horse unable to see its way along.

Wyatt cocked his Winchester and held his breath.

Another half-minute and Wyatt made out the silhouette of a man's head—a compact man, maybe an Indian after all—against the darker rock beyond him. Starlight picked out long black hair; the blue steel of a pistol shoved in his belt, and the eyes of the horse he led by the reins toward the light in the wagon.

Wyatt nestled the Winchester against his shoulder and took aim. "Not one step more, either way," Wyatt said crisply. "I've got a bead on the side of your head and I can't miss at this range."

The man stopped moving except to raise his head a little, and waited for the next command.

Wyatt lowered the rifle butt to hip level but kept the muzzle pointed at the stranger. "Drop that pistol on the rocks. Then move toward the wagon. I want you in the light."

The man obeyed, leading his horse, which Wyatt could now see was an Indian pony, a paint. And he could see something else: there was another man, someone small, on the horse, slumped over its mane, looking sick—or maybe asleep.

When they reached the pool of light around the wagon, Wyatt could see the lead man's face clearly. He was no stranger. It was Tomas Sanchez, the half breed Wyatt had saved from Hoy.

Awakened by the horse's sudden halting, the rider on Sanchez's horse sat up then, blinking, looking around.

"Where is we, Sanchez?" the rider asked.

"Hellfire," Wyatt said. "Henry McCarty, you damn fool, what the devil are you and Sanchez doing up here?"

* * *

They had a fire built from snags and dead tree limbs that Sanchez had somehow scavenged from a nearly barren hillside, and Wyatt was sitting on a heap of fallen gravel in the sheltered spot, warming himself at the blue and yellow flame.

Henry McCarty, hunkered across from him, was finally coming out with the full story. "Well sir, after you left town, Bessie Earp started saying that the Marshal was a dirty damned fool or a dirty damned liar, holding that Montaigne kilt that girl. She had some thoughts about who it might've been, but she wasn't saying." He broke off for a moment, staring into the fire, his buck teeth and wide eyes catching the light.

Wyatt threw a crooked gray branch into the fire, making sparks spiral upward. "Get on with it, Henry." The boy seemed to be coming at the story from every direction but the start.

"Well now, nobody told me that old Montaigne was arrested for killing that girl. I thought they took him in for bein' a nuisance. And it could be that I thought it best to keep my mouth shut about that night, anyways. I've *seen* that man that rides with Pierce. And he warned me . . ."

"How's Pierce come into it?" Wyatt demanded, startling the boy with the edge in his voice.

"Oh! As to that, now, you remember I was in the next shed over, that night the girl was killed—with Agnes—that colored lady Bessie set to watch over me. I was on my cot, but I couldn't sleep. I didn't tell you quite all I heard that night, Wyatt . . ."

"Is that so?" Wyatt said.

Henry missed the irony ringing in Wyatt's voice. "It is. I do confess it. I hear a commotion that night and I get up to look out what passes for a window and I see him come out of there, and with that Burke on his heels, and Mr. Pierce is saying 'I can't believe it was her' and Burke is saying, 'Hold on a minute, Mr. Pierce' and he says some other things I can't hear. But I hear him say 'let me talk to her' and he goes back in and Abel Pierce is marchin' up and down and then a few minutes later he's gassing something at that Burke about how they got to get out of there and Burke comes out . . . Well before he talks to Pierce, that yellow-haired man sees me pokin' my head out the door of our shanty. Over he comes with his hand on his gun and he leans close to me and says, 'This man here with me is Ace High around here, he's a big man, and if you go mentioning him—or me!—coming around this cat-house, you will shame him and I will kill you for it! I'd do it now was I not in a hurry. But maybe it wouldn't take so long, at that.' Then he grabs my neck and looks me in the eyes and he gives a squeeze on my neck, like to just show me how he might start in killing me. I thought my heart was going to dig out of me like a scared gopher . . . And then he hears Pierce call him and he lets go and walks over to Mr. Pierce . . . and off they go."

"He threatened your life!" Wyatt exclaimed, "And you never told me?"

"You never had him almost nose to nose, Wyatt, with his hand on your neck. All the way around, his fingers go! If I'd told you he'd-a kilt me for it. It fretted me some that I didn't tell you. Especially when you asked me about it later that night. But there was someone *else* told me not to tell you too . . ."

"Who?"

Enjoying Wyatt listening to him so closely, Henry seemed in no hurry to answer. "Well, it all seemed fair bad to me, that gunny and Pierce being there right that night, considering what you found: that pretty little Dandi girl, dead. I tried not to think about it too much but finally I hear talk on what happened to that Montaigne—stabbed to keep his mouth shut—and I had to tell Miss Bessie about what that Burke said to me. Miss Bessie didn't want me to tell you. Told me 'On no account tell Wyatt Earp . . .'"

"Bessie. Why'd she say that?" But he knew.

"I speculate it's because she thinks you and James are going to get into it with Pierce. And she don't want James in no gunfight. But she don't like Marshal Smith—so after you leave town, headin' for Deadwood, she said it was safe to tell someone, maybe the Judge—Well, I see the Judge on the street and I tell him about it. He didn't seem interested, not at all. But while I'm telling him, there was some fellas near, and a cowboy working for Mr. Pierce, that Hoy—he heard me tell it. Right away I hear that Burke is looking for me. So I . . . well . . . I borrowed a horse from Miss Bessie—"

"You stole a horse?"

"She said I could borrow it! I just didn't tell her how far I was goin'. I come across Sanchez here on the edge of town and he says, 'Boy what are you doing riding up alone into the big empty?' and I says I was going to back your play in Deadwood and he says, 'That young fella Wyatt Earp? I'll come along too,' and here we are."

Wyatt grunted. Much to think about in that story. He glanced at Sanchez. "Tomas—you have some *good* reason to come out here?"

"Wanted to get out of town. The cowboys was talking about hanging me. I'm not sure why. Maybe they hear I'm Apache—half Apache, half Mexico-Spanish—and they don't like the Apache. Some fights with them out in Texas, they say. So I got to go somewhere." After a moment he added, "And I owe you something. My father taught me to owe no man, but find a way to pay."

Wyatt shook his head. "You don't owe somebody for doing their job."

"Why have you leave your job, Wyatt?" Sanchez asked.

"I was fired." He shrugged. "I punched Deputy Carmody. And I was looking into things they wanted left alone."

Sanchez smiled and poured some whiskey into a tin cup. "What will you do in Deadwood?"

"I'll cut wood for sale to the miners. Wagonloads. They're short on it all the time—they need it for sluices and timbers for the mines and firewood. And I'll try my luck at some panning."

He had other reasons for going to Deadwood—or more accurately, for simply leaving Wichita for a while. He was afraid he'd make things worse for his brothers, for James and Virgil— who was in Wichita fairly often—if he ran into Marshal Smith and lost his temper with him. And then there was Mattie— Wyatt felt crowded. He needed some time to think. He hoped Bat and Virgil were looking after her, as they promised to do. And he hoped Bessie didn't tempt Mattie back into the trade. She had hinted . . .

He frowned at Henry. "Say, you tell anyone where you're going? Bessie'll be worried."

"I did tell her. I wrote her out a note."

"A note?" So he could read and write. Wyatt had forgotten to ask about the boy's reading. That was good anyhow. "I expect you're hungry?"

"Right enough we are!"

"Well then, Henry McCarty, you'll find some jerky and dried apples in a box under the wagon seat."

Henry fairly leapt to his feet.

"But," Wyatt said, staying Henry with a pointed finger, "before you get any food you fetch us some water from that pool—you got to earn your way in the world, boy. The canteens are in the back of the wagon. Sanchez, you have any supplies?"

"Some oats, that is all. And—" He shrugged apologetically. "Some whiskey."

"You can keep the whiskey," Wyatt said, remembering the shattered bottle on the bar.

"I'll have some!" Henry declared.

"No, you will not," Wyatt said firmly. "You will get us our water, then the food, and you'll forget the whiskey. And bring those extra blankets from the wagon . . ."

Henry hesitated a moment, looking at Wyatt, who watched him, expecting resentment. But all he saw in the boy's eyes was a kind of amazed fondness.

Then Henry set off, picking his way over the rubble.

"Tomas," Wyatt said, "what's an Apache doing so far North?"

Sanchez shrugged. "I am but only half Apache. My mother. My father, he worked up here for the railroad. He come back and die there, in Texas. They treated him like *el perro* there. Up here, he had work and respect. I come to find it." He toyed with the fire with the end of a stick. "Not much respect in Kansas either. I will watch for you, Mr. Earp—and I will see if there is work in Deadwood. Maybe no work—or maybe I'll find gold! There is someone waiting for me in Texas . . ." He broke off, staring into the flames.

Wyatt nodded noncommittally, moving his cold feet a little closer to the fire, pondering. He was past halfway to Deadwood. It wasn't sensible to send Henry back from here. Especially if Pierce and Burke were looking to shut the boy up. And if he'd told Bessie where he was going, she'd have told others. Pierce could find out . . .

But was Johann Burke really looking for Henry? Or was that an adolescent's drama, exaggerating his own importance? If "Joe Hand" *was* after the boy, would he follow him to the Badlands—and Deadwood?

Wyatt thought about the man who'd sat so motionlessly on his horse, out on the prairie. That man, Wyatt guessed, might be dogged enough to pursue anyone any distance if he thought they might be a threat. And if Pierce were paying him, that made it even more likely. A man like that lived for making other men into cowards or corpses.

There was threat of Indians too, out here. "Tomas—you talk to the Sioux much, since you been up this way? I mean—lately?"

"Some. I went hunting, come across some Lakota. I know one of them."

"They going to war on us?"

"Some want war, some don't. There was a treaty, to say the white man can't come here to the sacred Black Hills. Then comes Custer, finding gold—no treaty anymore. So some want to fight."

Wyatt nodded. "The President did try to negotiate with them. Tried to buy the land. They wouldn't sell."

"Belongs to the ancestors. The spirits. Not theirs to sell. They say Deadwood is stealing their land."

"That how you feel about it? The Sioux were cheated?"

"I feel about it . . . that maybe some other tribe had this land, long ago, and the Sioux took it. People push people. Some people are better than others but everybody has to move and push, sometime." He fell silent, drank liquor and stared into the fire, its flames doubled in his eyes. "But I tell you something—I don't like a . . . a *mentiroso*. A man who tells no truth."

"I do agree with you there, Tomas. Governments sometimes lie. There's so many people under them, why, if they tell the truth they're bound to make someone mad. Easier to lie."

Henry returned, and they passed around the jerky. Thinking to stimulate the boy's mentation, Wyatt waxed more eloquent than usual. "Couple-three years ago, 1873, we fell into a hell of a depression in this country. People losing their money, prices going haywire. It was bad. Some of the politicians said that finding gold would save the country. People were desperate . . . And I calculate that's when the Sioux really lost their land. The nation's bad luck got to be the

Sioux's bad luck." He shrugged. Tomas grunted, in a way that told Wyatt he understood.

The two men and the boy sat companionably, chewing jerky, resting, sharing the firelight—a single small breach in the fortress of night. Wyatt felt a kind of unspoken connection with Tomas Sanchez, then; two quiet men with a mutual understanding: the world was hard, no one was to blame for that, and all you could hope for was someone near you to trust. Someone who wasn't a *mentiroso*.

When the boy had curled up under a blanket, and was snoring steadily, Wyatt asked, "Tomas did you follow me here on the road, or did you go up on the ridge anytime, back there?"

Sanchez rubbed his eyes. "The ridge? No, not me. I stay down low, where it's easier. You see someone up there?"

"Thought maybe I did . . ."

It was just as well, Wyatt decided, to watch the horizon, on this trip. To watch the shadows—and watch close.

* * *

As the wagon rattled along through morning mist, wending its way along the trail toward Deadwood—Wyatt and Henry riding up front, Sanchez on his pony to one side—Wyatt found himself wondering if he could in fact trust Tomas Sanchez. He didn't know much about the man. Wyatt had probably saved Sanchez's life, and the half-breed had sworn to return the favor—but some men could change allegiances; some men could be lured by clinking of a few gold coins. And Sanchez was wearing an old Army pistol and cartridge belt. Even a rusty gun would serve if you wanted to shoot a man in the back.

As he had done more than once that morning, Sanchez drew his gun and trotted his horse to the bend up ahead, to see if anyone waited around the turn. He signaled that it was all clear and they went on. The miles crept by, the trail unoccupied except for Wyatt and his companions; a couple of mountain goats with great curled horns, and the shadows of buzzards, flying over. In a few days, the trail would be more lively. With the change in the weather, more miners would swarm into the Black Hills—Wyatt figured he was just ahead of them.

Sanchez holstered his gun and returned to pace his Indian pony alongside the freight wagon. He returned Wyatt's glance, now, as if wondering what was on his mind. And looking into the man's dark eyes, Wyatt felt a kind of loyalty in Sanchez that seemed as fundamental as the stony soil under the wagon wheels. Wyatt had always been a good judge of men—when he was sober. And cold sober now, he made up his mind that Sanchez was a man he could trust on the trail.

About mid-morning, they reached a pass between two stony hills. The occasional scrub oak grew on the hillside, along with small pine trees, larger spruce, ice in their shadowed lees. Between the sparse trees were tumbles of dark, angular volcanic rock. Sometimes they passed an acre of blackened ground, where wildfires had burned in the summer. Some said it was the many patches of ashen ground that gave the Black Hills its name. Others said it was the deep valleys of dark rock.

They'd gone only twenty yards into the pass when Wyatt tugged the reins and pulled the brake lever to stop the wagon. He'd smelled bear-grease and Indian leather—they tanned it differently than white men did. He had first caught those scents on the wagon train to California, as a boy.

Sanchez reined his pony in, backed it up to stand beside the wagon; he was looking the same way Wyatt was—up the trail ahead. He knew they were there too.

"What you two looking fer?" Henry asked nervously, shading his eyes to squint up the road.

"Sioux, maybe," Sanchez said.

They saw them, then—seven warriors, riding toward them, the group of riders dividing to go round a patch of snow frozen hard in shadow of the cliff; they came together again to spread across the trail, on roans and ponies, the beasts as painted as the Indians. Seven Indians that Wyatt could see—others could be posted on the hills. The Sioux wore a combination of scavenged white men's clothing and traditional garb, buckskin on their legs against the chill and tight rows of quills on their chests like a kind of breast-plate. Four of them had guns, as far as Wyatt could make out—he saw a pistol, a Sharps rifle and, held in the arms of an older man in the center, a Springfield. Riding saddleless, the Indian with the Springfield had long braided silver-streaked black hair, a broad, seamed face, and two eagle feathers drooping back from the top of his head. The others carried knives and war lances festooned with feathers. They seemed a poor band of Indians; only some of the braves had guns.

Wyatt and Sanchez both raised their right hands and tried to smile. The Indians drew up their horses, and looked them over. Wyatt felt the older man was sizing him up. He saw the Indian look at his gun, and his Winchester. The Indian was taking his measure, trying to decide, Wyatt suspected, if he were a fighter. A few words were passed between the Indians. The youngest one pointed at Henry, made a comment in his own language, and laughed.

Wyatt cleared his throat. "You speak their lingo, Tomas?"

"A little. I stayed four, five month with a band of Sioux, when I first come to Kansas. These are Dakota people. I don't know . . ."

He began talking in their language, using hand-signs when his vocabulary failed him. The man with the silver streaks in his hair—the senior warrior in this band, if not their chief—replied at length, pointing at Henry.

"Wyatt . . . What're they . . ." Henry began.

Wyatt signaled him to keep quiet. "Well, Tomas?" He'd let his right hand fall to his pistol but kept it there as if he were resting it on the butt of the gun.

"They say," Sanchez murmured, "they are not at war with us, unless we refuse them."

"Refuse them what?"

"The *chico*. Henry."

Henry sat up straight on the wagon's seat. "What!"

"They want him," Sanchez said, simply, shrugging. "And your riding horse. And some food. And any gold you have. And your Winchester. And whiskey. But they especially want the boy. The chief man there, he wants a servant. He had a Chinese girl for a slave but she died. He needs a new slave."

"The devil he does!" Henry burst out.

The Indians laughed at that, probably not understanding the words but realizing Henry'd been told what they intended.

"And if we give them Henry they'll let us go, eh?" Wyatt asked, winking at Sanchez.

"*Sí*, that's what he say," Sanchez said, his expression blank.

"Is it now . . ." Wyatt said, rubbing his chin thoughtfully and glancing sidelong at Henry. "The boy does eat a good deal . . ."

"Wyatt—you're not going to . . ." Henry began. He broke off, and looked close at Wyatt. Then Henry's shoulders slumped with relief. "You're making game of me, damn you."

Watching Wyatt and Henry, the warriors laughed again—which is what Wyatt had been hoping for. Men who will laugh with you might be less apt to kill you.

Wyatt sighed and shook his head. "I expect we'll have to keep you, Henry."

Sanchez spoke to the Indians again, pointing to Henry and shaking his head.

"What'd you say?" Henry asked.

Sanchez shrugged, chuckling at some private joke. "I say that Wyatt is a great warrior and you—you are *wakanisha* . . ."

Henry blinked. "What is that Walkin-Knees-a?"

"Means you is Wyatt's son—and sacred to him."

Henry looked at Wyatt, and then at the ground.

Sanchez made a gesture that was universal to white people and Indians—hold on, don't be hasty, it said. Then he turned to Wyatt, speaking in an undertone. "They are Yanktonai Sioux. It is Humpapa Sioux who fight with white men, not the Yanktonai, he says—but he says they will do what they must, to get what they need. He has decided he need the boy."

"They can't have the boy," Wyatt said, "and they can't have any of my horses. Or my guns. But they can have what supplies I've got, for we're almost to Deadwood. Tell them I'll give them all the coffee I have—all the tribes love coffee, from what I've seen. They can have a five dollar gold piece, all my jerky and oats, and they can have my respect. Don't leave out the respect, if you know how to say it."

"Almost the first thing I learned to say," Sanchez said. He spoke to the Indians, pointing at the wagon. The band conferred amongst themselves. They pointed at the horses, and again at Henry.

Wyatt said, "Ask the chief as respectfully as you can how good he is with that Springfield rifle. Tell him I've heard that men of his tribe are good shots. I'd like to know if he can shoot better than me. Just a friendly contest. We can shoot at pine cones. Make sure he understands I'm not threatening him . . ."

Sanchez smiled thinly, knowing that, in a careful, indirect way, Wyatt was doing just that.

He spoke to the Indians again, and waved a hand at the trees. The Indian with the silver in his hair—Wyatt thought of him as Silverhair—made an elaborate gesture which Wyatt didn't understand, then swung his left leg over the horse's neck, and slid easily off like a man jumping down after sitting on a high fence, the rifle held loosely in one hand. He gestured with the rifle, pointing at a lightning-blasted tree about sixty-five feet away—one side of the tree was burnt black and ashen, the other still green. One pinecone remained on the blackened side, easy to see between two twigs projecting down either side of it.

Wyatt gauged the distance to the pinecone. This would test his shooting, right enough. He was pretty good but not as good a shot as Bat, or a legendary shot like Hickok. Still, Wyatt had let himself in for the contest, now. He nodded his assent at the Indian.

The Indian popped his rifle to his shoulder, aimed at the pinecone; he became motionless as a pillar of stone. There was silence for the space of a breath, and then he fired.

The pinecone flew into pieces, as the sound of the gunshot echoed through the hills. Rifle smoke wreathed around the Indian's head, like laurels. The braves whooped with pleasure, and Silverhair gave a single barking laugh.

Wyatt nodded, smiling. He climbed down off the wagon, and cocked his Winchester, feeling his palms sweaty against the cold metal and wood. He hoped to God he didn't miss.

"Henry," Wyatt said softly, "sit still as ever you can and keep your damn mouth shut."

Wyatt brought the rifle-butt snug into his right shoulder, and aimed at a twig on the same branch.

He quieted his mind, and dropped his gun sights onto the twig. He pretended he wasn't shooting to save his life; he pretended he was shooting with his brothers, for fun, back on the farm in Missouri. He fired, and the twig snapped in half.

"Ah!" said the Indians, appreciatively: a twig being harder to hit than a pinecone. Wyatt looked inquiringly at the weather-beaten chieftain, and could see the Indian hadn't yet made up his mind.

So Wyatt put the rifle in the back of the wagon. He drew his pistol, cocked it, extended his arm, steadied his right hand with his left, aimed at a second twig on that distant branch—and fired in the way that Bat Masterson had taught him to shoot a pistol, out on the prairie: you look at what you're shooting at, not at the sights, and you hope for the best.

The sound of the gunshot racketed off the dark rocks of the hillside . . .

He missed the twig. But the bullet struck the branch, which broke in half, and hung down without breaking off.

The Indians murmured approval, assuming he'd been aiming at the branch.

Wyatt lowered his gun, hoping the Indians couldn't see his hands shaking. He rested the butt of the six gun on his upper leg, pointing at the sky; he put his thumb on the hammer spur, ready to cock it, and he looked Silverhair in the eyes.

Slowly lowering his gaze, Wyatt looked at the Indian's chest. He deliberately and consciously picked out a spot there, to shoot at. Just above the rows of porcupine quills, on the right side. He looked again into Silverhair's eyes—and back at that spot on his chest.

Then Wyatt waited, sitting with his back straight, ready for anything but trying not to seem hostile.

You'll be first, Wyatt was wordlessly saying. And I'm ready to make it so, if I have to. But I'm in no hurry for a fight.

The Indian grunted to himself and spoke to Sanchez.

"He say okay, he take only the coffee and the other things you say. And he ask, can he have that ax, in back there?"

Wyatt nodded. "Sure. I can buy another. I'll throw in a good knife too."

The Sioux spoke again. Sanchez said, "I think maybe he asks for ammunition. I do not know their word for it." He tapped his own cartridge belt inquiringly. The Indian nodded and made a sharp, decisive gesture with his hand. "Yes. And he makes up his mind for these ammunitions, because you make him waste a shot—he does not have many bullets."

Wyatt considered. They might use any ammunition he gave them against his own people. Then again, they seemed disinclined to fight. They weren't a warring bunch. Strictly speaking, what with the fighting that'd been going on in the Black Hills, he should give them no ammunition. But he had Henry to think of. And out here, a man had to be willing to bend some of his principles, just a little, if he was going to get through alive. He made up his mind. "Sure, I'll give him a box of shells, if he promises to use them only for hunting." It was not the first compromise on his standards he'd made in his life. Nor would it be the last.

When the gifts were given and the Sioux had ridden past them single file down the trail, Henry blew a long breath out and turned to Wyatt. "It's tolerable hard to hit something at that distance with a pistol, ain't it?"

"It is," Wyatt admitted.

"Well why didn't you use the rifle for your second shot?" Wyatt considered. "Because—I can fire the pistol more rapidly. There was plenty of Indians to shoot at, if it came to that. I wanted that six gun in my hand. And I figured it'd impress him more if I hit the target with the pistol."

"What if you'd missed?"

"To tell you the truth," Wyatt said, "I did miss. I was aiming at the twig." Sanchez laughed, and Wyatt went on, "But they seemed to think I was aiming at the branch. I reckon you got a guardian angel, Henry. Because the plain truth is, it's a miracle I hit either the twig or the branch with that handgun. I'm just not that good a shot . . ."

* * *

They had come to Whitewood Creek, the stream that ran through Deadwood Gulch, and found a rutted track running alongside it toward the boomtown. Every forty yards or so was a broken-down placer-mining sluices, built of splintery wood angled along the creek with here and there an abandoned rocker-box. Hillocks of earth were grouped randomly along the trail, some of them six feet high, as if giant gophers had been at work: miners had been digging exploratory shafts, in places where they'd found the right kind of quartz—or where some gold-dousing rod had seemed to tug.

The town was still some miles off, Wyatt guessed, thinking back to the crude map he'd bought in Wichita, and the going was slow with the rattling, second-hand wagon; now and then it slowed even more as the team labored through patches of snow.

A lot could happen, Wyatt reflected, between here and Deadwood.

They rounded a bend to see, across the creek to their right, the entrance to one of the deeply etched valleys typical of the Black Hills. Rising beyond the farther end of the valley was another set of darkly eroded hills, and above them, snowcapped in the distance, was Harney's Peak. But Sanchez was squinting south: he'd caught the flash of sunlight off metal on a hilltop, less than a mile back.

"Maybe a gun—or saddle-silver," Sanchez said, pointing. "You see it?"

Wyatt turned in his seat. He saw nothing but hilltops, but he didn't doubt Sanchez.

"Could be miners," he said. "Or more Indians."

"Could be Burke too," Sanchez said. "That looks to me like light on silver, Deputy Earp. I have seen his saddle . . ."

Wyatt nodded, not bothering to remind Sanchez he was no longer "Deputy" Earp. He remembered the silver ring around the base of Burke's saddle-pommel. "We've got some choices to think about . . ."

"We can get to town before he jumps us, maybe," Henry said, squinting so hard toward the man on the hill that Wyatt suspected he needed spectacles.

"Not unless I want to abandon this wagon," Wyatt said. "And I don't. But you two could go ahead on."

Henry snorted. "Then what the dickens is the p'int of coming along to this godfersaken parcel of ground? I come to find you. No sir, I'm staying with the wagon."

Sanchez nodded, looking toward the far horseman. "Could be it is not him too," he muttered.

Wyatt felt sure it was Burke. He didn't know why he was so sure. But he was used to having intuitions that turned out to be right.

"Tell you what we'll do, Tomas . . ."

* * *

Johann Burke was tired of this job. He had ridden long in the cold, expecting to get a Sioux bullet in his back at any moment; he had ridden hard, fording the Belle Fourche River, following deer trails and ridgelines, to get to this spot on the ridge, a place without women, without steak and whiskey—and no sensible man would go to any such place. He didn't care for country outings. He didn't even like to go to a city park. He liked to take a train from town to town, bring his horse along in the freight car. Ride out to the ranches if he had to, shoot whoever he had to shoot, collect his money, and get back on that train. Head to Kansas City or St. Louis, even Chicago for all the holiday he could afford. But working for Pierce was turning out to be a series of damned uncomfortable country outings. He'd even had to ride up to Kansas from Texas. He had sworn long rides off, after serving in the cavalry; after nights in the saddle hunched in the freezing rain, days baking in the sun. They'd done him a favor, reading him out of the cavalry. He had smiled, when the Captain had signed the papers, and thanked him for the dishonorable discharge—and then he'd laid for Captain Horton, one moonless night, and shot him from his horse. It was a matter of principle, even though he was glad to be out of the Army—it wasn't right he should be drummed out just for raping an Indian girl. That Horton was a self-righteous Bible thumper. Would Custer have cared he'd had his way with the squaw? No. And the girl had lived, after all. Probably.

Now he got down off that same horse, which he'd appropriated from the Captain. He squatted and stood, two or three times, to stretch his aching legs, wondering if he had a saddle sore. It felt like it. He'd have to get a plaster for it. He'd make Earp pay for that, in advance.

Pierce had sent him to silence that loud-mouthed Henry McCarty brat; not to go after Earp. But McCarty had joined Earp—whom Burke had hated on sight—and he figured that'd save him work in the long run. As for that half-breed, it was just bad luck for him.

Pierce had only wanted Burke to put a scare into the boy, to keep him quiet. The cattle baron didn't want his dirty laundry aired and the boy had spoken to a judge. Might be he wouldn't stop at a bribed judge. There was a newspaper in Deadwood who might pick up on it, for starters if the boy opened his yawp there . . .

But scaring people wasn't Burke's specialty. And they'd tried scaring Henry McCarty quiet already, at the whorehouse that night. The only way to be sure of McCarty's discretion was to shut him up for good. Burke figured he'd tell Pierce that the boy, old enough to use a gun, had tried to fire on him. Naturally, pressed with gunfire, Burk had to shoot the boy down. The McCarty kid might open up on him, at that.

Got to shoot him. *And that means, Mr. Pierce, you owe me an extra two hundred in gold. Considering this long ride, make it three hundred.*

Anyway, he'd would enjoy ridding the world of that goggle-eyed, bucktoothed little son of a bitch and that gaunt, self-righteous deacon of an itinerant lawman: a mere deputy, a fired deputy at that, who'd stared at him like he was some kind of vermin.

Burke got his spyglass from his saddlebag, and walked stiffly to the edge of the rocks rimming the cliff, then went down on one knee to peer over the edge of a low rectangular boulder. He focused the lens on the trail down below.

They'd pulled off the trail, right enough, though it was early in the day. He could just make out Earp, afoot, leading his team down to the creek. Looked like they were watering the horses, and getting some rest. They'd be long enough, Burke figured, for him to get within pistol shot. Or maybe the rifle was the way to go. He'd get the lay of the land as he went.

One way or another, he'd get them.

* * *

"Just stretch out there, Henry," Wyatt said, "and don't poke your head out no matter what you hear."

"Goddamn it Wyatt—" Henry began. "I don't want to lie around under the wagon while you do all the—"

"Don't swear that way, boy," Wyatt said absently, thumbing rifle cartridges into his Winchester.

Henry rolled his eyes. "I can shoot too, you know. Some."

"Just stay under there. He'll figure you're taking a nap—or you've taken sick. There's a shotgun next to you, loaded, but don't you touch it, Henry, unless he gets past us and comes right on down here. You don't use it unless you can make out the stitching on his boots."

Wyatt hesitated, pretending to check that his rifle was fully loaded, though he knew it was. He was wondering if he were making a mistake in stopping here. Maybe just setting himself up for Burke. The swishing and clucking of the stream offered no reassurance: it would go on, ceaselessly, though they were all shot dead.

"We should get out from this open place, Wyatt, you and me," Sanchez said. He started to look at the ridge, then remembered that Wyatt had told him not to. They were to pretend they didn't know anyone was up there.

Wyatt decided he was already committed. He nodded, and cradled his rifle in his arms, setting out as if he were going into the trees to hunt.

He and Sanchez started across the creek, leaping from rock to rock to reach the farther side in four jumps.

They started up the hillside under the patchy cover of the spruces, angling left, away from the rider, as if unaware of him. They kept going that way about a hundred feet, but once under thicker cover Wyatt gestured to Sanchez and they angled back toward the ridge that shouldered over their temporary camp, trying to flank the gunman.

They climbed the steep slope, wending between outcroppings and trees; some of the spruce and pine-trunks had beards of pocked snow at their roots, where their shadows had kept the spring sunlight off. The going got steeper; rocks rattled down around their boots and more than once Wyatt skidded back a yard and more, banging his knees. They kept on climbing, in silence, angling to keep the thicker copses of trees and brush between them and that hill to the south where Burke might be.

With each step Wyatt was more caught up in the hunt: the scent of the spruce trees seemed piercing; the colors of the lichen, splashed orange and yellow and gray-blue on the hillside's rocks, seemed bright as fireworks; the sky glimpsed between treetops was a more vivid blue than normal and his laboring breath was loud in his own ears.

There was something about going in search of an enemy that sharpened your senses, Wyatt thought. It made a man feel more alive. Until, maybe, all of a sudden he wasn't.

"Wyatt . . ." Sanchez said, as they neared the top of the ridge—just exhaling the name. He pointed to their right, between the trees. There was a boulder-strewn hollow between the southern edge of the ridge and the hill where they'd seen the rider, and Wyatt caught the tail-end of a movement there—might be a man slipping into the shadows of a big, egg-shaped boulder, about three hundred yards off.

"You see him clear?" Wyatt whispered. "I couldn't be sure."

Sanchez nodded. "Saw a man. Not sure who." He drew his pistol, and gestured with it, pointing down the ridge to the South. Wyatt nodded and Sanchez headed that way; Wyatt climbed farther up the slope. They hoped to catch whoever it was between them.

There was always the possibility it was just a curious Indian, or some lost miner. Wyatt had told Sanchez not to fire until he was sure. Hesitation might get him or Sanchez killed—but he'd hate to have to bury some innocent stranger out here in the middle of nowhere. A man would have to pretend it never happened . . . but he'd never forget that it had.

Wyatt continued up the steep hillside, moving hunched-over between an outcropping of granite on his left and a low sandstone boulder on his right, the Winchester heavy in his hands. He tried to quiet his mind down, focus on what he was doing. Don't think, he told himself, just stay alert.

But then again, if you didn't think about . . .

A bullet cracked the stone near his head, sending small chips of rock to score his left cheek.

"Son of a *bitch*," he swore, and dropped flat between the outcropping and the boulder, as the report of the shot echoed from the hollow between the ridge and the hillside.

Burke must be swearing now too, he thought. Missed me by a few inches.

He had a mental picture of what it would've been like if that bullet had struck him in the head. He forced the image from his mind.

But his heart was drumming and his mouth was cottony dry as he began to worm forward, between the rocks, looking for a vantage, a place where he could make a run for better cover.

He figured they hadn't fooled Burke after all; the gunman must've worked out where they were going and laid for them.

I should've abandoned the wagon and run for Deadwood, Wyatt thought, as he got to his knees. Should've headed for town on the stud; the boy could've ridden one of the team . . .

No. They'd still be slower than Johann Burke. He'd have ridden past, somewhere East, and ambushed them . . .

A crack as another bullet struck the boulder so close above Wyatt's back he felt it burn the air.

Wyatt launched himself toward a fallen pine tree, vaulted over its trunk, putting it between him and the shooter—as a bullet spat splinters of wood at his wrist.

He threw himself flat on the other side, starting to feel more angry than scared. Burke was making him feel like a rabbit dodging a hunter.

Wyatt decided he'd had enough of it. He wasn't going to be shot to pieces like a painted target.

He chambered a round, got to his knees and fired in the direction of the drifting gun-smoke in the hollow. The answering shot came almost instantly, hammering the log just a few inches below his right shoulder. Wyatt ducked low, slipped a few feet back down the hill where there was space to go under the log. He slipped through feet first, got up and ran behind a boulder, scrambling toward the place he thought Burke was, chambering another round as he went. Wyatt moved fast, ready to shoot in an instant—and then he fell headlong, flat on his face.

He'd tripped on a root-snag projecting from the hillside, and now he skated on his belly into the hollow, cursing without words, sliding, desperately holding onto the rifle.

He fetched up about halfway down the hollow, scraped up and grimy, in a pile of gravel and a cloud of dust. He felt foolish as he pawed at the dirt that'd gotten in his eyes. Damn, this was embarrassing.

Where was Burke?

"Hey—Kid Constable . . . !" came a mocking, Eastern-inflected voice, from behind him.

Wyatt leaned on his rifle butt, used it for leverage as he got his feet under him in a crouch, turned to look over his shoulder. There was Burke, standing on a shelf of rock about thirty feet above him. Burke had a Sharps rifle held casually in his left hand, its butt resting against his hip. His six-shooter was in his right hand—and it was pointed in a very business-like way down at Wyatt.

Burke grinned and cocked the pistol, centered its aim on Wyatt. "Didn't like you, from the moment I saw you . . ."

Wyatt knew he'd never be able to turn and fire in time—but he had to try.

"Wyatt!" came Sanchez's shout. He was scrambling up into sight, around a boulder about a hundred feet below.

Seeing Sanchez had a clear shot, Burke chose to fire at the halfbreed instead of Wyatt—his pistol discharging at almost the same moment as Sanchez's.

Wyatt turned, aimed the Winchester at Burke, pulled the trigger—and nothing happened. Dirt from his tumble had jammed the rifle. He dropped it and grabbed for his pistol as Burke fired again at Sanchez.

Wyatt snapped a shot off—but Burke was moving, slipping behind a spur of stone. Wyatt's bullet scored a white star on the granite where he'd been a moment before.

Wyatt saw no way to get up the slope directly to Burke—it was too steep here. He'd have to go down, across the slope below, and then up.

He picked up his rifle and jumped, leaping five feet down the hillside, to another pile of fallen rock, skidding from there to an anvil-shaped boulder that was the nearest cover. He threw himself behind it, just as a bullet skipped over its top. The shot rang off the hills. There was no answering fire from Sanchez.

Wyatt got his feet under him, but kept himself low as he turned to look downslope for Sanchez. Couldn't see him.

He put the rifle aside, took a deep breath, trying to work out where Burke was firing from. He decided to try a shot at Burke—get a reaction. He popped up, firing the pistol up toward the drift of Burke's gun smoke. The shot ricocheted from the empty shelf of rock where Burke had been.

Wyatt wasn't sure which way to jump. Go down to Sanchez or up to take on Burke?

Burke had the high ground and the advantage . . .

But Wyatt had to know if he was going to have to worry about Burke. The gunfighter had been wounded—he might be dying, somewhere up there.

Wyatt cocked his six gun and, moving in a crouch, rounded the anvil-shaped rock and struggled up the steep hill, scanning the boulders for sight of Burke. He saw no one; heard nothing but the thudding of his own heart and the crunch of his boots in the loose rock, the clicking of dislodged pebbles rolling down the hill.

He reached the shelf of rock Burke had stood on—there was blood here, and a fair amount of it. Some fallen brass. That was all.

"Burke!" Wyatt shouted. The name echoed back to him. There was no other response.

He could make out a couple of spots of blood—no, three, four, and more—speckling a mountain goat trail that threaded up the hill. Not a heavy blood flow there. If Burke's wound wasn't bad, he could easily lay in wait for Wyatt, somewhere up above. And he'd know Wyatt was coming—the loose rocks underfoot made a great deal of noise. Burke could be circling around to get at Henry too . . . And if Sanchez was wounded, no one was there to help him.

Wyatt shoved his pistol back in his holster, and went back for his rifle, staying under cover when he could. He made his way down, skidding toward the place he thought Sanchez had been. Loose rock tumbled down ahead of him; dust plumed around him to mix with the gun smoke still drifting up from Sanchez's pistol.

He kept his head down, scanning the ridge from time to time, expecting Burke to try to nail him with the rifle, from somewhere above. But no shot came.

* * *

Wyatt found Sanchez leaning back against the hillside, staring at the sky. He was sitting on the half-fallen trunk of a spruce tree projecting from the steep hillside like a cannon aimed at the opposite side of the valley. Sanchez had his gun in his right hand, lying across on his lap, and his left hand was over the center of his chest.

"Sanchez? Hey Tomas!" Wyatt said, coming closer. He reached out and pulled Sanchez's hand away from his chest. Blood from a bullet hole welled out, thick and slow. He checked Sanchez's pulse, knowing what he'd find. The emptiness in the man's eyes told the story.

Wyatt shook his head, his eyes stinging. Must be the dust.

He pulled Sanchez's body from its perch, and dragged it down to a shelf of clay under a ledge. He stretched him out there, crossing the corpse's hands over the pistol laid across his chest. He searched Sanchez's pockets, looking for some hint of relatives he might inform, and found a letter, written in Spanish, from a Maria Sanchez. Her name and the town of Laredo was the only return address.

Stepping back from the improvised bier, Wyatt looked around for Burke. No sight of him. No movement. Could be he was nursing his wound.

Returning to the body, Wyatt took off his hat, and said what funereal words he could remember. "Ashes to ashes, dust to dust . . . the Lord gives and, ah, He takes away . . ." He became aware that his mouth was gummy with dust, it was hard to talk. He spat it out, to the side. "Sorry, Tomas, no disrespect." Then he went on, "Uh, Lord, he was a good man, I will testify to that. Please take him in." He clapped his hat back on, used the butt of his Winchester to start loose rock from the hillside over the ledge, to bury him. It came down heavily, a small avalanche. Now and then check-ing the prospect for Burke, Wyatt carried more dirt and gravel over with his hands, and finished off with the heaviest rocks he could lift, to keep the coyotes off. The job was done pretty quickly. He turned away—then turned back long enough to say, "Wish I could do better for you. I hope your ancestors can find you out here, Tomas."

There was no time to rig up a cross. He had to see if Burke had gotten to Henry.

* * *

When Wyatt got there, walking along the creek, Henry was starting across the stream toward the ridge, the way he'd seen Wyatt and Sanchez go. He had the shotgun in his hands.

"Hey boy, where you going?" Wyatt called.

Henry turned, shaded his eyes, and grinned. "Wyatt!"

Wyatt waved, aching in his scraped-up limbs, and aching inside too. He kept under the trees along the creek as he came to the camp, peering up at the hillside for Burke. Was Burke dead? Or was he stretched out on a flat rock with his rifle, aiming it at Henry right now?

"Hey!" Grinning, Henry was running toward him, close beside the stump of a wind-smashed tree.

Then the boy tripped, fell face down, and the shotgun discharged. A chunk of the tree-stump vanished, shot away by the 12-gauge, and Henry yelped in fear.

Coughing with gun smoke, the boy got to his knees, patting himself to see if he was all there, as Wyatt ran up to him. "Wyatt? Am I shot?"

"Seems you aren't," Wyatt said. "Maybe you deserve to be, running with that damned . . ."

He broke off, thinking about what he'd done, himself, up on the ridge. Exposing himself; falling down a hillside. He'd done no better than this boy. It had been foolishness, running like that after Burke, throwing away all caution. If he'd been patient, controlled his anger, kept his head down, Sanchez would've probably flanked Burke, and got him.

Instead of the other way around. It was his fault, almost as much as Burke's, that Sanchez had died . . .

Wyatt took a long slow breath, as the sheepish boy came to him carrying the shotgun like a new infant.

"Was it Burke, Wyatt? Where's ol' Sanchez?"

"It was Burke," Wyatt said, taking the shotgun. "He's done for Sanchez. I don't think Burke's going to come after us, any more today, or he'd have done it by now. Sanchez winged him."

"Tomas is dead?"

"He is."

Henry looked over at Tomas's empty mount. "Well, shit. He was a good old boy."

"Yes. Yes he was."

Wyatt remembered that his father had told him: *When you make a mistake, own up to it like a man, but don't whip yourself for it. Even if you've hurt someone else by it. Just learn from it, boy.*

It was funny how things that his father had said—things that had seemed too obvious to say—seemed worth remembering, just a little later on.

"Now," Wyatt said, "I'm going to get the team hitched up. You perch over there, keep under cover, watch up that hillside for Burke. But give me that damned shotgun."

Henry handed him the shotgun and ran to do as he was bid. Wyatt took another look at the hillside. He had a strong feeling Burke had gone. But he had another feeling too. That Burke would be back.

He'd come on this trip to forget all about Pierce and Burke and that dead girl in Wichita. But there was no forgetting. Not after this.

CHAPTER ELEVEN

Wyatt and Henry rode the wagon into town just after sunset, the horses' hooves slipping jarringly on frozen ruts. Dirty scallops of snow edged the road through the mining camp. Sluices lay abandoned along the creek, right on the edge of town. Everything was striped by long shadows.

Straggled along Whitewood Creek and forking around a hill, the outskirts of Deadwood was mostly an assemblage of tents. Quick and dirty shelters for merchants and miners, some of the tents glowed eerily from potbellied stoves, stovepipes jutting through the canvas roofs spewing black wood-smoke. The silhouettes of men moved about in the illuminated tents like figures from a magic-lantern show.

"Some of those tents'll catch fire, with the stoves in 'em, if they don't watch sharp," Wyatt remarked. "I've seen it happen."

Wyatt's own sharp watch was for Burke. The gunman had probably come here, the nearest place that might have a doctor. Wyatt saw only miners, bullwhackers and merchants and Chinese laborers, and a few men who might be professional gamblers, and a couple of whores on their way to work.

But it was miners who thronged Deadwood, bearded men turned the color of dirt; street merchants hawked wares to the miners from carts and wagons. The crowd was almost entirely male; the occasional lady, gripping her husband's arm, picked her way over dirty boards between buildings, her lips compressed, eyes fixed on the ground ahead of her. The only women walking alone had the unmistakable brassiness of whores.

Gunshots were fired into the air, just a hundred feet up the road, so that Wyatt had to steady his horses. Gambling halls enforced their own laws, in Deadwood, and they were mostly rules about paying in advance and discharging firearms only out of doors; drunks in the street fired their guns at nothing much, whenever they felt like it, and a couple more felt like it as Wyatt's wagon lurched past the No. 10 Saloon. Tomas's mount, tied back of the wagon beside Wyatt's, whinnied and tried to pull free. Wyatt's horse shied and snorted. Henry climbed in back to calm the horses down.

Eyeing a wild-eyed drunk with matted hair waving a leather bag of gold dust and firing his gun at the rising moon, Wyatt reminded himself, again, that he was no longer a deputy. He must accept that Deadwood was only passingly acquainted with civilization. Indeed, Deadwood was an illegal town altogether, flagrantly in violation of the treaty of 1865.

"Once it warms up some, this here street's going to be stinking mud," Henry observed, returning to Wyatt's side. "Looks to be froze mud and manure now."

"I had warning of that. It's why I brought a pair of rubber boots," Wyatt said. "We'll get you a pair."

As the afterglow faded, lanterns hanging from the porches of the more complete buildings seemed to shine out all the brighter in the smoky air. Light spilled from open-air whiskey bars; the drinking sheds were not much more than lean-to's sheltering disheveled men passing jugs of "lightning".

They passed a group of miners, bearded men in worn, soiled clothes, in heated discussion of their disappointments and prospects. Some of the miners grinned in triumph, others looked stunned by their own bad luck.

Unless the U.S. Army was around, there would probably be no one to report Burke to. Anyway, Henry hadn't seen the shooting: it'd be Wyatt's word against Burke's. And Johann Burke worked for Abel Pierce, an influential man who numbered Congressmen as his friends. There was something else: Burke was a white man. Wyatt doubted he'd get justice for Sanchez.

Wyatt had to stop the wagon to let a buggy jump and shudder by; a small crowd of miners chose that moment to cross the road together, right behind the buggy. One of them slipped on an icy patch and went down, taking two others with him. They chose to laugh it off, but it was several minutes before the freight wagon had enough room to move on.

"More folks here than I thought," Henry observed. "It's a hustling larrup of a place, sure."

Wyatt nodded. "Homestake Mine's here, and it's turning out more gold than any other dig in the country. Word gets around."

"Gentlemen!"

A man standing on the boardwalk along the road had called out to them as their wagon creaked past. The stranger was shaped like a saltshaker, it seemed to Wyatt; he was wearing a butter-colored three-piece suit looped by a gold watch chain. On his head was a salmon-colored derby; his considerable jowls were broadened even more by bushy side whiskers and his ears were red with the chill. His nose, however, was red with whiskey, if Wyatt was any judge.

Thinking the man might be a merchant who'd want to order some wood, Wyatt pulled up and nodded to him.

"Gentlemen, well met," the man said unctuously, approaching the wagon and extending his hand—which Wyatt dutifully shook, not liking the spongy feel of it—"I chanced to hear you make a remark, as you passed—I believe you mentioned a gold mine. Opportunity, as you know, sometimes bounds as quick as an antelope—the slow hunter misses his game! I must away to St. Louis, tomorrow, to look after pressing business, and cannot hope to take any more gold out of my mine—the Lucky Wood-chuck mine, and a bedrock mine it is. But I'm getting ahead of myself. My name is Swinnington, J. Mundale Swinnington, Vice President of Swinnington-and-Swinnington Investments, Limi-ted—and you'd be—?"

"I'd be on my way," Wyatt said, clucking at the team.

The wagon trundled on, the man in the butter-colored suit sticking his hands in his pants pockets and gazing after them with an innocent, wounded air.

"Wyatt," Henry asked, "wasn't that kinda rude?"

"I suppose so. I'm tired and hungry, I buried a friend, I near got me and you both shot, I had to pay a toll to the Sioux to keep your hair from getting raised, and my patience is worn through. But Henry, I am not such a tyro that I do not know a swindler. We had 'em come through Lamar, often enough. I knew them in Illinois too, and Wichita."

This was a pretty long speech and Wyatt said nothing more till after they'd put their horses up in the livery and eaten elk steaks at a café with the odd name, The Inter Ocean Restaurant. Full of meat and potatoes, they sat in the corner by a window, drinking sarsaparilla; the window was made with cheap glass so warped the passersby looked like apparitions, rippling and unreal.

"What you going to do with Sanchez's horse?" Henry asked.

"Sell it and his saddle, and send the money to his . . . I suppose she's his mother, in Laredo."

Henry opened his mouth—probably to say something about finder's keepers—but he looked at Wyatt's face and changed his mind. "Where you reckon we gonna sleep, Wyatt?"

Wyatt looked at the boy, thinking he ought to send him on the first stage out—if there was one running through here—to whatever relatives he still possessed, or to Bat's care in Wichita. But he couldn't quite bring himself to do it. Henry was just so confident he could remain with Wyatt . . .

"'Where we gonna sleep?' If you want lice, we can sleep in what passes for a hotel here. But clean straw in the livery can be had, the fella says, for four bits a man, and with our bedrolls and the horses nearby, it'll be warm."

Henry shrugged. "I slept in worse places." He tried to look out the window, but it wasn't much use. Not only was it warped but now it was becoming steamed with the warmth of the room; miners, smelling sour and sweaty, crowded the other tables, talking or staring into space; there was a smoky iron stove in the farther corner, and a round-faced Chinese lady brought plates, some of Chinese food, some of venison—beef was harder to get here.

"How much?" Wyatt asked their waitress, when he was ready to go.

"Five dollar!"

"Five . . . !" Wyatt burst out. "For elk steaks and potatoes?"

"Five dollars, dammit-sure-yes," she said fiercely, balling her fists at her side, looking as ready to fight as any brawler. "Or maybe fifty you don't a-like five!"

"I'd pay the five, was I you!" someone called. "I have seen her use a meat cleaver to good effect!" The crowd laughed.

Seeing Wyatt's disgusted expression as he dug deep in his pockets for the money, a bearded miner at the next table winked.

"Welcome to Deadwood," he said.

* * *

"I heard a fella say a man was shot in the hills, he come in to the doctor last night," Henry said, walking up to Wyatt as he was picking up his one change of clothing from the Chinese laundry.

"Where the devil you been?" Wyatt said.

"You were sleeping and sleeping and it was an hour past dawn so I got up to look around. I hear 'em talking, when they come out that Inter Ocean place."

"We're not going to that damned restaurant again. Or any other around here." But his mind was on Burke. So Burke had found a doctor here. Was probably still in town. And Wyatt had confirmed there was no law in town. Now and then the miners would get up a deputation and lynch somebody. He didn't expect them to help a stranger—not Burke and not Wyatt Earp.

They stood on the wooden sidewalk, looking up and down the dirty street. Few people were about yet. Morning sun flashed from melting patches of snow; a chill wind gusted scraps of oilpaper, and bits of straw.

"How do we eat, if we don't eat at the cafes here?" Henry asked, with an intense concern.

"We'll cook our own meals, when we can, and do some hunting. I've got the makings of a tent."

"There's a feller down the street, got an open-air shed, he's selling hot oatmeal and molasses out of it. A dollar a head."

"That's a lot for oatmeal but we might avail ourselves of it."

"When do you figure we head up into the hills—?"

"Today. We won't go far."

Henry looked dubious, perhaps thinking of what might be lurking in the hills. "Hell, there's trees for wood right here, Wyatt, over yonder . . ."

"The bigger trees, good for lumber, have been cut down. Wood burning trees around here are on land that's claimed. Claimants don't allow forage on 'em so it's easier to hire wood hauled in. Any more questions?"

"Well let's get it done then, by God."

Wyatt smiled to himself at the boy's manly pretensions. "I'll take you up with me once or twice but I'm going to find somebody to look after you. Maybe I'll send for Mattie, if the stage comes in—it doesn't come often, they say."

Henry scowled down at his shoes, and Wyatt sighed, realizing he was going to have to disappoint this boy even more, some day soon. The boy needed a father, and Wyatt couldn't be that father. He felt neither qualified nor capable. And with Johann Burke around, Wyatt suspected that Henry was going to be increasingly in the line of fire. The boy might catch a bullet, if he trailed after Wyatt.

Still, Wyatt thought he might be able to teach him a few things— for a while. "Right now, Henry, let's get us some of that oatmeal, and some supplies, then I'm for the piney woods and a power of work. If you want to go, you'll soon have your reward: blisters, a complainin' back and a sour disposition."

"Be an improvement over working for Doc Black," Henry allowed, as he led the way to the oatmeal.

Wyatt kept watch for Burke, but didn't much expect to see him. He'd be laid up somewhere in town, convalescing most likely. He considered calling him out, for Sanchez's sake, but it didn't seem right to call out a man lying abed with a gunshot wound. And if it chanced that Wyatt were killed, what would become of Henry? Burke would most likely kill Henry too.

He'd make a fight with Burke, soon enough. He just hoped that he saw Burke first. A gunfighter "Joe Hand" might be, but Burke was quite capable of shooting a man in the back.

* * *

"Mr. Burke, I believe?"

Johann Burke, sitting up in bed, looked up from his newspaper, squinting through the lamplight at the man standing in his door-way—a stout man in a yellow suit.

"I locked that door," Burke remarked. As he spoke he lowered the newspaper over the bedclothes, covering his right hand, which closed over the butt of his pistol lying beside him.

"The lock's been kicked in, at some point, I believe sir," said the stranger. "It opened quite readily. The hotelier is unlikely to repair it, and unlikely to tell you it has been broken."

"I'll break his jaw, that's what'll get broken, if I live to see him. You a messenger from Mr. Pierce?"

"No sir, I am a free agent. I heard the woman who changes your bandages speaking to the hotel's cleaning lady about you. And it happens I'm on the same floor. They say you're looking for the man who shot you."

"The man who shot me is dead. I'm looking for the man who rode beside him. He should be dead too."

"That bespeaks a respect for symmetry, the harmony of the universe."

"It what? What the goddamn hell do you want?" He pulled the gun out from under the newspaper, but didn't bother to aim it.

The stranger took his point anyway. "My name is J. Mundale Swinnington. I manage investments, and do a bit of, you might say, private detective work. That is, I follow people, when asked. That sort of thing. Now our lady of the bandages says you were asking after an 'Earp'?"

"That's his name."

"I have seen him. I had an encounter with a rather rude individual—I remarked on his rudeness and a miner said to me that I had best keep my opinion to myself, for he had seen this man back down Ben Thompson, and some others. This worthy identified the individual as one Wyatt S. Earp."

"Is that right. I expect he's here to prospect?"

"He has business here, at the retail end of things, I understand."

"I'm laid up a day or two, maybe longer. But you keep an eye on that man. I'll tell you when to lead me to him."

"As for remuneration. . ."

"If by that you mean will you get paid, you will. I'll give you fifty dollars now and fifty when the day comes."

"That is agreeable to me, sir. Shall I help you find your money belt?"

* * *

The next morning, Wyatt sold Sanchez's horse and saddle for seventy-two dollars together. He added twenty-eight of his own and sent the total, with a note of explanation and praise for Tomas Sanchez, to the woman in Laredo. The letter went out with that morning's stage. Then he and Henry set off to work in the hills.

Henry complained most of the first day. Wyatt didn't say much to his complaints, except, "Is that so?" Then he'd hand him another tool.

They cut down medium-sized trees, white spruce and pine, mostly with a two-man crosscut saw, Wyatt doing as much pushing as pulling. Then they cut off the limbs with hand saws, stacked the small wood they wanted to keep beside the wagon, cut the fallen logs into sections, splitting them with a chisel to make planks long enough to be lumber for sluices and rockers and mine timbers, and loaded the lot. The weather, in this higher elevation, was still knuckle-stinging cold, and sometimes hail rattled through the tree branches overhead.

Henry had blisters and his back hurt but he lost his sour disposition about the time they came into town to sell their wood. They sold the entire load for a hundred dollars to a man who marked it up to sell to the miners and merchants. Some of it went to the Homestake Mine to help shore up the ceiling timbers, and to support new adits and drifts.

They spent the night in Deadwood, Wyatt feeling glum because he wanted to gamble but didn't feel he could safely leave Henry alone for any length of time. The boy would become bored, and wander about, and Burke might still be about.

There was no telegraph here, not quite yet, but Wyatt considered sending a letter to his brothers and Bat, on some outbound freight wagon. It'd be good to have someone to watch his back. But he wasn't even sure Burke was still in town. Reports varied on that score.

So they took their ease under horse blankets in the none-too-clean straw of the livery stable, Wyatt reading a dog-eared copy of Walter Scott's *Ivanhoe* in the light of the kerosene lamp. The book was a gift from Wyatt's younger brother Morgan, who had read it through three times. Now and then Wyatt read sections aloud to Henry, in the hopes that some of the book's refinement might rub off on the boy. It was embarrassing, however, when the boy asked him the meaning of words that Wyatt wasn't sure of himself. *Churlishness? Meeter?* Even more embarrassing was when Wyatt had to read Rowena's dialogue out loud. He didn't affect a woman's voice, but even so Henry would snigger behind his hand.

". . . Proud damsel," said De Bracy, incensed at finding his gallant style procured him nothing but contempt—"proud damsel, thou shalt be as proudly encountered. Know then, that I have supported my pretensions to your hand in the way that best suited thy character. It is meeter for thy humour to be wooed with bow and bill, than in set terms, and in courtly language."

Wyatt cleared his throat before the next part.

"Courtesy of tongue," said Rowena, *"when it is used to veil churlishness of deed, is but a knight's girdle around the breast of a base clown . . ."*

"Well, Wyatt!" Henry exclaimed. "It's but a damn girdle around a clown's breast, is it?"

"Hellfire! Read it yourself, boy!" Wyatt snapped, throwing the book at him.

Henry caught the book, laughing. "I might too!" But he contented himself with gawping at the illustrations. "Lordy I'd like to get me a crossbow—and a sword like that'n. You could cut old Burke down to size with that . . . You reckon he's looking for us, Wyatt?"

"If he isn't now," Wyatt said, lying back and tilting his hat over his eyes, "he will be."

* * *

"My father . . ." Wyatt paused in speaking to pull the crosscut saw, and take a breath. ". . . he liked to say . . ." He pushed the saw back as Henry pulled. ". . . that a thinking man can hardly bear the kind of toil that raises blisters . . ."

"I reckon I'm a thinking man," Henry said, rasping the words out as he struggled with the saw.

"That's not the whole saying," Wyatt said, as the log fell into two parts. "A thinking man can hardly bear that kind of toil, unless he learns to take pride in the work, and interest himself in it. Keeps the mind busy till he's done."

"Hard to find much interest in it," Henry said, looking at his hands ruefully. "Especially . . ." He looked at the sky between the treetops as a cold rain began to fall from the fast-rolling clouds. "Especially when I got a bad case of shivering the whole day through . . . Wyatt—don't you think I ought to be able to . . . I mean, I can shoot some, but . . . couldn't you give me a lesson or two? Suppose Burke finds us out here and you're away from camp?" With some reluctance, Wyatt nodded. "I've been thinking about that . . ."

So in the mornings, for half an hour before setting to work on the trees, Wyatt gave Henry shooting lessons. They fired the rifle and pistol at snags and pinecones. "Henry," Wyatt said, one morning, "I'm no great shot. One thing I know is, the winner of a gunplay is the one who takes his time. Never mind that flashy trick shooting. Fanning your gun, all that . . . you can't hit a damn thing that way. Mostly, the other fella's going to be nervous, and fire wild. Take your time and aim and keep a cool head and you'll come out all right . . ."

* * *

It was after their fourth trip out that Wyatt decided he'd pop his cork if he had to spend any more time around Henry—not that the boy wasn't good company, especially now that he'd learned to work some, but Henry was as talkative as Bat, and unlike Bat he had a boy's prattle about him.

"Henry," he said somberly, as they drove their wagon into Deadwood, just about dusk, "I believe I'll give you leave to spend an evening alone with Sir Walter Scott. I plan to get me a bath and play some cards."

"I'll come with you and watch fer cheaters, Wyatt!"

"Won't be necessary. You need a wash yourself. You're getting to be ripe. After dinner, you go on and have yourself a hot bath, and a haircut."

"I ain't got the spondulicks!"

"I'll give you some of your pay for cutting wood—and I'll meet you at the livery. Later on."

"Suppose . . ." Henry looked about at the miners, the ladies; the gamblers and saloon keepers bustling the muddy street.

"If you're thinking of Burke," Wyatt said, "I heard from Toothless Mike, when I went for water at the creek: Says he saw him ride out of town."

"Might not've been for good . . ."

"If you see Burke, give him the slip and find me. I'll be in the Number Ten Saloon, that place right over there, turning a card. But first, let's sell this load of wood and have us one of those expensive steaks . . ."

"Now that I can interest myself in . . ."

"Henry—make sure that's all you get interested in." Something else had occurred to Wyatt—he had seen Henry staring at the prostitutes and the town's handful of respectable women. Only natural, at his age. Still, they'd take him but good—and maybe give him a dose in the bargain. "Stay away from those working girls—don't even stop to talk to 'em. Raise your hat and hurry on."

* * *

The "No. 10" Saloon hadn't been built more than a year or so before, but already it had the sepia of antiquity: it had been prematurely aged in pipe smoke, cigar smoke, gun smoke—and wood smoke leaking from the bullet-dented Ben Franklin stove in the corner. It was given a distinct aroma too, from a thousand spills of beer and liquor.

"Supposed to be spring, out there," groused Toothless Mike, a bespectacled miner with a mane of white hair and, in fact, several teeth remaining. "But it's still cold as billy hell. Two cards."

Wyatt dealt out the two cards, and looked at his own hand. Aces and . . . a pair of nines. And a queen of hearts kicker. "Colder up in those hills," he remarked, as he considered the odds.

"Weather'll turn soon, Wyatt," said Charlie Utter tilting his cards a little to see them better in the light of the lamp hanging from the ceiling. "Colorado Charlie" was a long-haired, stocky frontiersman, in beaded buckskin and a weather-beaten broad-brimmed vaquero hat. Despite his frontier stylings he was clean as a whistle; he even kept his nails shining, though the mud got into everything here. He had an air of authority about him too, maybe earned in his many crossings of the Rockies leading prairie schooners to Oregon. Wyatt knew Charlie Utter from when they'd worked the railroads together, Wyatt hunting buffalo and elk for the men laying the track, Utter scouting for the surveyors.

"Damn these cards," Charlie said at last, and folded, mucking his hand into the discards.

The wind hissed over the roof, and rattled the window in its frame. Other than for the wind, the sound of glasses clinking, and murmured conversation, the saloon was unusually quiet. That night the No.10 had no music, its piano player, Thumper Jones, having been shot dead the night before. His noontime funeral had been well-attended, and several women were seen to weep at his graveside.

"Mike," Wyatt said, "I believe I'll raise you eight dollars."

Mike nodded sagely, studying Wyatt's face. Wyatt Earp was already known for his poker face: it was as expressionless, Bat once said, "as a Kiowa frozen solid in a Norther, right in the middle of horse trading."

"I don't believe I'll let you bluff me, Earp," Toothless Mike said, and saw the eight dollar bet.

"The mills are coming in soon, and you'll sell less firewood, Wyatt," Charlie remarked, putting his whiskey glass down and wiping his mustache with a tatted handkerchief. "They don't dig a shaft, or use a sluice—they just run the dirt through the cyanide mills, and pull out the dust."

"I expect I'm about done with this job," Wyatt said. "I just wanted to fatten my poke up some, and have a look at Deadwood."

"What you going to do?" Charlie asked, signaling the Russian girl for another drink. The round-faced, flaxen-haired Russian girl spoke almost no English, but she understood hand-signs for drinks and other hand signs not reproducible in polite company. "Thank you, girl, here's for the drink and four bits for yourself."

"I'll sell my wagon, do a little panning," Wyatt said, "and then I'm for Kansas—and just now I'm going to raise Mike another eight dollars."

A hand descended on Charlie's shoulder with an audible slap. Wyatt thought the rather delicate hand a woman's, till his gaze moved up to the tall man's Prince Albert frock coat, and the two pearl-handled Navy pistols, turned butt forward; he took in the red silken sash, the pale, broad-brimmed hat, silken string tie; the wavy, flowing, brown-blond tresses, parted in the middle; the thick blond mustache, itself long and flowing. The newcomer had a long nose that seemed to droop at the end, but a face that, overall, was handsome as a stage actor's although his lips were a trifle thin. The man standing behind Charlie studied Wyatt with affable, gray-blue eyes—eyes that seemed a little cloudy. Wyatt recognized James Butler Hickok. Most people called him Wild Bill.

Wyatt nodded. "Mr. Hickok, good to see you again."

"I know you from . . . ?" Hickok stepped a little closer and squinted.

"Kansas City," Wyatt said. "Wyatt Earp. Having some luck in Deadwood, Mr. Hickok?"

"Just got here yesterday, looking for Charlie and the gold, not in that order," said Hickok. His voice was mild, unassuming. "Charlie, which one of them big old hills around this burg has the gold in 'er?"

"The coldest, steepest, rockiest, furthest one from here, that'd be my guess," Charlie said, turning to look fondly up at his old friend Hickok.

Hickok laughed.

Mike chuckled and nodded. "You got the right of it, Charlie. Okay, Wyatt, I'll see you and call for a showdown."

"Just a miserable two pair, Mike," Wyatt said, laying out his cards. "Aces and ladies."

"Coon spoor!" Mike hissed, throwing his cards down. Then he laughed. "You do have the best poker face I ever seen."

"Well boys," Hickok asked, "is there a place for me at this table?"

"Pull up a chair, Mr. Hickok," Wyatt said. Hickok was an older man, in his late thirties, and one Wyatt respected. The ex-Marshal had been one of the best shots in Illinois, as a youth; as a young man he had been a wagon master and a stagecoach driver, then a spy and scout for the Union in the Civil War. He'd fought at the Battle of Pea Ridge and later he had shot Dave McCanles and James Woods in Nebraska; he'd scouted for Custer and the Seventh Cavalry and he'd escorted a passel of federal prisoners with his friend Buffalo Bill Cody. He had scouted too, for Charlie Utter's wagon train. He had shot Dave Tutt in a street fight, in Springfield, at seventy-five yards—a considerable distance for a pistol shot to the heart—and he'd let Tutt have his shot first too. He'd shot Jeremiah Lanigan and John Kile after they'd knocked him down in a fight and had pulled their pistols on him—he shot them down from the floor. It felt right to call Hickok 'mister'.

"I wonder, Mr. Earp," Hickok said, smiling wryly, "if you'd mind trading chairs with me. I like to sit with my back to the wall. It's a kind of superstition."

Wyatt would've liked that seat too, considering that Johann Burke might return to town, but he nodded and gave Hickok his seat. Hickok had even more enemies than he did.

A clean-shaven man carrying a Sharps rifle came in from the windy night, cussing under his breath; he removed his shabby hat, shaking a haystack of colorless hair free, flicked fine bits of hail from his shoulders, and hocked into a spittoon with unerring expertise. "Why," said the man, in a strangely high voice, "it's as cold out there as a . . ." This sentence was completed in expletive-rich language that was unprecedented in Wyatt's hearing—and having spent time in brothels, he'd thought he had heard every variation of swearing and cussing. Looking closer, he realized with a shock that this wasn't a man at all but a woman with a plain, mannish face and a man's clothing.

Hickok heaved a sigh, on hearing this harridan's voice and, without turning to her, said, "Hello, Martha Jane."

Martha "Calamity Jane" Cannary slapped her hat against her hip and crossed the room, bringing a rank smell of wet leather and unwashed clothing and sweat. "Jim . . ." she said, her piercing voice gone suddenly soft as she laid her dirty fingers onto his shoulder Hickok tolerated the contact, but only just.

"How's come she calls him Jim?" Mike asked, as Wyatt dealt the pasteboards again.

"It's his *name,* you goddamned . . ." Calamity Jane began, and finished cussing Mike out with an entirely new set of colorful adjectives. "He is James B. Hickok . . . 'Wild Bill' is nothing but the fancy of some hysterical idjit in . . . where was it, Charlie?"

"Sedalia, I think," Charlie muttered, looking at his cards. "Story I heard, Jim chased off a lynch mob, and some woman calls out, 'Good for you, Wild Bill!' Never understood why she picked 'Bill'."

"Sound better'n 'Wild James'," Mike remarked, chuckling.

"Truth is, it was my brother that chased off the lynch mob," Hickok remarked, stroking his mustache smooth. "Bill was a name he was sometimes called and he looked a lot like me—so they called him 'Mild Bill' and me 'Wild Bill', to keep from mixin' us up. My brother is a bit more mild mannered, but he can show steel when he needs to. When he stared down them lynchers, a woman said, 'Ain't he wild!' And someone else said, 'No, that's his brother.' And she said, 'Good for you too, Wild Bill!' So you see, a man's history when other folks tell it is a pitiful confusion."

"I believe," said Calamity Jane, "I have heard four different versions of that story."

"Having one version of a story is but a dull thing," said Hickok, signaling for another drink. Wyatt had noticed that Hickok drank with his left hand only, so that his right was free to go for his gun, regardless of circumstances and company.

Hickok swirled his drink in his glass. "And a pain in the ass that Wild Bill name has been too. Mr. Earp, I hope you never have the misfortune to become famous. They tell lies about you and saddle you with nicknames you don't want."

Wyatt Earp shook his head ruefully. "I'll never be famous. That I'm sure of."

"Surprised to see you here, already, Jim," Charlie Utter said, as he waited for the next hand to be dealt. "I thought you was going to bring an expedition, seeing you put those splendorous adverts in the newspaper . . ."

"So I am," Hickok said, fanning his cards out in his hand. "This here is by way of scouting the town. I'll have an expedition of miners up here in July, or August. I'll guide them, take a cut, and leave them to their own devices—and in this way I raise money for my dear Agnes."

Standing behind Hickok, Calamity Jane's eyes closed, as if in some inner pain, at the mention of Agnes—Hickok's new wife, a former circus performer—and she signaled the bartender for a bottle of whiskey.

As the game wore on, she sat silently at the empty table beside Hickok's, her rifle across her lap, muttering unintelligibly to herself and drinking. At last she fell asleep slumped in her chair, snoring with her mouth open. She snored louder than Wyatt's brother Virgil, and that was loud indeed.

* * *

"Ssss!"

Contemplating a possible straight and the odds against filling it, Wyatt ignored the odd hissing sound coming from behind him.

"Ssssssss—Wyatt!"

"I believe there's someone not much more'n five foot high hissing at you from the front door, there, Mr. Earp," said Hickok squinting at his cards. It was near midnight, and the smoke had thinned out in the saloon, as a number of miners had gone off to bed, but Hickok seemed to be having trouble seeing his cards anyway.

"Ssssssssssss!"

Wyatt growled to himself and turned to see Henry poking his head through the door. "He's probably saving me from making a big mistake," Wyatt allowed. "I'm out."

He threw down his hand, picked up his winnings—only three dollars over what he'd started with—and went to the door.

"Wyatt," Henry said, in a low, urgent voice, "I saw that Joe Hand Burke ride in. He was riding with the fella that tried to sell us a claim. I heard them say they'd been out at the Homestake Mine . . ."

"Pierce has a piece of that mine. He could be out there himself," Wyatt said, thinking aloud. "No use in courting trouble in town. It's late but we'll go out to the wood camp."

"Supposin' he follows us out there?"

"I was sort of hoping he might try . . ."

The door burst inward and Wyatt stepped aside, allowing a drunk to stagger into the saloon. The drunk stood there blinking in the sudden light, scratching at a louse in his thin beard. He was a stunted man, young, with watery brown eyes, one of them slightly crossed; he had a dirty-face, and a long, ragged duster over his overalls and red flannel shirt. There was a belly-gun sticking awkwardly out of his coat pocket.

"There he is by God!" the drunk whispered, staring at Hickok, breath like the steam out of a still.

Swaying, he clawed at the pistol—it caught in his coat, and then tore it free as he staggered toward Hickok, who was distracted by a close, laughing conversation with the barmaid—he was half-turned from the drunk. Charlie and Mike were staring fixedly at their cards.

Wyatt watched for half an instant, amazed that Hickok didn't see the danger. Then he drew his own pistol, and stepped up behind the drunk just as the man raised his .36 revolver to point it at Hickok.

"Hey *you!*" Wyatt said sharply.

The drunk turned to see who was behind him and Wyatt brought the Colt down hard, before the turn was complete. Neatly buffaloed, the man fell like a sack of grain from the back of a wagon, out cold.

"Now who's this you're buffaloing, there, Earp?" Charlie Utter asked, looking over with raised eyebrows.

"Trying to save this foolish drunk's life. He was pointing a gun at Mr. Hickok," Wyatt explained. But in fact he suspected he'd saved Hickok's life.

"What's that you say?" Hickok demanded, getting to his feet. He walked carefully—very carefully—over to the man on the floor and hunkered down to squint at his face. "It's that son of a bitch Jack McCall. I took his gold dust with three deuces, yesterday. He got himself drunk and decided I cheated him." He stood up and nodded to Wyatt. "You did well to stop him—I'd have killed him, for certain."

Wyatt looked at McCall speculatively. There was something about the man's face—even in unconsciousness, so fixed was the cast of his features—that suggested he wasn't quite sane. His mouth seemed pulled into a permanent, crooked snarl. "Might be best to post this McCall out of town, when he comes to," Wyatt suggested. "Give him an escort a ways down the road. He wasn't coming at you straight on—he's a back-shooter. I'm heading out anyhow—I could take care of the matter myself, Mr. Hickok."

Hickok snorted. "Don't you bother with it, Mr. Earp. When he sobers up, the goose-egg you've given him will give him pause enough. I will not show concern over so low a man. He is the worst kind of street rat. Too cowardly to be a real danger to anyone."

Wyatt shrugged. "Whatever you say. Good night to you, Mr. Hickok. I'm for the hills."

Hickok gave a slight, courtly bow, touching his hat, to acknowledge that Wyatt had done him a good turn, and went back to his game. He didn't even bother to take McCall's gun . . .

* * *

It was a sunny afternoon, the weather finally allowing it really was springtime, when Wyatt and Henry returned to Deadwood with another load of wood. This time they sold their load to three separate merchants, and for a much lower price. There was a good deal of competition in the lumber business now that the weather was improving.

"You want to carry your share of the money?" Wyatt asked, as they stood outside the livery.

"Sure! I—" Henry broke off and his face went pale, as he stared at something behind Wyatt.

Wyatt let his hand drop to the butt of his six gun.

"That's it, Earp," said Johann Burke, behind Wyatt. "Pull it. Or don't. There's no law here, and I don't give a damn."

Wyatt could tell from the direction of Burke's voice that he was on his horse. He heard the animal snorting: a sound coming from pretty close by. He heard another sound, then: a chillingly familiar sound that made the hair stiffen on the back of his neck. A pistol cocking.

There were miners and working girls, blinking in the sunshine, gawking from the wooden walks along the buildings, no more than fifty feet away. A yellow-haired woman watched, eyes shaded by her hand. No one moved or spoke or made to interfere. They had the look of people taking in an exciting theatrical event.

"This is funny," Burke said. "Twice now I caught you from behind. You're not terribly alert, are you boy."

"What you mean is, that's twice you came at me like a coward, Burke," Wyatt said. "What do you say to facing me?"

"It's like hunting wild pig," Burke said. "I don't care which way it's facing—this way'll do."

Wyatt wondered if he might push Henry clear, at least . . .

"You on the horse!" came another voice, coming from the boardwalk. "I dislike to see a man shot in the back."

Wyatt glanced to his right. Wild Bill was pointing his pistol, with studied casualness, at the man behind Wyatt.

Another voice, only as melodious as a crow's but a blessed sound all the same, came from Wyatt's left. "You'd best give the notion up, mister."

Wyatt looked, and confirmed it was Calamity Jane, aiming her Sharps at Burke. Wyatt hadn't really made her acquaintance. You couldn't count sitting next to someone while they snored off a drunk. But here she was, backing Hickok's play.

Knowing Burke was stymied, for the moment, Wyatt turned very slowly, to look up at the gunfighter.

Pointed at Wyatt's breast now, the gunfighter's pistol wavered as he looked at Calamity Jane, then at Hickok.

"Hickok, do y'say?" Burke asked, his hoarse voice dripping acid. "That'd be Marshal Hickok, of Abilene?"

"I held that position, yes indeed," said Hickok. "That voice of yours—" he added musingly. "—I have a notion I might've posted you out of Abilene."

"If you'd tried to run me out of anywhere," Burke said. "You wouldn't be here talking."

Hickok stiffened with the cold fury that had foreshadowed a number of deaths. "Why you dirty damned boasting—"

"Burke!" Wyatt interrupted.

He had noticed that Hickok was squinting at Burke; that he had mentioned recognizing Burke's voice, not his face. The rumor that the ex-Marshal was losing his eyesight could be true, and Wyatt wanted this stand-off ended before Burke struck on Hickok's vulnerability and—perhaps underestimating Calamity Jane as a back-up—took a shot at Hickok. It'd be tempting for Burke to enhance his reputation by being the man who'd brought down Wild Bill.

Burke had turned his glare to Wyatt, who continued, "There's three guns, and any one of them could do for you, Johann Burke. This isn't the time."

"That's Joe Hand Burke?" said Calamity Jane, mostly to herself. "I heard about him, some, and it wasn't nothing good."

Burke looked at the three guns; Wyatt's was still holstered, but Hickok and Jane Cannary were ready to open fire.

Burke grunted, and holstered his six-shooter, shaking his head in a sneering mock of awe. "You're a man struck by luck, Earp. I'm a bit slower than usual, seeing as I had a bullet dug out of me not long ago. So I won't push it. But I'll tell you what, boy, everyone's lucky streak ends, come the midnight hour. Everyone."

Burke's gaze shifted to Henry. He gave him a look that made Wyatt think of a buzzard looking at a sickly calf. Henry shrank back a step.

"Burke, if you want to make a fight with this man," said Hickok, "you will not do it in Deadwood. There's us three, and Colorado Charlie'll come if I give a yell. You will ride out, you damned braggart, and you will not return a-tall whilst I am here."

Burke took one last look around. Then he gathered up his reins, backed his horse a few steps, and turned to ride away down the street, moving his mount only a little faster than a walk to show a contemptuous unconcern.

Calamity Jane gave out a long jeering whoop, and spat in the gutter. "That's right, ride off you yellow-feather offspring of a pig and a whore . . ." And off she went with it.

Wyatt noticed Swinnington, the confidence man in the butter-colored suit, scowling to himself on the sidewalk back of where Burke had sat his horse.

Seeing Wyatt looking at him, Swinnington made as if he were suddenly interested in the weather. He gazed earnestly at the sky, nodded to himself, then turned and hurried away.

And Wyatt suspected, then, judging from Swinnington's manner, that the swindler had heard that Burke was looking for Earp and Henry McCarty—had kept watch and, confirming Wyatt's whereabouts, had sought Burke out and sold the information.

Hickok holstered his pistol, gunbutt-outward, his hand performing the action in a single smooth, flowing motion. Wyatt and Henry went to shake that hand.

"I owe you a debt, Mr. Hickok," Wyatt said. Wyatt remembered Jane, and turned to her, touching his hat. "And I thank you too—Miss Cannary."

Calamity Jane shrugged and scowled, but seemed pleased. Then she turned and stalked into a saloon.

"Me, I sure owe ya both too," Henry said, shaking Hickok's hand rather longer than he needed to.

Hickok squinted down at the boy and grinned. "No sir, you both watched my back fer me last night and I won't forget it."

Henry beamed at that.

"But you'll have to keep a watch by your lonesome, after this," Wild Bill went on. "I'm leavin' town, to see my wife. I am thinking to return to Deadwood later this summer, perhaps in July. Could be I'll see you boys then."

But Wyatt was never to see Wild Bill again . . .

* * *

Though his back ached from bending over, his face was getting sunburnt from reflected sunlight, and he sometimes slipped into the creek, Wyatt never tired of prospecting. He was half hypnotized by the glimmer of sun on the water, and the occasional flecks of gold.

Just now he was panning, using a big tin pan brimming with water to separate gold flakes out from the sand in the creek, but for all his effort he had accumulated a little less than a gram of the precious stuff. He had been assured by Toothless Mike Spears, who'd passed by with his mule not ten minutes earlier, that panning a gram of gold in half a day wasn't so bad at all—more was heard of too. Sometimes.

But it wasn't the gold dust Wyatt liked. Mostly he liked being out here under the spruce trees; he liked the sound of the creek and the living smell of the water, and the craftiness of the crawfish slipping under the rocks and how the color of a small trout seemed to be almost the same shade as the firs. And he liked the freedom of panning, feeling like he was finding treasure, a glittering bounty hidden away in the Earth just for him . . .

He and the boy Henry had been working at it since dawn on a waterway branching to the East of the "hotter" area frequented by the other miners—Henry, however, had given up an hour before and was now dozing, an arm thrown over his eyes, in a newly green meadow just up the hill. Wyatt figured if he found enough promising color some place where there wasn't a claim, he'd build a sluice, do his own placer mining . . . But he'd have to send for Mattie—or cut her loose. In his saddlebags was a letter from her overflowing with melancholy. She declared herself unwilling to come to Deadwood, "a place known for its women of low virtue" and she couldn't bear waiting for him alone in Wichita. Women of low virtue! She was doing her best to forget . . .

"Wyatt S. Earp?"

Wyatt straightened up like a bent sapling released, all in a snap, wishing he'd kept his gun on his hip. About thirty feet away a man sat on his horse with the sun behind him, its glare making it hard to see his face. Wyatt silently cursed Henry for not keeping a watch like he was supposed to. The man who'd spoken his name was a shorter man than Burke, anyway.

"You *are* Wyatt S. Earp?"

Wyatt's full name was actually Wyatt Berry Stapp Earp—his namesake was a commander his father had served under in the Mexican war, a Wyatt Berry Stapp. But Wyatt *B.S.* Earp not having the right ring, he usually went by Wyatt S. Earp.

"That's right."

"Sorry, didn't mean to ride up on you like that," the man said. He slipped off his horse and approached, leading the horse, his hands in plain site to show he wasn't toting a pistol. A modestly sized fellow in a dark suit and a pencil thin mustache, he was not much older than Wyatt. "My name is Isaac Gray. I work for Wells Fargo. I've had a dickens of a time finding you. If not for Mike Spears I'd have given up and gone back to Deadwood."

"Finding me for what purpose, Mr. Gray?" Wyatt asked.

"Well sir, our shotgun messenger's been killed. I have heard that you're the brother of Virgil Earp, who's done some work for us, and I esteem Virgil highly. I'd like to offer you a job."

"As you can see, I'm prospecting."

"I can offer you the certainty of a hundred dollars above the going rate for the job, as opposed to the uncertainty of panning for gold. It's the Cheyenne and Black Hills express, do you see, with a Wells Fargo shipment of two-hundred-thousand in gold. There's a gang of owlhoots we're worried about . . . I know it's risky but I'm in terrible need of a good man."

Wyatt put a hand to his back and stretched, grimacing. He was half inclined tell Gray to just ride away. But this was a chance to make another mark—someday he might run for Town Marshal, in Deadwood, or Wichita. Protecting a gold shipment put you in the good books of the local merchants. And it'd make Mattie happy— from Cheyenne, if he was remembering the route accurately, he could continue with the stagecoach to Wichita.

At length he nodded, and stepped up onto the bank of the stream. "I expect there'll still be gold, somewheres, later on, when I'm ready to look for it."

Wyatt offered Isaac Gray his hand. Gray had a firm handshake, and, in a way, Wyatt was shaking hands with Wells Fargo too.

CHAPTER TWELVE

Jerome Mundale Swinnington was relieved to see the spring water trickling down the rough granite base of the cliff. He didn't have to urge his mule toward it, the thirsty animal sped up to a quick trot, eager for the pool of clear, cool water fed by the spring.

It was a hot day, though scarcely past midmorning. When the weather turned in the Dakotas, Swinnington reflected, it turned like a marching soldier doing a left-face.

Swinnington dismounted, rubbing his rump and grimacing with pain. He was not a seasoned rider. He knelt at the small pool, and drank deep, so thirsty from three hours ride in the twisty trail through the Black Hills that he didn't mind ducking his own muzzle beside the mules.

Finally he sat up, cupping water in his hand, taking off his hat so he could splash his forehead. He was so taken with the water he didn't notice the two men walking openly up to him.

However, the first remark they made got his attention. "I think we should kill the son of a bitch, Dunc," said the man stepping up to the spring on Swinnington's left. "That suit alone deserves it, seems to me."

"Fair enough, just don't shoot holes in that vest—I hanker for that vest," said the other man, standing not more than six feet away, on Swinnington's right, pistol in his hand. "And that watch—don't hit the watch neither. I'd surely like to learn how to read a watch."

Though Swinnington had just drunk deep, his mouth was once more bone dry. He managed to croak out, "Gentlemen—wait! I come with an offer!"

"Anything you want to offer we can take anyhow!" said the shorter of the two men—almost midget-short but with an air of command as, gun never wavering, he sidled over to stand near his partner. He had a black mustache that seemed to grow out of his nose hairs, a week's growth of beard, his hair stringy and greasy; eyes so small and sunken they were hard to see. It was difficult to tell too, what color his clothes were, for all the dust and dried mud. This would be Dunc Blackburn, the man Swinnington had come here to find. Blackburn and the taller man, grinning under a brushy mustache and a floppy brown hat, looked to have spent some time camping out in the wilderness.

"Right you are, gentlemen, you can rob me if you choose," Swinnington admitted, in his most conciliatory tone. "But I've got little enough for you to take. I left my money in Deadwood—as only seemed prudent—and I've come here to—"

"You left your money—because you figured we was going to *steal it?*" Blackburn demanded, in a tone of outrage. "Why, that's an insult, you just *assumin'* I'd rob you! Made up your mind I was dishonest, right from the get-go!"

"Well I, ah . . ." Swinnington was rarely honest himself—but now he was honestly confused.

Then Blackburn let out a peal of laughter, his tongue sticking out as he laughed, and his companion laughed with him.

"You sure twisted him up with that one, Dunc!"

Swinnington got to his feet, chuckling companionably in his relief. "Most amusing. Boys, I'm here with some intelligence of interest. It was known that you were holed up this way, and might not know about the shipment—they've been varying the shipping just to confuse any stage robbers, and it seems a dirty trick to me. But tomorrow it goes out—two-hundred-thousand in gold, shipped by Wells Fargo on the Cheyenne and Black Hills express line, leaving Deadwood at seven, headed for Cheyenne itself."

Blackburn scratched his thorny chin with the sights of his pistol. "You don't say. *How* much gold?"

"Two-hundred-thousand. It's the spring clean-up, all at once. Now you'd think they'd have a cavalry escort, or some such. No gentlemen, nothing of the kind."

"We done for the last shotgun messenger," Dunc said musingly. "All to get nothing much. They must have a new guard ridin' along."

"Yes, but he's a stripling, practically an infant, name of Wyatt Syrup, something like that. He will give you no trouble."

"And why," Dunc Blackburn asked, tilting his head to gaze shrewdly at Swinnington, "are you bringing us this here *intelligence?*"

"Well sir, I've been paid to offer you this little tip. There's a certain party who would like to see that shotgun messenger dead—him and his young companion both. This party, himself having been wounded, and being somewhat outgunned in Deadwood, and having business some ways to the West, why, he cannot take care of the matter himself. So knowing you boys were out here . . ."

"And how'd he know we were camping nigh to *this here spring?*" the taller man asked, the question cracking like a whip.

"Mr. Burke works on the, ah, fringes of your profession—he knows some of your associates, it seems."

Burke wouldn't like his name brought into this, but Swinnington was afraid these men would kill him for his watch and mule alone—or for sport. Burke's name might convince them that they'd be making an enemy if they killed him.

"Burke . . . *Yo*-han Burke?" Blackburn muttered. "Why didn't he come hisself?"

"I told you, my friend, he had business elsewhere. He'll be back. I believe he expects—that is, *we* expect—a cut of anything you obtain." Swinnington suspected that there were other reasons Burke had kept himself in the shadows. If Pierce knew about this little deal Burke would wake to find a rope around his neck—because some of that mining gold in the shipment was Pierce's.

"Well now," Blackburn said thoughtfully. "*Yo*-han Burke . . ." He and his partner exchanged glances—and shrugs. "All right—you can go. But keep quiet."

"Dunc—what if he's lyin' about Burke?" the taller man mused. "What if this is some kind of ambush set up? He could be an agent for the gov'mint . . ."

Swinnington drew himself up to his full height. "Sir, I'm shocked at the suggestion. The government indeed! That is an insult! I hail from Virginia, and I do not approve of the so-called Union. In any event, I am not long out of the Federal Penitentiary myself. Just a year ago, it was, that I departed that kindly institution. A matter of so-called 'land fraud', so they said. A miscarriage of justice, is what it was, in truth."

"I don't care what kind of carriage you rode in," Blackburn said. "Keep your mouth shut. And get the hell out of here. We'll take care of that gold shipment . . ."

Swinnington simply tipped his hat, mounted his mule, and rode back toward Deadwood with all the dignity he could muster.

* * *

Wyatt wasn't terribly concerned when he woke in the stable to find that Henry was missing. The boy was probably at the outhouse.

He dressed, and cleaned himself up at the water trough as much as he could, shivering in the morning chill, then returned to the livery stall—and only then noticed that Henry's bedroll seemed to have been untouched; it was rolled exactly as it had been the night before. He remembered that the boy had sat up with the lamp burning, paging through *Ivanhoe*. Had he slipped out in the night? It had been a mistake, it seemed, to give Henry the money he'd earned . . .

Wyatt looked at his pocket watch. He was due to meet Gray at the stage in forty-five minutes. With a mingling of irritation and anxiety, Wyatt gathered up their effects, and went in search of Henry.

The morning was crisp; it smelled of wood smoke and horses and spruce trees. Only a few miners were about, and a couple of sleepy merchants. But here was Colorado Charlie Utter, coming out of the No. 10.

"Charlie, have you been playing the night through?"

"I have, Wyatt, and I regret losing both the sleep and the cash. But say, I saw that boy of yours, stumbling through the bar, around three in the morning. He was headed toward the Dancing Lady with a gypsy girl who can be counted on to show up about the time the miners are too drunk to stand . . . He was carrying a jug of Old Orchard."

"The devil you say! Why the little . . ."

Charlie laughed, and then waved wearily and set off for his tent. Wyatt went in search of the Dancing Lady. He found Henry in less than ten minutes, on the ground outside the dance hall. The boy was huddled against a rain barrel, alternating between snoring and moaning to himself, and smelling strongly of spirits.

"Come on, Henry, we have a stage to catch! Unless you plan to stay here in Deadwood."

"What?" Henry sat up straight with a start, and then whimpered, clutching his head. "Stay here? No . . . don't . . . wanna stay here . . . by myself . . ."

"Are you sure? You think you're man enough to drink. You ought to be man enough to take care of yourself."

"If that's . . . if it's what you . . . Oh Lord . . . My head . . ."

"It isn't what I want," Wyatt admitted, taking pity on him. "I just hate to find you sleeping in the street like a goddamned bindlestiff. But this isn't a fit place to leave a . . . to leave anyone. Is your money gone?"

Henry fumbled through his pockets. Then he nodded mutely, his mouth buckling.

"I thought it'd be. She just bided her time. Some lessons are expensive. I learned a few hard ones myself." Wyatt patted the boy on the shoulder. "You come with me . . . we'll get us something to eat and get on the stage. I expect some of that oatmeal and molasses is hot, about now. Maybe we'll get us some eggs too . . ."

"Molasses . . . eggs?" Henry clutched his stomach, and bent over. Wyatt stepped hastily back, just barely fast enough to avoid getting vomit on his boots.

* * *

Blinking in the dusty wind, Wyatt held the sawed-off shotgun across his lap with his right hand, his other hand gripping the rail edging the coach's box as they rollicked along between steep hillsides, under a clear blue sky.

Conscious of the long journey ahead of them, John Slaughter drove the stagecoach at a breakneck pace; he was a gangly, long-chinned, rusty-mustached, wolf-eyed man somewhere past thirty-five, his shoulder-length red-brown hair tied back with a leather thong.

The stagecoach, an aging and trail-worn Concord imported from the East, rocked when it hit a rut, shuddered at every stone, and leaned precariously when they took corners. The motion made Wyatt redouble his grip on the small iron rail next to the shotgun messenger's side of the box. Down below, curled up alone on the stagecoach's passenger seats, Henry groaned when they struck the rougher spots.

Slaughter chuckled and ducked his head whenever he heard Henry groaning—and he had to be groaning loudly to be heard over the perpetual creaking of the coach on its decaying bolsters, the rattle of the wheels, the clatter of the horse's hooves. "That'll sure teach that boy not to get a sore head before taking to the road . . ."

Wyatt nodded, admiring the way Slaughter handled the team when they came to a sharp turn. The driver eased around the curves with fine adjustments of the reins and gentle pulls on the brake lever. Wyatt had never driven a stagecoach himself but he thought he could manage it, with a little training, though the team was a big one: the "hitch" consisted of three pairs of horses, of successively smaller sizes.

The nearest horses to the coach were the "wheelers", the biggest and best trained. Guided by the driver's lines, they started the turns; the center pair, the "swings", weighed a bit less but did their share of pulling; the lead pair was usually the smallest horses in the hitch, and they helped lead by watching the road. Wyatt sat behind the "off" horses, on the right; Slaughter drove from behind the "near" horses on the left.

"How do you get all these animals guided around some of these sharp turns?" Wyatt asked, having to shout over the noise of the stagecoach. "I can figure for two horses, but six . . ."

"I'll tell you, when it gets twisty, you got to turn each pair of horses separately—I got reins in hand for each pair, do y'see—otherwise they get themselves tangled up!"

"You don't whip 'em, I see."

"Nah, I need both hands for all these lines! A fella whips 'em, that's just showboating, that is. Ruin a good hitch with whipping. Yet some folks will persist in callin' the driver 'the whip'."

"You figure us close to the Cheyenne River?"

"I do. Then we follow it West toward Wyoming territory, oh, fifty some miles. We'll come to a station, if the Sioux haven't burned it out . . ."

"Good long distance into Wyoming after that, before town, I expect?"

"Helluva long way, sure enough. But I don't spend no time there, not more'n a night—my pa's sheriff too, but we don't get along. They've got strange notions in Wyoming."

"How's that?"

"Well sir, women can run for office 'n' vote local elections in Wyoming territory. Governor's wife must've barred him from the bed till he give in. It ain't natural, allowing a woman to vote. You with me on that?"

"I know what you mean," Wyatt said diplomatically. "But don't you think that's the direction of history, in a kind of way? First the Negroes freed, then the women get the vote."

"Why next you'll be saying the Chinese and the red savages will have the vote!"

Wyatt suspected it would happen some day, but he didn't want to try to explain the idea of historical inevitability over the racket of the coach. He didn't much like long discussions anyway. So he changed the subject, patting the boot under the driver's box where the gold shipment rode: "Are there many in Deadwood who know about the gold we got on board?"

"We tried to keep it quiet. But I reckon it got out. You'd better watch sharp at the fork up ahead. That's where old Hank Degg got himself shot last time . . ."

Wyatt nodded and stowed the shotgun and pulled the Winchester rifle from its scabbard. He wasn't sure why he made the switch. Some instinct for the best play. He had a sense that they were being watched; that the coach was being followed.

He wondered if he'd made a mistake, bringing Henry on this trip. Should have sent him by one of the wagon trains heading to Kansas for supplies. This trip was too dangerous to bring a boy on.

He reflected that they hadn't heard from Henry in awhile. The boy had finally gone to sleep. Maybe when they got to the station, a few miles ahead, he'd be ready to eat. As he looked at the silvery glint of the lowering sun on the slow-running Cheyenne River to their left, Wyatt decided he was ready for food and rest, himself. He was hungry, tired, and he suspected that the driver's box, though thinly padded, had permanently changed the shape of his pelvic bones. Anyhow it felt that way.

It was Slaughter who saw the riders first. "On your right!" he shouted, jerking his head that way.

Wyatt cocked the Winchester and turned to see the riders a few hundred yards off, angling toward the coach from the northwest; riding to cut it off. The studied way that the four riders were pacing the coach suggested outlaws, and not some harmless group of horsemen. Threading their mounts through a stand of spruce, then out into the open, they leaned into a single-file gallop, stalking the stagecoach. Sun glinted off steel as the riders drew their pistols . . .

"That lead man," Slaughter shouted, snapping the reins to urge the tired horses on, "that's Dunc Blackburn, the son of a whore who killed Hank! He ain't bothered with a mask and that's a sign they mean to kill us!"

They were just within pistol shot and then Wyatt heard the .45 rounds crack through the air close behind, the bullets outflying the report of the pistols; holes appeared in the right side of the coach.

"Henry! You okay?" Wyatt called, aiming the Winchester as best he could with the rocking of the coach.

"I'm in one piece, Wyatt!" the boy shouted. "Give me a gun!"

"Just lay low, flatten down—!"

Another fusillade of bullets sang by; two more, scoring splinters from the coach. One of the riders—gun smoke from his pistol streaming behind him—shouted for them to *"Brake 'er, brake 'er and stop, damn you, or die!"* As if to underscore the warning, a bullet sang by Wyatt's head. Another chipped the scrollwork above the passenger window.

Wyatt had never before been under such heavy fire and he felt terribly exposed atop the stagecoach. He had an impulse to jump off and find cover. But he remembered Newton's advice: *Sometimes you say to yourself it's up to the Lord if you live. Got to accept you might not live—or you'll be afraid and your gun-hand won't work for the fear. And that'll kill you right there . . .*

The coach's sidelight shattered from another shot as Wyatt fired back. He fired one, two, three times—his shots showing no effect. The riders drew closer, and closer, angling to cut them off. Bracing in place with his feet, Wyatt aimed and fired again, but it was hard to hit anything, frustrating to try to shoot with the coach making the rifle jump and waver out of true. He had one shot left in the Winchester and it'd be hard to re-load with all this bumping around . . .

"They're going to shoot the leaders!" Slaughter shouted, and it took Wyatt a moment to realize Slaughter meant the lead horses. Blackburn, now almost to the road ahead of the stagecoach, was turning in his saddle, pointing his pistol at the lead horse on the right side.

"They will, will they," Wyatt muttered, aiming the Winchester. No time to reload: He'd noticed that the men, riding single file, were close to one another, their horses almost nose to tail . . .

Wincing, Wyatt sighted on Dunc Blackburn's horse. He fired the last round in his Winchester, the bullet smacking home behind the animal's left shoulder, just missing the outlaw's knee.

Wyatt hated to do it; he'd been raised to cherish horses, but a horse was easier to hit from a stagecoach going full bore—and he had another reason too.

It paid off. Blackburn's horse went down just as he fired his pistol at the stagecoach's leaders—the pistol shot going wild as his horse seemed to dive into the ground. Blackburn leapt free at the last moment but the following horses crashed into the fallen animal, then slammed hard into one another: Wyatt could almost hear the bones breaking.

The stagecoach left the tangle of men and horseflesh in its dust. Slaughter whooped in triumph and the coach rocketed on down the trail.

* * *

Swelling left arm dangling like a dead thing, Dunc Blackburn walked unsteadily over to inspect his horse. It was already dead. One of the other horses was dying, its neck broken. Its rider, an Irishman named Mulrooney, his right leg shattered, sat near the shuddering horse, weeping openly. "Oh my Savior Jesus," he sobbed, "My horse . . . I stole 'er with me own hands three years ago, and a fine *cinealta* horse she was since . . . O the *lach* horse . . ."

Weeping the whole time, Mulrooney picked up the pistol lying beside him. Hand shaking, he shot the animal through the head.

The remaining two horses and their riders were bruised but intact. Hound Farraday, the tall man Swinnington had seen at the Black Hills spring, was picking up his own pistol, returning to his spooked horse—it reared, afraid it was going to be shot too, and he had to grab the reins till he could gentle it down. "Easy, you buckethead, easy . . . Dunc, we could still go after 'em, two of us anyway, might catch 'em up . . ."

"No, you damn fool, the station ain't far off, and there's men and ammunition there. We get any closer we'll have a pack of 'em on us. No . . . We're going to bide our time . . . Maybe have us a talk with Mr. *Yo*-Hann Burke . . ."

"Oh Lordy Lord, my leg . . ." Mulrooney burbled as he tried to straighten the leg out. "Jesus, Mary, Joseph and Patrick too. Sure, I'm gonna need a splint . . . I don't think I can sit a horse, Dunc, you'll have to make a . . . now what do you call those things the Indians drag behind their horses, when they've got a man hurt?"

"I don't think we need to know what to call them, Mulrooney," Blackburn said, checking to see that he still had a bullet into his six-shooter. One, but that was enough. "For I don't think it's going to be needed at all . . . We haven't got time for your broken leg or your whining."

Seeing what Blackburn was about, Mulrooney stared a moment, gathering his courage. Then he spat at him and said, "May the cat eat you, Dunc Blackburn, and may the devil eat the cat."

Blackburn grinned, and shot Mulrooney through the head, just as Mulrooney had shot his horse.

He holstered the pistol, and said, "I need a horse. One of you is going to have to walk. Hound, you and me, we're going to do something about this shotgun messenger who kills a man's perfectly good horse just to save his skinny little neck . . ."

* * *

Henry had a bullet hole in the back of his right shoulder. One of the outlaw's bullets had cut through the leather flap over the window, ricocheting off a brass fitting to wound the boy crouching between the seats.

Shirtless and facedown on the cot in the log-cabin coach-station, Henry tried to show he was game, biting his lip to keep from crying out. But with Slaughter digging in the point of a knife to pop the bullet out, and pouring raw spirits on the wound, Henry went pale, sobbed aloud once—and lost consciousness.

"Now if only he'd had the good sense to do that before I started digging out the durn bullet," Slaughter muttered, reaching for the bandages.

Wyatt sighed and shook his head as he went to find a place to bunk.

It was late the next morning before Henry was awake and strong enough to take in some broth and climb aboard the coach. They were set to take passengers out again, including an elderly missionary woman in a bonnet who'd learned some nursing during the Civil War, and she volunteered to look after Henry on the trip to Cheyenne.

Helping Henry up into the coach, Wyatt said, "Henry, we have to think about your future, and think serious."

Wyatt was worried that Henry would catch another bullet in his company. The next one would likely be fatal. Burke might well return to Kansas—and even without Burke, Wyatt seemed to be a magnet for gunfire, lately.

Henry took his seat and, grimacing with pain, leaned to look out the open stagecoach door at Wyatt. "I figure to heal up and practice my gunning and become a deputy . . . And watch your back for you."

"You're getting ahead of yourself. You need to grow up first."

Looking out from the shadows of the coach, Henry looked like a trapped animal.

"I know: I'm 'between hay and grass'."

Something about Henry, right then, gave Wyatt a shiver. Anger seemed to pull shutters in Henry's eyes, as the boy went on, "If the one side won't have me, maybe the other will. Until you shot the horse out from under that Blackburn, I thought those ol' boys were doing it up pretty slick out there . . ."

And he reached out and shut the coach's door in Wyatt's face.

CHAPTER THIRTEEN

"My horse and saddlebags get here, okay?" Wyatt asked, as he and Bat strolled through the long shadows of early evening. Wyatt was less than twenty minutes back in town, still carrying his handbags; Bat had met the stagecoach, pretending to chide them for being late—as if he hadn't noticed the bullet holes.

"The freighters dropped the horse and the bags off at the livery this morning, in good shape. Your pockets full of nuggets now?"

"I made some pretty good money, and didn't throw much of it away on cards," Wyatt allowed. "Another one-hundred-seventy-five for riding shotgun."

"Good pay for one trip."

"A riskier trip than most. But I will need work in town. I was thinking of going out to California, after I save up. Mattie might like that. My father gave up on California too easy. Lost his temper with the whole territory."

"Wyatt, there's work for you right here in Wichita . . ."

"What sort of work?" Wyatt asked, wondering if Mattie would still be in the hotel at this hour. He took out his watch—and stared at it in raw surprise. There was a crimped bullet lodged in the shattered face, right where the hands came together.

Bat gaped at the watch, and whistled. "Will you look at that!"

"I never even felt it!" Wyatt shook his head, adding ruefully, "I'll need a new watch." He looked at his vest, found the hole—right over his liver. The watch had been in a vest pocket. "And a new waistcoat. There's the hole . . . Never noticed it neither. Did feel some kind of bruise . . ."

"Is that all you can say, 'I'll need a new watch and weskit'? Do you know how close you came, Wyatt, to taking that bullet in your gizzard?"

"What sort of work were you talking about?" Wyatt asked again, closing his fingers over the broken watch. He didn't want to think about how close he'd come to dying.

"Special Deputy work. The U.S. Marshal, Meagher, him and some of the merchants hire men—'on assignment', they call it. For things the town deputies don't want to do."

"You mean fixing the sidewalks? Shooting stray dogs? I've done my share of that."

"No, I mean repossession—and tracking men out in the prairie. Tracking's long, hot, dirty work and I myself take no joy in it. But they'll pay for it. Marshal Smith likes to claim it's the *U.S.* Marshal's job, and Meagher, he claims it's the *Town* Marshal's . . . Say, how's young Henry McCarty?"

"Well enough. Bessie's looking after him. I've got a mind to get him out of harm's way." Which brought a question to mind. "You seen Johann Burke in town? Or Pierce? Or that Hoy?"

"None of them for a good long time." After a moment Bat added, "If Burke comes looking for you, you send for me. I'll back your play." He said it simply, without drama, as he watched a frilly lady with a lacy parasol cross the street nearby, but Wyatt knew he meant it; meant it all the way.

"Thank you, Bat. I'm not too proud to do just that. But . . ." He handed Bat the bullet-shattered watch. "There's a present for you. You might want to look at that before you come running."

They both watched the lady crossing the street: a woman with delicate features and big brown curling-iron tresses spilling down the back of her neck. She had no need of the parasol, now, with the sun so low, but she kept it propped on her shoulder and spun it in her white-gloved hands as she whisked along in her bustled skirt, careful never to look their way but quite aware they were watching.

"Word is, Pierce and Burke are down in Texas," Bat said, in a low voice, his eyes following the sway of the lady's bustle. "Pierce got his friends to drop the lynching charges and now he's chasing squatters off his land—people that came in when they thought he wasn't coming back."

Wyatt shrugged. Pierce would be back in Kansas, at some point. "You got my note?"

"Way you tell what happened in those hills, though . . . I'm not sure how it'd come out in court. I asked Meagher about it, since it happened in territory supposed to be controlled by the federals—he didn't feel inclined to arrest Burke. Said it wasn't clear who was hunting who. Your word against Burke's."

Wyatt grunted. "That's what I figured."

"And it doesn't hurt, even with Meagher—who isn't a bad sort—that Burke is Pierce's hound."

"Figured that too."

"Seems to me it's gotten to be as much a feud as anything else . . . Or it'll look that way to people."

"It *is* a kind of feud." It was funny, Wyatt thought, how you could lose sight of what had started a feud in the first place. First that night in Ellsworth, running afoul of Pierce. Then Wyatt asking a few too many questions about a girl he didn't even know.

Dandi LeTrouveau had died—and that death had led to other deaths. Montaigne and Plug Johnson, and Sanchez. It was like a bullet ricocheting through a tightly packed room. And maybe the bullet wasn't spent yet.

It might be wiser to leave Wichita, he thought; to head west, avoid the conflict. But it'd haunt him, if he did that. He'd have to watch his back forever. And he hated leaving things unfinished. "Meagher won't care that Smith fired me?" Wyatt asked.

"Nope. He won't give a shied penny."

"I've got to see Mattie," Wyatt said. "But tomorrow morning I'll have a word with Meagher about that work—I expect John Slaughter reported the attack on the stage already."

"You truly want me to keep this pocket watch, as a souvenir of your sorcerous luck?"

"I truly do. I'd rather not see it again."

"I'll show it to my brother Ed—he'll want to know where you buy watches that take a bullet for you . . ."

Wyatt said goodbye to Bat on the porch of the hotel, and got only a few steps into the lobby before almost running headlong into Mattie on her way out. She was dressed in a red-trimmed white gown, cut low at the bosom and sewn so its skirts hitched up on the sides to show her legs.

"Could get chilly tonight, for that outfit," Wyatt remarked.

"Wyatt!" And she ran into his arms.

* * *

Later, as they lay cooling off in their bed, Mattie in Wyatt's arms, her cheek against his shoulder, he asked, as gently as he could, "That get-up you were heading out in—you weren't thinking of going to . . . to 'work' in that thing?"

"I . . . Well . . . no. Only . . ."

He could tell that she wasn't sure she should tell him the truth. He drew back, fixed her with his gaze. "Go on ahead, Mattie. Tell me."

She made a little moan. "I didn't think you were coming back."

"I sent you money, and letters."

"Two little scribbles! I didn't know how long the money'd last—or if there'd be more. I thought you'd found someone else. I hadn't heard from you in a while. And I was so *bored*."

"Saying you wouldn't come to Deadwood because of the 'ladies of low virtue'!"

Her mouth quivered. "I was more afraid I'd . . ." She shook her head.

He was surprised at how angry he felt, thinking about her going back to her old profession. His own past only seemed to stoke the anger.

She began to sob, her face in her hands.

He relented, leaning back and putting his arms around her. "You've got no cause to fall into that life again. I'm here now. You'll learn to make fashionable dresses, you'll go to ladies circles, go to the theater. Keep busy. You understand me?"

"I understand, Wyatt," Mattie said softly, nestling closer to him with a sigh.

He noticed there were no tears on her cheeks.

* * *

"Marshal Meagher?"

The U.S. Marshal looked up from the circulars on his desk. "It's that youngest Earp boy, isn't it? I thought you moved out of town."

"I thought so too. I'm not the youngest Earp boy, Marshal—but I'm sure the one here looking for work."

In a linen "sack suit", for the coming of summer, and sporting a waxed handlebar mustache, Meagher might've seemed jaunty but for his broad, rugged face and his enormous frame—he weighed 275 pounds, Wyatt had heard. Now Meagher scratched his chin and looked Wyatt up and down.

"Marshal Smith says last fall you came in drunk and cold-cocked his deputy. Trying to let that killin' Canuck go."

Wyatt answered without hesitation. "Sir, I don't like to say anything hard about a peace officer. But Marshal Smith is a lying son of a bitch. I wasn't drunk, I never tried to let Montaigne go, and I had a reason to smack that dunderhead who keeps Smith's jail."

Meagher smiled. Then he suppressed the smile and tried to scowl. But after a moment he gave in and laughed aloud. "Damned if I don't agree with you about Smith and Carmody!" Meager fell to chuckling, straightening papers on his desk and shaking his head. Then he sobered, looking narrowly at Wyatt. "But you're getting into gunfights up in the Black Hills, Masterson tells me."

"Johann Burke's a hired killer, Marshal. He was stalking me, and I ran him off. Happens he killed a friend of mine too. Later on in Deadwood he threatened my life. Marshal Hickok backed my play and sent him packing."

"J.B. Hickok? I don't think he was ever a U.S. Marshal, if that's what you mean. Town Marshaled in Abilene some. Hickok gets into trouble when he drinks. They're calling him a vagrant in Cheyenne just to get him out of town before he kills someone. But you know—I always liked him. Hell of a fella." He lit a small cigar and puffed thoughtfully. "Well . . . Truth is, I don't mind crossing Smith by hiring you on—he don't like me none anyhow because he knows I'm going to run against him for the Town Marshal's job—my federal appointment's coming to an end, don't you know. Let's see now . . ." He drummed his fingers on the desk, cigar clenched in his teeth, gazing out the window. After a moment he took the cigar out of his mouth, blew smoke at the ceiling, and went on, "Couple of drovers rode off without paying their bill. Took a wagon they didn't pay for too, this morning. They come from another territory, making it a Federal matter—or so Smith claims. They're a good distance from town by now. Mr. Moser's wagon, it was, and he's asking me why don't I give chase, but I've got to stick around. Now, Moser will pay a bounty of seventy dollars, entire, plus expenses, if you want to bring those boys back—bring them or the money they owe for the wagon and the bills. I've got another man, Behrens, willing to go, but he don't want to go alone—seems he dislikes being outnumbered. What do you say, are you game?"

Wyatt reflected that seventy dollars split between two men wasn't much for risking his life out on the prairie. But if he completed this job, it could lead to others, and he knew he was under a cloud with the local peace officers. He wanted his good reputation back.

"All right," he said. "Which way'd they go?"

* * *

Mattie was sitting up in bed, dressed only in her drawers, clipping a piece from the *Wichita City Eagle* with her sewing scissors when Wyatt came in about midnight, the day after he'd gotten back from chasing the deadbeat drovers.

"Here you are, Wyatt," she said, passing him the clipping. "They spelled your name wrong but I like it anyhow."

Wyatt sat on the bedside and read a brief account of the pursuit of the deadbeats by Special Deputy "Wiatt Earp" and Special Deputy John Behrens. They'd gone almost to the Indian Territory just to bring back some minor thieves.

> *The Higgenbottom outfit, among other games, stuck M.R. Moser for a new wagon, who instead of putting himself in communication by telegraph with the outside world just got two officers, John Behrens and Wiatt Earp, to light out upon the trail. These boys fear nothing and nobody. To make a long and exciting story short, they just leveled a shotgun and sixshooter upon the scalawags as they lay concealed in some brush, and told them to 'dough over', which they did, to the amount of $146, one of them*

remarking he was not going to die for the price of a wagon. It is amusing
to hear Moser tell how slick the boys did the work.

Wyatt snorted. "Makes it sound like the work of a minute. I thought we'd never catch them. And all for thirty-five dollars, on my end. We let 'em go, after they paid up, and surrendered that wagon. Didn't want the work of bringing them back. We're just debt collectors, is all."

"I suppose they weren't big fish," Mattie said, taking the clipping back and pressing it into her scrapbook. "But Bat said it shows how much sand you've got, going that far to do a small job. It sure makes me proud to read about you."

He shook his head and leaned back against the headboard. "I just wish I was making more money. It's all kind of piecemeal. But Marshal Meagher says when he's elected Town Marshal, he'll re-hire me onto the city police."

She looked at him, affecting a little-girl shyness that wasn't particularly natural to her. "Do you think, then, we could get us a house, Wyatt? Just a small one?"

"We could rent one. I don't want to buy property here—I don't know how long I'm staying in Wichita."

She pouted, still playing the little girl. "You're leaving me again?"

"I meant . . . how long *we'd* stay here. I'm thinking of moving on to California, after I've worked here a while longer. Or one of the silver towns in Arizona territory, maybe. Get in at the start of something growing."

There was no good reason to stay in Wichita for long—a job as Deputy Town Marshal was just something to do before he found his real road in life. He should have left town by now, really. Except he kept hoping that some way he'd find out exactly how Dandi had died, and why—and then he might get her some justice. Her—and Sanchez and Montaigne.

But he sometimes worried that maybe he wanted to get to the bottom of the murder just to prove he was right. Maybe it's my own vanity, he thought. Pride. He remembered a line his mother had liked to quote from Proverbs: *Pride goeth before destruction, and an haughty spirit before a fall.*

He wondered if his pride would destroy him; and if he did fall—would he fall alone? Or would he take Bat Masterson and Henry McCarty down with him?

"Arizona . . ." Mattie said, seeming to try the place on, in her mind, the way she'd try on a hat. "Arizona . . . You think we could settle some place like that, have our business and maybe . . ." She glanced at him. "Children?"

"Could be." He couldn't bring himself to speak decisively about it. He didn't want to deceive her, and though he might want to have children, he wasn't sure he wanted to have them with Mattie.

"I wish I had a business to take care of," she went on. "A dry goods store, maybe. Or a dress shop. I get so bored. I tried to sit at one of them sewing circles. That Mrs. Donaldson—she's the wife of that new preacher—she brought me in to sew. But those women wouldn't hardly speak to me. I expect word got around . . ."

She fisted her hands in front of her mouth and began chewing a knuckle, staring into space. After a moment she repeated, softly, "Word got around."

CHAPTER FOURTEEN

The summer shone relentlessly on, August overtaking Wichita hot and sudden as a prairie fire. Henry mended quickly and dogged Wyatt's footsteps, looking sullen. When they went out on the plains to hunt, Wyatt taught Henry to ride and to shoot from horseback. They never spoke of the harsh words at the stagecoach—Wyatt figured Henry had been in low spirits, feeling testy from his wound.

Now and then Wyatt asked quietly around about the night Dandi was killed in Bessie's brothel, but found out nothing new. He had still heard nothing from the U.S. Marshal in Louisiana.

Otherwise, Wyatt dealt Faro for his brother James, played some cards himself, and he did the occasional Special Deputy's job. One Saturday night in August an assignment took him to Ida May's place in the Delany district.

Her sign read:

Ida May's Emporium of Gambling
~and~
the Delights of Genteel Companionship

Ida May's was an ambitious if unfinished combination of brothel and gambling hall. It aspired to opulence. She had purchased an old saloon, rebuilt it piecemeal, and the trappings of the new, velvet-draped, gold-trimmed establishment only partly covered up the raw wood and warped floorboards of the old one. The new pool table stood crookedly on the uneven floor, despite attempts to level it with shims, and the imported mahogany bar, carved with bare-bosomed nymphs, didn't match the unstained green lumber of the bottle shelves behind it.

Wyatt and Bat took all this in as they made their first inspection of the place, at about ten on a warm night.

"You ever notice, those velvet draperies and cushions are all somewhat reminiscent of soft human flesh, and not accidentally," Bat remarked.

Wyatt raised his eyebrows at this; Bat was given to high-flown observations.

"The flesh is all up those stairs, there," Wyatt said. "Except for the bar girls. But what we're here for is that piano . . ." Wyatt was weary and wanted the job done. They'd been out hunting with Virgil and Morgan and Henry, most of the day. They had gotten this last minute assignment from a merchant who'd cornered them in the café.

Wyatt's brother Virgil came in, waving his derby at them. He was not as lean as Wyatt and his droopy, sandy-blond mustache had grown, as Wyatt's younger brother Morgan had observed, "to compete with the mighty walrus of the Far North." Virgil wore a small diamond-shaped Special Deputy's badge, pinned on the lapel of his dark suit for the evening, as did Wyatt and Bat.

From across the room, Wyatt pointed at the piano, on the other side of the modest crowd of cowboys, peddlers, shopkeepers, hostlers and gamblers; Virgil nodded and crossed the room to meet them there. Wyatt noted Mannen Clements, a trim, hard-eyed man in a cowboy's working outfit, and Pierce's current ramrod, Hoy, playing poker at a table nearby—Hoy was incongruously dressed in a florid suit with checked pants, perhaps trying to be natty for Ida May's girls.

Clements was a cousin to the gunman John Wesley Hardin; though not the notorious hard-case his cousin was, it was said he could get himself worked up into a fighting mood pretty easily.

Hoy and Clements were a quarter the way through a bottle of George Dickel Tennessee Whiskey and it showed in their unfocused eyes and red cheeks as they glowered at the lawmen passing their table.

"Hoy's got a snootful," Wyatt murmured, as he, Bat and Virgil converged at the piano. "You see any more of Pierce's hands in here, Virgil?"

Virgil mopped his forehead with a red kerchief as big as a cavalry banner. "Seven or eight of Pierce's boys. They've been trickling into town—he's got a herd a few miles South and some have come ahead. There's another 'tribe' of Texans here from the 'Circle C' outfit too."

Bat gave the piano an experimental push. "This piano's on wheels but it's heavy as an opera singer fond of ice cream."

"Well," Wyatt said, "let's get it done. We'll explain to Ida May as the piano's going out the door." He was not looking forward to loading a piano onto a wagon, on this warm, somnolent evening.

But at that moment a would-be ivories tickler sat down at the upright and began to bang away at the keys: a merry, drunken cowboy with his dusty sombrero pushed to the back of his head and an unlit rolled cigarette disintegrating in his yellow-toothed grin.

"I believe the gentleman has decided to put the screws to 'Buffalo Gals'," Bat observed dryly.

"Friend," Virgil said to the pianist, "We're going to have to take this piano out from under them talented fingers. It seems Miss Ida

May has laid out for more than she can pay and, with the utmost regret, we must repossess this instrument."

"I'm damned if you are!" the cowboy said, the statement making his cigarette butt fall onto the piano keys. But his grin never wavered and he banged away with ever greater alacrity.

Wyatt made to draw his gun, with a mind to buffaloing the drunken pianist, but Bat shook his head at him. "Don't need to do that, Wyatt. Let's just push it out of here and if he wants to go with it, let him."

Wyatt shrugged and the three deputies took up positions around the piano, rolling it toward the door. The piano bench was on wheels too, and the pianist pushed it along sideways with his feet to follow the piano, banging away as it went, stretching his arms out, maintaining at least some of the familiar song.

The cowboys started by laughing at the piano player but soon turned to shouting outrage at the deputies. "Where the hell you going with the lady's pianer!"

Miss Ida May swished down the stairs, waving a silk kerchief to get their attention. "Whoa, hold on, boys, what are you after!"

She was a dark woman, perhaps part Indian, in a low-cut scarlet gown that could have served as the cover for a velvet sofa; she had wavy black hair, showing some gray, large black eyes, and skin the color of milk with a liberal splash of coffee in it. Her breasts had fallen some, and her makeup failed to conceal crow's feet at her eyes. She had worked a long time in the cattle towns before saving enough money for her "emporium".

"Ida May," Wyatt said, halting the slow roll of the upright, "You owe five hundred dollars on this piano." She was a petite woman, but emanating dominion as she swept over to them.

"I paid them two hundred fifty dollars already!"

"It's a seven-hundred and fifty dollar piano."

"I am over-reached, boys—that imported bar there nearly broke me. Next time the herds come in . . ."

"We've been appointed to repossess it tonight, Ida May—or to collect the five hundred dollars. They're not going to wait for the next drive." Adding, with real regret: "I'm sorry."

"I haven't got that much cash on hand—I just paid off the rest of the money for the property, this morning." She took a step closer and looked at the three men meltingly, her voice softening. "But if you boys would like to take it out in trade, I have three ladies upstairs who're feeling blue for want of company . . ."

"Well now . . ." Bat began, musingly.

"No," Wyatt interrupted, giving Bat a sharp, reproachful look, "No ma'am, we have to have the money or the piano."

"What do you mean by taking Ida May's piano?" Clements demanded, throwing down his cards.

"It's a low thing to do, right enough, Mannen!" Hoy declared, throwing his cards down too.

"It tain't my fault," Wyatt declared, struck by an idea. "It's *your* fault that piano's rolling out of here—it's laid on all of you men in here!"

"What the devil are you on about, Earp?" Clements demanded. "How is it our fault?"

"Here's a lady in need, she's wanting a mere five hundred dollars, which all you boys'll throw away in a card game in an hour or two. If you were to pass the hat, why, she could have this piano back."

"That's it, gents!" Bat chimed, in amusing himself by adding: "You can have the tune-box here if you pony up *to the tune* of five hundred dollars!"

Some of the cowboys laughed but no one reached for their pokes as yet.

Wyatt shook his head dolefully. "You boys are mostly from Texas, aren't you? Well that explains it. I don't suppose they've got much but skinflints and dirt scratchers in Texas—you talk big but when it's time to show . . ."

"Here's fifty—no, *sixty* dollars for your pian-y!" said a cowhand as long and thin as a willow.

"And here's another seventeen, eighteen . . . nineteen dollars!" shouted the drover on the piano bench, digging the money out of his vest pocket.

Bat took off his hat and circulated through the room, encouraging the Texans to dough over. The scowling Hoy and Clements had little option but to contribute, and in short order the five hundred dollars was handed to the astonished Madame. She ceremoniously passed it over to Virgil.

"Paid in full!" he shouted, waving the money and prompting a cheer from the crowd.

"One free drink for everyone!" Ida May declared—she was judicious in her gratitude.

Most of the assemblage crowded to the bar but Hoy and Clements simply stood by their table, hands dangling near their pistols. Clements snarled, "Earp—what was it you said, about Texans? I didn't like the sound of it. You goddamn better well apologize!"

Wyatt snorted and looked at him in disbelief. "Apologize to *you?*"

"To me and every man here, you string bean son of a bitch!"

Wyatt shook his head. "You keep on with me, Clements, you'll get something into you can't buy your way out of."

Bat exchanged grimaces with Virgil at this—at Wyatt pushing out the limits again.

"Something I can't . . . ?" Clements turned to Virgil in puzzled outrage, demanding, "What the hell does he mean?" Clements demanded of Hoy. He turned back to Wyatt. "What the hell do you . . ."

But Wyatt turned on his heel, and strode toward the door.

He could feel Clements' eyes watching him go. He half expected to be shot in the back. But he went out through the swinging doors without incident. The incident came later.

About eleven-thirty, Wyatt and Virgil were heading up Main Street, Wyatt to his hotel room and Virgil to his boarding house, when they heard a staccato crackling of gunshots from the direction of the bridge over the Arkansas.

The two men turned as one, to look back toward the Delano district. "I don't reckon that's a call for us," Virgil said. "We get one job at a time."

Wyatt nodded. But both he and Virgil stayed where they were, hesitating, thinking they were probably not needed at the ruckus— they weren't regular town lawmen—yet not quite able to turn their backs on it. . .

"Wyatt!"

It was Dave Leahy, trotting his mustang up the street toward them. He reined in and leaned on his pommel. The mustang, barely broken, stirred restlessly, eyeing them fiercely. "There you are, Wyatt! Smith's out of town, and Meagher asked me to get you—there's a few deputies on the bridge already but I don't think they're going to be able to hold those boys."

"Anybody shot?" Wyatt asked. "I heard gunfire."

"Firing into the air, so far. Seems it was some remarks from you that started it and Meagher thinks if you set the fire you ought to put it out." Virgil grunted. "You see there, Wyatt? Sometimes you push it a button too far."

"Could be you're right," Wyatt admitted. "I'm coming, Dave. Virgil, you don't have to mix in."

"No, I sure as Hell don't," Virgil said, but he set off at Wyatt's side toward the bridge over the Arkansas River.

Bat was already there, with Behrens and Cairns and two other deputies, facing off a milling mob of Texas cowboys gathered in the middle of the bridge—under a mob of blazing stars. Several of the Texans carried lanterns—all of them flourished guns, glinting silver and blue-steel in the angry starlight.

A horseman trotted onto the bridge from the Delano side, and the crowd parted for him—he rode into the overlapping circles of lantern light, and Wyatt saw that it was Mannen Clements, a Dragoon pistol in hand

"We should have brought a shotgun," Virgil murmured.

"Here's one I'll gladly give up to you," Behrens said nervously.

"I'll take it," Wyatt said, and, shotgun in hand, he took two long strides up onto the bridge, ahead of the other deputies. He figured Meagher was right: this was his fire to put out.

Finger on the trigger, Wyatt held the shotgun firmly in his hands—pointed at no one, as yet, but clearly ready to pop to his shoulder. Held in that way it was a message understood by every man there: *Push any harder and the shotgun swings your way.*

"Mannen!" Wyatt shouted—his tone rang with authority, but he also gave it a kind of respect for the man he was addressing. "Hold that stud up, right there!"

Mannen Clements looked at the shotgun, and the men blocking the bridge—and reined in his horse.

"What's all this about, Mannen?" Wyatt asked. For a moment he thought his heart was beating so loud the men could hear it. But his face was the one he used for poker—with just a glint of warning in his eyes. He couldn't let these men know how scared he was.

Clements' horse, sensing the tension, was almost dancing in place as the cowboy held the reins with one hand, the pistol tilted up in the other. He glowered balefully down at Wyatt Earp. "'Scared to show', you said, Earp. You're just a damned day-labor deputy but you have insulted every man in the territory of Texas. All the Texans I was able to locate in Wichita are here to ask for satisfaction."

There was a cheer from the Texans, at that.

"Quiet down and let them talk!" Virgil bellowed. He'd drawn his pistol and he held it in the air like a baton, to draw their eyes—and as an unspoken warning of his own.

"Maybe *now* you'd like to apologize, Earp!" Hoy suggested. He was standing beside Clements' horse, his own weapon drawn but so far pointed at the boards of the bridge.

Wyatt was faced with a kind of dilemma. If he apologized, he'd be backing down in front of these men—and his sway over them, come a hard situation, would evaporate. He expected to work for Meagher, when Mike was elected Town Marshal. He'd need that authority.

On the other hand if he told Clements and Hoy to go to Hell, there could be a bloodbath. Men had been killed for less in a mob situation. These men were drunk and angry and, most of all, each had something to prove to the others.

The only way to stop this, he calculated, was to stop their leader—and that seemed to be Clements. But killing him wasn't the way to do it, unless there was no other choice.

"Most of you men work for Mr. Pierce, or the Circle C," he said at last. "Do you think your bosses want you to get shot up, or locked in the city jail? You'd best ask yourself what they want you to do!"

"They'd want us to make you answer straight!" Clements burst out, drawing his other pistol. "Do you apologize or *not?* And that means putting down your gun and . . . I think he ought to pay a fine, don't you, boys? Maybe we'll have his boots and guns too!" The cowboys cheered at that.

Wyatt said, "Can't apologize when I didn't make the insult. You didn't understand me, is all. I can say I'm sorry I didn't make myself understood. I've ridden with many a Texan and I've plenty of respect for them."

"There!" Bat put in. "That shows Wyatt's heart's in the right place, boys! Let's have some peace and quiet so you boys can get your business done! There's ladies at Ida May's sighing for you right now!"

There was a smattering of laughter at that; a little easing of tension.

"You've all got to go on back, now!" Wyatt said. He made eye contact with Mannen Clements, and hardened his face.

And very slowly and deliberately, he cocked the hammers back on the shotgun.

"Mind me now, Mannen!" Wyatt whispered, in a voice only loud enough for Clements and Hoy to hear—but his tone was insistent. "Put up those guns and go on home!"

Clements looked at the cocked-back hammers of the shotgun. Then he shrugged expansively, holstered his gun, and said loudly, "I accept your goddamn apology!"

And he turned his horse, riding at an easy trot through the crowd, back to Delano. Talking and laughing and grumbling, the others trailed after him.

"That was as close to a local war as I ever want to see," Virgil said.

"It's not over yet," said Bat. "Pierce, Burke, and the rest of that bunch will be in town in two days."

CHAPTER FIFTEEN

Bat found Wyatt playing poker in James Earp's gambling hall, about five in the afternoon in late August. Seeing his friend waving a folded newspaper at him, Wyatt threw in his cards, gathered up his slim winnings, and went to join him at the bar.

"What's rustlin', Bat?"

"I just thought you'd like to know—as you had some acquaintance with the man. My brother Ed brought this from Deadwood . . ." He handed Wyatt the front page of a newspaper.

It was a recent copy of Deadwood's *Black Hills Pioneer*. Wyatt read:

ASSASSINATION OF WILD BILL
HE WAS SHOT THROUGH THE HEAD BY JOHN McCALL
WHILE UNAWARE OF DANGER
ARREST, TRIAL, & DISCHARGE OF THE ASSASSIN
WHO CLAIMS TO HAVE AVENGED
A BROTHER'S DEATH IN KILLING WILD BILL . . .

On Wednesday about 3 o'clock the report stated that J.B. Hickok (Wild Bill) was killed. On repairing to the hall of Nuttall and Mann, it was ascertained that the report was too true. We found the remains of Wild Bill lying on the floor. The murderer, Jack McCall, was captured after a lively chase by many of the citizens, and taken to a building at the lower end of the city, and a guard placed over him. As soon as this was accomplished, a coroner's jury was summoned, with C.H. Sheldon as foreman, who after hearing all the evidence, which was the effect that, while Wild Bill and others were at a table playing cards, Jack McCall walked in and around directly back of his victim, and when within three feet of him raised his revolver, and exclaiming, "damn you, take that," fired; the ball entering at the back of the head, and coming out at the centre of the right check causing instant death, reached a verdict in accordance with the above facts . . .

Wyatt felt his heart sinking within him. "Shot from behind! Hickok always tried to sit with his back to the wall. I told him not to let that drunken lunatic stay in Deadwood. But he didn't want to show himself afraid of such a man. And McCall was too low for Hickok to call out." He pored over the article again, and shook his head. "I don't believe it—they let the murdering bastard go!"

Bat nodded sadly. "Yes they did, Wyatt. It seems that Wild Bill had enemies in Deadwood. One of them was a man named Johnny Varnes—he had a run-in with Hickok in Colorado. It seems McCall worked up a grudge for Hickok but put it aside after you clobbered him. Then this Varnes got McCall fired up again and fanned the flame with cash. Offered him two hundred dollars to backshoot Hickok. Ed thinks Varnes and his friends got McCall released. They paid off some of the jury and tried to make Hickok look like a red-handed murderer, with that phony story about his brother—from what I hear, McCall *has* no brother."

"He won't get far," Wyatt mused aloud. "Charlie Utter or California Joe or Jane Cannary will kill him if no one else does . . . And if I come across him . . ."

"You won't have to. Ed says there's determined talk of re-trying him in another town. Agnes Hickok has hired a man to pursue him. McCall will swing if he's not shot down first."

Wyatt had scarcely known Hickok, but he felt sorrow for the loss of a man he'd admired from boyhood—Wild Bill had been a legendary Civil War spy, and a plains scout, before getting a reputation as a gun hand.

It was a bitter thing. You might give up lawing, but some no-account would pop up from the underbrush of the past and shoot you in the back.

"I'm going riding," Wyatt said. "I need to think . . ."

Bat nodded, and turned to order a drink, as Wyatt walked out of the gambling hall and went to find his horse.

Henry was in the livery, rubbing the horse down for him. "You going riding, Wyatt? Can I go?"

Wyatt wanted to go alone, but he had gotten a telegram about Henry, and decided that now was as good a time as any to tell him. "You can borrow that roan I bought for Mattie—Lord knows she almost never rides her, and that horse needs exercise. There's things we need to talk about."

* * *

They rode along beside the Arkansas River, where they could get relief from the sun in the shade of an occasional cottonwood.

"We goin' any place in particular?" Henry asked, at length.

Gazing out across the plains, Wyatt just shook his head. The sky and the prairie vied for endlessness. The vast vault of blue was broken by the occasional perfectly white, cottony cloud, moving along at a good clip in the welcome breeze. Wyatt watched the shadows of the clouds ripple over the rolling plain. Men came and went that way—like the shadows of clouds. Some men went quicker than others . . .

At last, Wyatt said, "Henry, I wired some money to the Pinkertons—their man found your step-daddy for me."

Henry's mouth dropped open like a confused child, showing his buck teeth, once more seeming a much younger boy than he was. He took a deep breath. "Well. So you're sending me away."

"I'm sending you to someplace you'll be safer. We're expecting Burke back here in town. He thinks you know too much—although you saw and heard little enough that night. But I think Pierce paid him to kill you. And until he does, he doesn't collect the money."

"We could shoot him down. You almost got him last time."

"This isn't the Black Hills, Henry. And it's not just Burke. I just feel you need to grow up somewheres safer—where you've got family."

"That man Antrim ain't my family." Henry swallowed, hard, looking away. Wyatt knew the boy was hiding tears. "Shit, I don't need to hang around with you. I'm staying here—without your help."

"Mr. Antrim is expecting you. He's telegraphed me about it . . ."

"He wants a slave, like that Indian did. That's what he wants me for. A worker he don't have to pay."

"If that's the case, contact me, and I'll look into it."

"I don't need to be his slave," Henry said, as if he hadn't heard. "I don't need that kind of life no more. I can find other ways to make a living. One way or the other."

Wyatt frowned. Was this another hint that the boy was thinking of turning outlaw? Once at camp, in the Black Hills, Henry had asked him about the outlaws he'd known, and his interest seemed to have a glow of admiration about it—for the outlaws. And he'd talked that way about Dunc Blackburn, at the stagecoach station.

"Henry, you're not thinking that outlawry is the way to go, are you? Most of 'em do it because they're too damn stupid to do anything else. They all get caught."

"Cole Younger ain't stupid and he ain't been caught."

"He'll be caught or killed. His time'll come."

"At least they make their own way in the world, and be damned to needing anyone else!" the boy said angrily. He climbed down off the roan, and started walking determinedly back along the riverbank toward Wichita.

"Where the Hell you think you're going, boy?"

"Wichita. I don't need your help—or your whore's horse, either."

A ripple of fury went through Wyatt, and he rode up to the boy, slid off his horse, and grabbed Henry by the collar. "What'd you call my woman, Henry? What'd you say?"

"Well ain't she? And you should know about whores!"

Wyatt kept a grip on the boy's collar with his left hand, raised his right to slap him. And then in his mind's eye he seemed to see himself, standing there, about to smack someone half his weight and a foot shorter. He lowered his hand, and let Henry go. He walked back to his mount, shaking his head. "Just get on the damn horse, Henry, it's too far to walk back to town."

But Henry turned and trudged toward Wichita.

Wyatt took the reins of Henry's mount, climbed onto his own horse, turned it with a nudge of his knees toward Wichita. He led the roan behind him as he walked his horse alongside the boy.

"You want to ride shank's mare that's your decision," Wyatt said.

They made their way slowly toward town. A couple of long, hot, dusty, fly-tormented miles crawled by, and at last Henry said, "Oh I don't give a damn."

He climbed up on the roan and, silently, they rode back to Wichita.

* * *

"Burke," Abel Pierce was saying, as they sat together in Ida May's place, one evening in early September, "I want you to forget about Wyatt Earp. And the other matter. I have settled my mind about it and it's done."

Burke shook his head. "It's gone too far for that, Mr. Pierce—for me anyway. Far as I'm concerned, it's a matter of pride and reputation. I can't do for Hickok, with him dead by another's hand—"

Pierce snorted. It was his opinion that, even if it was true that Hickok's eyesight had been fading, Wild Bill would've shot Burke dead; he'd have nailed him with a single shot out of pure, unerring killer instinct. When they asked Jack McCall why he shot Hickok in the back, instead of facing him, McCall said, *Because I didn't want to commit suicide.*"

"—but I can do for Earp, right enough," Burke was saying.

"I'm paying you well, Johann, and I've decided I don't want unnecessary trouble here. I've got business to do. Now if Earp makes me wrathy, I'll give you the go-ahead. But he's just a Special Deputy, he can't do a damn thing."

"Can't he? Suppose he starts pushing on that girl's dying?"

"Burke—shut up about that."

"Well, sir—just suppose?"

Pierce poured himself a shot of Kentucky bourbon, and drank it off. He looked up at the upper landing of the stairs sweeping to the second floor, where a freckled chestnut-haired girl caught his eye and waved to him; she was wearing a blouse cut down to her nipples and a dark blue dress hitched up in her fingers to show a length of pale thigh.

He winked at her and then shook his head, looking away. He had difficulty looking at them at all, now. He judged he'd get over it, some day. But it was strange to think about—regardless of what he'd told Earp on the street that day—these girls having families, somewhere. Mothers and fathers. Even children of their own . . .

Chewing his lip, he poured himself another bourbon. "I made up my mind. Don't push it, Burke."

"What about the boy?"

"Will you keep your voice down? If they were going to use that boy's testimony against us in court, they would've by now. He don't seem to have seen much."

"But he'll talk, sooner or later. Maybe there won't be any court case—but you'll be tried and found guilty another way, Mr. Pierce. You don't seem like a man who wants to be gossiped about. You talked about running for governor of Texas someday. If the tongues are wagging, well . . ."

"I drink with the boys who run this town, Burke. My money's in their pockets. No one's going to talk me down."

"You think you can do what you like here, Mr. Pierce? How about a little test?" Burke lowered his voice and leaned closer. "How'd it be if we hurrahed the town tonight. Shoot up the place, ride into some saloons like old times, bust a few windows—just to show that you can. And if Earp just happens to get in the way of a bullet . . ."

"He's not a city policeman, right now—he won't be called to deal with a 'hurrahing'."

"Earp will be there." He signaled a man at the bar. Over-dressed and pompous, the man sauntered over and tipped his hat at Pierce. "Mr. Pierce," Burke said, "Let me introduce J. Mundale Swinnington . . ."

* * *

Wyatt was playing poker in James's place, about half an hour before midnight. He was distantly aware that the noise in the gambling hall had grown over the last half hour to a crescendo of argument, laughter, the chatter of chips and the clinking of bottles; it was filled out by shouted betting, demands for drinks, drunken declarations of love and dutiful giggles from the saloon girls. The musicians had to blow and thump and squeal even louder to be heard, adding to the din. This climax of noise was as normal for a Kansas gambling hall late on a Friday night as the rising tide was to the sea. In about an hour, those who'd lost money steadily all evening or who simply had no more funds for drinking would make their way regretfully out the doors; those too drunk to stand would sag into a chair, only to have the bouncer nudge them into leaving. None but the hard-core gaming element would remain. The place would ease down to serious, quiet gambling, and Wyatt was looking forward to it.

Mattie was with him tonight, sitting at his elbow, chatting condescendingly with the saloon girls, pretending not to see the men who winked at her. She got tired of staying home alone in the evening and James's place was almost respectable, compared to some in Wichita.

Contemplating a pair of Jacks and wondering if they augured well for staying in the hand, Wyatt was thinking too, that as he'd won two hundred dollars tonight, he could afford to take Mattie up to St. Louis, to see a show and do a little shopping. She needed an outing, to get over being so restive.

Someone passing the table jostled his arm and he looked up in mild irritation. Then he stared.

It was that swindler from Deadwood. Swineton, or whatever his name had been. Swinnington, that was it. His yellow suit was getting dingy and frayed—and it appeared he might pop a seam himself as he recognized Wyatt. "Sir I do . . . I do, ah, apologize, I didn't mean to interrupt a gentlemanly game of—that is—Oh, say . . ." He started to turn away—then something seemed to occur to him and he turned back, licked his lips. "Do I understand that you were interested in information about—" He lowered his voice and leant near. "—about that poor girl who died at Bessie Earp's establishment . . . If you were to provide a small, ah, gratuity . . ."

"People who come and offer information for money are prone to making it up," Wyatt observed, looking hard at Swinnington.

"I see . . . I . . . well perhaps not. Actually it might be best . . ." He swallowed and backed away. "Excuse me." He turned and headed hastily for the door to the street, with many backward glances at Wyatt.

It seemed to Wyatt that Swinnington was acting guilty—acting like a man of the theater. Still and all, Swinnington had some connection with Burke—asking around Deadwood, Wyatt had confirmed that they'd been seen together. A connection with Burke was a connection with Pierce. What else would this Swinnington know about?

Wyatt turned to Mattie, seeing her smother a yawn. "You're tired," he observed. "And this hand doesn't look promising." He threw in his cards, surrendered his ante and collected his winnings. Not bad, just under three hundred dollars . . .

He walked Mattie to the door, almost dragging her by the elbow, hastening to see where Swinnington had gone. The yellow suit was easy to spot, even in a darkness scarcely moderated by the oil lamps—the confidence man was headed toward the bridge over the Arkansas River. He wanted to follow but he had to take Mattie to the hotel . . .

"Wyatt, Mattie—how are you folks this balmy night?" It was Dave Leahy, strolling down the wooden sidewalk toward them.

"We're very well, Mr. Leahy," said Mattie, with the ghost of a curtsey—she liked to play at seeming ladylike on the streets. But if she had a bit too much to drink, or an extra swallow of the pain medicine she sometimes got from the pharmacist, the sewing-circle lady in her tended to disappear.

Wyatt was still watching Swinnington, who was becoming hard to see as he went farther from the street lamps. "Mattie—I've got to look into something. It concerns that girl who was killed. There's a gent I want to talk to." He turned to Leahy, giving him a meaningful look. "Dave, could you . . . ?"

"I'd be honored to escort the lady home. But Wyatt—you will give me the story, later?"

"I'll give it to you—then the question will be . . ." Wyatt left the rest unsaid: The question will be: Will they let you print it?

Leahy compressed his lips, looked at the ground and shrugged.

Mattie took Wyatt's hand. "Wyatt—don't leave me now . . ."

"I'll be there soon enough, Mattie," Wyatt said, patting her hand gently.

She made an exasperated noise in her throat and let Leahy take her arm. She spoke loudly, so Wyatt would hear, as they walked away together. "*Dear* Mr. Leahy—you look *very handsome* tonight in your coat and tails! Truly very handsome!"

Wyatt hurried after Swinnington. He was thinking he might catch him somewhere alone. He could apply some pressure to discover just what Swinnington knew of Burke and Pierce—and Dandi LeTrouveau.

He was within fifty paces of the bridge when he realized that he'd lost sight of Swinnington. And there was an uproar coming from the Delano side of the river. Gunshots, then whoops and hollers.

Wyatt peered through the darkness, trying to see what was happening on the other side of the bridge. He saw flashes, heard the crack and thump of gunfire, a clatter of hooves.

Out of the corner of his eye Wyatt glimpsed someone hurrying toward him. He tensed, spinning on his heel toward them, starting to draw his pistol—

"Don't shoot, Wyatt, it's me!" It was Bat, carrying a shotgun. "I was over at Meagher's office and I heard shots—he let me borrow the shotgun."

"I'll take the 12-gauge, Bat, if that's all right—will you get Virgil for me? You know where his place is, down the street . . ."

"Are you sure? Maybe we should get Smith!"

The clatter of hooves became a raggedly rolling drumbeat as the horses struck the wood of the bridge.

"He isn't in town. Sounds like the drovers are hurrahing the town. I can't let them get over the bridge. We got to keep them bottled up. Just go! When you get back, come through that alley there by the blacksmith!"

Bat nodded, tossed him the shotgun and hurried off on his errand.

Wyatt started toward the bridge. But some inward voice told him he was being foolish. He suspected, now, that Swinnington had been sent to lure him here. And he was a bigger fool to put himself in the line of fire when he was no more than a Special Deputy. He didn't have the legal authority—unless you counted citizen's arrest.

That would have to be sufficient. Because now he saw that the riders, coming off the bridge with their guns cracking, firing at street lamps and windows, were bent on hurrahing the town—there would be wreckage, probably someone shot from a stray bullet. Hurrahing was something Wyatt could not bear. And he made out Abel "Shanghai" Pierce riding a big horse in the lead.

They were coming right at Wyatt, some of them pointing at him—he heard someone shouting, "There's that Earp!"

He needed to think about tactics. He stepped back, hurried to the shadowy-draped corner of the blacksmith's workshop, and set the shotgun down, leaning it against the wall.

Another flurry of gunshots came. Window glass shattered somewhere and a woman screamed. Hooves thudded the street.

Drawing his pistol, Wyatt stepped back around the corner of the building, still in shadow—and found himself facing Shanghai Pierce who was just climbing down from his horse about forty feet away. With him were George Hoy, Grigsby, Dudley, Creighton, Mannen Clements, and three cowboys whose names he didn't know, including the one who'd tried to play piano at Ida May's—the amateur pianist looked less affable now. No sign of Swinnington.

Not seeing Wyatt yet, Pierce seemed to be headed to a closed and locked grocery store. A sign in the window advertised whiskey by the bottle. "We'll get us some drinks to take with us," Pierce was saying, flipping his pistol and raising his arm preparatory to smashing the window with his gun butt. "We'll let this town know it's been annexed to Texas!"

"Mr. Pierce!" Wyatt shouted, drawing his Colt. "Do not break that window!" He leveled his gun at Pierce.

Pierce froze, arm still cocked—then he let the gun droop by his side and turned toward Wyatt. "Here you are, Earp, sooner'd I'd hoped." He smiled crookedly.

Wyatt heard another horse and turned to see Burke riding into view, coming up behind the others. George Hoy, Creighton, Clements, and Grigsby were already pointing their pistols at Wyatt.

Wyatt kept his gun on Pierce—and he backed up, toward the narrow alley by the blacksmith's workshop.

"Look at that!" Hoy chuckled. "He's fixing to run!"

Wyatt did make haste, then—into the alley. He holstered his pistol and swept up the shotgun. Bat and James Earp and Deputy Potts were in the alley, as he'd hoped, coming toward him. Bat had come across James before Virgil—and Meagher had sent the chunky, nervous deputy Potts. They were all armed.

Wyatt put a finger to his lips, pointed back down the alley, then gestured for them to circle the blacksmith's low wooden building. They hurried back through the alley . . .

"Earp! You hiding back there?" It was Burke, trotting his horse up close to the alley's mouth.

Wyatt stepped out into sight, leveling the shotgun at Burke's chest and thumbing the hammers back. "Just went for my artillery, Johann."

Burke hesitated, knowing that if he fired a shot, Wyatt would pull the trigger as he fell—the shotgun wouldn't miss at this range.

Wyatt saw Pierce move closer—bringing his pistol into play. Clements cocked his gun . . .

"What's your orders, Mr. Pierce?" Hoy asked. "Seems to me this here is real opportunity . . ."

Pierce hesitated. Then his eyes hardened. Wyatt tightened his finger on the shotgun triggers, deciding that he would take Burke down with him . . .

"Mr. Pierce!" Bat shouted, stepping out into the street, behind Pierce. James, Potts, and Bat spread out behind the cowboys, guns in hand.

"Look here, you damned yahoos!" James shouted, pointing his pistol, his voice gravelly with thousands of nights in smoky bar rooms.

"The law's here now!" Potts shouted, but more tentatively. "The fun's over, fellas!"

Shanghai Pierce and his men turned to take in James Earp, Bat Masterson, and Deputy Potts, spreading out behind them— Bat was aiming his Winchester at Pierce himself. Pierce saw that he and his bunch were outflanked. "Now that's a helluva sneaky tactic, damn you . . ."

Wyatt allowed himself a small smile. He had used classic military tactics, retreating a short distance to draw an enemy after him, so that he could move into a position of strength while his reinforcements outflanked his enemy. It was another thing Newton had told him about. "Burke—put that gun away."

Burke licked his lips. He looked over his shoulder at James, who was pointing his pistol at Burke's back. Then he holstered the gun. "All right, boys. But I'm not spending the night in jail. The accommodations aren't up to my standards." He turned and galloped away.

Bat swung his Winchester after Burke—he seemed to be thinking about shooting the gunfighter off his horse.

Wyatt called out, "Bat—he's got away. Let's just take these others in . . ."

Wyatt heard cheering and turned to see a group of assorted local citizens, some in their nightgowns, across the street, watching.

"The hell you're taking me to jail!" Pierce snorted.

Wyatt turned back to Pierce, stepping close—Pierce's gun was now pointed at the boardwalk.

"I'll say it twice!" Pierce declared. "I'll be damned if you'll arrest me, boy! You haven't got the authority."

"You can call it a citizen's arrest if you want," Wyatt said softly. "Or you can say I'm backing up Potts there. But you're going to jail. You shot holes in every damn wall and window this side of Wichita. Now give me your gun." He raised the shotgun.

"Go to the devil! You won't shoot me with that shotgun for disturbing the peace!"

"No, I won't shoot you." Wyatt eased the shotgun's hammers off cock. "But Mr. Pierce . . ." Wyatt met Pierce's eyes, and he spoke simply, clearly, and with conviction, straight from the center of his being, as he slapped the shotgun barrel down hard into the palm of his left hand. ". . . you give me that gun, or I'll bust your arm in two."

For a long moment, Pierce searched Wyatt's face.

Then he handed over his gun.

* * *

At nine o'clock the next morning, while Pierce's new attorney was paying the cattle baron's fine—contemptuously tossing fifty dollars onto the court clerk's table—Wyatt was tossing Henry McCarty's grip up to John Slaughter. Henry stood silently next to the stagecoach's open door.

Slaughter was working full-time for Wells Fargo now and he'd be driving the stagecoach from Wichita to points West and South.

"You could work for us anytime, you know that, don't you, Wyatt?" Slaughter asked, as he stowed the grip in the rack behind him.

"If I'm in the mood to have my hair parted by a bullet, I'll sign up," Wyatt said.

"By God, I think Wyatt just made a joke," said Bat, walking up to them. "That's the second one this year!"

"I heard him make one once, about giving me to the Sioux," Henry mumbled.

"Sounds like Wyatt's light-hearted humor," Bat said.

Wyatt and Henry looked at one another, neither speaking. Henry was wearing a catalog suit that Mattie had picked out for him, with knee breeches and tweed cap, and he didn't seem comfortable in the outfit.

"Henry," Wyatt said, at last, "You have a hundred-forty dollars now—and besides that I've given you money for the telegraph, so if there's any *real* problem with Mr. Antrim, you're to tell me. And . . . write me. Let me know how it is for you, in New Mexico."

Henry shrugged. "Maybe I will," Henry said. He bit his lip. He seemed morose—but there was another feeling showing in his eyes too.

Wyatt cleared his throat. "I uh . . ."

Henry shook his head decisively, and climbed up into the stagecoach. "I'll find my way, okay."

"You think about what I told you," Wyatt said. "You remember. Some trails only run downhill."

And wondering if he were doing the right thing, Wyatt closed the door on the stagecoach.

Henry turned away from him, as if refusing to say goodbye—then suddenly he turned back and thrust his hand through the window.

He and Wyatt shook hands, for the last time. "Thanks," Henry said, his voice choked with emotion. "Whatever happens—I thank you."

He let go of Wyatt's hand and sat back in the coach, staring straight ahead. Slaughter waved to Wyatt and gave the reins a snap. The horses whinnied, and the coach rolled away, sending up plumes of dust from the wheels.

Bat and Wyatt looked after the coach, watching it all the way down the street. Then they went to find some breakfast.

"I wonder what'll become of him," Bat said, at last.

Wyatt shook his head sadly.

And in fact, he never would know what happened to Henry McCarty, because he hadn't known him by the other names that Henry adopted later. One of those names was William Bonney.

But most people would know him by his nickname.

Billy the Kid.

CHAPTER SIXTEEN

"They call it the Atchison, Topeka, and Santa Fe . . . but it don't go to Santa Fe," Pierce grumbled, "Maybe some day. I've got to get off the train in Medicine Lodge . . ."

Pierce was in his seat, Burke standing in the aisle, in the first class passenger car of the 6 p.m. train to Points South. They could hear the engine snorting as the boiler got up steam; the smokestack was beginning to gush ash and some of it spiraled in through the open window. But the train hadn't budged an inch yet.

"Shut that window up there, for me, Johann, would you? The goddamn train . . . Getting ash on my suit . . ."

Burke went to close the window, and returned, thinking that Pierce's grumbling about the train was cover for what was really eating at him. "I'm sorry you spent the night in jail, Mr. Pierce," said Burke, in a low voice, leaning near him, "but I tried to tell you the man has no respect for you."

Pierce looked around the car before answering. The only other passenger in first class was a fleshy man with oiled back hair, already snoring, at the back of the wood-and-silver trimmed lounge car. "I'll tell you what, Johann—Wyatt Earp humiliated me in front of the whole town . . ."

Burke nodded. "Adding insult, City Council voted unanimously, this afternoon, to offer him a job as Assistant Town Marshal. Smith doesn't like it, of course, but he's stuck with him."

"So I heard. Your damn fault Earp got that job, Johann. That hurrahing was your idea. I had this town sewn up. The whole mess is your fault. Including me getting arrested. Uncle Fergus, he . . ." His voice trailed off.

"No sir, wasn't my fault. I blame Earp—he didn't have to arrest you. No real harm was done. He could've just taken the guns for the night, sent you to your hotel. Let you pay a fine. But the bastard just had to humiliate you. How far will he go? Hell, the real question is, what's to be done about it?"

Pierce thought for a moment, watching the smoke blackening the window. "It don't matter whose fault it was. Not now. He shamed me. And he's too damned nosy. It's a matter of pride as well as prudence . . . I'll give you seven hundred dollars."

"What about the boy? That McCarty runt."

"Happens I heard Earp sent him to New Mexico. Never mind, Earp's your target."

Burke tapped the butt of his gun with his forefinger. "We understand what the money is for, Mr. Pierce? We're clear on that?"

Pierce nodded grimly. "It's to take care of a son of a bitch who made me look like a fool in front of my men. And it's to make definite-sure he isn't around to stick his nose into anything he shouldn't be sticking it into. That clear enough?"

"Yes sir. I'll need expenses out front . . ."

The train shrilled its whistle as Pierce took out a checkbook and a pen. "Here's a bank draft for half. Take it to the Wichita Bank of Commerce. They'll honor it without blinking. When it's *all done*, and done completely, telegraph me like this: *Wolf will no longer trouble herd.* You understand, Burke? Say nothing else in the telegram."

The train gave a wrench, not quite rolling but seeming to strain at the bit; the whistle shrieked again, and the billow of gray black smoke eclipsed the windows completely so that the train car darkened as if the sun had set.

Burke smiled. "I understand you perfectly well, Mr. Pierce." He touched his hat, and hurried to get off the train. He had a wolf to hunt.

* * *

Wyatt, Mattie, and Bat were walking down the sunny street in search of coffee. Wyatt yawned—he'd been up till four in the morning. He waved through the open door at Marshal Meagher as they passed his office. Seeing Wyatt, Meagher got up from his desk, gesturing for them to hold on.

"You got a letter, Wyatt," Marshal Meagher said, coming out and passing over a linen envelope. "They sent it care of me because it come from a U.S. Marshal . . ."

Seeing Meagher was waiting for an explanation, Wyatt said, "I wrote for information about Dandi LeTrouveau."

Hearing that, Meagher winced and went back into his office.

Wyatt opened the envelope and read:

Salutations, Officer Earp

 I regret so much the delay in responding to yours of ____. We had a busted dike here, and much land flooded. I had to abandon my office for awhile. I was then distracted by the depredations of a local feud. On reclaiming my office I found your request for information high and dry on a cabinet. Accordingly, when the occasion took me to that county, I have visited the orphanage you named and was informed that the former resident Miss Dandi LeTrouveau was the daughter of a woman named Belle LeTrouveau and a Mr. A. Pierce, as indicated by Belle LeTrouveau. She did not indicate

what the A stood for. He was only here a few weeks. She made the arrange-
ments for her daughter on her death bed and this is all the information she gave.
Belle came from a good family here, but they died out with the yellow jack in
'57. No other family is known. I am sorry I have no further information for
you at this time. Most of our records were destroyed in the recent flood.

H. Liam Cay,
U.S. Marshal, Louisiana

Wyatt shook his head. "I'll be damned!"

"What is it?" Mattie asked, frowning at the envelope.

"It appears Dandi was the daughter of a woman named Belle LeTrouveau. Dandi didn't take her daddy's name because there was no legal marriage. He was a young fella who visited New Orleans some years ago . . ."

"Anyone familiar?" Bat asked.

"Her father's name was Pierce. Marshal doesn't know his first name, except the initial 'A.'"

Bat stared at him. "'A' as in Abel? As in Abel Pierce?"

Wyatt nodded thoughtfully. "Seems too big a coincidence to be anyone else." He folded the letter and put it in his shirt pocket. "Pierce left yesterday on the train for Points South. He's going west, taking the train far as Medicine Lodge. He'll ride south, after that, I expect . . . I might be able to catch him in Medicine Lodge."

"Oh, Wyatt!" Mattie shook her head. "The girl is gone—and whoever did it is long gone from around here. Now it's a shame, what happened, and I'm sorry for her but it's a fool's errand to chase it any more. Stay here!"

"I've got to know—if I confront Pierce with this, he may feel he's got to tell me the whole truth . . ."

"But that killing happened before you had this job—that was a different agency. And who will pay you for this?"

"If I can solve it, I will bill the city for solving a murder. If they don't want to pay, I don't much care." He thought of Sarah. He thought of Urilla. "I've just got to know . . ."

An hour later, after a quick meal and quicker packing, Wyatt was at the ticket window in the train station, buying passage to Medicine Lodge for himself and paying a freighting fee for his horse. The noon train, which had been forty-five minutes delayed, was about to leave, but there was just time to get the horse aboard a stock car.

He didn't notice the man watching him from the shadows at the back of the train station. The man was sitting on a bench in a corner, between a grandfather clock and the wall, smoking a pipe, and you'd have to peer into that corner to see him clearly.

* * *

Some hours later, the same Johann Burke was cantering his horse down a half-overgrown dirt road winding through the low hills of Southern Kansas, looking for the trail to what was left of the town of Ghost Corners. You wouldn't see the trail if you weren't looking sharp for it. Could he have ridden past it?

He reined in his horse, listening. Yes—he could hear a horse coming up the road behind him.

It was a region marked with stony outcroppings and this late in the day it was still warm here, with the September sun bouncing off the granite, sparkling the veins of quartz. Burke didn't care for people riding up behind him, but he was grateful for an excuse to pull his horse into the shade of a copse of cottonwoods. He dismounted under cover of the brush and, drawing his pistol, moved to where he could watch the road. Could be that it was just another traveler coming, with no thought of Johann Burke.

But it could be one of the Earp brothers, or Bat Masterson. They might've guessed what was coming, and they were said to be ridiculously loyal to Wyatt Earp.

Instead, he saw, it was that gilded lump, Swinnington, inexpertly riding a mule; bobbing about in his saddle, wiping his forehead and gawping at the hills.

Burke slipped through the brush, and stepped into view. "Swinnington!"

Startled, the portly swindler's mount reared, nearly throwing him. "Whoa you cretinous, foul-smelling mule!" he shouted—which only made the animal more jumpy.

Burke stepped into the trail and caught the mule's reins. "Take it easy, there, easy. That's it . . . Swinnington, what are you doing here?"

Swinnington removed his derby, which had developed a flapped hole in the crown like the top of a half-opened tin can, and wiped his glistening forehead with his forearm. "Mr. Burke, I've been looking for you. You said to watch Wyatt Earp. I heard Smith say Earp'd be taking a train out of town, so I waited over there at the station, biding my time—"

"Get to the point. Where's he gone?"

"Medicine Lodge! He's trying to overtake Abel Pierce. He's sent a telegram ahead asking the Sheriff to stop Pierce—I got the telegraph operator to tell me. Don't know if they'll hold him in Medicine Lodge, Mr. Pierce being a well-regarded gentleman, more well regarded the farther south you go, as I understand it, but—"

"So Earp took a train south, did he? When?"

"Earlier today. The only train. Have you anything to drink, Mr. Burke? I have only a canteen of water. Just . . . water. It has been a trying journey in the heat. My hat fell off and this idiot beast trampled it into the dust. I was just about to turn back, thinking I could not overtake you. When I came up here before it was with a large party, before the Indian trouble—"

"Yes, yes, here's a pint of whiskey, help yourself."

"You're a saint, sir."

Burke snorted. This Swinnington rattled away, saying things without a thought for their meaning.

So Earp was going to Medicine Lodge? A railroad car—that could make for difficulties.

There would be witnesses on a train. And Burke had a bad feeling about calling Earp out. He'd rather not take a chance like that. Then too, Earp was now Assistant Town Marshal—shoot a lawman in the back and there'd be a real investigation. Witnesses might be located. He couldn't kill them all.

He knew of some other folks, though, who had little to lose by killing young mister Earp. And Ghost Corners, where they liked to meet, was just up west in these hills . . .

"Now as to the payment you promised me, Mr. Burke," Swinnington was saying. "That would be, ah, four hundred dollars in gold."

"I promised you a hundred, you lying sack of shit," Burke said absently, his mind on the train to Medicine Lodge.

"Oh but this arduous journey I've made, sir—well, two hundred-fifty will fill the bill, I believe—"

Burke looked at Swinnington. Seeing that look, the swindler closed his mouth, and swallowed.

"Or . . . or, Mr. Burke . . . a hundred would be fine."

"In town, I might be inclined to give you the money," Burke said, his voice ominously soft. "But out here? I don't think so. And I can't just let you ride out because you might try to sell information to, say, Bat Masterson."

Swinnington's eyes widened. "I'd never do that, Mr. Burke!"

"You'd sell your mama for a bucket of beer, Swinnington. No. I don't want to pay you and I don't want to let you go. So let's see. What does that leave me? Besides—there's some creatures . . . Back home we have a bug called the Jerusalem Cricket—big as your thumb and the ugliest crawling thing you ever saw. Whenever I see one, I have to step on it. Can't bear it otherwise. You give me much the same feeling, Swinnington."

Swinnington tried to back his mule up, but Burke still had a grip on the reins.

"Now see here, sir!" Swinnington wailed. "If I just disappear, why, then, ah, people will . . . they will . . ."

"They will? Who will search for you, Mr. J. Mundale Swinnington? A bloodsucker like you, why, nobody'll miss you when you're gone. If anyone does notice, they'll say 'Good riddance'." He cocked his pistol, going on relentlessly, "I doubt if even *one single person* comes to look for you, Swinnington."

"No—!"

"I'm 'fraid so." He fired his pistol into Swinnington's belly, blowing him off his mule. The confidence man fell heavily onto his back, groaning at the impact, shot through the belly. "Nope, no one'll look for you at all, Swinnington. Kinda pitiful, that is." Burke felt a little pity too, looking at Swinnington writhing on his back in the dirt—like a half-crushed bug. Anyway he felt something close enough to pity to use up another perfectly good bullet, finishing Swinnington off, when he could have saved one by leaving him there to die slowly.

Then he went through the dead man's pockets, taking the watch and the eighteen dollars he found.

He took the mule too. He'd sell it, somewhere along the line. No reason to let a perfectly good mule just wander off.

* * *

Wyatt slept badly on the train, waking jumpily every time the locomotive stopped for water or screeched its brakes on a downslope. Come morning, with the train still chugging onward, whistling now and then, he woke from a dream of Urilla and Dandi walking hand in hand beside a river of jet-black water, the two dead women coming slowly, very slowly toward him with sad smiles of greeting on their faces . . .

Glad the dream was fading, Wyatt rubbed his eyes, grimacing. The train was not as uncomfortable as a stagecoach or a wagon, but it was no featherbed, either.

There were a few other people in the car: an elderly woman gazing forlornly out the window across the aisle from him; a swarthy, lank-haired plainsman snoring in the rear; a couple of young women leaning on one another, dozing, toward the front. Both women had worn their flowered hats all night and both hats were now tilted wildly askew.

He held his new watch up to the gray light coming through the window, and sleepily puzzled over why it said two-fifteen, when it was clearly dawn. He realized he'd forgotten to wind it.

Winding the watch, he looked at the sun rising over the rolling plain, its rays returning color to the stands of oaks and cottonwoods, patches of sere corn in farmland, and judged it to be about seven-thirty in the morning.

The locomotive's whistle gave out a shriek, and this time it kept whistling, sounding almost frantic. Again and again it screeched—then the train braked, the cars slamming their couplings together with the suddenness of it, and Wyatt had to grab the seat in front of him to keep from being slammed himself. He almost lost his grip on his watch.

The locomotive stuttered jerkily to a halt, hissing steam that was caught up by a breeze sweeping from the south so it dewed the windows. Startled awake, the other people in the car were asking one another in frightened tones what was afoot.

There was no station here. This was a stop of some urgency, unscheduled. Wyatt put his watch away, got up and drew his pistol, keeping it low so as not to needlessly alarm anyone. He started for the front of the train.

"There's a feller with a gun up there!" the plainsman shouted. At first Wyatt thought the man meant him, and he turned to tell him that he was a Deputy, then he saw the plainsman pointing through the window on the right side. "Now there's two more . . . coming from a whole 'nother direction. Why, they're sewing us up from all sides!"

"It could be Jesse James!" one of the young women said, excitedly, pressing a hand to her bosom, the other hand straightening her hat. "He robs trains whenever he feels like it! He just . . . takes 'em!"

It wasn't likely to be the James Gang, Wyatt figured. They were too well informed to rob this train. As far as Wyatt knew, the train carried nothing valuable. Either he was misinformed or the robbers were. There were scarcely any passengers to rob, and none likely to carry much cash.

But then, he thought, stepping through the door to the iron walk over the coupling, a stupid mistake wasn't unknown amongst outlaws. As he'd tried to tell Henry, it was not usually a profession chosen by smart men. Wyatt had only flirted with outlawry when drunk. And drunk was the same as stupid.

Wyatt stepped down onto the cinders of the railroad bed, looking right and left, seeing no one.

Leaning to look toward the front of the train, past the locomotive, he saw someone had dragged a slender felled tree across the tracks. Not a big tree trunk but it might've been enough to derail the locomotive. Wyatt stepped out of the train for a better view of the front, thinking whoever had put the blockade up was still there . . .

"Hey—horse killer!" The shout came from behind him and Wyatt knew it'd be too late as he spun and brought his gun up to find a target.

He had just time to see Dunc Blackburn, forty feet away, grinning past the rifle he'd nestled into his shoulder, aiming at Wyatt's head—before Blackburn went spinning to one side, spraying blood from the left side of his chest, shot by someone hidden between the train cars.

Who was doing the shooting? The plainsman?

Blackburn fell, gurgling, without having fired a shot—and Blackburn's man, Hound Farraday, jumped down behind the fallen outlaw, coming off a coach. He'd been on the train searching for Wyatt.

"Dunc!" Hound shouted, firing wildly at Wyatt with his dragoon.

Hound missed. Wyatt snapped off two shots. But rattled by nearly getting his head shot off, Wyatt missed his aim. One of his shots chunked into Hound's right shoulder. Hound swayed, grimacing with pain, but didn't fall, his gun leveling at Wyatt—another pair of shots came from the unseen gunman between the railroad cars, then, the first catching Hound in the side of the neck and the second punching through his left temple.

Hound staggered to the right for a few steps, as if for a square dance, and then fell in a heap, dead before he hit the ground.

Wyatt cocked his gun, stepping back from the train, looking for the other gunman. Whoever it was might think he was with the outlaws. "Who's there?" he called.

"Hello, Wyatt," said Ben Thompson, grinning as he came out from between the cars, smoking revolver in his hand. "How are you?" He glanced at Hound and holstered his pistol.

"Ben!" Wyatt blurted, momentarily confused. "You weren't on the train, were you?"

Ben chuckled. "I was not. Wyatt, it's like this . . ." He beckoned to Wyatt and the two of them went to examine the bodies of the dead men as Thompson spoke, keeping his voice down so the train's passengers wouldn't hear. ". . . I went to see my brother Billy, at a place where the owlhoots hole up. Ghost Corners . . ."

"That old trading post? I thought it was closed down."

"Not much left of it—just a few shanties, and something like a saloon. Dunc Blackburn and this fella Hound had been there before me—somewhat more animated than they are now. Billy tells me this Blackburn tried to hire him into his gang. He said Blackburn had to take care of a fella named Earp on a train, first, and they'd rob the train while they were at it, and then they'd hit a stage somewhere. Billy declined their generous offer, and told me about it. Not liking Dunc Blackburn, and owing you a favor, why, I followed them to see exactly what they were about, and here I am . . . My horse is over yonder."

Wyatt let out a long, unsteady breath. "I'm beholden to you. Either one would have shot me dead for sure, the way things were set. How'd they know where to find me, I wonder . . ."

"Story is, they were sent by a man named Joe Handle Burkett— or a name not far from that. I do not know the gentleman. I don't think I'd care to." He looked at the bodies. "Wyatt, I'd rather not take credit for this shooting—just say it was some wandering citizen, if you will. Or say you did it yourself, if you want."

Wyatt shook his head. "I don't care to have any more of that kind of reputation than necessary."

"I understand—sure as bloody hell, that I understand."

"You know, Ben, you committed no crime, in killing these men," Wyatt pointed out. "They were firing on a peace officer."

"I'd have to make a court appearance to back it up—and that, my friend, would be bloody inconvenient. I've got reasons to avoid the police in Medicine Lodge." He grinned, rubbing his chin. "Let's say it was done by a mysterious, public-spirited gunman. First now, what do you say, shall we move these stiffs into a freight car, put my horse aboard, and move that little bit of a tree? Then we'll be on our way and I'll ride the train with you to the next town."

Wyatt nodded, noticing the locomotive's engineers leaning out of the engine cab, trying to see past the smoke and steam, not wanting to come down until they were sure the shooting was done.

It was time to get these bodies out of the way, and report the 'mysterious gunman' to the engineers. He bent over and grabbed Blackburn's body by the collar, started dragging it toward a freight car he knew to be empty. Thompson dragged Hound by the ankles. They made a strange pair, walking backwards and dragging dead men, side by side.

"I'll be getting off in Medicine Lodge too," Wyatt remarked, as they dragged the bodies along. "I've got business there. Pressing business."

CHAPTER SEVENTEEN

It was deep into a hot afternoon when Wyatt parted with Ben Thompson, and headed for the Sheriff's office just off the main street of Medicine Lodge. To get to the office he had to weave carefully through a stream of cattle herded down the middle of the side street, the steers harried by whistling and chirruping mounted cowboys, on their way to the pen at the freight station. He was careful where he stepped.

Wyatt found the sheriff reading a dime novel at his desk: *Wild Bill, Slayer of Badmen.* Sheriff Purcheson was a balding, pot-bellied man in a rumpled brown suit, with side-whiskers that merged into his mustache, and a bulbous, broken-veined nose.

"I'm Earp, deputy from Wichita," Wyatt said.

"Are you?" said Purcheson, putting the dime novel aside with a sigh. "*Must* you be indeed? I reckon you must."

"There was a shooting on the train—or close to the train, when we made a stop. Two men shot dead."

"Speak up, all the caterwauling from them cattle is soaking up your voice. You say a shooting? What's the particulars?"

Wyatt gave him the story he and Ben Thompson had agreed on, saying "some gunman with a grudge" had shot the two outlaws down, probably someone from the train; the gunman didn't step forward afterward to claim credit, perhaps fearing retaliation from Blackburn's gang.

Wyatt didn't mention Thompson. The story wasn't exactly a lie—Thompson had gotten onto the train, later, after all. As it happened, shortly after arrival in Medicine Lodge, the plainsman on the train took credit for the killings; holding forth in a saloon, he described his gunfight with the outlaws in hair-raising detail, and afterwards was widely regarded as a dangerous *pistolero*.

"Why was you on the train?" the sheriff asked, rubbing his eyes.

"I sent you a cable saying why."

"Oh, so you did. You're looking for Abel Pierce. Well . . ." Purcheson shrugged. "Pierce was here. But I could not detain him without a clear-cut reason. And the fact is . . ." He bit off a plug of chaw, chewed it for awhile, staring into the distance, while Wyatt waited, quietly steaming, for the rest of the story. Finally Purcheson completed his sentence. ". . . and the fact is, Mr. Pierce left about an hour ago, maybe more. Rode out on his horse, with his traveling bags strapped behind him. I figure he's far from town, by now. Might've headed south, or east, I ain't sure."

"He 'left'? You mean you let him go," Wyatt said icily. He knew it wasn't politic to put it that way, but he couldn't keep it in.

"I had to let him go—" Purcheson said, spitting at the cuspidor and missing. "Damn! Now I got to get that squaw in here to clean that up. Now as to Pierce—he's an important . . . he's a citizen with rights and you had no . . . well, you didn't give me no clear and legalized reason to hold him."

"I cabled you that he was to be questioned about a murder. That's reason to hold a man for a day at least."

Purcheson worked on the rest of his plug, meditating his reply.

Wyatt didn't wait for it. He turned and walked out of the office. There was no use wasting more time with a bribed Sheriff.

At the train station Wyatt was told that no train had left in the last hour nor would one depart for another several hours, the engineers having to turn the bodies of the outlaws over to the coroner, and sign affidavits. The stationmaster said that Pierce had taken a big, black horse from the holding corral used by the train station. "I assume, sir, that it was his own horse."

Wyatt retrieved his own mount and set off southward, galloping as long as he felt his mount could take it. The Sheriff had seen Pierce leaving town on horseback—and south was likely the way he went.

* * *

The sun was dipping behind the poplars and pines, and the weather was cooling off considerably when Wyatt caught up with Abel Pierce. The cattle baron had stopped to water his horse at Chance Creek. When Wyatt rode up, the water was striped by the rouged shadows of the poplars lining the stream.

Pierce was just standing up from filling his canteen; even before seeing Wyatt he had a dour, put-upon look on his face, probably stewing over having to ride out early to avoid a mere Assistant Town Marshal.

Seeing Wyatt canter up, pistol in hand, Pierce dropped his hand to his side and said, "Boy, you have vexed me one time too many. You better have a damned good reason to point that pistol at me." His voice was guttural with barely-controlled anger.

"It's in case you get ambitious with your own weapon, Mr. Pierce." Wyatt turned his horse so he could keep his gun leveled at Pierce as he dismounted. "Drop your gun belt and move away from it. Sit on that little rock over there, and we'll have a talk. I have a letter to show you . . ."

* * *

"It was long ago," Pierce was saying," when I was young. Belle LeTrouveau was a little slip of a girl, not much more than eighteen . . . I fell for her hard, first time I saw her, in Baton Rouge . . ." He broke off, again squinting at the letter from the U.S. Marshal in Louisiana. "It don't say much about her. But see here, boy—I don't see what you're followin' me for. How is this the law's business?" He tilted his head back, giving Wyatt his best imitation of a judge looking down at him from the bench.

Wyatt felt it was best to holster his gun, for the moment, so that Pierce would feel he was talking freely and keep on. But he kept his hand on the holster, in easy reach of the gun butt. "Mr. Pierce, I expect you know the girl who was killed in Wichita was Belle LeTrouveau's daughter. I can prove you were there, in the building, the night Dandi was killed. I have a witness." Mostly he was bluffing, since Henry had left town. "Too much of a coincidence, your being her father, you seeing her that night, then she turns up dead. Maybe you took her for a whore, since she was in a whorehouse. And you didn't want a whore around calling you daddy."

"You're accusing me of her murder? You got no real proof of that."

"If I poke around a bit more . . . it's at least enough to get it in front of a jury. Could be they'd acquit you. But you wouldn't like sitting in front of that jury. If you've got another story, better tell me now."

Pierce looked at the letter, then at the stream. He seemed on the fence about whether to talk. Finally he turned fiercely to Wyatt, firing the words like bullets from a Gatling gun: "I'm too damned big a man to scare that way! I'm a big, wide man you couldn't ride across in twenty days!" He stood, and commenced pacing up and down, crumpling the letter in his fist, his voice getting shriller, his face redder. "Why if you was to say Pierce Country instead of Texas, people'd know you meant Texas! I'm as much as I want to be and that's ten times more than any other man! I am kin to John Alden and President Franklin Pierce! I am a laird of the land! *Damn* your impertinence!" His eyes glittered, the pupils sharpened to points.

The hint of madness in those eyes reminded Wyatt he did have one more card to draw. Something Dudley had mentioned. "Mr. Pierce . . . maybe you'd like to take a moment and think about it. Maybe—say a prayer."

The cattle baron stopped pacing and blinked at Wyatt in angry confusion. "A prayer!"

"Or—ask advice. Some folks like to ask advice of those who've gone on before . . ."

Pierce's eyes went distant, glassy. His lips moved without sound. It seemed to Wyatt that he was saying, *Uncle Fergus . . .*

"Maybe . . . Maybe I will take a turn up the stream, and think a bit . . ." Pierce allowed.

Wyatt reached out and gently took the letter back from Pierce, nodding affably. "You go ahead, sir," Wyatt said, careful to sound respectful. It seemed smart, just now. "I'll watch your horse for you. Just stay where I can see you, if you please."

Pierce snorted. "If I please! Or even if I don't!" He stuck his hands in his trouser pockets and went stalking up the bank of the stream, muttering.

Asking advice, Wyatt figured, of Uncle Fergus.

* * *

Time passed. The creek slipped endlessly by, chuckling at human vanity. Somewhere overhead, a red-tailed hawk keened to its mate that *here, here* is meat to be had; a fat ground squirrel, a mouse. The sun eased itself a little lower yet . . .

Maybe half an hour went by, before Pierce returned. He sat on the little boulder on the edge of the creek; Wyatt sat on a tussock of earth and grass nearby. Wyatt's gun was not pointed at Pierce but it was under his hand, laid flat across his right knee, and it'd be but the work of a split second to take aim and fire. Though Pierce had settled down to talk, appearing ready to relieve his mind, Wyatt didn't trust him.

"Where do you want me to start, Deputy?" Pierced asked at length.

"How about all the way back. Right at the beginning . . . With Belle LeTrouveau." Wyatt reasoned that if Pierce got involved in his story, he'd have less chance to work up a lie.

"From the beginning?" After a long moment, Pierce sighed, and nodded, and went on, "Well, Belle LeTrouveau, she was a respectable girl, but her family had died on her . . . She had no money left. She thought a man might save her. A good marriage . . ."

He paused, and Wyatt thought of Mattie. Her family had died on her too. There was all too often no one there to help when a woman lost her family. Maybe Mattie had fallen too quickly into prostitution. Pierce's Belle had tried something a little better—anyhow, a "huckleberry above a persimmon better", as Wyatt's mother would say.

Pierce licked his lips, and continued, "Belle was down to what I suppose was her last two dollars. She went to a spring dance—I expect she was there to angle for a husband. Now I was in Baton Rouge on my way to New Orleans, with a friend of mine from Louisiana, a party-loving body who'd been working the cattle with me. I was just a poor drover, but I'd had a stroke of luck—I won me five hundred dollars in one night in a hot poker game. Nearly got shot out of that game, but I got away with my skin and the pot. I bought myself a nice suit, and went to the dance. Then I met Belle . . . and like as not she danced with me the first time just to be on display out on that dance floor. Little thing, she was, but the eye took to her and she knew it. Her interest perked up some when

I flashed my roll of bills, sort of by accident, mentioning I was staying at the Crystal Hotel. That was the best hotel in town, a pricey place. In fact I had rented no room there—but I figured I could get one. I let on like I was . . . oh, like I was the man I am now. A man of property. I always said, if you believed it enough, and you fought for it, you got there. That's what my . . . what an uncle of mine told me. You got any liquor in that saddlebag, boy?"

"No sir, I don't. So she figured you were a high roller before you were one?"

"She did. I confess I deceived her. But she liked me, I could tell, so I calculated to clear it up later once we were good and truly tangled up. I took her with me to New Orleans—but she wouldn't share a bed with me, not at first. She said we could be 'genteel traveling companions, like friends in the philosophy of Plato'." He chuckled at the memory. "She let me kiss her once or twice, nothing more. We got to New Orleans and I took her any place she wanted to go to. I bought her a seventy-five dollar necklace—worth a deal more than that too, but I bought it from a man who'd lifted it somewhere himself—and I wined and dined her, but she made fun of me, saying I'd come into riches knowing nothing of cultured things. Seems my cultivation in Rhode Island was sparse. Still, she seemed to like me, so it happened that the night I was about to run out of money she had a glass of champagne too many and she let me into her room . . . And she gave herself to me." Pierce smiled unhappily, his eyes unfocused. "The next day . . ." He paused to swallow, to clear his throat. A moistness gleamed in his eyes. ". . . the next day she wasn't feeling so good and asked me what my intentions was. I had to admit I was just a poor cowboy, and was now broke. I expect she had been stringing me along to be a husband, waiting for me to come out with the question. I come out with it right then but she just laughed in my face. Why, a lady like her couldn't hook up with me, a man who stares at the rumps of steers all day, nothing but holes in his pockets. She would soon enough meet a rich man, she said—and in the meantime she had an offer to work in a hotel of class, in New Orleans, supervising the housekeeping.

"I could not persuade her to go with me. I was embittered too, with her laughing at me. So I walked out and took the first coach to Texas. Then I got caught up in the war. I heard no more of her, till after the war I chanced to be in New Orleans. I heard that the hotel she'd worked for had been swallowed up in the Reconstruction by some carpetbagger, and a man who'd worked with her said she'd been put on the street. So now Belle was living with a daughter somewhere, and had taken to drinking. She was taking in laundry and such. I might've had an uneasy feeling about that daughter. The age was right. But I remembered Belle laughing at me when I asked for her hand. Still and all . . . sometimes I've wished . . ." He shook his head. "What it comes to is, I didn't look her up. I went back to Texas . . . and heard no more of her till that night in Wichita."

"When you met Dandi," Wyatt prompted.

"That's when I met Dandi," Pierce agreed, his voice soft. "The only time . . . Now, I like to bed a certain kind of woman, and the younger the better. Why, as young as thirteen's not too green for me. Johann described what I liked to Bessie Earp—he used the name Johnny Brown. So he makes the appointment and I go to that place in Delano where she has her women working—I guess your brother James can't have his little bit of a casino on the respectable side of the river if she works her girls up there—"

Wyatt shifted uncomfortably at all this talk of his brother's connection to whoring. He suspected that Pierce was dwelling on it to encourage that discomfort. Maybe to send a message: *You're no better than me, Earp.* If Pierce heard about the gunboats, he'd crow over that too.

"—Anyhow, Johann Burke and I went there to have us some girls. Ol' Johann—why, to tell you the truth, he has started to give me the skeeries. Some as said he's a 'raw-head-and-bloody-bones' monster, and I laughed at it, for he's a handy man to have, but he takes too easily to killing. Enjoys it. Me, I do it when it's got to be done, but . . ."

Pierce fell silent, for a few moments, perhaps sensing he was in danger of saying too much. Staring into the darkening creek, he broke a poplar twig from a fallen branch, began to shred the twig into small pieces, as he went on. "Anyhow, I was in your sister-in-law's place waiting for a girl, and in comes Dandi. She seemed reluctant to get to it, nor was she dressed like a whore. I was staring at her, seeing a ghost: the eyes were different, but most ways she's the spitting image of her mother. Johann is there with me and he says 'Seems like she's got you smitten right off, Mr. Pierce.' And the girl's eyes get wide and she says, 'Then it is so—you are Mr. Abel Pierce!' I blurt out yes, I am, and she seems like she can't make up her mind to speak. Finally she tells me that I'm her . . ." He broke off again, clearing his throat to hide the hoarseness of emotion. ". . . her papa. She reaches into one of those little bags a woman wears on a string around her wrist, pulls out a rolled up photograph of me and her mother together . . . I thought I'd jump through the ceiling. 'Papa!' she says again. Insisting, do y'see. 'It's me—I'm your daughter!' She goes on with a speech about how she never thought to see me in such a place, but she would not judge me because here she was herself. Perhaps, she said, I was only there to find her. She had only just commenced to work here—a man had bribed a lady in Louisiana for her, and taken her to Kansas City, she says, and then she run off to Wichita, because some cowboy in Kansas City—that was Choppy Blanchard, whom I fired first chance—Choppy had told her he worked for Abel Pierce. And Abel Pierce, he tells her, is in Wichita. So she goes with Bessie Earp, and comes looking for me. A great weeping speech she made about it. She insisted she had done no whoring but she had to come here only because someone said Mr. Pierce was here. I could see she didn't want to be in that whorehouse." Pierce had to break off to keep from tears himself. He didn't entirely succeed.

Wyatt waited. Cattails waved in the increasing breeze; frogs commenced to call out.

At last Pierce wiped his eyes, and went on, "Deputy, I was filled with horror. I had suspected that girl of Belle's was mine and I had not gone to look into the matter and—now she was in a brothel, and housekeeper or not—how long before she became a whore? I suppose I should have taken her out of there. Maybe if I'd had time to think about it, I would have. I reckon so. But right then I says, 'No, girl, maybe you're the daughter of a woman I once took to bed, but she mocked me, and there could have been other men, there's no telling I'm your father—and I deny you, and will have none of you!' Yet I know she was my daughter—I could see it in her. She has my mother's eyes. And you just know your kin . . . I did not believe she was not a prostitute in that place—and it tortured me to know my daughter was a whore. Later, I heard that it was true, she was but a housekeeper . . ." He let out a long, slow breath that whistled softly as it came.

"There's more, I believe," Wyatt prompted, gently as he could manage. His hand still on the gun.

Pierce scratched his chin. "Believe it or not, Johann Burke suggests, right then and there, that I could still bed Dandi anyway—I nearly hit him, but it would've been worth my life to do that, so I just turn and walk out. She's back there weeping, and weeping. I can still hear it . . ." He threw the twig in the creek, watched it float downstream, his eyes glistening. Then he took another deep breath and went on, "So Burke and I go outside—then Burke, who'd been drinking absinthe, an indulgence of his, he says he's going back in, to have a run at one of the other girls, and I said do whatever you damned please. I couldn't quite bring myself to leave yet—I'm just standing shufflin' my feet outside for a little while, in that dirt track out behind the place. Maybe thinking I ought to go in for her, after all. I'm not sure how long I was out there—just pondering and pondering, feeling lost. Standing in the smell of the outhouse and feeling like I was smelling my own soul. Finally I make up my mind. 'Maybe I *can* do something for her. I don't want folks to know my kin's a whore, or about to be a whore—but I can send her to a finishing school, far away somewhere. Get her out of that life. Maybe someday she can come and see me and I'll feel all right about it . . .' Then Burke comes out and says, 'Mr. Pierce, that girl killed herself. She's twisted the sheets up and hung herself. I took her down but she's beyond saving.' Then . . ."

He had to stop and clear his throat again, swallowing hard. He knuckled at his eyes.

Wyatt felt a jarring, unwelcome sympathy for Pierce, then. He thought of Urilla—Pierce surely blamed himself . . .

But Pierce went on, with an angry abruptness, "Then I figure that what I'd said, it made her hate herself and despair. I had driven her to suicide. Well, I thought maybe she's still alive, maybe Burke is wrong. So I go back in and there she is, on the floor, with that twisty sheet by her— I shake her, and I call to her, and I slap her cheek—" He mimed all this for Wyatt as he said it. "But she was dead. Then I hear people coming and I rush out of there. I yell for Johann to come on. I didn't want the . . . the association."

"You didn't tell anyone," Wyatt said, shaking his head in disgust, "that you thought it was suicide—even when a man was accused of her murder?"

"I was ashamed of the whole thing—it's one thing being in a whorehouse with a bunch of range-dirty drovers and another if it's talked about in the newspaper. We managed to keep some things out of the paper, but there's only so many holes you can stop up in a leaky barrel. I've been thinking of running for office, back in Texas. And then her being my daughter—"

"So you made arrangements with Smith. You let them kill Montaigne and you killed Plug Johnson to keep him quiet."

Pierce shot him a defiant glare, his natural arrogance rising up in him again. "They were both no-account scum! You know that! One doomed to die in the shavings on the floor of a saloon—and the other a crook bound to be lynched!"

Wyatt looked Pierce in the eyes—eyes going dark and hollow in the dusk. "And you tried to get me killed, Mr. Pierce—me and Henry McCarty. All because you didn't want people to talk about you."

Pierce scowled—and shrugged it off. "Burke was only supposed to scare you."

"He sent Blackburn to kill me, on the train to Medicine Lodge. That wasn't just a scare either. You know about that, Mr. Pierce?"

"Not . . . well . . ." Pierce smirked, his smile twisty. "You went too far when you arrested me in Wichita." His confidence was returning—putting Wyatt in his place made Pierce feel more like himself. ". . . Dunc Blackburn, was it? I kind of thought Burke was going to do it himself." His fists balled on his knees as he turned to Wyatt, lowering his head like a bull. "But I'm telling you, boy—don't think I'll admit any such thing if it comes to court! I'll say you're makin' it all up. I'll get the best damn attorney in Kansas! You won't touch me for any of that!"

The two men glowered at one another. Then a worried, thoughtful look came over Pierce. "You said—what did you say about the suicide?"

"I said, you *thought* it was a suicide, Mr. Pierce. Burke wanted you to think so. I expect he told himself the girl would make problems for you. But that was just an excuse to do what he wanted to do anyway. Why do you think the coroner went with murder and not suicide? Because the sheet was pulled down? No sir. The coroner looked at her throat, and saw the marks there—the marks of a man's fingers, Mr. Pierce. Your daughter was murdered. Strangled by Johann Burke—that's how I figure it. Because she was alive when you left her. And then Burke went back in, and in a minute or two she was dead. And if it wasn't suicide . . . then your own man killed her."

"No." Burke shook his head violently. "That's . . . *no!*"

Wyatt leaned toward Pierce and went on earnestly and implacably. "He pawed her, and strangled her, Mr. Pierce. I expect he likes killing. You can see it in the man. And you *know* it's so—when you were talking about how he likes killing, just a moment ago, it was in your mind that maybe he'd done it. It seems to me you already knew."

And Wyatt could see it in Abel Pierce's eyes: he knew the truth now. Pierce had suspected all along. But Burke worked for him and Pierce didn't want to believe it. Because that was something even worse than believing your daughter had killed herself: knowing that your own hired killer had strangled her . . . just for the hateful joy of it.

They were silent for awhile. The shadows of the poplars reached farther and farther, to be joined by other shadows, of shrubs and outcroppings and clouds, all merging with the gathering evening. Crows sent derisive cries from the treetops as the wind picked up, making the poplars switch about. Midges rose in a cloud from the reeds, and mosquitoes hummed over to investigate the two men . . .

Finally, anger simmering in his voice, Pierce said, "I expect it's so." He swatted at a mosquito. "Damn these gallnippers. Yes I reckon so—Burke seemed crazy-fascinated with Dandi, the moment he saw her. Maybe there's a sickness in him." He swallowed, and the next words were growled: "God *damn* him." He spat into the creek. "But Earp—I had nothing to do with what he done. I didn't know."

Wyatt looked hard at Pierce and after a moment he nodded. "I believe you. But don't you think Burke should pay for killing your daughter? He should hang for it. You could testify against him."

Pierce shook his head. "I don't want to testify—bring all this out in public. That business with Plug Johnson, I can see now that was poor judgment. I shouldn't have done it. All that could come out, in court, was I to testify against Burke. But I'll tell you what, Deputy. I'll tell you where Johann Burke is likely to be, now that you know for sure he's the one. If—*if* you give me your word on two things."

"Which two things, Mr. Pierce?"

"Just that you'll do your best to see to it he dies at your hands. I don't want him talking to a judge. And second . . . after it's done, you don't tell anyone about any of this. If you swear to that, I'll forget about your Henry McCarty, and I'll tell you where you can likely find Burke."

Wyatt didn't much like it. Making a deal with Pierce seemed wrong—Pierce had murdered Plug Johnson. And he'd let Smith arrange Montaigne's murder. Maybe even paid for it to be done. But it was true: with Pierce denying everything, no one would believe Wyatt's theory about why Pierce had shot Johnson. The letter he had didn't prove for sure that Pierce was Dandi's father. It was hearsay. The great Shanghai Pierce could claim it was another A. Pierce—it was a common name. Pierce would say he'd shot Johnson in self-defense and he'd be believed. Smith would back him up.

Wyatt judged that he could bear to let Pierce go. But not Burke.

Johann Burke had to have killed others the way he'd killed Dandi. It'd come too naturally to him. Burke would go on killing. And Wyatt had promised to avenge Sanchez.

Still, to hunt Burke down the way Pierce wanted . . . Even up in the Black Hills, Wyatt had hoped to get the jump on Burke and disarm him.

"It doesn't sit well with me," Wyatt said, musing aloud about it, "to hunt a man just for the purpose of killing him. If I have to kill him when he resists arrest, that's different."

"You make up your mind to do it this time, and I'll give Burke to you. Now you know for sure he killed her—you know he deserves to be shot dead, like a mouth-foamin' dog. And you know he won't let you arrest him. I can tell you where to find him but I'll need your word you'll keep silent, after. Is your word good, Earp?"

"It is. And I give it to you—but there's one condition. I've got to tell Masterson. He was there with me that night when we first looked at her body. He'll keep quiet. Bat Masterson can be trusted."

Pierce peered like a crystal gazer into the stream. Then he nodded.

"You just missed me in Medicine Lodge, Deputy—Sheriff Purcheson told me about your telegram. Then I saw you get off that train. I saw to it you didn't see me—and I wired Burke about where you were. I figure he's on the way to Medicine Lodge. And he'll look for you on the trail you took to get here . . ."

* * *

Wyatt and Pierce didn't even say goodbye. Abel Pierce simply rode south, and Wyatt headed north.

It was as dark as murder out now, with the only light from a sliver of moon and a clutch of stars half hidden by thickening clouds. Wyatt's horse seemed confident of the road, but Wyatt wasn't—he wasn't sure he was on the right road, at all.

There was no turning back. He was going to hunt Burke down and kill him. No judge, no jury. Just kill him. And leave his body for the vultures.

He knew he'd crossed a line, inside himself, deciding to do it that way. He knew that having crossed that line, he would be able to do it again some day.

Thinking about that, he shivered, and rode into the night.

* * *

About midnight Wyatt was able to see the lights of town reflected on the clouds at the horizon. Just a flicker, but it was unmistakable. He decided he'd rather face Burke in the daylight, after a rest. A cold wind was blowing from that direction, like an outrider for winter, and Wyatt hadn't brought along a heavy coat.

It was tempting to ride into Medicine Lodge, check into a hotel room—but Sheriff Purcheson would keep track of travelers, and he couldn't be trusted. Come morning, he might well tell Burke that Wyatt was in town, and where he was staying. Right now, Wyatt figured, the gunman was probably still somewhere well North of town.

On the edge of the Gyp hills, Wyatt found the thread of an antelope trail, barely visible in the starlight. He followed it off the road into an area of crumbling rock and thorny scrub. The ground rose to a modest hillside and there, almost a quarter mile off the road, he camped near a spring that was just a trickle on the rocks, icicles in the shadowy parts. He chose a small flattened patch of ground about thirty feet above the trail.

Wyatt staked his horse behind a granite outcropping, fed and watered the sorrel, then made a fire of scrub oak. After a scanty supper of jerky and spring water, he sat with his back against a mossy rock, watching the flames snap when the wind wormed close. He was uncomfortable, sitting there with his gun belt on, so he took it off and set it on a low rock nearby, next to the sawed-off shotgun John Slaughter had given him as a gift.

The fire was too far off the trail to see, wasn't it? But maybe not. Maybe he ought to put that fire out . . . Lord he was tired . . .

Weariness washed over him and carried him into a fitful sleep shot through with red, fragmentary dreams.

Wyatt woke at dawn to the breath of a horse in his face.

My horse pulled up its stake and wondered over here, he guessed sleepily, sitting up.

But it wasn't his horse. This was a big gray horse, with jet black eyes. Johann Burke was smiling down at him from the saddle. He looked like a living corpse, sitting up there, with his face gray-blue in the early light.

But it was Wyatt who was closer to death. Burke had his pistol pointed down at Wyatt's heart.

"That's three times, boy. Twice I catch you with your back to me, and now I catch you sleeping. Your hands are in clear sight—no guns in reach. You see? No one's that lucky three times in a row—your luck's run out. It stands to reason that if a man don't watch his back, he's gonna die. And you keep forgetting to be watchful. Now you're going to eat breakfast in Hell."

Wyatt tried to think of some way to keep Burke talking. "You kill the girl for that *mafie* bunch in Kansas City? Or for fun?"

Burke shrugged. "I did get the word to look for her. I was thinking of bringing her back to them. But she bit my hand, when I took hold of her, so I had to make her sorry . . . Should have taken her alive, though. They wanted her alive. Good money gone to waste."

"How'd you find me out here?" Wyatt asked. Hoping he didn't sound as desperate as he felt. Hoping Burke couldn't hear his heart pounding—it seemed to him the sound was echoing across the hills.

"Kind a got lucky myself, boy—lucky you're a fool!" Burke said, grinning. "Rode all night, to catch up with you. Would've passed you this mornin' if it weren't for that smoke. Just a little. Just enough. Now stand up."

Wyatt looked at the fire. It had burned down to embers but it was still smoking. He saw that his weapons were where he'd left them—but he'd never reach them before Burke shot him dead. There was a box of shotgun shells, near his left foot, at the base of the rock, but they were of no use to him.

"I said stand up," Burke repeated, backing his horse up a step.

Wyatt stood, letting the blanket drop away.

"Was me," Burke said, "I'd never, ever sleep out in the open like this with an enemy within traveling distance, and not have my gun under my hand. You've got a lot to learn, boy. Too bad you won't have the chance." His thin smile widened, then, and he cocked his gun.

"Pierce knows you killed the girl. I told him so," Wyatt said, quickly. Both he and Burke knew he was stalling—but he could think of nothing else to do. He would make a dive for that shotgun. Burke wouldn't miss, with that pistol, up so close—but maybe he'd be able to shoot Burke with the shotgun as he was dying himself. That'd be some consolation.

Burke's face went blank, but it was a blankness that covered a cold, killing fury. "You told him that? You're a dirty sneaking little back-climbing son of a bitch." Burke's head cocked to one side as something seemed to occur to him. "You know, with your back to that rock . . . why . . ." He chuckled. "This horse is pretty well trained. He's a fightin' horse. A Comanche warrior taught him this trick . . . now watch this . . . watch as he kicks your face through the back of your head . . ."

Wyatt looked at the big gray horse, the breath steaming from its twitchy muzzle, and seemed to see in its black eyes that it'd been brutalized into obedience; into thinly bridled violence.

Burke shouted "Hy-*yah!*" and the horse reared up, slashing out with its forelegs—

—Wyatt kicked very deliberately at the ground near his weapons—

—as the horse gave out a sound that was more shriek than whinny, striking at Wyatt with its fore hooves. He ducked back, a shod hoof grazing his right cheek, cutting the side of his face under the temple; the hoof, coming back down, struck sparks from the stone behind him, and the other hoof's fetlock glancingly struck his left shoulder, making him suck in his breath with pain. The horse reared back for a killing blow . . . as Burke laughed and hooted.

Then three of the shotgun shells that Wyatt had purposely kicked into the embers went off, almost at once: three miniature thunderclaps just to the horse's right, peppering its legs with shot and coal.

The detonations of the shotgun shells terrified the appaloosa. The horse fishtailed to get clear of the blasts, its whole body writhing in fear and pain, bucking away from Wyatt, Burke clinging to the pommel like a rodeo rider, cursing. The gunman fired his revolver but couldn't aim from the back of a bucking horse and the round hissed past Wyatt's head as he swept up the sawed-off shotgun, double-cocking it in the same movement. Wyatt took a step to the left for a clearer shot and fired, from six feet away. Both barrels.

Burke's gun-hand vanished and the flesh on the right side of his face went with it, carried away by the double barrel of shot.

Burke screamed and lost his grip on the bucking horse, fell from the saddle. But his left foot was caught in the stirrup, and the horse—running from the shotgun discharge—twisted away from Wyatt, dragging Burke down the hill.

The whinnying horse dragged Johann Burke through patches of thorn and over craggy rocks and across spiky stumps of dead trees.

"Oh God in Heaven," Wyatt muttered, his stomach lurching. He managed to control the retching, as he set the shotgun down, and found his pistol. Cocking it, and setting his boots carefully on the slope, he started after Burke. It appeared the horse had dragged Burke a good ways . . .

But the trail of blood, torn flesh and ripped clothing ended about forty yards away. He was surprised to see Burke struggling upright, leaning on a boulder, standing on his right foot; on the limb that wasn't broken. The stirrup and saddle, pulled from the horse, were still attached to his shattered left leg. Burke's great gray horse was nowhere to be seen.

Burke had lost his six-shooter—he was gasping, whimpering. Coming closer Wyatt saw that Burke's body was torn by the dragging to expose the bone of his ribs and breastbone: shreds of skin mingled bloodily with shreds of clothing; his face was a ruin, his right arm ended in a bloody stump. Burke was wracked by long shudders, going from head to foot, again and again . . .

The young deputy shook his head, not sure what to do—and that's when what was left of Burke jerked a Colt's Pocket Pistol from inside his coat with his intact left hand, and brought it into play.

Wyatt fired his pistol, aiming for Burke's heart but the angle was awkward and the round caught Johann Burke high in the right side of his belly. Burke quivered back against the stone at the impact, yelling hoarsely: "No!" Wyatt cocked and fired again, his second bullet smashing into the gunfighter's left shoulder. Burke jerked and sobbed at the impact of the bullets, convulsively squeezing off a shot from the pocket pistol. His shot went in to the ground—and then the stubby gun slipped from his drooping fingers.

Seeming to collapse in on himself, Burke slid down the stone.

Wyatt went closer to the dying man, wanting to say something, and not at all sure what it was. But he was careful to kick the pocket pistol out of reach.

"Please," Burke said, his ruined mouth bubbling with blood. "Just . . . kill me. Kill me. Please . . ."

Wyatt took a deep breath.

Then he cocked his pistol—and he accommodated Johann Burke.

You should regret it, he'd always felt, when you had to kill a man. But the truth was, when he shot Burke dead it was as if the recoil from each shot was the gun just leaping for joy. To Hell with Johann Burke.

* * *

Wyatt spent the night in the best room he could find in Medicine Lodge. The next morning, after a light breakfast, he set off
on horseback for Wichita. He might've taken the train, but he felt
strange, within himself, and he wanted time to digest all that'd happened. Time to think, in quiet.

The cold wind had subsided, but the clouds moved too fast in
the sky, and it was still overcast, and chilly. He could smell mes-
quite and moldering leaves and something dead—a deer, or buffalo, probably, decaying out in the plains.

Along about noon, when he was wondering where to find water
and forage, his horse twitched its ears forward, lifting its muzzle in
a way that told Wyatt there were riders coming.

Ten minutes later, Bat Masterson and Virgil Earp came riding
around the bend, emerging from a screen of cottonwoods.

Virgil waved his hat, in that way he had, and Bat grinned as the
two men cantered up. The three riders reined in, their horses snorting curiously at one another.

"Ben Thompson sent a wire," Virgil said. "Suggested you might
need some watching over."

"You're late for that," Wyatt said. "But it came out well enough."

"You finished what you were about?" Virgil asked.

"I did," Wyatt said, in a way that hinted he didn't want to talk
about it any further. Virgil caught the hint, and just nodded.

"I told you he'd be riding, Virgil," Bat said. "Why, a sturdy
plainsman like Wyatt here would scorn the train."

"Still wish *I'd* taken a train," said Virgil. "Wyatt seems just fine
and I'm longing for a warm hotel room."

"Town's not so far back," Wyatt said. "There's good pasteboard
play there, I hear. Cattlemen in town wanting to throw away their
money on cards. You might do nicely."

"By God," Virgil said, "there's no reason to head back to Wichita
right quick. I believe I will act on your suggestion. Bat?"

"I'll ride on with Wyatt."

"Then be damned to you both—I'm for Medicine Lodge!" Virgil chuckled, clapping his hat on his head, and rode off at a good pace to the South.

Wyatt and Bat rode on toward Wichita in silence. At last Wyatt said, "Burke killed Dandi. Told Pierce she committed suicide. Pierce was covering up his shame at the whole thing. That's about it. Except . . . I made a deal with Pierce—gave him my word I'd kill Burke myself and speak of all this no more. I can't tell Leahy; I can't tell anyone. No one's to know about him and Dandi. And I said you could be trusted to keep quiet too."

Bat nodded. After a moment he said, "Burke's done for?"

"He's cold as a wagon wheel. And buried, more or less. He nearly did for me. But I had some luck."

Bat nodded again, squinting off into the Eastern distance. "But . . . isn't that Burke's horse?"

He pointed—Wyatt turned in his saddle to see the unmistakable horse, the color of storm clouds, running unsaddled along the top of a low ridge some distance to the East. It paused, and looked toward them, then shook its head fiercely and turned to gallop out of sight.

It was gone. But that sickly, murderous horse would continue wandering out there somewhere. Dandi would still be dead and Sanchez and Montaigne were still dead. And Urilla . . . Urilla was dead.

Right then he didn't feel much better, having killed Burke. He just felt like going home to Mattie.

* * *

"He said *what?*" Wyatt demanded, one chilly afternoon, at the smoky bar in James's place.

Dudley leered—he'd recently lost a front tooth and the gap showed black. "He said you was working out some kind of scallawaggin' deal with Marshal Meagher." He looked at his empty whiskey glass intently, and licked his lips.

Wyatt growled to himself and signaled to the bartender. Dudley's glass was refilled, he drank half of it down, wiped his mouth, and went on, "Marshal Smith said he heard you'd back Meagher for Town Marshal if he'd go easy on them whores your sister in law has and if he'd hire you and your brothers on for some cooshy job. Said Meagher was taking bribes and you was turning your back on them bribes and . . ."

"And when did he say this?" Wyatt asked, between clenched teeth.

"Why, an hour ago, in Red's place. He was just heading back to his office and—*Whuh oh.*"

This last, as Dudley watched Wyatt Earp stalk toward the door, his hands balled into fists.

Dudley chuckled. "Want to see this. Glad I stayed on in Wichita. Entertaining kinder town."

He and a few other no-accounts shuffled out the door to follow Wyatt down to Smith's office.

* * *

Wyatt knew he ought to hold back. He knew he ought to take a ride in the country and think it over. He might call Smith out in court, sue for slander. But this was just one button too many. Smith had jailed Montaigne, then allowed him to be killed; Smith had stood by while Plug Johnson was murdered and Smith had obstructed investigation into Dandi LeTrouveau's murder. Had ridden with that murderer Burke in his posse. He had cut Wyatt from the town police on a pretense, and now he'd slandered him, lying about Meagher and lying about the Earp brothers. He had gone just exactly one step too far—And thinking about it Wyatt felt a long-capped wellspring of chill fury bursting up, driving him unstoppably down the street.

Marshal Smith was stepping out of the jailhouse, just then, calling out to Carmody, who was heading off on some errand. Smith seemed to want to remind Carmody of something. Forgetting all about it when he saw Wyatt Earp striding toward him.

"What are you saying about my brothers?" Wyatt demanded. "What are you saying about me and Meagher? What's all this business about bribes and dirty deals, Smith?"

Carmody rushed up to them as Smith sputtered, "Why I— there's been talk, that's all I—now you just back off, boy, you just—"

That's all he got out before Wyatt cracked him on the jaw with a sharp right, making him reel back.

"Here now!" Carmody shouted, as amazed as he was angry, fumbling for his gun. Wyatt turned and drove a fist into Carmody's gut. The big deputy folded over and sat down, wheezing, his face mottled.

Smith was reaching for his gun but Wyatt slapped it away with a hard left backhand, snapping his right fist to catch Smith with an uppercut. Smith went over backwards, moaning, to slide down against the wall. He ended up sitting beside Carmody, his head wobbling.

The two men looked comical that way, sitting side by side, one with a wobbling head, the other gasping for breath like a landed fish, and the small crowd that had gathered behind Wyatt laughed and hooted.

Wyatt turned and looked at them. Saw that one of them wasn't laughing: a stout man with flaring mutton chops he knew to be on the town council. Wyatt knew then, as sure as winter follows autumn, he'd be fired. He shrugged and turned back to Smith.

"You say anything you want about my family," Wyatt told Smith, "except I require it be the truth." He turned and walked back the way he'd come.

* * *

Wyatt found Bat Masterson playing cards in James's, and sat down at the table, shaking his head at the dealer to indicate he didn't want into the game, which was itself a prodigy.

Bat looked at him, then folded his hand and nodded toward a small, quiet corner table. Wyatt nodded and they went silently over to the table, sidling through a pack of drunken cowboys to get there.

Bat turned a chair around backwards, sat leaning his elbows on it; Wyatt ordered them drinks and sat across from him.

Wyatt drank a glass of beer, occasioning lifted eyebrows from Bat, before he finally spoke. "I just beat the dickens out of Marshal Smith . . ." He looked mournfully down at his swollen knuckles.

Bat grunted. "You came out on top—but you don't look happy about it," he observed.

"I was starting to get some kind of steady life here. Give it a little time I might've been appointed U.S. Marshal. But I just heard that Smith was telling lies about me, saying I was corrupt and my brothers were getting special deals . . . And I thought about all the rest he did and . . ."

"It all came out at once."

Wyatt nodded. "It did. Can't take it back now. I'll be arrested— or fired."

"I think they'll decline to arrest you, in consideration of your record. But the job . . . You beat up a town marshall. That is frowned upon. You'll be fired."

Wyatt snorted. "One mistake after another. With Urilla. Then in Illinois . . ." He shook his head. He didn't want to talk about the gunboat and the drowned girl. "Nearly let Burke kill me, making mistakes. I *did* let him kill Sanchez—failed to stop the bastard, anyhow. Sanchez was a good man. Then this—should have kept my temper. Another damned mistake." Wyatt spun his empty beer glass on the table. It whirled—and fell over with a *clunk*.

Bat waited—but Wyatt said nothing else. He had been as open with his thoughts as he knew how to be.

At last Bat said, "If you don't make mistakes, you're not a real man."

Wyatt looked at him. "How's that?"

"Out there in the world, taking your chances like a man, you're going to make mistakes. Anybody lives so careful he doesn't make mistakes—that's not a man."

Wyatt thought about it. He took a long, slow breath. He decided that Bat was probably right. "Not sure I needed whoppers that big . . ."

"You want another beer?" Bat asked. When Wyatt shook his head, Bat leaned toward him with a smile. "How many times you wallop him?"

Wyatt shrugged. "Two or three. Him and Carmody. They were sitting on the sidewalk looking kind of startled when I left."

The two men looked gravely at one another. Then Bat laughed—and after awhile, Wyatt had to join in.

More than one patron of the gambling hall looked at Wyatt with some surprise. *Is that Wyatt Earp . . . laughing?*

After the laughter faded, Bat took a deck of cards from his jacket and said, "How about I make you feel better by taking all your money?"

Wyatt shrugged and said, "Let's get a fresh deck."

"Here's your last clipping in a Wichita paper, I expect," Mattie said dourly. She closed her nightgown, then sat up on the bed and dropped the clipping from the *Beacon* onto the sheets where he could see it.

He was lying on his side, wearing only his trousers, head propped on his fist, gazing out the half-curtained window at the gray late morning sky. Occasional spits of snow slanted by. He could hear bullwhackers cracking their whips, wagons rattling, people calling to one another. He was not really in the mood to go out, yet—it had gotten cold again, he had no work in Wichita, now, and was feeling low in his spirits. The only good news had been hearing that Jack McCall had been hung in Yankton, Dakota Territory, for the murder of Wild Bill Hickok.

Bat had left town a couple days earlier, taking the train to help his brother Ed with some lawing over in Dodge City. Virgil was out of town, James was in a bad mood, Mattie was peevish with cabin fever—and Wyatt had not been making friends of late . . .

"I don't believe I want to read that newspaper hogwash," Wyatt said, irritably. But he picked up the clipping anyway.

> *. . . On last Sunday night a difficulty occurred between Policeman Erp and Wm. Smith, candidate for Town Marshal. Erp was arrested for violation of the peace and order of the city and was fined on Monday afternoon by his honor Judge Atwood, $30 and cost, and was relieved from the police force . . . The remarks that Smith was said to have made in regard to the marshal sending for Erp's brothers to put them on the police force furnished no grounds for an attack, and upon ordinary occasions we doubt if Erp would have given them a second thought. The good order of the city was properly vindicated in the fining and dismissal of Erp. It is but justice to Erp to say that he has made an excellent officer and hitherto his conduct has been unexceptionable.*

"Now why would you want to clip that?" Wyatt demanded. "Not exactly high praise. They didn't even spell my name right—this time my last name."

Fired twice in Wichita, he thought. Not a good record. It really was time to move on . . .

"I kept it," Mattie was saying. "because it says you were an excellent officer, is why. Most people don't hold it against you, what you did—but you shouldn't have knocked Marshal Smith down like that."

"I know it. I just lost my temper. I suppose some of the other things Smith did, before that, they kind of lit the fuse."

"Well, you've got a long fuse, all right. Can we get something to eat?"

"I suppose."

"We're going to California, pretty soon, aren't we? Or Arizona?"

"That's what I'm thinking."

A knock sounded. Wyatt slid off the bed, took his pistol from the bedside table, and went to the door. "Who is it?"

"It's Dave Leahy!"

"A moment, Dave." Wyatt stuck the gun in his belt, picked up a red undershirt from the floor, and pulled it on before opening the door.

"Sorry to disturb you folks but they asked me at the telegraph office if I could bring this to you . . ."

Wyatt opened the envelope and read the telegraph—and his spirits rose.

To Wyatt S. Earp, Wichita

Heard you free for new job. Need help Dodge City. Hard noggins here need creasing. Job on offer. Good pay. Come quick.

Bat

Wyatt smiled and folded up the telegraph. "Seems Bat needs my help . . ."

Mattie called out from the bed, "Where's he need your help at?"

"He's still over in Dodge. I haven't decided to go for sure, Mattie. But maybe we should. Maybe I can be of use in Dodge City, somehow . . ."

The End